Karina Natalia Vasquez is a fantasy romance author based in England. She is of Peruvian and Spanish descent and adores anything that has dulce de leche in it. When she isn't writing, she is reading fantasy, romance and fangirling over Star Wars. You can usually find her holed up in her room, cuddling her two dogs, collecting crystals for her superstitious mind or daydreaming in the hope that she will magically end up in a Fae kingdom one day.

By Rina Vasquez in the Solaris and Crello *trilogy*

A CITY OF FLAMES
A KINGDOM OF SHADOWS

Coming soon:

A WORLD OF RUINS

A
KINGDOM
OF
SHADOWS

RINA
VASQUEZ

WILDFIRE

First published in paperback in 2024 by
WILDFIRE
an imprint of HEADLINE PUBLISHING GROUP

2

Cataloguing in Publication Data is available from the British Library

ISBN 978 1 0354 1438 3

Offset in 10.18/14.8pt Adobe Caslon Pro by Jouve (UK), Milton Keynes

Printed and bound in Great Britain by Clays Ltd, Elcograf S.p.A.

HEADLINE PUBLISHING GROUP
an Hachette UK Company
Carmelite House
50 Victoria Embankment
London
EC4Y 0DZ

The authorised representative in the EEA is Hachette Ireland, 8 Castlecourt
Centre, Dublin 15, D15 XTP3, Ireland (email: info@hbgi.ie)

www.headline.co.uk
www.hachette.co.uk

To everyone who is terrified of something and is too embarrassed to share it. Remember, it is okay to be scared.

Zerathion
Emberw
Aurum Castle
City of Flames
Aeris
Isle of El
Undarion
Sea of Serenity

OCEAN OF STORMS

NARALIA'S VILLAGE

SCREAMING FORESTS

ENTS

OLCAR

TERRANOS

THALORE

MELWRAITH

CHAPTER ONE

'What's someone like you doing in a tavern all by yourself?'

I turn to look at the man sitting beside me at the bar. A man I've grown all too familiar with.

My gaze wanders around the tavern, taking in the scene of inebriated patrons knocking their mugs against one another and drenching the nearby benches with mead, before coming back to rest on the man who is next to me. When I look at the fine strands of his brown hair, I can't help but grin, even if a part of me is secretly repulsed by him. 'I felt like I could use a drink.'

I begin to fill with a sense of relief as he gives the bartender the signal to pour us both a tankard of ale. He smiles gently. As he looks at me, he slides the mug across. I make an effort not to move at all because of how uncomfortable I am.

'Have we met before?' he asks.

We have.

I draw out the word 'depends' on my tongue while angling my head to the side.

His chuckle vibrates, a heinous sound. A laugh I closely associate with the rust of iron gates inside a dungeon. Old, distasteful, and unpleasant to the ear. 'I'm not entirely sure. Have you asked me for favours before?'

As I reach for the mug, a strained smile crosses my face. 'Never.'

'Really?' He feigns surprise. 'I can recall all the ones you made for your brothers when you were just a child.'

I fix my eyes on the tankard as the reflection of his grin bounces off the surface of the metal. I quickly reach for my blade, and with one fluid action, I thrust the tip against his abdomen. Nobody takes any notice, nobody even bothers to look in our direction. I had been discreet enough. When I see that one of Ivarron's brows have now raised, I speak softly and ask, 'How did you know it was me?' Darius had placed a glamour over me. It should have worked.

'Stupid girl,' he says, unfazed by the blade. 'I know everyone who lives in this village, and I can recognise when someone is trying to trick me.' His eyes shift to my left hand. 'And there is also only one person I know who always favours wearing one glove to cover something they hate.'

The memory of a specific man with whom I came to share my first kiss crosses my mind, causing me to press the blade's tip further into Ivarron's stomach. 'The maps you had at your place. Where are they?'

'My, my, confessing that you've broken into my place now, are we?' He clicks his tongue; mocking disappointment as his lips split into a crooked grin. 'I taught you better than that, Naralía.'

'You treated me like a slave.'

'Don't act like you don't miss working for me since it seems –' he eyes my clothing. '– That your Venator dream didn't pan out.'

My cold mask falls. Ivarron chuckles over whatever revealing expression must be on my face. 'Just tell me where you have the map to the Screaming Forests.' Despite the pressure of my blade on him, my voice is barely a whisper, much to Ivarron's pleasure.

'I would listen to her if I were you.' These words don't come from Ivarron's mouth.

Looking past his shoulder, I see Darius resting an arm against the counter and flipping a gold coin between his fingers.

'She can be quite the menace when she wants something.' His voice oozes his usual playfulness as his charming gaze flickers to meet my furious one.

'What are you doing?' I grind my teeth at his evident inability to listen to my plans. I had told him to wait outside with Tibith.

His response is to smile at me just as Ivarron clasps his hands together and the many rings on his fingers clink as he says, 'Well, now this is fascinating. My old trapper is working with the infamous Golden Thief. I must say I expected someone more –' he gives Darius a once over '– Intimidating.'

Darius's lips tug into a fake smirk as he inclines his head forward. 'Brave.' His whisper is a threat slicing the air between them. 'I like that in a man – well, those of my age, of course. Now, why don't you go ahead and give us that map?'

Ivarron's eyes dart down to where Darius's palm carves a blade out of shadows.

My need to scoff is immediate. If my blade did nothing to scare Ivarron, then—

'With pleasure.'

I furrow my brows at Ivarron's complacent answer. He looks at me with a sickly smile and rises from his seat. Turning to the barmaid, he gives her a firm nod before saying to us with a derisive gesture of his hand, 'Follow me.'

Darius and I share a look: *do we trust him?*

I had informed Darius what type of person Ivarron was on our way here. From how his firm jaw had tightened in the pale rays of sun, I assumed he didn't like the idea of going to Ivarron for help.

Neither had I.

'Stick to my side,' Darius whispers into my ear, resting his hand on my lower back.

I'd retort with an insult if I weren't too distracted by the various looks shooting our way. However, a traitorous flutter spreads across my spine like the comfort I'd experienced the moment after I saved him from the dungeons.

I remove his hand. 'May I remind you I know him better than you do?'

His murmur is a chuckle vibrating against my ear. 'And may I remind you, I managed to pay off your debt, Goldie.'

I glare at him, at the cocky gleam in his golden eyes, before I choose to ignore him and tread behind Ivarron. He leads us through a doorway on the left side of the tavern. Putrid scents of urine and mould hover in the air of a long corridor, but after being so accustomed to spending far too long in the dungeons, I push past the smells. The floorboard creaks, drowning out our heavy footsteps until we enter a smaller room at the end. Sunlight darts through a shaft window on the side, and I watch Ivarron make his way around a table full of clutter. All his jars, trinkets and books decorate a wooden shelf behind him. It's as if he's displaying each prize he's won for hurting various magical creatures.

For so long, I had watched his collection of claws, fangs and pixie wings grow. I would dream of them in my sleep so often that it soon became a reality of nightmares every time I visited Ivarron.

'It's been a while since someone's asked me for a map of the Screaming Forests.'

'Why has all your stuff moved here?' I don't bother explaining why

Elliot Sweeney is a community psychiatric nurse from London. He was awarded the Fisher Scholarship to attend the Curtis Brown Creative novel writing course, and he's also been supported by Spread the Word through their London Writers Awards Scheme. The Literary Consultancy has showcased him as a Spotlight Author, and he's written for *Alfred Hitchcock's Mystery Magazine* and *Switchblade*, amongst others.

Praise for *The Next to Die:*

'A promising and hard-hitting debut'
Sunday Times

'*The Next to Die* is a remarkably assured debut. It oozes the sour tang of authenticity, mingling psychiatry and crime with the mean streets of London. Kasper has the hallmark of the classic crime fiction protagonist, brutal but with an underlying compassion.'
Andrew Taylor, bestselling author of *The American Boy* and *The Ashes of London*

'With pitch-perfect tone and quality to the writing, *The Next to Die* is a great new piece of London noir and a terrific debut.'
Amer Anwar, author of CWA Debut Dagger-winning *Brothers in Blood*

'A superb, heart-thumping thriller that sucks you in with its breathless action, *The Next To Die* is, without doubt, my favourite read of the year.'
Carol Wyer, bestselling author of the DI Kate Young and Detective Natalie Ward series

'*The Next to Die* hooked me immediately with its formidable pace and fluid style. Kasper is a fascinatingly flawed but honourable character very much in the Chandler mould. A wonderfully assured debut, perfect for fans of dark and gritty thrillers.'
James Oswald, bestselling author of the Inspector McLean series

I need the map. I don't need to tell him what I plan to do with it anyway.

'Change of scenery.' Ivarron gestures to the entirety of the room. 'I own this place now.'

I can imagine all the unpleasant things he must have done to own it.

'So, Nara.' He settles into a chair, clasping his hands once again. 'What do you have for me in exchange for this map.'

'Money – since you love it so much.'

He makes the sound of unabashed agreement. 'I do.'

This was almost too easy. He is so predictable.

'But I don't need money this time.' He leans back, his glass eye unblinking. 'I want something else.'

Annoyance churns in my stomach. 'We don't have anything else.'

Darius slowly moves closer to me as Ivarron's eyes sharpen with a smug smile. 'It is not an object you can steal. I want to know a hidden secret . . . your greatest desire.' Curiosity fills his one working eye as it slices towards Darius. 'How far are you willing to go for this map?'

I remain silent, pondering his words. If there is one thing I will never forget about Ivarron, it would be his nefarious deals and his greed to blackmail anyone by obtaining information from his victims. He'd done it to people I'd known from my village. I'd seen them step into Ivarron's old home and come out thinking they'd made the best decision of their life, when they'd given everything away.

'What if I trade you a valuable pendant?'

I thought I misheard; I glance over at Darius. I give him a puzzled look as he holds a firm gaze on Ivarron.

Pendant?

Since when—

My thoughts freeze as he takes out the Rivernorth pendant from his pocket. The gold glints and reflects in Ivarron's eyes as if he were in a sudden trance.

Darius dangles the chain on one of his fingers. 'A pendant that belongs to the previous rulers of this land. The Rivernorths.' He tilts his head, and a smirk carves his full lips. 'Wouldn't you rather this than a silly little secret?'

The last time I saw the Rivernorth pendant was the day before Darius's arrest.

'Tempting.' Ivarron taps his fingers against the desk, then rises and walks towards Darius, reaching for the pendant.

Darius pulls his hand back and snaps, 'The map.'

Ivarron's fingers curl into his palm, unsatisfied with that retort. Still, he turns back to the desk. Taut silence stretches the room as his hands skim the top layer of wood before fishing out a set of keys from his coat pocket to unlock a drawer. He lifts a rolled-up parchment and heads towards Darius again. Each step is precise and heavy with tension as he hands it over. Hesitation crosses Darius's eyes, but his gaze briefly meets mine before he drops the pendant into Ivarron's palm.

Despite our success, the pressure in my chest doesn't seem to lift off.

'It's been a delight seeing you again, Nara.' Ivarron turns to me. An unwelcoming grin shapes his thin lips as Darius unfurls the map in his hand.

'I wish I could say the same.'

He laughs, raising the pendant towards the light. 'How I've missed you, Trapper.' He pockets the pendant, and I can't help but watch his movements. 'You were my best one yet, although Idris wasn't far off in terms of his skills. I wonder if he picked that up from your father or –' he pauses '– *Illaria*.'

My eyes flare up at him as he says my mother's name. 'Don't ever say her—'

'This isn't the map.'

The anger on my face shifts into confusion at Darius's accusatory words, and when I look at him, I can almost taste the anger pulsing off him.

'He gave us a fake map.' He tosses it onto the desk, much to Ivarron's curious amusement.

No, there must be some mistake— 'How do you know?'

Darius's eyes don't leave Ivarron's once. 'Well, Goldie, in my many years of thieving, I've come across a few cartographers who have shown me how to spot a fake. Whoever you got this from, I assume they drew this fake map and hid the real one instead.'

It had been too easy.

'I underestimated you, Golden Thief.' Ivarron angles his head, his lips curling into a menacing smile. 'Immortal blood or not, you do prove useful.'

Whatever Ivarron's intentions are, neither of us wants to play his game any longer. I'd dealt with it for too long in the past.

'Where is the real map?' Darius demands, inching a slow step towards him.

'How about we make a different trade?' Ivarron raises his hand, tapping his forefinger against the others. 'You, for the map.'

The tension rolling off Darius's shoulders thickens the air, making it hard to breathe as his rage grows at Ivarron's request.

'After all,' Ivarron's smile only grows, 'I've always wanted a pet dragon.'

Silence takes over the room, but Darius's anger is loud enough to rupture the walls to dust.

'Oh? It seems I've struck a nerve with the—'

Not even half a second goes by before Darius takes a single stride and grabs Ivarron by the throat, slamming him against the shelf. Two jars smash onto the floor as Ivarron wheezes out a sadistic chuckle.

I immediately rush after them, touching Darius's shoulder as I say his name in warning before Ivarron exclaims, 'Careful. Even a powerful shifter like yourself can be tamed with just a single drop of this.' He rummages through his pocket and lifts a vial—

'Neoma blood.' It slips past my lips in a whisper as the blood shines bright, brimming with something beyond extraordinary.

Darius lets go, and I leap in front of him as Ivarron rubs his neck with the same deranged smile lingering on his lips.

'Word travels fast,' he says. 'After the news that the Golden Thief had been captured thanks to the glorious Neoma tree, I knew it was because of you, Nara.'

My muscles tense at the reminder.

'I'd had many of my men retrieve vials of blood from that tree for my collection. Labelled them as something entirely different, so I was never caught. And when you'd mistakenly grabbed it, I decided to look into it.' His chin dips. 'Until I heard word on the street that the Venators were using blood from a Neoma tree against shifters and dragons. It didn't take long to figure out it had to be because of you, Nara.'

Memories of the night Darius was captured pierce my mind like shards of glass. *His hand clutched an arrow shaft as blood pooled from his chest . . .*

The second those thoughts flashed into my mind, a stampede of horses braying from outside causes me to whirl my head to the window.

Solaris, no.

'You've become quite the star fugitive in Emberwell, Nara.' Ivarron's words drip with mockery as Venators swarm the market square. 'Venators have been patrolling the village for days on the Queen's orders. How could I refuse such a hefty reward?'

I bite the inside of my cheek to dial down the fury enveloping me. 'You alerted them.'

He raises a finger as if to correct me and grins. 'The barmaid did, though the Queen gave me a generous offer for you and the Golden Thief's capture if you did turn up here.'

A funny feeling, a lot like betrayal, punctures through me. I must remind myself that Ivarron has always been this type of person.

'We need to go.' Darius grabs hold of my arm, tugging me towards the door, but I halt and stare at Ivarron, my molars grinding the longer I have my eyes on him.

'I wish you could have been different,' I dare to say, and his brows rise with the faintest amusement. 'Because there was once a time when I thought you were like a father.' An incredulous laugh slips out as I shake my head. 'But what would a thirteen-year-old know?'

The unexpected comment breaks that constant brash confidence Ivarron always carries around. His smile fades into a straight line as Venator voices echo nearer outside, and the last I see before I let Darius take me away from the room is Ivarron sinking onto the chair with a bleary gaze. I try to forget that image as Darius and I rush through the tavern, pushing past people before we barge through the doors. Bright light springs down on us, and the first thing I see is Tibith waving from the ground.

'Hello, Miss Nara! Did you get the map?'

Darius and I exchange frustrated looks. I heave out a breath as I say, 'Not exactly.'

Tibith simply blinks at my answer just as a Venator spots us from afar and yells to alert the others. Darius quickly places another glamour upon us, masking our looks from the Venators as we make our way through the village square. Civilians brush past us while I keep my head low, praying we make it back to the forest before someone realises who we are.

'Shit,' Darius mutters beside me.

'What is it?'

'My magic, I can feel it fading. I've overused it today.'

No, not now. Not when we are so close.

I look both ways. Sections leading off into fields and other villages cover my view before—

'Over there!' a Venator shouts, and panic blankets me completely.

People stop to look, and Venators unsheathe their swords, darting our way.

'Come on,' Darius grunts, fingers closing around my upper arm as we move through the crowd, dodging and sliding between gasping men, women and children.

Once we are out of the market square, the long grass, the fresh crops, the empty fields I'd once spent my childhood in pass me by as I start to run. The galloping sound of horses and shouts from Venators behind us do not compare to the heavy thud of my heart, just remembering how my home was not so far from here.

Sunlight carves through the trees ahead, and a cart full of hay enters my vision. The second we near it, I unlatch the side, and all the fodder falls out, blocking their path and slowing down the Venators.

'Always knew you were a criminal at heart,' Darius laughs, and I shake my head at him as we careen through the woods. A scowl forms on my face as I try to ignore him despite the smile begging to part from my lips. Tibith rolls ahead of us before Darius leaps over the same broken tree I'd seen with Illias the day I killed that rümen. He sticks his hand out to help me, but I shoot him an irked look and jump over it myself as I run past him.

Stubborn as I may be, I know these woods better than anyone else. This is why, as I approach a certain cluster of branches and lichens, I stumble to a pause, panting at what is in front of me.

Thorns and shadows mark the entrance to the Screaming Forests, the thinnest opening a person can get through. Hundreds of times, I'd wondered what it would be like to go through them, curious about what lay hidden ahead.

Male voices tug away my transfixed gaze, and I look over my shoulder at the Venators appearing between nearby trees.

'Goldie,' Darius says, his voice a gentle command as I turn to him. 'We need to go.'

My eyes connect with his, warm and compelling, and I can't help but nod. I take one last look at the entrance, and my stomach plunges at the idea of the mysteries of the forest before Tibith, Darius and I cross the threshold into Terranos.

CHAPTER TWO

As we leap over logs, we are surrounded by endless verdant trees. We don't stop, even if my legs are tired and my breath heavy. Branches latch on to the sides of my cloak, and I hide my face to avoid being scratched.

Darius slows down when there are no Venators in sight, and we finally stop for breath at a clearing. I inhale the forest air and slowly turn, glancing at everything around me. The forest is covered by ancient roots, the trees are tall enough to obscure the sun, towering over us as if they intend to capture anyone who dares to walk into their forbidden territory. The only light that does enter, dapples through the trees before disappearing into the mist.

I turn to Darius, I see he's also assessing the forest. My temper is still high from our interaction with Ivarron. 'Why on earth were you carrying the Rivernorth pendant and didn't bother to tell me!'

He releases a surprised chuckle, running a hand through his hair. 'Is now really the time to argue, Goldie?'

Yes, always with you.

'We don't have a map.' I stomp my feet across the long grass as I stalk up to him. 'We are currently *in* the Screaming Forests with no direction to head in, and not to mention we were almost captured.'

His brow arches at the aggravation waving off me, but then Tibith trots between us. 'It's okay, Miss Nara. Darry can use his powers!'

Darius glances upward, letting out a stiff sigh. 'No, Tibith . . . my powers won't work in here.'

'But-but why not?'

'According to different sources, the Elven King wants to ward everyone off his lands.'

Tibith takes in Darius's answer, blinking twice before letting out an excited squeal. 'Then Miss Nara can use hers!'

'*No* magic works here,' I emphasise, though Tibith's innocent tilt of his head suggests he still doesn't understand. 'And besides, I have no powers in the first place.'

'And here I thought you were special, Goldie.'

Excuse me?

I point my index finger at Darius. 'Are you trying to provoke me?'

'Always.'

The crease between my brows tightens the longer I glare at him. I step towards him until the tip of my finger touches his chest, and his lip curls with amusement at the sight of it. 'Look, unlike you, I don't need magic to survive, so don't come crawling to me when something attacks you.'

'I don't crawl to people, Goldie.' His voice lowers, dark and lustful. 'They usually crawl towards me instead.'

My lips purse with annoyance as I stab my finger harder into his skin, hoping it can somehow hurt him. 'Why anyone would like you is beyond me.'

'Well, Goldie.' He gently flicks my hand away, and we're millimetres apart from each other's faces as he leans down to match my height. 'You only think that because you haven't had the pleasure of sleeping with me.'

I scoff. 'I would rather kiss a goblin.'

'Done that.' He grins. 'And I must say, Treet was a great kisser.'

An infuriating sound urges to come out of my throat, but gets stuck. He seems to know the perfect way to annoy me, he has a witty response to anything I say to him. And instead of wasting my time here, listening to him, I just stare him down and call out for Tibith because *he* is someone I'd much rather spend this journey with.

But he doesn't respond. Darius and I immediately look around where Tibith had been standing. Where has he gone?

I take a few steps, trying to spot a peek of orange fur anywhere. 'Has someone grabbed him?'

'I—' Darius's words freeze. A twig snaps behind us as a shadow darts across. We both pivot to the sound, with our blades unsheathed at the ready, pointing them outwards.

Another rustle between trees drifts closer in our direction, then stops. My previous annoyance is quickly replaced with worrying anticipation. *I can handle it*, I remind myself.

'What do you think it could be?' I whisper, my back pressed against Darius's. 'Trolls? Dangerous Nymphs? Soul-sucking faeries?'

'If you keep talking, they might end up sucking your soul first.'

I hope he gets eaten. 'Just—'

Suddenly, a small creature jumps out, caramel hues reflecting off its fur as it jumps through speckles of light. 'A rabbit?' I ask, sighing as I sheathe my blade again and turn back towards Darius. Of all things, a rabbit is what I least expected.

'Wait.' Darius holds a few fingers to my face, narrowing his eyes over my shoulder. 'That's not a rabbit.'

With a frown, I look as the rabbit leaps in the opposite direction. It screeches a horrible monstrous sound before it begins convulsing and morphs into a deformed hairless creature with no eyes and rows and rows of sharp teeth in ring-like circles protruding from its head. I grimace, watching it disappear into another set of high trees.

That's an image I will never get out of my head.

'I found fruit, Darry!'

I whirl to find Tibith toddling out of the bushes, holding bright red berries in his palm.

'Don't eat that.' Darius shakes Tibith's paw to rid him of the fruit. 'We can't trust anything in these forests, much less tempting berries.' He huffs a breath, glancing around. 'We should camp here for the night, then figure out the rest of our route in the morning.'

For once, I can't argue with that idea. 'Agreed.' I nod. 'Which one of us should keep watch throughout the first half of the night?'

'I will,' Darius says. 'I can imagine you're much more volatile if you've had no sleep.'

Hilarious.

A forced smile touches my lips as I saunter up to him. 'The opposite, actually.' Walking past, I hear that deep chuckle of his from behind me.

I glance over Darius's shoulder at the makeshift bed he's made from piles of leaves and let loose a soft chuckle. 'Looks almost as good as the made-up bed in your cottage,' I say as he turns to the sound of my voice. I recalled the time fondly, when he'd laid me to rest on a pile of clothes and cured my wounds.

His gaze darts down at the leaves, then lands back on me before resting his forearm against the tree. 'Beds are overrated; besides, I haven't slept in one for over twenty years.'

I frown at the strange admission, it seemed to convey a hidden pain. 'You haven't?' I ask. 'Is that a shifter thing?'

He chuckles, pushing himself off the tree. 'I suppose.'

Short and succinct. That is not a typical answer I usually receive from Darius.

I can't help but give him a commiserating look, though I'm sure the last thing he wants is my pity. My lips part in an attempt to ask him if he would like to talk about it when loud snores interrupt us instead. Looking to my right, Tibith lies flat on the grass, his fur belly rising and falling as he breathes in and out of a deep sleep.

A smile blooms on my lips, and I find myself asking something else. 'How did you meet him?'

'Does this still count as part of your five questions for me?'

I arch a brow as I look over at the cocky grin on his lips. No, if anything, I will always have a question for him, despite what I'd won playing the Liars, Dice game.

He observes my resolve before giving in with a soft sigh and nodding as he stares at Tibith. 'I was thirteen when I found him being pushed around by a few people. I ended up confronting them, and since then, Tibith started following me wherever I went.' He chuckles at the memory, looking down at the ground. 'The first time we robbed a place together was a bakery, which is when he took up such a liking for bread.'

A silence charges through the night breeze of the Screaming Forests, in such a way that no one would think it is crawling with dangerous, deadly creatures. I let a small smile take over my face at the image of everything they must have done together since they met.

16

'And then you taught him how to speak,' I say quietly, not holding back the admiration in my voice.

'Wasn't easy, but I managed just fine.'

'Well, I don't think I've ever seen anyone take time to teach a creature to speak or care for them the way you do with Tibith, especially in Emberwell.'

When he doesn't respond, I tilt my head up at him. His gaze brands into my own as a smile lingers on the corner of his lips. 'Is that a compliment, Goldie?'

'You wish,' I retort.

'I don't need to,' he says, mischief glinting in his eyes. 'If anything, I already know you secretly have a thing for me.'

And there he goes again, annoying me beyond words. 'You know, every time I think we are having a decent conversation, you decide to go ahead and ruin it.'

He hums with a lazy smile, crossing his arms over his chest. 'What can I say? You bring it out in me, Goldie.'

My previous irritation surfaces again, twisting inside my stomach like a whirlpool. 'You're the worst person to be stuck with for this journey, I can't believe I'm doing this with you,' I sputter annoyedly without fully realising the consequences of my words.

For a split second, I almost see a hurt look in his eyes. 'I'm not particularly thrilled either,' he responds, feigning amusement. 'But what option do I have?'

'Maybe exercise the option of shutting up right now.' I give him a firm look before leaning into his face and pointing my index finger at him. 'And don't even think about doing anything weird while I sleep!'

'Weird?' His lip quirks as if he's trying not to laugh.

'You know what I mean – placing bugs on me, scaring me awake. And, by the way, I don't scare easily, so you can forget that idea—'

'Are you sure you don't scare easily?'

I hesitate for a second, staring at the challenging gleam in his eyes before lifting a brow. 'Do you?'

'I asked the question first, Goldie.'

'And I asked the question second,' I quip, and he chuckles in resignation.

'You know, you're the most stubborn person I've ever met.'

'Thank you.' I smile curtly. 'Now, goodnight,' I add in a harsh tone, shutting out any other possible chatter as I curl up and rest on my side, facing away from him.

I regret the second I close my eyes.

Thoughts plague my mind. Memories, the dungeon, the Ardenti I had to kill, and . . . Lorcan, all come rushing back to me like a crashing wave in a storm. I can't fight the tightness in my throat gripping at me so firmly that I clutch on to my chest. Too mulish to say a word, I lie here, waiting for my thoughts to dissipate into an empty void.

What *are* we doing here?

CHAPTER THREE

Another day has passed in this forest, another day where we did not encounter anything vaguely threatening or dangerous. I should consider myself lucky, but every few hours Darius would tease me about not falling headfirst into a bog, and so I began to reconsider the meaning of this word 'lucky'.

Unsurprisingly, quite a few arguments have sprung out of my impatience, causing Tibith to quickly try to make us see how this was no place to fight or bicker.

We have yet to listen.

This brings us to now – we have decided to sit down and rest in another clearing within the forest.

Tibith is further away from us, rolling along the grass, and when I turn to look at Darius beside me, he is staring at Tibith with a smile.

'What's it like?' I ask. His gaze cuts to mine in question. 'Without your powers, what does it feel like for a shifter?'

He cocks his brow, and I already know what he's thinking.

I roll my eyes. 'It's a genuine question, and it doesn't count towards the ones that are part of the bet we placed.'

He tips me a curious glance beneath his dark brows. 'Are you that interested in shifters then that you want to know more about us? Or am I just that special to you?'

Why did I even ask? 'Never mind.'

I'm about to turn the other way when he sighs and says, 'It feels like something is blocking my powers.'

I pause, then look up at him as he leans back, his arms straining as he rests all his body weight on them.

'A lid to a jar screwed on a bit too tight, if you will.' His brow furrows the more he stares out ahead. 'I can feel my magic there on the surface, burning to be let out, but I can't make it work, no matter how hard I try to summon it.'

'Not even when you would like to shift?' I cannot deny that when I saw him in his dragon form, I was not floored by the power he exuded . . . because I was. Terribly so.

He casts me a sideways glance, shakes his head and flashes his teeth, showing his sharpened canines. 'Still have these, though.'

'I'm sure biting will come in handy when we're deeper in this forest,' I tease, a soft laugh leaving my lips as he chuckles and shakes his head at me.

Moments like this make me think about how everything has changed for us. The girl who had promised her boss she would capture a powerful dragon shifter is now working together with him to bring justice for his kind.

'It's odd, isn't it?' I stare at him, chewing on my bottom lip. 'When we're not at each other's throats, I seem to quite enjoy your company.' There's that cocky gleam in his eyes as he tilts his head. So I quickly say, 'Don't let that get to your head.'

His grin slowly stretches across his lips, beautiful yet seductive like always. 'Already has, Goldie.'

Of course it would.

I exhale a breath as a pleasant quietude cascades over us. I can't force my stare on anything else except that smile of his, and with everything that has happened, the topic of our first kiss has never been brought up since that night in the woods, and I don't think Darius wanted to be the one to mention it first.

I still tell myself it was a mistake, a momentary lapse of chaotic thoughts stringing us together.

Still, it doesn't help that I think about it more often than I should.

His eyes flicker to my lips, the smile on his face fading as he watches me breathe. 'Nara,' he whispers, but I look away, flustered and embarrassed.

'I should probably eat some of the food Gus packed for us—'

Darius grabs my right wrist before I can rummage through anything. 'I just want you to tell me something.'

Panic fights its way through my heart.

'Last night . . .' His words draw my wary gaze back to his. 'You said something in your sleep.'

Fragments of a nightmare I had last night re-emerge. The same one I have been having since I killed that Ardenti.

I shrug one shoulder and swallow in heavy gulps. 'So I speak in my sleep. It's not the first time I have heard that.' Getting up, I look everywhere else but at him as he lifts himself from the ground and takes a worried step towards me.

I hate that he does that.

It shows he cares, despite telling me he did not.

In the face of what my heart fears, I would rather him consider me an asset. It's easier.

'You mentioned a dragon,' he says, gold eyes darkening with concern. 'And Sarilyn.'

'I don't see why you suddenly need to mention my silly dream. Of course I dreamt about Sarilyn. After all, we are here in this forest thanks to her.'

He doesn't believe me.

'Don't listen to my heartbeat,' I whisper, rather protectively. It's a long shot to think he can, when it could potentially be a part of his shifter powers.

His jaw moves back and forth. He's used to this side of me, the stubborn, defensive Nara who prefers hating him.

'I don't have to,' he mumbles, and though I wish to say more, I bite the inside of my cheek instead as we stare at each other. Neither of us makes a move.

'Darry, Darry!' Tibith runs towards us, but Darius doesn't look away from me. 'Is there any more bread left?'

I force a stiffening breath between my lips and break our stare as I look down at Tibith. I reach inside my satchel for some bread wrapped in cloth and give it to Tibith. 'Here,' I say, eyes darting up at Darius. 'I've lost my appetite.'

CHAPTER FOUR

I gather water into the palms of my hands, sipping it as I sit by a stream which looks pretty normal compared to the thick bubbling lakes we have encountered so far. Thankfully, my aching thirst is quenched as I shake the last few droplets off my hands and continue on our path.

We'd woken up at dawn, and never stopped for a rest. What felt like hours of walking were merely an hour or so, treading carefully and testing the ground for any signs of quicksand. It would be a lie to think I'd forgotten everything from my conversation with Darius. And waking up has only emphasised my troubling thoughts more.

'You're awfully quiet today.' Darius chuckles behind me as my fingertips brush past the dry moss of trees. It's the first time we have spoken since last night. 'Usually, you would have insulted me a few times by now.'

'I've just been thinking,' I mumble miserably, watching Tibith roll ahead of us without a care in the world.

'Of what?'

'Of different ways I can murder you.'

I can envision the smile on Darius's face as he coos, 'Go on.'

'So, you can survive all my attempts? Nice try.'

'Ah, clearly no creatively murderous plans are actually on your mind then.'

'Believe me, I've thought about hundreds of ways to kill you. I even made a new list for it.'

'What was your other list?'

'My hate list.' I huff and stop to catch my breath. 'I wrote you down ten times.' I turn to him, but all I can focus on is the soft glow of the sun caressing his onyx hair and the glimmer of his gold eyes.

His lips tug to the side. 'Sounds more like an obsession. Did you kiss my name after you wrote it?'

Pig.

'Dream of me?' He smiles harder as he notices my ever-growing aggravation. 'Imagine me naked?'

My brow lifts, knowing he's waiting for me to insult him, get even more irritated by everything he says because, strangely, I think this is his way of wanting us to be normal again.

Pursing my lips, I blow out a relaxing breath before my features soften. 'Yes, I did.'

All the amusement disappears from his face, and I know I've got him as I saunter towards his tense body. 'And then I thought of all kinds of scenarios,' I whisper, sliding my fingertips up his arm.

How unexpected and tempting of me.

Another game between us.

Back to normality.

'Like?' There's a rasp to his voice as his brow furrows.

'Well,' I breathe, eyeing his upper arm, the taut muscles visible even through his sleeve. 'They'd start off with you touching me.' My hands reach down to grab his and place them on my waist. 'Here.'

He watches me closely, tracking every movement. 'Then,' my whisper is a graze upon his skin. 'You'd lower them to my thighs.' And I do exactly that, grinning as I look up at his throat, stretching while he swallows hard.

I win.

Pushing his hands off, I step back as his arm suddenly encircles my waist, pinning me back to his chest. 'Seems very unlikely of me to do, Goldie,' he murmurs in a dare.

'Oh?' I cock my head, raising my brows. 'Why is that?'

He smirks like my challenges mean nothing. 'Because what you just showed me is minuscule compared to what I would do and what you secretly desire.'

My façade drops.

'It's too tame, too *safe* when it comes to you,' he says, a laugh vibrating deep in his chest. 'And we both know you're not like that, Goldie. You want to know why?'

I don't say a word as he keeps going.

'Because you want to feel everything. You want to experience what it's like to go over the edge. But it doesn't stop there.' His voice drips with seduction, warming my veins until it's scalding. He wets his bottom lip as he stares at my own. 'See . . . you want to be punished; you want someone to be as dominant with you as you are in person, and not just that, Goldie. You also crave the desire of a release that only a dragon – one you *hate* – could ever give you.'

What is happening?

My palms crackle like wildfire, heating under his chest. His lips hover over mine, and a voice inside my head tells me to push him away, but I'm solid on the spot. My mouth is slightly ajar, and my eyes are half closed as his hand glides down my back, making me lose all sense.

'But of course,' he whispers, and my gaze tracks the thickness of his lower lip, the vibrations of his neck as he talks, 'that is only hypothetical, though I'm glad to know I've had somewhat of an effect on you, Goldie.' He lets go and winks as he walks past me. 'Knew you had a thing for me.'

'You—' Frustration builds in my chest, and I screw up my face as I whirl towards him 'You fliptwit!'

'Fliptwit?' He carries on walking carelessly. 'I've never heard of that before.'

'I made it up.' I grimace to myself at the childish need to admit that.

He turns to me, placing a hand on his chest in fake offence. 'You sure know how to wound me with your words.' His voice drops to a whisper as he scrunches his nose with glee. 'Wretched mortal.'

I force the bout of anger back down and step in front of him, causing him to halt. 'Wretched mortal or not, I am still the only one who got you out of the dungeons.'

We're standing just as close as we were before, and noticing the glare I must be throwing his way, he inclines forward.

'And I got you out of the trials.'

I clench my fists. 'I had a plan.'

'You have a lot of pride in yourself, Goldie.' His voice rings with laughter. 'Never want to accept the truth even when it's right in front of you.'

My teeth grind together, partly wishing he didn't have to be so right.

'It's almost like,' he says, 'everything is a game to you.'

'You started it that way!'

'And who is winning so far?'

Blanking on that question, I stammer, watching his lip curl into a victorious grin.

'Miss Nara is!'

I blink at the sound of Tibith's voice and glance to my left, where he flaps his ears and looks over to Darius.

'You always give in to the arguments, D-Darry.'

Well, Solaris be damned.

I clap once, and a single laugh, loud and full of mockery, escapes my throat as I turn to face Darius. His frown tells me how offended he is as I say, 'For once, I am winning against you, and not just at Liars, Dice! Actually, you know what? I always win –' I walk backwards with a tight smile '– because *you* have lost the ability to argue against me and I—'

Am on the ground.

Except it's not the ground, it's thick, cold and wet, drenching me completely.

Mud.

Putrid-smelling mud.

I look up from the ditch I'd fallen into, and this time the sound of laughter comes from Darius as he appears at the top, holding his lower stomach in hysterics. 'What is it you were saying, Goldie?'

I'm sure a feral snarl explodes out of me.

'Something about always winning?'

Another grunt of anger expels from my lips as I stand, only to slip and fall on my backside.

'Dirt suits you, Goldie. It's quite—'

My knees quiver as I get up again and reach around his ankle, pulling him into the mud pit with me.

We topple over each other, rolling even deeper into the dirt. Round and round and round until both of us show not a single speck of clean skin.

'You're the most infuriating person I've ever met!' I hiss, throwing mud at his face as I land before him with my legs on either side of his. He chuckles, gripping my waist, causing me to slip off him and fall as he hovers above me. As I hit his chest, some raging animalistic noises bubble out of me. But he snatches my wrists, pinning them down into the squelching clag.

'You know this won't end well for you, Goldie.' His nose touches mine, and both of us breathe manically. 'Acting irrational always makes you lose against me, even if you think you've been winning so far.'

He makes me act irrationally.

He's a rush of adventure I can't get rid of.

'Then release me,' I breathe, mustering the little patience I have left in my voice.

He stares down at me, not letting go. I can hear our breathing align at a rhythmic pace, fast and hard. Even with mud all over him, his eyes shine through like a rich golden honey.

When he finally breaks away, cold rushes right through me, and suddenly it's the worst feeling in the world.

He slowly rises from the mud and rests his hand around my lower back, lifting me. And for once, I don't fight him. In fact, I'm too numb to say something or let our bickering ruin the moment when—

'Um, Darry?' Tibith's voice trembles with apprehension, causing us to look up.

He's standing at the edge of the grass, staring at something ahead of us, and a weird sensation climbs up my throat as I look over my shoulder.

Bones of animals and possibly humans are piled up in the ditch.

The ground shakes, and I swivel to Darius, clutching his forearms as we try to remain upright. 'This isn't just mud,' I say, and looking towards the depths of the forest, we watch as something underneath the ground hurtles towards us.

CHAPTER FIVE

The mud ripples as a massive centipede-like creature with a strong and unbreakable exoskeleton bursts through it. It releases a loud screech, revealing thousands of razor-sharp teeth circling inside its mouth.

One bite, and we'll be in pieces.

Thin tentacles sprout from the top of its head, and my eyes widen as it spits a bright green substance in our direction. I push Darius onto the ground, landing on top of him while Tibith panics above us, and I look up to see him rolling around in his self-made cocoon, yelling, 'Monster, monster, monster—'

'What is that thing?' I press my palms against Darius's chest.

His brow furrows. 'Aren't you supposed to be the genius when it comes to creatures?'

'Not ones like this!'

He grips my waist, looking over my shoulder before he rolls us aside. I'm under him as a shot of that liquid substance hits the ground beside us. Mud sizzles and burns – acid. It has to be.

The creature spits again, missing us by a hair. 'See that vine over there?' Darius tips his head towards my right, and I nod, looking at the end of the ditch. 'Use it to climb out.'

What? 'You're not going to act all sacrificial now, are you?'

He doesn't seem amused by my comment, even as his lip tugs up at the side. 'I'm trying not to get us eaten.'

I scoff as he pushes himself off me. That gives me the chance to get up and rush towards the other side. The creature's shrill roar ricochets against the trees as I sludge through the mud, nearly slipping before I clutch on to the vine and steady myself. Glancing behind, I see Darius kneeling by the pile of bones with a blade in his hand.

'Miss Nara, look out!' Tibith's warning has me darting my gaze just as the creature spews its acid in my direction. Alarm takes over me as I drop to the ground, and the acid burns through the vine. I stare wide-eyed as leaves disintegrate and imagine how that could have been me. Stumbling to a stand, I reach for the remaining vines to try to haul myself out.

'Hold on, Miss Nara!' Tibith squeaks, attempting to heave me out of the ditch just as I land on my hands and knees. 'We need to help Darry!'

I'm up from the ground, whirling to where Darius is fending off the creature.

I unsheathe my blade, watching him roll out of the way before he is hit with the acidic venom. Automatically my gaze goes to the creature as it shuffles around like a bug and rises, readying to drop and attack.

A thought occurs.

The creature resembles a centipede.

Its nest is a humid, wet mass of mud.

Centipedes detest the warmth . . .

'It needs heat,' I whisper to myself, the realisation trembling out of me as I shout to Darius, 'It needs heat!'

He frowns at me as he ducks while the creature lunges at him. I search the area, my heartbeat in my throat as I lock my gaze on stranded logs of oak wood.

'Tibith, grab me as many sticks as you can find,' I order, my knees slamming onto the ground as I grab one and carve out the bark. The mud on my skin is still wet, making it hard for me to keep my grip steady as my fingers slip.

A roar of pain comes from behind, and I look over my shoulder. Darius has injured the centipede on its side, but that still isn't enough. 'Any day now, Goldie!' he says as Tibith appears dragging some sticks larger than his small figure can carry.

Perfect.

I steal one from his pile, thanking him as I place my blade between my teeth and rip a piece of material from my long-sleeved tunic. I tell Tibith to hold on to it while I carve a small hole through the oak wood. Kneeling up on one leg, I rest the log beneath my foot and put pressure on it as I rub the stick with both hands against it, faster and faster. A few worrying minutes pass before I see thin strips of black smoke. I huff out in relief and blow, breathing life into it.

'Come on, come on, come on—' I pause my frantic mutters when another shriek vibrates the forest. Sweat trickles down my brow, and Tibith whimpers in panic.

A flame soon enough ignites, and I freeze. I glance at Tibith and almost smile, but I know I need to act fast. I stretch my hand over to the other logs and take one as Tibith hands me the piece of clothing back, and I use it to wrap around the log.

I move up from the ground, lighting the makeshift torch on fire, and don't even stop to think as I jump into the mud ditch, joining

Darius. His eyes immediately lock with mine. There is a slight shift in his brow as the creature focuses on me. He tries to divert it back to himself, as I push the fire in the centipede's direction. It screeches in horror, spitting its venom at me as I twirl away from it and jam the fire straight into the spot where one of its many legs joins its torso. The centipede roars, flailing its body around as it heads straight for me. I roll onto the mud, dropping the torch as I look up in time for Darius to lunge from his feet, aiming his dagger towards the wound. The thrashing centipede doesn't see it coming as Darius latches on to it, piercing the thick gravelled skin underneath its hard exoskeleton and sliding it down as thick, blue gunk begins to gush out.

The creature shakes, roaring as its tentacles spurt acid in every direction to defend itself. Darius yanks the dagger out and plunges it into one of the tentacles as the centipede goes down with him, slamming onto the mud and causing its fluids to splatter everywhere – mainly all over Darius.

Breathless, I rise, casting my eyes over him. His brows pinch in disgust as he picks at the unpleasant viscous substance plastered over his clothes. Even with Tibith's cheers over our victory, I can't help it. I burst into uncontrollable laughter.

I laugh until my stomach squeezes, and I can no longer breathe.

I laugh . . . like I'd once done at the den.

Wiping wet tears from my eyes, I dial down my laughter and look at Darius. His head is tilted, staring at me with an expression I can't quite read.

'What?'

He shakes his head, and a smile now beams at his lips. 'Nothing, it's just . . . you should laugh more often, Goldie.'

I cease my grin, slowly and carefully at the lack of his usual mockery despite those words. My fingers slide up to the corner of my lips, the tips caressing the cracked mud on my skin before I withdraw the hand and clear my throat. 'We should carry on before it gets dark. Who knows if there's more of these giant centipede creatures around.'

He goes quiet, nodding as he looks at the deceased creature, and I try my best not to think about how freeing it felt to be joyful, even if just for a moment.

Our fire burns bright in the centre of our clearing and illuminates the night. Terranos is already colder than what I'm used to in Emberwell, and though Darius's powers are useless in these forests, he also knows how to make a firepit from scratch. But I doubt he is as affected by the cold when shifters already carry heat from within.

I make my way towards him when my stomach rumbles ferociously, and I huff at the thought of the only block of cheese we have left from what Gus gave us.

Darius doesn't seem to hear it as I settle beside him, bringing my knees to my chest. After the earlier dispute, I'd bathed in a nearby river and dressed in the only other set of clothes I had left in my satchel – a white shirt and corset with a pair of leggings.

Warming up my palms by the fire, I look over at Darius. He is wearing a set of clean breeches and shirt, while Tibith sleeps on his lap.

'You should get some rest this time,' I say.

He stares at the flames in a hypnotic state. 'I'm not tired.'

Liar.

'You haven't slept in days.' I had not seen him for a whole week after the trials, but I couldn't get past the hollow darkness beneath his eyes when I saw him at the meeting with Gus. 'I know because I can barely ever sleep myself.'

He breathes out an incredulous laugh and finally looks at me. 'A few hours ago, you fought me inside a mud pit. Why are you acting like you worry over me, Goldie?'

'I could ask you the same every time you've saved me.'

We slip into silence, and his eyes pry away from mine.

My chest squeezes when there's no annoying retort, and I wonder . . . He's definitely not the same because of what happened. Everyone deals with grief differently. While Illias and Iker dealt with it more openly, Idris and I never did – still don't.

Most people expect to feel sadness, but what they do not expect is the profound emptiness you are left with when someone dear to you perishes. I've become changed from each death I've experienced, and after Lorcan's, I've ended up feeling confused . . . lost.

I clear my throat when I remember something and pick at my fingernails. 'I know we haven't spoken since—'

'Don't.' His voice is a dejected warning. He knows what I was about to say.

Swelling forms in my chest, the size of a rock. 'He told me to tell you to go after what you wish for,' I say softly.

His jaw tightens as he shifts his gaze towards the fire. A taut second passes by, wind curls through the woods, and the trees almost seem to be screaming for help, before Darius finally whispers, 'It's not so simple.'

'No wish is simple to achieve.'

'It is when it's absolutely unattainable.'

'And how would you know that it is?'

He looks at me with a heartbroken gaze full of secrets and devastating promises. 'I don't deserve such a wish to come true.'

Tension spikes the atmosphere around us.

It's a good thing I adore being hated.

Something *he* had said to Erion at the trials.

I will never understand your desperate need to be hated by so many.

Something *I* had said before his capture.

I snap back when Darius's fingers trace the skin of my cheek, and my breath halts.

'Still got mud on you, Goldie.' The pad of his thumb slides downwards, lingering on my lips for a while. 'Do you ever wash properly?'

He's straying from the topic.

Pushing his hand away, I shake my head. 'Are you ever serious for more than just one minute?'

He grins effortlessly, looking down at my hand still on his. I remove it like he's scalding hot. 'I think you know my answer to that,' he says.

'I don't know why I even bother trying to speak to you like a normal person.' I stand, dusting off any dirt from my backside. Darius watches the motion hesitantly before I say with a huff, 'I'm going to get more wood for the fire.'

'Be my guest.' He gestures to the different sections of the forest, separating into four paths.

Glowering at him, I start towards the same path he took to find wood, when I stop halfway. I inhale a quick breath, tapping my foot impatiently on the ground as I decide to turn and look at him.

His eyes are on me. Curious amusement sparks through them against the raw fire.

'You should know everyone good deserves to have their wishes come true,' I say, and his smile dims. 'And if Lorcan wanted you to go after something, you should go for it, because the only person stopping you is yourself.'

I turn around and walk away before I witness another defeated reaction from him that I might not like.

CHAPTER SIX

I mumble to myself like a madwoman while walking down narrow pathways. Sharp twigs and leaves stick out from wildly growing bushes, and I swat at them with my hand. Leaving Darius with my harsh words makes me wonder if I should have said them at all. I've only come to know one side of him until recently. Some moments I want to ask him hundreds of questions, despite whatever I'd said the day I won against him at the den. And other times, I think things should be left unspoken.

Sighing, I shake my head and have the uncomfortable urge to take out my sun carving, which Lorcan gave back. Instead, as emotions swell in my throat, I draw out my double-ended blade.

During the days I'd spent in one of the shifter's rooms after the trials, I carved the exact figure I'd once done at my old cottage.

The Ardenti dragon.

My thumb glides over the intricate markings of scales made from ebony wood. A reminder that the dragon should have lived, and *I* should have been brave enough to go against the Queen from the beginning.

'*Solaris incarnate.*' Something stops me in my tracks. '*Protector of land and life alike.*'

I slowly turn, and my brows furrow at the ethereal voice.

'*Solaris, Solaris, Solaris.*'

As if I'm unable to resist, I begin following in the direction of the sound, like I am being pulled towards it, whether I like it or not.

'*The sun blooms again, for she has found her moon.*'

Leira's vision.

'*Death,*' it hisses. '*Reign . . . resurrection.*'

Parting a bush to make way, I come to a stop, surrounded by tall trees and shrubbery. My eyes dance across a fluorescent lake as blue and gold colours sing through the ripples, and a waterfall lies ahead of me.

I've never seen a more enchanting sight. It feels like a scene from an utterly beautiful dream, even with the roar of the waterfall crashing onto rocks.

Tilting my head, I walk closer and closer until my feet touch the banks of the lake and I watch my glowing reflection among the ripples.

'*Naralía.*'

I hear it again. It's clearer this time, like a choir of voices.

'*Join us.*'

'What are you?' I ask, my voice almost in a sleepy daze as my blade slides from my grip onto the grass.

'*Freedom.*'

A smile spreads across my lips, and naturally, my eyes close as I remove my boots. I'm far and near, mesmerised and fatigued. I do not know what it is, but I can't stop as I dangle my left foot over the water before dipping it in. It's enough to entice me as warmth spreads throughout my body in a calming blaze, and I plummet into the water.

If there's a splash, I don't hear it as I submerge myself. It's like my release – a gravity pulling me further into this so-called freedom.

Laughter echoes distantly in my mind like the rippling effect of the lake, and soon I'm taken back.

Taken back to a memory I'd long forgotten.

I laugh brightly, running down the streets of an old town my mother loves to visit.

They have the best woodwork shops here.

She tells me to be careful as two marbles she bought for me at the market roll onto the ground. As they pass by, people click their tongues in disapproval, watching me race to catch them.

I smile once I manage to grab one, but the other comes to a stop, hitting the front of someone's shoe.

Glancing up, I see that someone is a boy with short brown hair and a scraggy tunic.

He picks up the marble, inspecting it between his thumb and forefinger as the sun glistens off it.

'That's mine,' I say, nearing him.

His head shoots up, and hazel eyes widen with fear. It's like he doesn't know whether to speak or not.

I must have scared him.

'You can have it if you want,' I say, rocking on my toes. 'My mother says I should be kinder.'

She tells me that so I can make friends.

Except I can never make friends.

Only my brothers are my friends.

Maybe this boy can be my friend now, but he still looks scared . . . hesitant even.

'Does that mean you are not kind?' at last, he replies.

Although his question irritates me. 'Of course I am.' I lift my chin up with confidence, then drop it slightly. 'Well, only when I want to be.'

His lip twitches into a smile, and I frown, wondering why I have never seen him here before. I've visited this village hundreds of times with my mother.

'How old are you?' I step forward, but he takes a skittish step back. 'It's okay, you don't have to tell me,' I amend and stick my hand out, hoping he will see I'm nothing of the evil sort. 'I'm six.'

His eyes dart towards my hand, blinking with uncertainty on whether he should take it or not.

'My hand doesn't bite.' I smile. 'Unless you provoke it.'

That earns a small laugh from him, and he accepts it, though he quickly frowns when I shake him with enough force that his arm flails up and down.

He goes quiet again, making me open up my other palm to show him my marble. 'They're Solaris and Crello marbles, see.' I point to his hand, and he looks at it.

Mine has a sun crested inside it, and his, a crescent moon shape.

'Do you believe in them?' I ask, and he stares at his hand for a while, perhaps a little too long.

'I—' he considers his words for a moment. 'Believe that—'

The memory fades into nothing before it can finish, and my mind fills with a sense of terror as new memories, ones I do remember, pop up.

Ones I remember too well.

Kill it, or you leave me no choice but to set forth a punishment.

No . . . no.

Lorcan was the first to get bitten by me, the one to stay strong, shift, unlike me and everyone else down here, who are weakening by the day.

Something heavy floods my chest. I thrash against the weight of the water, but spindly hands wrap around my ankle.

Tell Darius to go after his wish.

You can tell him yourself.

Why should the Queen take an interest in you? You'll end up just like your father.

Voices . . . images overlap, and I want to yell; I want to cover my ears to stop it.

So, let me ask you again, the Golden Thief or me?

You used me just how everyone else seems to.

After all, you're right. I do think of you only as an asset to me.

Asset to me.

Asset to me.

Asset to me.

The words echo even as everything goes dark, and I'm . . . free.

CHAPTER SEVEN

As I cough and hold my hand to my neck, water sputters from my mouth. I jolt up from the ground, taking in a gasp of fresh air. My corset is ripped in half to my side as my gaze travels to Darius kneeling with my blade in his hands.

'It's a good thing I decided to go after you,' he says. 'Seems like I can't leave you for more than a minute; otherwise, you're getting yourself in danger.' No teasing voice, no humour. He's annoyed.

I watch as he runs his hands through his wet hair. I must look confused as my eyes dart around, listening to the waterfall's delicate patter against the rocks.

I don't remember much.

Hell, I hardly remember jumping into the lake.

Could it have been Sirens?

It can't be, though. They're known to reside in Undarion.

I look at Tibith's worried eyes beside Darius and think how badly I underestimated the creatures of this forest challenging my abilities.

Then again, this forest isn't normal.

'I t-told you Miss Nara is always drowning, Darry!' Tibith's feet pad along the grass as he walks up to me. 'I think you need swimming lessons, Miss Nara.'

A startled laugh escapes me at the seriousness in his tone. 'I think so too,' I whisper, lowering my head towards him. As my eyes lift to Darius, I notice his brows narrow, and his gaze is fixed on the ground. A flicker goes off in my stomach, much like nerves. 'Thank you—'

'What were you thinking?' he asks quietly.

I nibble on my bottom lip as I realise this was all my fault.

If Darius hadn't come, I might be nothing more than flesh and bone waiting to decay at the bottom of the lake by now.

'I wasn't,' I answer, and his eyes flash to mine.

He waits for me to go on, but I don't know what else to say. Not when he's looking at me as if I mean something.

I can hardly feel my legs as I push myself off the ground, and Darius lurches towards me, holding my forearms to maintain my balance. Spotting Tibith chasing a few fireflies in the background, I tell Darius, 'There's no point turning back. By resting, we are just taking up more time.'

He scans me from top to bottom and raises a brow in concern. 'You're also soaking.'

'As are you.'

A slight chuckle. 'For a dragon, that's nothing.' He sighs after I shoot him a glare. 'Look, you're cold, and I can help you warm up.'

'I don't need a dragon shifter's body heat to help me dry. I can warm up just fine on my own.'

'Clearly,' he murmurs in a taunt as he watches me wrap my hands around my body, shivering, and with a huff from his nose, he steps forward. My heart drums, and I almost want to step back, but I don't.

Ironically, I'm frozen on the spot as his hand tentatively reaches out and slips under my shirt.

I let out a little gasp at the tender touch of his palm. He pauses as I drag my gaze up to him.

'I can stop if you really don't want me to.' I don't think he meant to whisper those words, but he did.

I consider his suggestion but find myself shaking my head instead.

He places his other hand on my skin, gliding both up to my sides. It is the first time I feel conscious of my curves.

Our eyes remain on one another as his thumb curls under my breast. Goosebumps pebble my skin, and a shivering laugh climbs up my throat. 'You're going a little too far north, don't you think?'

He stops; a faint turquoise glow from the lake lights half his face. 'Would you rather I go south?'

One of my brows curves upwards. 'I'd rather not have to break your hand.'

'Progress.' He grins. 'You said you'd rather *not*.'

'Don't push it.'

I feel his chuckle rumble through his body and into mine before he lowers his hands to just above my hips.

Silence engulfs us for the next minute as I stare at him, the way anyone would, being this close to someone and feeling the smooth strokes of their fingers on your skin.

Whether I'm making him uncomfortable or not, he doesn't care because he's also staring back at me.

'I have my next question,' I say.

I don't, actually.

But anything to stop the strange silence between us.

He smiles. 'After this one, you only have two left.'

We'll see.

'Have you ever fallen in love?' The unexpected question leaves my lips before I've even thought it through.

His hands tense on me, and gold eyes – usually bright – darken. For a moment, I don't think he will answer at all until— 'Yes.'

A single word that makes my heart speed.

Before my time in the city, I rarely questioned someone, but now? I want to ask when? With whom? What happened? But I hear myself ask, 'What's it like?'

My heart dips even further between the crevices of my chest, thinking of Lorcan again before Darius inhales a deep breath and says, 'Frightening.'

That's not exactly the answer I expected, but what answer did I want? 'Is that all?'

'Love is different for everyone, Goldie.' The heat of his hands now spreads to my upper back. 'Sometimes, a simple glance is all it takes to fall in love with someone.'

I snort, and my lip twitches into a smile. 'I've only ever heard that in stories my mother would tell me.'

Curiosity creeps into his eyes. 'And how did your mother and father fall in love?'

My smile falters as my expression turns pensive. 'On Noctura night, when they were children. My father saw her dancing as the gold dust fell from the sky, and he's always said that's the moment he knew he loved her.'

He smiles at my response, proving him right with his point on love.

'Well then—' I pause, tilting my head. 'How can you know when you're *in* love with someone?'

A crack of sorrowful silence consumes him as he stares at me intently, and then . . . he answers, 'When it hurts.'

When it hurts.

The repetition of that sentence claws at the barriers of my mind, shredding the thought that love is the most painful thing one can ever experience.

Who hurt you, Darius?

That is all I care to know at this moment, but he backs away, his hands no longer warming up my skin as he kneels to pick up my blade and give it to me.

'I think you're warmed up now. We should go,' he says, avoiding my gaze and calling for Tibith before walking away from me.

CHAPTER EIGHT

Insects hum in the air, and the rustling of animals between shrubs reaches my ears as I stare at Darius walking a safe distance ahead of me.

Quiet.

He is always so quiet.

When we are arguing, we are too busy to focus on anything else; when we are not, the world is too much to bear. And perhaps he is right about love. Eventually, it is all supposed to hurt one way or another; in death, heartbreak, lies or deception.

That doesn't mean you shouldn't be willing to take some risks in life.

'Miss Nara?' Tibith's voice breaks through my thoughts, and I glance down at him. 'Can I ask you something?'

I think I nod as a reply because he goes ahead and says, 'Why-why do you wear that?' He points to my hand where the black fingerless glove rests.

Leather tightens against my skin as I curl my fingers into my palm, staring at it under the shadowy moonlight. 'To cover my scar,' I answer.

'But I like your scar, Miss Nara.' He sounds sincere. It makes me smile. 'And so does Darry.'

'Really, now?' My brow tugs up in vague interest.

He hums as he nods. 'He says its shape is like a river of dreams.'

A river of dreams. Huh, I've never looked at it that way. All it's ever been is a reminder of when my father died and who caused this scar in the first place. It's always been a river of nightmares in my eyes.

I cut a glance towards Darius. He keeps a steady hand on the hilt of his blade as he observes every part of the forest. Once this is all over, I wonder if he will finally rest.

'Tibith,' I say, sliding my focus back to him. 'Since you asked me a question, can I ask you one?'

'Of course, Miss Nara, I love questions!' His bright orange ears flap like a bee's wings, and a smile stretches my lips.

'Is there . . . a reason why Darius refuses to sleep on beds?'

Tibith takes little time to think it over. 'That's easy! He is not used to them, Miss Nara.'

'Not used to them?'

'The man who looked after him never let him sleep on any,' Tibith says, plainly. Hearing this, a hole grows in my chest. He must mean Lorcan's father, Rayth. He's the only one who looked after him when Darius's mother died. 'Darry doesn't like talking about it. He tells me nice stories instead. Ones of giant bread houses all for me to eat!'

It's hard not to smile when Tibith radiates with virtuous excitement. But as my gaze flickers from Tibith to Darius again, the corner of my lips are weighed down with the possibility that there may have been a reason for Darius killing Lorcan's father after all.

I excuse myself and separate from Tibith, stalking towards Darius in the hopes of talking to him or questioning him perhaps. Whatever it takes, even if it ends in an argument.

But he halts just as I reach up behind him.

'Why did we stop?' I find myself asking instead. Surrounding us are large trees almost blackened by night, and detritus fills our pathway.

He looks over his shoulder at me and then points towards the ground. 'See that pile of leaves?'

Indeed, I see it once my eyes travel to it. A large circular pile of green, orange, and ochre leaves covers the dusted ground.

'It's too neat to have just landed there,' he says, frowning.

He's right.

I immediately recognised this trap, I'd used one similar to hide my nets.

Scanning the trees for any hidden rope, I say, 'Trap?'

Darius keeps his eyes narrowed on the leaves. 'I don't think it's just animals in this forest.'

'Humans?' Tibith's voice squeaks from below, causing Darius to look at him with a look that's just as unsure as Tibith's.

It is clear that this well-thought-out trap couldn't have been created by the creatures we've encountered so far. But humans? Most, if any, have never survived in this forest – that we know of, at least.

'Or it's the Elven King,' I suggest, and those amber-brown eyes – gold and honey specks – lift.

'Maybe,' he replies, but something unspoken lingers between us.

I want to hate it.

I choose to always hate it.

Hate him.

But the second it looks as if he is going to say something more, my eyes catch a spiralling vine, alive and covered in ivy and thorns, slithering up a tree, like an ominous snake behind him. It coils around the branches, and my eyes grow wide as I watch it shoot out in our direction. I shout for Darius to look out, and he dodges to the left as I grab my blade, chopping the vine in half.

The three of us stare down at it as it sizzles into dust.

Tibith gasps. 'Like magic, Darry!'

Darius chuckles. 'Ever experienced something like that in your trapping days, Goldie?'

I throw Darius a sarcastic look. 'I'd say you were much worse than this.'

'Impossible,' he teases, and strangely it eases me to see him smiling again.

When I go to smile back, something wraps around my ankle and knocks me down. My chest slams against the ground, and a dull ache reverberates through my entire body before being dragged through the dirt.

Darius yells my name, with Tibith panicking in the background. I twist onto my back, glancing at my leg where a thicker vine pulls me along.

Give me a break, for Solaris's sake!

I try slashing it with my blade, but this time it seems indestructible, angry even. Jamming the dagger into the ground, I resist its pulls as Darius catches up to me, attempting to cut it with his blade. Another vine twists around his sword, yanking it out of his grip. He swears when one tries to grab him but successfully evades it.

My fingers go taut, the pressure of holding on to my dagger begins to hurt, and a desperate cry comes out of my throat as my grasp slips.

Darius catches my hand in seconds, falling onto the ground as he tries hauling me towards him.

Tibith climbs up his arm, trying to help him before a mouth hidden between the tree trunks opens, and we meet with a cave filled with slime and darkness.

Panic sharpens like a knife in my gut, and I look at Darius, his forearms straining as he tugs at me. 'If I live through this—'

'You can thank me.' His voice is low and forced. 'I know.'

I manage a scowl before he grunts and finally yanks me from the grip of the vines. I wince as they scrape my skin, and then I'm on top of Darius as he falls onto his back.

Tibith growls at the tree, and I press my hands on Darius's chest, lifting my head to look at him.

We're both panting as I ask, 'Will there ever be a day when we stop saving each other?'

'I hope so,' he says, in an obvious way that shows he doesn't mean it. 'I can't stand any more of your stubbornness.'

'And I can't stand you,' I reply with a smile as I get off him, and he helps me to my feet.

His usual cocky grin broadens, only to vanish as he watches me.

He must see it before I can feel it as his face becomes a blur, and I can't focus straight.

'What's wrong?' his voice echoes.

I stumble. Burning sensations swell beneath my skin, and pain shoots from my ankle towards my thigh. Collapsing into Darius's arms, he kneels on the ground as his features carve into an edge of concern. It feels like my lungs are swelling, and it only gets more painful every second I inhale. It's like someone is stabbing my ankle over and over.

'The vine,' I muster. 'It must have been poi— poisonous.'

Darius looks at my ankle, and I hear Tibith's frightened gasps as he says, 'Darry, her leg.'

I'm losing consciousness, but Darius shakes me in his arms. 'Nara, look at me.'

I do.

'I'm going to try to give you some of my dragon blood so it triggers the healing process.'

I'm nodding, but it hurts. Everything hurts.

Each breath is shorter than the last.

My vision swirls, causing nausea to coat my throat before I look as Darius bites down on his wrist. My lips part just enough for a droplet of blood to get inside my mouth, and for the strange taste of sweetness like honeyed fruit to brush against my tongue. I swallow, my head resting on Darius's chest as we hear, past the distant whispers of the forest's breeze, multiple voices inch closer and closer.

Darius turns his head, and I can just about make out shadowy figures coming through the bushes.

'Darius,' is the last thing I whisper before succumbing to exhaustion.

CHAPTER NINE

I cringe as light shines through the gaps of the twig roof above me; I raise an arm to protect my eyes. And as I lay here, my hand curls around what might be straw. It's a bed of sorts, but the way my head is pounding makes me think back to the day I fractured my bones after falling out of a tree when I was a child.

When I gaze to my left, I turn to stone as I'm greeted by a smooth green face with obsidian eyes and leaf-shaped ears standing there, watching me.

I let out a noise between a gasp and a scream as I scramble off the bed. My back hits a wall made of branches while the Elf continues to stare with curiosity. Blinking further at what I'm seeing, I notice it's a beautiful female with a human figure. She's long and slender, wearing a dress made from whole green leaves and vines holding it together around the neck. She leaves nothing to the imagination, showing her toned stomach and silky long raven hair ending below her waist. Her skin glistens as she steps forward and tries to approach me.

'Who are you?' I ask, my palms sliding along the wall as I move to get away. My eyes dart around the small hut, taking in the frame of the wooden bedposts and straw I was lying on. 'Where am I?' I try to slow my breathing, piecing together what I last remember.

Vines.

The forests.

Poisoned.

I glance down at my ankle, now healed because of . . . Darius.

My gaze darts up as panic skids along my spine. 'There was a man with me and a—'

'They are safe, just like you.' The elf's voice is soft and tranquil.

I stare at her, unsure whether to trust her words. 'Take me to them.'

She bows her head. 'Of course.' And extends a slim arm towards the door.

Sensing that I won't move until she does first, she nods once and leads the way.

I follow her out of the hut and across a wooden plank bridge. It creaks and quivers beneath my feet, and I can see we're high above, amid trees, by gently gazing over the ropes keeping it together. If I jumped over, I'd almost certainly die. More bridges cross over others in the middle, going to shelters and further down into the forest. Elves in leaf-like attire, such as the one in front of me, stop what they're doing and stare at me. But my attention is drawn to one who appears youthful as he tilts his head, and his eyes follow me every second I walk. I turn away, a huge pressure building in my stomach. I was just in Darius's arms last night, poison running up my leg, and now I'm in this strange place.

'How did we get here?' I ask the female in front. She does not turn as she carries on walking.

'You were brought here by our kind,' she answers. 'Woodland Elves.'

I'd heard of woodland Elves, but I'd not known they'd reside in the Screaming Forests.

'Our leader,' she continues, 'Renward runs this part of the forest. Rest assured, though; he poses no harm.' She climbs up a small step from the bridge and onto a wooden platform.

A crowd of woodland Elves surround a weeping willow tree, whispering to each other as they notice me. I stare back at them, eyeing how some have an earthly flesh to them and obsidian hair varying in length.

My eyes soon land on Darius and Tibith on the side. Darius's gaze connects with mine, and relief fills me so that I cannot help but start rushing towards them. He immediately does the same but an unpleasant rasping voice startles us halfway.

Everyone goes silent, and I look to my right, where the weeping willow tree stands. Beneath the arching branches, a male Elf sits on a throne made of bark.

Renward, I assume.

He rises, revealing black painted marks on his lean chest and hollow cheeks. 'Bring her forth,' he says, and I'm dragged by the arm by the same female Elf I'd walked up here with.

I come to a stop in front of Renward. He looks down at me with no expression whatsoever.

'A human,' he says, night eyes darting to the other side. 'A Tibithian and a dragon shifter together. We haven't seen such a thing in—' He gestures his hand in vague thought. 'Ever!'

The crowd laughs at that.

Renward silences them by raising his palm. His eyes narrow in on me. 'What is your name?'

I take a sharp breath. 'Naralía.'

'Naralía,' he repeats, and his tongue darts out like a reptile.

'Tell me, what is it you seek that you've dared to cross into our borders?'

I glance towards Darius, and his expression is tight as he studies Renward. Returning my gaze, I warily say, 'We wish to meet the Elven King.'

There is nary a murmur or sound from anyone.

Renward strides closer to me, curious. 'What is the reason behind that wish?'

I raise my chin. 'It is for something that can hopefully bring peace to all of Zerathion.' I refrain from mentioning our intention of gaining access to the Isle of Elements or that we are wanted by the Queen in Emberwell.

A snicker falls from Renward's mouth. 'And you think the king can help you there?'

Another laugh explodes from the crowd. They must assume it's a stupid reason. 'We can only pray that he does,' I say, and they quieten. 'We've not gone through the forest intending to attack or harm anyone. We just want to survive long enough to meet the king.' I lower my head for him to see how serious I am. 'If you show us the way to him, we'd be eternally grateful.'

'Why do you think we would show you the way?'

'I don't.' My answer has him tipping his head to the side. 'But it is only a humble request.'

He hums to that, his stare scrutinizing. 'I see.' Minutes pass by before he says, 'Very well, if I am to take you to him, I only have but one condition.'

Of course, there is going to be a price to pay. How foolish of me to think otherwise. 'Name it.'

Renward smiles, sharp teeth gleaming. 'We are to be wed.'

Well, that is unexpected.

I'm sure my surprised look reflected off Renward's blackened eyes.

From the corner of my vision, Darius steps forward. 'What—'

'Why?' That is all I ask, cutting Darius's attempt at a protest.

'It is a tradition in our tribe for the leader to find himself a bride. I've searched for months for someone suitable.' A gaunt finger reaches out to touch my hair, and I inwardly shudder when his slippery skin briefly strokes mine. 'And now I've found the perfect one . . . a human.' He throws his head back and laughs. 'Oh, I can already envision the looks on the rest of the Elven lords' faces, but most of all, the king of Terranos himself.'

Darius is beside me within seconds, his words fierce as he aims them at Renward. 'If you think I'm going to let you—'

'Yes,' I say simply, sensing Darius's eyes snap in my direction. 'I will marry you.' Renward's smile is sly as he takes another step, but I lift my palm to stop him. 'But only after you have taken us to the Elven King.'

It's a risky deal, but I've made risky bargains all my life.

Renward moves back and inclines his body. 'Of course. In the meantime, why don't you accompany us tonight for a celebration as my betrothed?'

I agree with reluctance, giving him a bright fake smile before he gestures for the crowd to depart and strolls back up to his wooden throne.

I turn to go back to the hut when Darius's firm hand clutches my arm. Looking up at him, I realise we are too close for comfort.

He lowers his head, lowers his voice too. 'Do you have any idea—'

'I know what I'm doing,' I say past gritted teeth. 'I've made plenty of deals before, remember?'

He doesn't reply for a few seconds, and we're both staring at each other with absolute conviction as he says, 'We don't know if we can trust them or the king.'

I know that. 'I'm not asking you to trust them. I'm asking you to trust *me*.'

He looks over at Renward, and a muscle twitches in his jaw before he sighs. 'Fine . . . but if for any reason –' he turns his head and his eyes shift to meet mine '– he does anything I don't like, then I'm taking you out of here, and I don't care if we're dealing with monstrous centipedes or deadly vines, I will get us to the Elven King myself.'

The solemn promise in his words wraps around my heart, tightening it until it hurts. 'I don't doubt that for a second.'

A slow smile makes its way onto his lips as he lets go of my arm and then says, 'Glad to see your ankle is at least healed.'

Without much thought, I glance down at my foot. 'I suppose I have you to thank for that . . . *again*.'

His laugh is like silk against my skin, enticing me to wrap myself up in it. His head dips, and my cheek brushes along his as he whispers in my ear, 'So, what now, Goldie?'

I grin. 'Didn't you hear? A celebration is being thrown in my honor.' I give him a once over, humming in thought. 'I say you'd make a great servant for the king's betrothed, for the time being.'

His smile takes on a mischievous glint, and his expression overall says he loves the idea.

'What about me, Miss Nara?' Tibith asks, appearing beside Darius.

I smile down at him. 'You're my protector, of course.' My gaze flickers to Darius again, giving him a final look of confidence before walking away and saying over my shoulder, 'Coming, Tibith?'

He buzzes with elation and rolls by my side as we make our way to the hut.

CHAPTER TEN

Satiny hands brush against my torso, adorning me with leaves and peony flowers. Two Elven females had entered our hut earlier to dress me for Renward's celebration tonight. I'd planned on wearing what I already had on, no matter the state of my shirt. But they insisted on adorning me with Elven wares.

'You look wonderful, Miss Nara,' Tibith says, bouncing up on one of the wooden stools opposite me.

I smile, feeling uncomfortable on the inside as I look down at the ivy wrapping around my calf. Leaves sewn onto sheer fabric come to a point at the end of my knees with slits high enough to show my thighs on both sides. I admire the effort these Elves are going to, but my back is completely exposed, with only two leaf pieces crossing over each other to cover my breasts. I'm worried that one clumsy movement and everything will fall apart.

One of the Elves murmurs something in a different language to the other – a clicking sound with their tongues as she fastens the top part around my neck.

'Miss Nara,' Tibith makes a noise I'd imagine a child would make when curious. I thank the female Elves, then usher them away as he asks, 'Why did you accept the frog's marriage request?'

My lip twitches, biting back a laugh, yet I can't help but draw my brows together. 'Frog?'

He nods. 'Darry said he was a toad.'

That makes more sense.

'Well,' I say. 'You were there, weren't you, Tibith? It was just a deal.' Walking like I need to go to a privy, I head towards the other side of the hut. There is no mirror in here, so I make do by brushing out my hair with my fingers. I frown as I stumble upon a wilting peony and pluck it out, placing it front and centre over the flower wreath around my head.

'I wish you could marry Darry,' Tibith mumbles, causing my hands to stop midway through brushing.

I drop them to my sides and turn to Tibith.

He's staring up at me with glistening, hopeful eyes.

Not even in my wildest dreams would have been my usual response, but a funny tilt in my stomach makes me laugh awkwardly as I say, 'I'm sure if he could, he would marry himself.' I nibble on the corner of my bottom lip as Tibith tilts his head, urging me to go on. 'And besides, why would you want me to marry him? We hardly get on.'

Tibith lowers his head, swinging his feet over the stool. 'Because then we would finally be a family, Miss Nara!'

An invisible knife shatters through my heart.

Family.

A sharp pain shoots behind my eyes, and I blink it away as I rush over to him, not caring if I rip apart my dress. I drop to my knees and rest my hand on his soft pelage. 'What about the shifters back home?'

His eyes are enormous compared to the roundness of his face as he lifts his gaze. 'It is not the same, Miss Nara.'

I exhale, silently agreeing with him. It took me a while to get used to not having my parents around. It's not the same without them, but I wouldn't trade my brothers for the world.

'Tibith?' I whisper, watching how sorrowful he looks when he's always cheery. 'Do you want to know what I do when something saddens me?'

He perks up a little, and I smile. 'I carve,' I add. 'Do you want me to show you?'

Something a lot like excitement flickers in his gaze. He nods, hops off the stool, and treads towards the wooden bedposts. I slowly stand up, looking at my leather glove and dagger on the dresser beside the bed. As I grab the blade, my hand hesitates in picking up the glove too.

I release a long breath before swiping the dagger and not the glove.

I step onto the platform watching the Elves as they parade around, dancing to the sound of others clapping their hands as a form of music. Torchlight lanterns hang above vines, causing shadows and suffusing everything in green light.

Tibith runs off from my side, and I go to chase after him when Renward steps in front of me, grinning. 'You fit right in.' He glances at me wholly. It doesn't sit right with me, but I still smile at him as he takes my hand. 'If I may have your attention,' he announces to the crowd. The music and dancing stop as they all turn their heads to us.

I hardly pay attention to Renward's words once he begins talking, as my gaze skips over males, females, and even children before it catches Darius's. His toned chest is bare, with the same black paint Renward has smeared across him. The only piece of clothing covering him is the brown cedar breeches.

My eyes eat it all up until our gazes clash, and every sound fades. We stare before he lets his eyes linger on my dress with a heated spark.

I'm suddenly aware of my breathing, the soft air intake . . . the heavy exhale. I scold myself for feeling this way . . . for feeling vulnerable.

'– I expect you all to treat her with respect.'

I break eye contact with Darius, looking up at Renward as he says that. My body tingles, still imagining Darius staring at me, but Renward quickly erases that thought as he gives me a slow smile, showing how menacing he can look.

'After all,' he says. 'She is my bride-to-be.'

This time, I can't fake a smile as I snatch my hand away, and the celebrations resume. He tells me to enjoy the night, but I don't reply, and with a courteous nod, he heads to his wooden throne.

'You make an awful bride,' Darius says, and I look at him just as he approaches me with a coquettish grin.

'You make an awful servant,' I retort, my upper lip curling with disdain.

He chuckles, swallowing up the space between us. 'Well, for me to be your servant, you have to give me orders.'

'Fine.' I flash him a tight smile. 'Dance with that Elf over there.'

He looks over his shoulder as my eyes stay on an Elf with long hair waves and glowing skin.

'She seems to have her eyes all over you,' I say as he faces me again with a superior, arrogant gleam. I try to remain calm and unbothered. 'If only she knew how dreadful you are.'

His head dips. 'I wonder the same thing with Renward choosing you to marry him.'

I pout with mockery. 'Upset he didn't choose you?'

'Obviously,' he murmurs with a smile, but it disappears the longer he looks at me.

I hum with a lilt of sarcasm in my tone. 'Have a wonderful dance, Darius. I'm sure you won't have a problem wooing her with your narcissistic tendencies.'

Just as I'm about to go the other way, someone grabs me by the waist before I can make the complete turn. Darius presses me against him, and my hands instinctively touch his chest as my feet are slightly raised off the floor.

Damn him.

Damn him and how small my palms look against his chest.

'What are you doing?' I hiss quietly, glancing around in panic. 'Renward could be watching us right now.'

'Let him.' A glint of dark promise thrums through his words, causing my heart to race. 'Or are you afraid?'

I pinch my lips together with frustration. 'I'm not afraid. Now put me down.'

He doesn't. 'Let me ask you something that I have been dying to know.' He adjusts his arm around me, pulling me closer and eliciting a gasp from me. 'If you were so curious the other night as to knowing what love is, does that mean you've never fallen in love before?'

The question startles me. I frown as every bit of my frustration crumbles. 'Why are you asking me that?'

'Does it?' his whisper comes across strained, a plea even.

I think back to what he said . . . *when it hurts.*

Of course it hurt when Lorcan lied to me, and when he died, it hurt more because I had still grown to care for him despite his lies. But that was never love.

Darius searches my eyes, dark gold chipping away at my pride and stubbornness.

'Never.' The word comes out so softly you would think I said nothing. Yet Darius seems taken aback by it.

His grip loosens, and he lowers me to the ground as I stagger away. We stare at each other in a way that consumes us both with despair. He drops his head pensively, and a numb sensation buzzes through my veins as I turn around. I pass through the crowd, making my way towards the high table.

I lay my palms flat against it, dragging in slow breaths for relief. But all that fills me is shame – the shame of knowing that perhaps Lorcan truly had meant he had loved me, and I didn't love him.

I love you too much for this to ruin everything.

I squeeze my eyes shut at the memory, and my knuckles ball into fists before I gaze at a bowl of exotic fruits. An assortment of jackfruit, papayas and a strange, teal-coloured fruit the shape of a plum. As my stomach growls, I snatch it from the bowl and sigh, praying my thoughts about Lorcan will vanish as soon as I bite into it.

A surge of every sweet fruitful flavour I've ever tasted bursts on my tongue. It doesn't take long until I forget all my problems, and the world around me slows down like a dream.

CHAPTER ELEVEN

ours have passed as I smile dreamily, raising my hands and dancing like everyone else around me. Leaves begin to fall off my dress, but I don't care, for I enjoy every moment I move to the Elves clapping.

My body feels light and airy as I create a figure of eight while swaying. I can't think of a time other than at the den where I've felt like this – without any worries weighing me down. Tipping my head back, I inhale and close my eyes before my back bumps against something hard, and I twirl around to find Darius.

I stop dancing as he looks at me with a tense jaw.

I try to keep my eyes on his, but it's too late as I trail the tight muscles of his chest, the density and strength of his abdomen, and how it's caressed by the light of the lanterns above us. 'I see now why everyone calls you handsome.' I stifle a grin; however, a titter escapes me.

He's far from pleased. 'What did you take?'

'Take?' My laugh is never-ending. 'I haven't eaten or drunk anything except for a lovely piece of fruit.' A delicious glowing teal fruit I'd hope to have the pleasure of eating again.

Darius sighs sharply, and I frown at how stern he's acting. He looks around before grabbing me by the elbow. 'I think I should take you back to your hut.'

Unsure if it's the clothes I am in or the command in his voice, my skin feels like it's on fire. I try and tug my arm away, but it's a weak attempt. 'I compliment you for once, and you're trying to drag me out of here?'

His smile is strained. I'm considering offering him one of the fruits I had. 'I'd rather you just keep insulting me,' he says, taking me through the crowd. I see Tibith having a blast at the other end with females stroking his fur, and I chuckle, looking back at Darius.

'Oh,' I say. 'Well, I have a lot of those for you.'

He keeps me close to his side, still holding my elbow. 'Save them for when you've sobered up.'

'I'd rather say them now.'

He stops, and I almost bump into him. Sighing, he turns to me. His eyes are so beautiful, so gold they make me think of golden arrows firing at me – far too dangerous to look at.

'You know, Goldie,' he says low, with no trace of humour. 'I always enjoy a challenge with you. But this time, I need you to listen to me before I do something that you will absolutely hate.'

An amused scoff comes from the depths of my throat; I'm positive I'm spitting. 'That's hardly a difference when I hate every—' I yelp as he puts his arm under my legs and scoops me up against his chest. My hands, on instinct, come around his neck before I scowl down at him as he saunters his way out of the crowd. Embarrassment floods me like a harsh wave as some of the Elves stare at us, and I pray Renward doesn't.

'Will you stop picking me up!' I say, and he ignores me. 'Darius!' I shake my legs, kicking them in the air as he walks without even a smidge of strain while holding me. 'Darius—'

'Keep saying my name. We'll see where that gets you.' His eyes never stray from the front as a smirk gleams off his lips.

I make a vexed face. 'You are intolerable.'

'I thought you said I was handsome a few minutes ago, Goldie?' His eyes jump to mine. 'If you were lying, I'd have to disagree with you there.'

Arrogant ass. 'I was doing just fine until you interrupted me.'

'You had three Elves staring at you the entire time like you were their next conquest.' His words baffle me, how he tightens his jaw as he says it. 'You're lucky I didn't make them swallow their testicles.' The rage and disgust in his voice pierces through my chest. I can only swallow my surprise as we pass the bridge and he pushes open the straw-latticed door to my hut.

He settles me onto the floor, and in some way, I hope to regain the strength in my voice as I say, 'Either way, you have no right to—'

'No right to what, Goldie?' he says quietly. The brush of his hand against my waist makes me look up at him. Any anger is gone, replaced with genuine concern, and when he sees I'm unsure of what to say, he tips his chin towards the bed. 'Get some rest.'

I can't rest.

He turns from me, strolling to a wooden chair in the corner of the room. He sits down, and my eyes slowly pinch together at the action.

'What are you doing?' I ask.

He leans back, taking out a coin from his pocket and flipping it. 'Waiting until you fall asleep.'

I am momentarily shocked. He's waiting until I fall asleep?

Is it to protect me? To save me from those Elves he'd mentioned?

I expel a breath, having nothing to say because falling asleep is just as hard for me as it is for him. Climbing into bed, I turn my back to him. It doesn't help to know he's watching me with guarding eyes, so I toss and turn, my mind buzzing with thrill and too much energy.

Minutes pass by without so much as a word from either of us. I blow out an aggravated breath and sit up. My gaze snaps to him, and his brows jerk up almost amusingly before I say, 'You sitting there and watching me isn't helping.'

He rises. 'Then, as your humble servant, I will stand guard outside.'

He starts for the door, and I don't know what takes over me when disappointment catches me by the throat, and I jump from the bed. 'Wait!' As he turns, I am already standing in front of him. My eyes are glued to his chest. I quickly forget whatever it is I want to say, allowing my hand to do what it wants instead.

I slowly drag my palm up his abdomen, fingertips touching the grooves and curves of his muscle. Through the midnight blue light of the forest and the darkness inside this hut, our eyes fixate on one another. He's not saying anything, but I know he wants to. He wants to say a lot and does not know where to begin. His eyes are practically begging for a sense of reality to kick in.

Or perhaps that's part of my mind saying it for me.

'Nara,' he says my name almost in a warning. 'Go and rest—'

'What does it feel like?'

He wears a frown on his features. 'What does what feel like?'

My gaze again falls to his chest, and heat races between my legs. I want it to stop, but I cannot. I'm hypnotized. 'To experience something that is not tame with someone else?'

I can feel the deep heaves of his breathing as his chest moves beneath my fingers. As I look up, he swallows hard.

'I think you know the answer to that already, Goldie.'

I shake my head, not knowing what I need. I just know I'm aching. 'I have never done anything more than a kiss,' I whisper. 'Maybe – I want more.'

'What you need is to lie down. Who knows what kind of fruit that was.'

'*What you need is to lie down.*' I wiggle my finger in the air, imitating his stern voice, before I loosen a laugh and whirl around to face him. 'Why must you be so serious when I decide I finally want to have some fun?'

He ignores me, trying to get me onto the bed.

I pat the straw as I plop down on it. 'Now you're acting just like Idris. Whenever I did something wrong, he either ignored or chastised me.'

He watches me move across the bed, messing with the waves of my hair until I lay on my stomach. I prop my elbows up and rest my face against the palms of my hand. 'But do you want to know a secret?'

There's a smile, and he bends down, caging me in with his arms at my sides. 'Enlighten me.'

I grin. 'I *lived* to defy him.'

If I won't live to serve, I will live to defy.

'Well, it looks like that has rubbed off on everyone else you've met.'

A lazy smile sprawls across my face, dimming when he straightens up and starts to leave again. I quickly grab his arm. 'Don't go.' I gesture towards the extra room beside me, and my cheeks burn at the invitation falling from my lips. 'Stay here.'

Time seems to pass the longer he doesn't answer. He stares at me, and I stare back. Whatever is going through his mind is a struggle of its own.

Finally, he nods, and my heart picks up as he lowers beside me. His eyebrows pucker together as he tests the bed out. Palms steadying him and his shoulders tensing before he lies down, staring up at the ceiling. His legs dangle over the edge, not adjusting to his full size, and I can tell he's uncomfortable.

I turn to the side as my hand rests beside my head. 'I know . . .' I falter. 'I know why you don't sleep on beds.' The words come out with a shuddering breath I hadn't intended. When he looks at me, I add, 'I asked Tibith.'

He faces me, and the tips of our pinkies touch in front of us. He smiles. 'Gathering enough information on me to later blackmail me, Goldie?'

'I was curious.'

'You still are.'

I am.

The silence drifts in like a soft breeze. He sighs, giving in, and doesn't focus on me any more. 'I was his pet more than a son.'

Deep twisted hurt flows from his voice, and a chill runs down my back at his revelation. My mind recalls Ivarron's words and how furious Darius had gotten when he'd called him a pet.

'For Rayth, I had to act like the creature I am.' He lets out a forced laugh. 'Suppose I got used to it.'

I listen to him as he tells me of the times Rayth would feed him leftover bones and scraps of food lacking the nutrition a young boy needed. The person who managed to look after him the most was . . . Lorcan. At first, they never saw eye to eye. In fact, they were always pinned against each other, but then one night, after Darius was punished and made to sleep outside, Lorcan went to him. He brought him a blanket, and that's when Darius began telling him stories. Made up ones where it always ended victoriously.

It reminds me of when I'd beg my brothers to tell me stories of adventure and freedom.

But the way Darius believes he deserved what Rayth put him through causes a shift in my heart. I touch the side of his face, and his eyes flicker up at me. 'You are no one's pet.'

I mean it.

Intoxicated or not, I do.

His smile doesn't reach his eyes, but he glides the back of his hand across my collarbone, affectionate and thankful. A buzz circles inside my stomach, zapping at every part of me with his touch.

He shuffles closer, and I try to hide how it's not affecting me when in truth, right now, all I want is to lean into him.

I blame whatever was in that fruit.

His fingers trace up my arm, warmth radiating from them, making me slightly arch my back. It's comforting, yet a flutter of goosebumps invades my skin, and I hold back a sigh, trying to think of other things, *normal* things.

I can't.

'Tell me something.' Anything to get rid of these feelings.

'Like what, Goldie?'

'Something that will annoy me.'

His low sensuous laugh doesn't help. 'It's no fun if you're asking me for it.'

I shift my body even closer to him; the creak echoes within the hut like a broken ship. I'm confused with myself, but I can't help it. And he can't either. His hand brushes my cheek, and I turn my head as the pad of his thumb collides with my bottom lip.

He traces it, and the tickle of his faint touch makes me tremble. It's too short for him to notice but not short enough for him not to feel it.

Between the slits of moonlight from the walls, I see his eyes glaze with something unknown. 'I hate these,' he murmurs, dragging my lip down with his index finger.

Warmth unfurls inside me, triggering a realisation within.

His voice says he hates my lips, but his eyes say he doesn't.

'What else do you hate?' I ask. My voice is hardly my own as he looks at me.

'Your hair.'

He loves my hair.

'Your stubbornness.'

He loves my stubbornness.

'Your strength.'

He loves . . . my strength. Something I don't believe I ever have any more.

'Your laugh,' he whispers, and it goes straight to my heart.

It annoys me that I start smiling, but it's inevitable, causing a wide one to bloom on his lips. My hand reaches out to his chest, and I press it flat against his skin, feeling how taut he goes. It's not long before his breeches stretch and grow hard around my lower abdomen.

I close my eyes, breathing hard. I'm suddenly dizzy, hot and flushed all at once. *Think of something else, think of something else, think of—* 'Why do you carry a coin everywhere you go and leave others behind after you've committed a theft?'

My eyes pry open over my random question. Darius's brow lifts, amusement tinging the edges of his lips.

'That's something I can't answer right now, Goldie.'

'Why not?'

He has this cocky smile as he answers in mock confidentiality, 'It's a secret I hold dear to my heart.'

My nose scrunches as I smile at him. 'You're the worst.'

He grins. 'And you, Goldie.'

Tipping my chin back, I hum. 'Fine, answer me this. Why are

dragons so fascinated by gold?' I had always known about how they are drawn to it, but I was never interested in learning more about them, not before my bond with the Ardenti dragon.

Darius thinks carefully for a few moments. 'Gold to dragons is like how humans need sun. Without it –' his fingers drag down the length of my arm and goosebumps attack my skin, '– there is no life to live.'

I lick my lips as though they are dry and clear my throat. 'In other words, it's an obsession.'

He chuckles. 'Yes. I can't explain why, but whenever we see it, or someone entices us with it, we need more.'

We're silent until I whisper in a bid to change subjects, 'Tell me a story.'

'What about?'

'Surprise me,' I say, slowly . . . sleepily.

He chuckles quietly, grabs a peony from my hair, and begins a story that makes me instantly smile. A tale of an adventurous girl brave enough to go against her enemies. His voice soothes me like a melody as he goes on, and eventually, I drift off beside him, too content to think of where we are.

Chapter Twelve

The smell of freshly chopped wood awakens me. I think I'm at home as I stretch out my arms and legs with a wide smile.

Prying my eyes open, sunlight glows above me, and as I blink a few times, I hear the straw hatchings, the sounds of woodcutting and the clicking of tongues from outside.

I turn my head to the side, and it's then that I see no one there except for a note, causing a flood of last night's memories to come back with a surge of emotions.

I'd invited Darius to lie beside me.

I shoot up from the bed, still wearing my dress, and look around the hut until my gaze snags on Tibith at the foot of my cot.

He tilts his head and smiles. 'Hello, Miss Nara, you're finally awake!'

'Where is Darius?' My voice is hoarse and dry from the morning, and disappointment holds me captive for a second. Why had I expected him to still be here? Mulish, I would have likely kicked him out, knowing me.

'He left early this morning to fetch you some breakfast from one of the Elven people!'

My head darts to the side table again. I pick up the note and flip it open to find a scribbled mess.

Did you know that you snore incredibly loudly? I will make sure to remind you of that, Goldie.
In the meantime, freshen up. I will be back soon.
Yours truly,
The ever-so-dashing thief.

I glare at the note as my lips fight off a smile.

'What does it say, Miss Nara?' Tibith bounces on his toes, and finally, I smile.

I fold the parchment and place it on the nightstand. 'It says how he agrees with me on why he is such a pig.'

Tibith frowns as if to say that doesn't sound like Darius, but as I slip off the bed, leaves crunch around my waist, and I smile, heading for the door.

'Where are you going, Miss Nara?' Tibith asks from behind.

'To find him,' I say, stepping onto the bridge, looking left and right. I don't want to wait until he returns, and I do not even know what I plan to say to him. A thank you always leads to us bickering, and a demand to know why he says he doesn't care about me when he obviously does leads to another disagreement.

But for the first time in a while, I had slept the entire night. No night terrors, no memories of the Ardenti, Lorcan, my father – nothing.

I half run, half walk, greeting a few Elves coming out of their huts. I make it onto a separate platform, turning in a slow circle as the sun beats down on my skin. I was not familiar with how things worked here, I had no idea where to go and most likely, I will need to descend more bridges until—

'Naralía,' a voice says, and every muscle in me hardens.

Twisting to the sound, I see Renward by his door. Fresh raven paint adorns his glistening skin, and his thin lips oddly purse in thought as he notices how I'm wearing the same attire that I had on last night.

'Care to join me?' He turns to the side, motioning his hand to the inside of his hut. 'I won't accept a no.'

My lips curl into a grimacing smile. I don't think many people dare to say no to him.

Faltering on my legs, I glance over my shoulder before unwillingly agreeing to his offer and entering the grand space of his hut.

'Please take a seat.' As he walks past me, he gestures towards the chairs that are covered with straw. There is a table made of oak in the space between them, and when I sit down on one of them, I nod and gather the edges of my dress.

I shift awkwardly, wondering how anyone can consider these to be comfortable. Renward sits opposite me and picks up a small, round fruit from a bowl on the table, offering it to me.

I recognise it in less than a heartbeat.

Teal, plum-shaped – the one I had last night.

The moment I shake my head, he puts it down, and I continue to take in my environment. His shack is considerably more spacious than the others that are located here. There's a desk on the other side of the room, handmade shelves, and the smell of pine lingering in the air. My eyes draw back to his desk. Scrolls of parchment lie underneath books just as something catches my attention – lines, drawings – a map.

'You left the celebration early last night,' Renward says, drawing my attention from the desk to him as he hands me a timber cup and steam rolls off the top with a herbal scent. 'Why is that?'

'Exhaustion,' I answer. 'You must know how tiring travelling through the Screaming Forests must be.'

His hum is thoughtful and curious as he rubs his upper lip. The tips of his fingernails are dark moss green and slender – likely to snap in half with hardly much force. 'The dragon shifter . . . who is he to you?'

Why do you want to know? 'His name is Darius,' I correct him with a frown. 'And he is –' A pause as I think of a term for what he is. Frenemy, arrogant ass, *past* enemy? '– My ally.'

Disbelief rakes over him as he laughs. 'Last I recalled, mortals and shifters did not get on.'

'They don't.' I choose not to offer him more information on the matter. 'Have you been living here since the Elven King created the forests?'

His chuckle is shrill and unpleasant, like a boiling iron pot whistle. 'Is that what everyone believes? That he created—' He gestures to the space around him. 'This?'

My brows bunch together, full of doubt. 'It's what we've grown up to be told.'

He shakes his head like it is a travesty that we know little – that *I* know little – of our world. 'Our kingdom is the largest of Zerathion, yet we are always forgotten.'

Or perhaps the constant hatred between kingdoms gets in the way of uniting us all.

'You know,' he says, the words slow and thoughtful. 'Three hundred years ago, we lived in the woodlands outside the borders of the city of Thalore. Sadly, that is all now owned by Dark Elves too.'

'Dark Elves?'

'Thalorians,' he corrects himself. 'Elves of shadow and destruction. They've never gotten along with other Elves in Terranos.' He mentions a few of the main cities of Terranos, Thalore, Melwraith – a territory that belongs to mountain Elves near the West, and Olcar – the city where the King and most high Elves reside.

It's all very new to me, but the question that keeps running through my head is the one Renward posed: *is that what everyone believes?*

I cut him off halfway through with a shake of my head and a scrunch of my brows. 'I'm sorry, I must ask . . . if the King didn't create the Screaming Forests, then who did?'

He grins like he was expecting that question. 'Sarilyn Orcharian.'

Shock wraps around my neck, suffocating me for a moment.

The air becomes uneasy around us before he says, 'Your Queen.'

My mouth dries. 'How?'

Renward waves his hand with a contemptuous expression. 'She was a powerful sorceress – a shame it's how she lost it.' Creating this must have taken a toll on her powers. 'To think, a shifter such as a Rivernorth is all it took for her to become who she is now.'

My hand grips the cup even tighter. There's something in the way he says it that I don't like. 'Aurum didn't make her the person she is today.' I look up through narrowed brows. 'She did that herself.'

Surprise mixed with interest flickers across his eyes. 'Is that so?'

'Vengeance can turn us blind at times.' I would know. It's all I thought I wanted since my father's death. I despised dragons, thinking they were at fault.

Renward seems fascinated by this answer, tilting his head as he leans forward in his chair. 'Would you have done the same as her?'

I consider it, and a thousand thoughts pierce my mind, enough to give me a blazing headache. 'I would have thought about it,' I say, not bothering to hide that statement. 'Anyone would, out of anger, spite and heartbreak. Whether we choose to act on it, in the end, differentiates us. Sarilyn happened to have chosen that path, but no matter what she might have accomplished – shifters dying at her mercy, an army of Venators and hundreds of mortals at her side – she's still alone . . . nothing can ever replace that void.'

Renward's stare never falters from me. My stomach hollows, not for fear, but because he has that same stare with which Lorcan would look at me – *intrigued*.

Someone interrupts us, barging past me. It's a male Elf who ignores my presence and says to Renward, 'Meridi wishes to speak with you.'

Renward's slit-like eyes don't move from mine. 'Send her in.'

I rise from my seat, seeing this as my cue to leave. I bid Renward farewell and start heading towards the doorway.

'Naralía,' he calls out to me, and I tense. 'Do you know if all the Rivernorths were killed?'

Like a shiny object catching the attention of a creature, he has me interested. 'Yes, I believe so,' I say over my shoulder.

'Then you should have nothing to worry about when it comes to bringing peace to Zerathion.'

I'm about to whirl around when Meridi enters, rambling about not catching enough creatures from the forest. I don't think anyone realises my hesitation or the confused expression on my face as I look back.

A breeze beats through the air, trees howl, and for a moment, they sound as if they are . . . *screaming*.

Souls trapped, wanting freedom.

Something unexplainable then skitters along my back. My blood hums, in tune with the strange energy in the air, nature and the forest. But this feeling quickly disappears as the sounds of a struggle emerge from one of the bridges. I turn my head and rush quickly to where my hut is. Outside the door, Darius holds up a young male Elf by the back of his moss green shirt with Tibith beside them, growling on all fours.

I'd smile at Tibith's need to fulfill his protective duties over us if it weren't for the fact that I recognised the boy in Darius's grip and recalled how he had stared at me the day I first went to meet Renward.

'Goldie.' Darius grins as he spots me. 'Glad to see you're well.' His gaze darts down to the young Elf. 'Look who I found rummaging through your things inside your hut.'

The boy looks to be around twenty, maybe younger. 'I mean no harm, I promise!'

Darius's voice oozes coolness, but his eyes flicker with impatience. 'Then what were you doing going through her things?'

The boy panics, his gaze jumping from Darius to mine. 'I wanted to know more about her!'

Surprise jolts inside me before I look at him with a skeptical glare. 'Why?'

'Because,' he quietly whispers, 'you are putting yourself in grave danger by agreeing to marry Renward.'

CHAPTER THIRTEEN

The word 'danger' registers in my mind, but I'm not sure I'm even blinking properly at the boy. It is almost as if I've become so accustomed to danger being part of my life that I'm almost desensitised.

Darius lets go of the boy, his brows creasing as he stares at him. 'What do you mean "danger"?'

The boy straightens his shirt, huffing as his eyes dart to mine. His moss-coloured skin shines emerald as the sun hits his head. 'Renward won't take you to the Elven King. He is just saying that to get you where he wants you. Our kind isn't like the rest of the Elves in Terranos. We hold very little nature magic, and Renward loathes that. Especially after the King mocked him at an annual competition between Elven lords. After that, he tried to have the Fallcrown Princesses of Terranos murdered and made the King so enraged he banished all woodland Elves to the Screaming Forests. He hates us, and all Renward wants is to dangle you in front of him like a trophy before killing you.'

'So, we're dealing with someone who is out of his mind,' says Darius in no shape of a question but a knowing statement.

I had never planned to marry Renward. When I asked Darius to trust me, I meant it. I just needed time to figure out the next step. I shake my head; everything this boy says makes my stomach turn. 'Why would he need a human for that?'

The boy's eyes wander in all directions before he speaks quietly, 'Over the years, being inside this forest has made him grow crazier and slowly lose his mind. Nothing he does now makes any sense.'

Tibith lets out a frightened squeak and hides behind Darius's leg. 'Darry, the Elf wants to harm Miss Nara!'

Darius's eyes flit to me. Restrained anger clouds the streaks of gold like a storm hiding the sun. 'He won't.'

He watches me suck in an unsteady breath at the assurance in his voice.

For as long as I live, immortality or not, I will make sure nothing ever happens to you.

'Listen,' the boy says. 'You need to be careful of him and anyone else here, and if they offer you a Mullvern berry, you must not eat it.'

'Mullvern berry?'

'It's a type of fruit harvested by the faeries of the forests. The more you eat, the more you grow weak. It's what he uses to make sure no one ever leaves.'

My mind immediately thinks of a particular blue fruit.

Darius and I glance at each other, he must have thought the same. *We must leave.*

Returning my gaze to the boy, I ask, 'Why are you telling us this?'

The sheer panic in his eyes is disrupted by something sorrowful. 'Because . . . My mother died at the hands of Renward, he sent her deeper into the dangers of the forest alone. I . . . I don't have anyone else.'

My heart twists into the tightest knot hearing the boy's painful story. Maybe it's seeing a young boy with no mother or father that makes me fight to keep my emotions in check. 'What is your name?'

'Aias,' he replies with a bow of his head.

I turn to face Darius. He's staring at me with such concern that he forgets I can see how much this bothers him as well. He never met his father, and when he finally had someone that he could call family, Darius lost him as well.

'Aias,' I whisper as I turn to him, already thinking I can't leave him behind. He has no one else. 'Do you think you can get us out of here?'

'I don't exactly know the way, but—' His lips pinch in thought. 'I know Renward has a map back at his hut, we could use it to figure out a safe route out of here.'

A flutter of relief cascades over me. It must be the one I saw on his desk. 'I think I know which one you mean.' Wasting no time, I turn to the side and glance at the ground. 'Tibith, you go and gather any supplies we might need, food, weapons, anything—'

'I'll go with him,' Aias interjects. 'And once you have the map, you can meet us over the bridge.' He points to where I first saw him, outside a caved-in hut.

I nod in agreement before he and Tibith dash off, leaving Darius and I alone. We're in the same clothes as last night, which reinforces my memories of us sharing a bed. It had to be the fruit I ate; whatever was in it turned me insane.

My cheeks heat up, and I clear my throat. He speaks before I can, 'And what am I to do, Goldie?' There's a mischievous undertone in his voice as he smiles, making my breath scatter.

I lift my chin. 'I want you to use your skills as a thief to steal a map on Renward's desk.'

Excitement flashes in his eyes – a thief in his element. 'As you wish.' He bows rather theatrically to show his allegiance.

I roll my eyes and shake my head, turning to push the door open to my hut when Darius's hand grabs mine. My shoulder knocks against his chest, and his rosewood scent fills the air around us, citrus and the warm summer air blending into one. As my gaze slides from our hands to meet his eyes, I'm captured by the fierceness in them.

'And you?' he asks, voice thick. 'What are you to do?'

'I'm going to distract him.' My voice comes out small. I detest that it keeps happening so much lately.

His lip quirks into a closed smile. 'That should be easy.'

My brow arches. 'Why do you think that?'

He hasn't let go of my hand yet, and he doesn't appear to be in any hurry to do so. He moves his head closer to mine as he glances ahead of me. 'You're already quite distracting as it is, Goldie,' his murmur reaches my core, sending goosebumps up and down my spine.

I tilt my head, our lips a breath away. 'Is that so?'

He hums. 'It's terribly annoying.'

'Now you know how I feel about you.'

He smiles, his eyes hooded as he looks down at me. 'I distract you?'

I glower. 'You annoy me.' Which is just the same in many ways.

He chuckles, the tips of our noses touching. 'I'll see you in a bit, Goldie.'

I don't have the chance to reply as he takes his hand off mine and walks towards the platform. Unable to stop myself from smiling,

I head inside my hut, grabbing my sheath and taking out the sun carving I have been carrying since Lorcan returned it to me the day of the trials. I run my fingers over it before putting it away and rushing out of the room.

My knuckles rap against Reward's door, and he opens it on the second knock.

'Renward!' I say with a forced smile as his forehead scrunches over my abrupt return. 'I believe our conversation from before was cut too short.' I peek inside his hut to where the desk is, only to find the map isn't there any more. Hiding my frown, my gaze cuts back to Renward. 'Do you have a moment to spare?'

He guffaws with a pompous attitude. 'You do not need to ask, Naralía. As my bride, you hold the same title as I do.'

I hold back from cringing at his lie.

A bride whom you will likely try and kill.

He turns to go back inside. My eyes widen, and I shout, 'No!' making him jump as he looks back at me.

My smile stiffens unnaturally. 'It's a wonderful morning. Why don't you show me around?'

Renward looks at me with slight concern. My knotted hair and the crown of flowers falling around my head likely make me look deranged.

He presses his lips into a firm line. 'Certainly.' He steps out, and his hand touches the small of my back, leading me to a different bridge at the other end of the platform. I look over my shoulder with a sly glance as Renward's voice becomes a distant murmur, and I see Darius casually standing by one of the trees near the other huts. He walks towards Renward's hut but gets interrupted by the same female who'd ogled at him at last night's celebration. He gives her a tight smile as he looks down at her, but his eyes quickly shift to mine.

His stare urges me not to worry, but it's not worry I feel. And before I can admit to what it might be, I steel myself and look away.

Chapter Fourteen

I have difficulty listening to Renward's words as he shows me the open-air kitchen. Smoke sizzles from logs as woodland Elves place speared animals on top of them and others come through, carrying bowls of fruits.

All I can focus on is whether Darius has found the map, or is he still talking to that Elf?

Renward brings us around, my arm linking with his as he walks across the bridge. We've barely been out here more than ten minutes. With just a few things to exhibit, he had mentioned most Elves go down into the forests and hunt. I'd gathered where the trap I'd seen the night I got poisoned came from.

'As you can see, Naralía, we don't have much to offer,' Renward says as my eyes search for Darius, but I don't see him. Relief sinks into me before Renward continues, 'After the forests were created and the Dark Elves took over Thalorian woods, this is the only place we can call home.'

A lie.

You were banished here.

Trying to keep up the role of ignorance, I ask, 'Why don't you just try to retrieve those woods?'

He laughs as if I've asked something absurd. I have, *obviously*. 'We could never go against Thalorians. They are creatures of the shadows that practise dark magic.'

Right, and Aias had said woodland Elves possessed little magic.

When we pause outside his door, I purse my lips to the side and turn to him. 'About what you mentioned earlier,' I say. 'What do you know about the Rivernorths?'

He chuckles, waving his hand. 'I won't bore you with all my theories, sometimes I think they are nothing more than my own belief in folklore.'

I stop him from entering his hut. 'I insist.' I truly do. It's what I originally intended to ask, even after I left his place this morning.

From the easy smiles he was giving me earlier, his gaze becomes solemn. He exhales deeply and says, 'The Rivernorths were powerful shifters, as you know. Nothing could kill them. Their history was derived from the Northern rivers of Emberwell, and according to their stories, they were born under the light of a full moon, harbouring the moon's power in those very same rivers.'

They controlled the oceans, the light and the skies. The shifter from the dungeons had said the same.

'But despite the fact that Sarilyn managed to kill Aurum, many believe there is another reason she also slaughtered the rest of his bloodline.'

My brows furrow up at Renward, and a fraction of his sharp teeth peek through his smile.

'She wanted to ensure there was never anyone remaining that could bring Aurum back.'

Dread forms like chunks of coal in the pit of my stomach. What he is implying is that King Aurum may not be entirely gone. 'That's impossible.' I shake my head. 'You can't toy with life and death.'

'You're quite right, but if you truly open your mind, it is a world of endless possibilities. In fact, I recall, Aurum was obsessed with the concept of death.' He lets those words mingle between us, coldness settling over my bones before he gestures towards his door. 'Come, I want to show you something.'

No, I don't want to. I can't think of anything else other than the Rivernorths and their gruesome fate. As someone calls out to Renward, nausea begins to roll up in my throat. I am not looking at him as I place my palm on my stomach and try not to move. Renward informs me that he will be there in a few moments and motions for me to go inside the hut. As I walk into his shack, my eyes clash with those of Darius's and I freeze.

'What are you—' We blurt out simultaneously, causing me to let out a frustrated breath.

He raises a pointed brow at me. 'I'm still trying to find the map.'

Oh, you have to be kidding me.

My lips part, alarm spreading over my features when I hear Renward's footsteps. Darius ducks, heading behind the desk to hide as Renward's shadow forms behind me. I whirl too fast, making me almost slip and fall.

Renward's eyes narrow at my sudden jerky movements. 'Are you alright?'

'Yes!' I beam, letting out a shaky laugh. 'I'm just ever so nervous to be around you.'

He chuckles, partly confused, and then walks past me. I turn, watching him approach the desk, and my stomach buckles in the hope he doesn't spot Darius.

Slow seconds pass in silence as Renward picks something up from the desk and approaches me. He holds an oak box and opens it, stunning me with an emerald stone shaped like an oval. Leather bands are tied around it as he takes it out and hangs it from his fingers like a necklace.

My fingers delicately trace it as its glow reminds me of magic connected to grass and nature. 'It's beautiful.'

'It's yours.'

My gaze shoots up at Renward, and I gape at him. 'Oh, I can't possibly take—'

'I insist.' He makes me turn my back to him, and I watch as he places the stone around my neck, fastening it at the back. I grasp it between my thumb and forefinger, staring at the depths of the shades of green it reflected back at me.

'It is perfect,' Renward says. 'You will make a gorgeous bride.'

I crack an awkward smile. 'You must know I detest compliments.' Turning, I notice Darius holding a rolled piece of parchment. He gives me a nod as he creeps towards the door.

Renward notices my gaze wandering off, and his ears twitch as if he hears something. He turns his head, making me panic before I spin him back to me and my lips smack against him in a closed-mouth kiss. My eyes open to see Darius's wide gaze on us and his jaw tightening the longer I kiss Renward. I wave my hand towards the door, allowing Darius to escape as I fight off the need to gag at the slimy feel of Renward's lips on mine. It's wet, warm and slippery, like a frog. Only a frog sounds like a better option right now.

We part, and I press my lips together, nausea thickening my throat.

'That was quite unexpected.' He chuckles, holding me by the sides of my arms.

I surprise myself at how saccharine I can be as I smile at him. I can't bring myself to speak, unless he wants his chest covered in my vomit.

He closes his eyes, leaning into me again. I grimace before I hear a thump, and then Renward collapses.

I look up from Renward's motionless body to Darius, with his fist in the air. 'Are you serious right now?'

This makes escaping all the more complicated now that he's knocked Renward unconscious.

'He's tried to murder the princesses of Terranos before, and you're concerned over me knocking him out cold?' He tamps his anger down as he takes another step towards me. 'If anything, he has been let off lightly.'

I snort. 'I'd agree if it wasn't for you having hit him out of jealousy!' The accusation sounds foreign on my tongue. It had slipped out.

'Jealousy?' he repeats, brows high as he comes even closer, my breasts touching his chest, and though baffled by my own words, I still nod with defiance, tipping my nose up at him. Eventually, the longer I stare at him, he blows a frustrated breath and grits out his words, 'Fine, you are right. I am jealous, Goldie, satisfied?'

His confession takes me off guard. I blink as if I've misheard or imagined what he said. But the resolute look in his eyes tells me otherwise. For many reasons, I expect him to always say something meaningless whenever I confront him. But I didn't expect his admission to be this blunt.

He stalks out of the hut and my breath comes out in rapid panicked bursts as I look back at Renward one last time before following Darius.

CHAPTER FIFTEEN

I rush out after Darius as we make it onto the bridge and see Tibith and Aias waiting for us. Darius doesn't look at me. He won't mention what he'd said back at Renward's hut. His sole focus is on getting us out of here. But I can't shake it off, and a sickening part of me is happy he was jealous.

'Did you get the map, Darry?' Tibith asks, and Darius waves the rolled-up map in return, passing it towards Aias.

Aias places it inside a leaf sack while carrying a quiver and bow in his other hand. 'Come, I—'

A piercing shriek blasts through the air and we all turn to see Elves heading towards Renward's hut.

My panicked eyes dart to Darius. His jaw is stiff as he says, 'We need to go. *Now*.'

Aias lurches on his shoeless feet, and we sprint after him. Without even a second thought, Darius grabs my hand while Tibith races on all fours along the ropes that hold the bridge as we make it onto a lower level. An arrow flies past us, missing me by just an inch. I look up to see a group of male Elves chasing after us. They make it onto one of the bridges opposite where we are, and as I run, I realise someone had to stall them long enough.

Darius seems to read my mind as he turns his head to me, his eyes darting to the Elves, then Aias.

'Aias!' I shout. 'Hand me the quiver and bow!'

He nods, launching it towards me. I catch it and halt, nocking the arrow as I whirl around. I line it up to where the rope is. My eye zeroes in on it as I inhale and release with one big exhale. As the arrow pierces the rope and jams into the tree, the rope snaps. Elves yell as they struggle to keep their balance; however, I quickly grab another arrow and aim it at the rope holding up the other side of the bridge.

With a sound like a whip cracking through the air, the entire bridge collapses with Elves holding on to the wooden planks.

I pivot with a satisfied smile and frown when Darius throws me a charming smile. 'What?'

He lifts his palms in mock surrender as if he's readying himself to say something, but Aias interrupts, informing us to carry on.

We do, jumping onto a smaller platform to fit the four of us. Ropes suspend it in the air, with bamboo sticks surrounding it like a cage. Aias starts lowering us with a rotating mechanism on the side, feeding the rope through as we go. I race towards the edge, looking down at how far up we still are.

With other Elves recovering from the bridge, I look over my shoulder at Aias. 'How fast can this thing go?'

'Not fast enough,' Darius answers for him, glancing skyward. His gaze snaps to the Elves approaching from other bridges and then at all of us. 'All of you head down. I'll meet you there.'

I gape in horror at the audacity of this man as he jumps onto a bridge. 'What is with this hero complex of yours?'

Aias starts lowering us just as Darius flips a blade in his hand and winks down at me. 'It ensures I always appear better than you.' He charges down the bridge without hesitation.

It bothers me so much that a grain of worry is already growing inside me as I watch him go against the Elves on his own. And I know he expects me to stay out of danger and make sure we get out.

I grunt in defeat, and the lever creaks as we descend. Throwing the quiver over my shoulder, I take a few steps back, heaving my upper body onto the bridge and roll my eyes at my terrible choices. Tibith yells at me for being unsafe, but I instruct Aias to keep rotating the device and get out of here as I quickly haul myself out of our make shift elevator. I throw the sword my brother gave me to Aias and pray that they don't collide with anything as I focus on Elves coming for me with spears from various connecting bridges. They keep saying something to each other and pointing towards my neck, but I can't make out what they're saying as I pull the arrow back on the drawstring and aim straight ahead. I release arrow after arrow, missing at times as I begin running and reach the end of the bridge. I jump onto the next, searching for Darius, and find him at the end, slicing an Elf's throat.

My legs kick off, darting across planks, but as I reach for another bolt, something grips my ankle, dragging me down. My head pulses as everything around me quakes, and my eyes struggle to adjust. I wince, trying to raise myself onto my palms and notice my bow is far out of my reach.

I'm about to grab it, but my attacker is too fast. A hand grabs my hair, yanking my head back.

'Now, where does my bride think she is going?' *Renward.*

He releases me with brute force just as the bridge begins to collapse from the weight of other Elves getting closer to Darius. Vines snap, and I lose balance, rolling off the bridge and dangling off the edge. I'm trying to pull myself up but Renward doesn't take long to regain his footing, and a diabolical look flashes in his eyes as he kneels and wraps a hand around my throat.

My scream is filled with rage and agony. I'm clawing at his hands when the silver gleam of one of my arrows draws my eyes to Renward's right.

'Pity,' Renward laments. 'I quite liked the idea of having a human bride. I guess I'll have to wait for another instead.' His fingers squeeze the air out of me as he stares down at my neck, at the stone necklace he's given me, and moves to take it. But he doesn't get the chance, as I reach for the arrow and jam the tip into his chest at the last second.

He howls, letting go of me as he stands up and stumbles backward. Luckily, I manage to grab on to the edge of the planks again, my feet flailing in the air as Renward cries out and fails to catch himself. He falls off the bridge onto the next, and as I look down, I grimace at Renward's neck bent at an impossible angle and his wide lifeless eyes staring up at me.

I don't have long before my fingers slowly slip, and panic takes over as the plank boards crack. 'No, no, no—' I say and shriek as it breaks.

A hand catches me before I can fall to my death, and I look to see it's Darius. Thick blood coats half of his face and chest as he pulls me up. We don't talk, and I don't thank him. Instead, we're breathless, chests touching and taking in one another.

'Darry!'

Our heads whip towards Tibith and Aias inside the same platform as before.

'We came back for you!' he shouts, ears fluttering as he sits atop the lever Aias is holding.

At the same time, a spear lands beside me, missing us by a small mark from one of the upper bridges. Darius keeps a hold of my hand as we jump over the gaps on the planks and sprint to where Tibith and Aias are.

As soon as we get on, Aias pushes the lever, only for a spear to strike between the iron contraptions. The platform squeaks to a stop, and we jerk forward.

I look at Darius wide-eyed when Aias says with a strained voice, 'It's stuck.' He tries to move the lever, but it won't budge. Another spear hits the floor near Tibith's feet, and furiously, I yank it from the wood, twisting around to aim it at the same Elf who threw it.

Turning back to Darius, he scans the platform and what holds it up before settling on the lever.

'What are you doing?' I ask, purely baffled as he angles the knife in his hand.

'Getting us out of here.' He looks up and sends me a smarmy wink as he says, 'Though I suggest you hold on to something too, Goldie, unless you'd rather hold on to me.'

I eye him with a judgmental glare, placing my hand on the bamboo railing instead. He smiles as he glances at the device in front of him and slams the blade between the iron, breaking the lever.

Once, twice, thrice.

Clanging sounds whip through the air, causing sparks until I hear a snap, and I shut my eyes, clinging on to the bamboo as the rapid force of the rope makes the platform fall. Each beat of my heart pierces through my chest, sending bolts of something so freeing to my stomach.

Upon impact, I lurch forward. The platform splinters and breaks in half as Darius yanks me towards him, and I peer up at him, my palms on his bare chest.

'Is anyone hurt?' he asks, though all the while he's only looking at me. Tibith and Aias say no as Darius's eyes trail over my lips, cheeks, nose and more. 'Are you, Goldie?'

I shake my head vehemently, wanting to say something, anything, an insult at the least.

He moves a strand of my hair from my face and places it behind my ear as he smiles. 'Then let's get out of here.'

We wander for miles, following the map and discovering hidden trails that beckoned us with silence and safety. We eventually relax when we reach a clearing and the sun is shining through the trees onto the grass.

I sit cross-legged on the ground, staring at Darius and Tibith ahead of me, sprawled on the grass, talking and pointing at the trees. For the first time since stepping into this forest, I feel safe. My gaze settles on some roses growing on the bushes nearby and lilacs dotted around us. They make me wonder about Freya, what she must be doing now, if she's arguing with Rydan, if Link is with Illias, or whether Iker and Idris are settling into the den just fine.

I miss them. I miss them greatly.

'Thank you for taking me with you.' Aias sits beside me, handing me my blade. 'I owe you greatly.'

I look at him with a frown and take back the dagger. Owing me is the last thing he needs to do. 'You're the one that told me the truth about Renward's intentions.' Even if I knew I ultimately wasn't planning on marrying him at any cost, Aias had betrayed his own kind for us. 'At least now you're free.'

Aias hums as though he disagrees. 'I don't think I can believe I'm truly free right now, but soon, I know I will be.' His smile is warm and gentle. I want to ask why he believes he is not entirely free yet, but he points towards my other hand and says, 'What is that?'

I unclench my fist, showing him the sun carving I've kept safe throughout our chaotic escape. 'It is a carving of—'

'Solaris,' he says to me.

I smile, flipping the carving over. 'Do you believe in it?'

He shrugs, shaking his head solemnly. 'I used to until my mother died.'

That saddens me, and I think of Lorcan, whether he's with Solaris, whether my mother and father are too.

As I look up between the caved trees circling us, my breath comes out in waves. 'Regardless of everything that happens, there may be a reason for it. When my mother died, she told me to chase all the adventures that came my way. Now I am.'

No matter how dangerous, exhilarating, or painful.

As my gaze flits back to the carving, I'm not sure what possesses me to do this next thing, maybe it is the realisation that I do not need this any more. Yes, it is a memory I had cherished for too long, but it is no longer necessary. I don't need it to remember Lorcan, and I don't need it for good luck.

I pull my arm back and throw the carving out into the bushes.

Aias's eyes blink in bafflement as I look at him. 'You're throwing it away?'

I shrug. 'I don't need it any more.'

He hesitates to come up with words, but he doesn't have to say anything as droplets cascade over my skin and a blissful shower of sweet rain begins to fall, under a golden sun and velvet clouds. It is cold, inviting and refreshing as I tip my head back and let each raindrop kiss my skin. When I look back down towards Darius and

Tibith, they're in their element too, Tibith trying to catch each droplet in his mouth as Darius just takes in the rain, like every single drop lights up within him, like . . . it strengthens him.

Automatically, I stand up and walk over.

'Goldie.' He smiles as I sit opposite him. 'You have never looked worse.'

I can't hold in the laughter that spills out of my lips. 'And you have never looked so atrocious before. I can hardly look at you.'

The rain beats gently along the ground as Darius chuckles. He looks to his left and reaches for a rose, picking it off the bush. He hands it to me, and I snort embarrassingly, remembering he'd done this with a jasmine flower in Chrysos Street.

'What is this for? Do I smell like roses now?' I tease, bringing the soft petals up to my nose for a sniff.

'No,' he drags out the word mockingly, grabbing it off me and inspecting the stalk. 'It is because you are prickly, just like its thorns.'

I should have seen that coming.

I scoff and try to grab it from his grasp, but he puts it behind his back. As I lunge for it again, my earnest smile grows more irritated, and he moves his arm away from my reach. Low, then too high for me to catch. He's laughing in the same way that vexes me all the time yet has my heart drumming dangerously against my chest. Before we know it, we've chased each other quite a way further from where Tibith and Aias were.

The rain trickles down his face and chest, and as he leans back on his elbows, my knee slips as I try again to grab the rose. His arm catches my waist, sliding me so I am beneath him, and my hands come around his neck. My bright laugh mixes with the patter of the rain. I close my eyes briefly before opening them to find Darius's gaze fixed on my lips. A shade of green casts a shadow from the trees, darkening his golden tan. Water drips from the tips of his hair onto my cheeks, and we don't make any sudden movements to get up.

'I've decided,' I say, and his eyes dare not leave my mouth.

'Decided what, Goldie?' he whispers, and I forget where we are, what our task is, and how much we've gone through.

'I—' An intake of breath. 'I want to change the rules from the night I won the Liars, Dice.' He tips his head to the side, his muscled arms never letting go of me as I continue what I'm trying to imply. 'For every question I have, you can ask me one.'

His face breaks out into a grin. 'Five weren't enough for you?'

I shake my head. They really weren't. 'If we don't want to answer it, we don't have to.' I figure it's the best balance for both of us.

'Alright,' he concedes with a nod of his head. 'I'll go first, then. What were you like as a child?'

I smile, thinking he'd have asked me a more challenging question, but he did not. 'Chaotic,' I say, and he laughs. 'Night or day?'

'Day.'

For me, night.

'Favourite story?'

'The staff of Aithne.' It is a tale of a valiant nobleman on a quest to find the queen of stars, Aithne.

He can't help but smile shamelessly at that, his eyes twinkling like golden stardust. 'I heard the lead in that story has a temper. Sounds like someone I know.'

My brows squish together, and I playfully smack the back of his neck. 'Well,' I say. 'No one tests my temper like a certain shifter who loves to steal.'

'He sounds like an amazing shifter. What's he like?'

'Vain . . . likes to irritate everyone—'

'I only like to irritate one person in particular, Goldie.'

I arch an eyebrow. 'So, you admit to being vain?'

His lips carve into an unabashed smile. 'Of course.'

I wet my bottom lip, and we succumb to a comfortable silence. He waits for me to ask him something as I let my right hand slip from his neck, tracing my index finger along the stubble of his jaw. His breathing is slow, hardly steady, as the pads of my fingers now run over his lips.

What else do you hate?

Your hair.

Your stubbornness.

Your strength.

Your laugh.

'Darius?' My whisper as soft as it can be as the rain around us settles. 'Am I still that same asset to you?'

His eyes meet mine, and it's like he stops breathing. His face hardens, not from anger, not from annoyance, but regret.

Many things haunt me from my time in the city, and I *know* he had lied that night of his capture. His heartbeat may have been steady, but his eyes told me something else.

Answer me, I want to say, *tell me what I hope to hear.*

But I don't get that answer as branches crack and split from the other side of the forest like something is approaching us.

Darius keeps his arm around my back and carefully lifts me up with him. I remove my hands from his neck, and I see Aias and Tibith catching up to us. I suddenly see a shadow behind them, someone I do not recognise and I protectively push myself in front of everyone. What appears through the trees is a woman – no, an Elven woman. Pointed ears peek through the loose curls of her raven hair that falls down to her hips, and her skin glistens in a deep bronze tinge.

She has an arrow pointed at us as her grey eyes narrow at our state. Her clothes are made up of a long-sleeve green tunic, fitting her slender figure, with a hood and high ochre woven boots that make her blend in with the forest.

Another second ticks by, and Tibith hugs my leg from behind as more Elves emerge from behind trees. Emerald armour plates cover them as they rest a hand on their hilts, differing from the female Elf before us.

'Who are you?' she asks us, her voice melodious and clear. 'And what is it that you are doing in our lands?'

Chapter Sixteen

The female Elf watches us as Darius speaks of what we've endured the past few days, our encounter with Renward leading up to his death, and the need to meet with the Elven King.

I chew the inside of my lip, growing heavier with unease as she listens intently, hardly blinking.

She slowly lowers her arrow, and what comes from her lips is not the response I had at all expected. 'You all look terrible.' She doesn't sound compassionate, nor does she even smile at the least.

Darius scoffs beside me. I can sense that he is about to object to her and possibly throw a jab my way, but I smack the back of my hand against his chest and say to the Elf, 'Yes, yes, we do, which is why we only ask for safe passage towards the Elven King.'

She stares at me as though searching to see if I am speaking the truth until Tibith steps forward, waving at her.

'Hello, miss,' he says. 'You are very beautiful! My name is Tibith. What is yours?'

She looks down at him with a frown. 'Arlayna.' Then her eyes cut to us. 'A Tibithian who speaks. How?'

Simultaneously, Darius and I look at each other.

'He was taught,' Darius answers.

Arlayna's brows lift, slightly impressed, before masking her expression with a shadowy look. She clears her throat. 'If it is the King you wish to speak to, I can take you there.'

'Your Highness, you know the King despises woodland Elves—' *Your Highness.*

Surprised, I frown as one of the Elves in armour tries to protest. He must be a warrior for the King.

Another Elf, who is tall with light-tanned skin that looks ethereal against the sun, takes a step forward. His dark blonde hair falls in soft waves down to his cheekbone, and I glance at how he folds his arms, built in a way that I imagine he could break every bone in my body with just one hand.

A carved crown made of branches and stars is engraved on his chest plate, along with the other warriors surrounding us. 'I believe it is not up to us to decide whether to take them back. Isn't that right, Princess?' He dips his head towards her, but Arlayna almost looks annoyed by the emphasis of her title.

She tips her chin up and turns her back to us. 'Gather the horses. We will ride with them into Olcar.'

All the guards nod as the blonde's gaze lingers on the princess, like there is more than a professional boundary between them. Arlayna goes to pass him before she pauses and says, 'Aeron.'

Aeron bows his head and glances over at us who are drenched from the rain and barely clothed. I look at Darius, not knowing if this is a good thing that we are finally heading to meet the King. But somehow, he lets all that worry inside me disappear as his fingers thread through mine, squeezing my hand in reassurance.

We make it out of the woods and onto a narrow sloping pathway. I ride with Darius on a white horse while Aias and Tibith are on another beside us. The princess is in front of everyone, leading us through vibrant fields of tall grass. When I look up, there are no grey skies above, and I inhale the fresh air, thinking about how we are finally out of the forest.

As we journey through valleys and stone paths, I keep close to Darius, clutching his torso as I'm overwhelmed by the vastness of Terranos. I never thought I would be here as I spot the castle lying further up on steep hills, standing out against townhouses and treehouses stacked in certain areas where lakes and docks rest. It's larger . . . *taller* than Aurum Castle, and so different to Emberwell as I imagined it would be. It's like some place conjured out of a dream.

Elves all cheerfully talk to one another, their friendly chatter bringing peace of mind as bright skies continue looming over us. We travel across stone bridges with vines and trees growing along buttresses as the city folk stare at us – at Arlayna – gossiping and wide-eyed. Some kneel and bow to her as others offer her goods from their carts, yet she only gives them a small smile and declines when another guard leans towards her on his stallion and whispers something.

My curiosity makes me wonder what was said, but we soon arrive outside iron gates covered in thorny vines and roses wrapping around its bars. Behind it, I can see the giant towers of the castle and other guards standing sentinel with swords sheathed along their backs.

Thick waves of silence roll over us as the guards look at each other hesitantly once they see who the princess has brought back with her. Yet with one order for the gates to open, the guards do as they are told, raising a hand towards the other sentry by the mosaic towers.

Heavy gates lift, the iron grinding and rasping. Tibith covers his ears as I glance at him and Aias staring in awe at the castle.

The inside is so grand. If I were to say something, it would echo for eternity as I gaze at the pillars and the glass ceilings emitting the sunlight through the green squared patterns. Between every post, a guard looks upon us, and at the end, where the dais is, I see the King sitting on a throne made of emerald shards with vines travelling towards the podium and wrapping around the arms of the throne.

My gaze lingers on the long ash-blonde hair draped across King Dusan's shoulders as he leans forward, wearing a crown made of branches and thorns – similar to the crests on the guards' armour. 'Arlayna.' Annoyance brews deep in his hoarse voice as it echoes off the throne room walls. It's a startling sound. 'What are a woodland Elf and two outsiders doing here?'

I try not to show the word 'outsiders' unnerves me.

'Renward is dead,' Arlayna says, and the King's brow arches in intrigue. 'The mortal took care of that.'

Dusan's jade eyes lock on to my neck where the emerald gemstone Renward had given me rests. He drops back onto the throne as he says, 'Mortal?'

'A dragon shifter and a mortal,' Darius replies, low and taut.

'Now that's interesting.' Dusan runs a hand full of silver jewelled rings over his chin, his fair skin so smooth and pale compared to his contrasting rich green tunic and cape. 'I should congratulate you on surviving the Screaming Forests and Renward. Quite brave, although if you're looking for a reward, we do not offer one.'

'We've not come for a prize.' I'm hoping I don't sound too harsh; this is more frustrating than I thought it would be. 'We've come all this way because we would like access to the Isle of Elements.' Surprise flickers in his gaze as I continue, 'We believe it can help us stop a potential . . . *war* outbreak.'

'A war?' he repeats like I've uttered the most unbelievable sentence in the world.

I nod, taking a shaky breath. 'More a great battle predicted by Seers – a battle that can destroy all of Zerathion, should we let it happen.'

'The Isle of Elements has nothing to stop a petty battle; we've had far too many of those in our lifetime to concede to one human's cowardly wish to not stand up and fight.'

'But it possesses power that—'

'That is far too valuable for me to let just anyone enter.' The King raises a brow as if to say he tires from this conversation. He signals for Arlayna to escort us, but I'm not finished.

'I know it was Sarilyn that created the Screaming Forests.' As a last desperate plea, I launch a few steps forward, but Darius places his arm over my chest, like a protective barrier when guards seem to reach for their swords. His eyes shoot me a penetrating glare, calming me before he looks at the King.

Dusan stares at us, narrowing his eyes as he tilts his head. It's a scrutinizing stare that almost lasts as his slim fingers tap against his knee.

I clench my eyes shut and open them as I exhale. 'And I know she crafted the Northern blade, powerful enough to end the reign of shifters. We only ask for one chance to help our lands, to help *you*. We have travelled and tried to survive in the hopes of protecting our world, please do not deny us this possibility.'

'And the woodland boy?'

'He is only a past victim of Renward's maddened mind.'

Everyone is quiet. I can sense Arlayna's eyes are on me as I pray for Dusan to heed my urgency, and another suffering minute lingers between us.

'There are four Elemental Stones that, once joined, open up a portal to the Isle of Elements,' he says, and I'm suddenly filled with hope. 'You already have one around your neck.'

I touch my skin, looking down at the emerald stone.

Relief blooms in my chest that Renward was foolish enough to gift it to me.

'One other is hidden in Melwraith, upon the mountains.' Dusan's lips purse as he looks at the rings on his fingers. 'Another is protected by trolls and finally one is in Thalore.'

The Dark Elves.

My stomach hollows.

'You need all four to open the portal, and if the Isle of Elements is truly where you seek to go, then you will have no problem retrieving these stones.' His eyes cut to mine, assessing my reactions though I do not give him one.

We've come this far, I am not backing down now.

I look up at Darius. His eyes don't need to tell me anything. He knows why we came here.

'How long do we have to retrieve those stones?' he asks, stepping away from me and turning towards Dusan.

'As long as you like.' Dusan smiles for the first time since meeting him. 'You are welcome to reside here in the meantime.'

Darius and I give each other another look, and I nod at Dusan.

He clasps his hands together, motioning his head to a lady in a green kirtle dress. 'Golrai, you may direct them to the spare rooms of the castle.'

She comes forward, bowing her head. Dusan now turns his attention to us. A slow smile paves his lips as he says, 'Welcome to Olcar, the High-Elven city of Terranos. I expect you to succeed.'

Golrai shows Tibith and Aias a room to share in a different section of the castle. As she shows us around the castle, I can't help but zone her out, I'm distracted by the idea that Sarilyn was once here in Terranos, just like us, before . . . before everything.

We stop as Golrai leaves us by two bedroom doors opposite each other along a wide, dimly lit hallway. I fiddle with my fingernails, looking over my shoulder at Darius.

He's quiet. I'm quiet. It's intimidating.

We went from the forests to this.

Something new again.

'Nara,' he says, not his usual 'Goldie' and not an insult in sight as our eyes catch each other. 'You should know that you were never an asset to me.'

I inhale deeply at seeing his relief after that confession. 'I know,' I say before entering my bedroom quarters.

CHAPTER SEVENTEEN

I'm sitting on a squab cushion by the windowsill, overlooking the silvery mist spreading across Olcar. Despite the glamour of my chambers – ivory drapes, green silk curtains, covers and soft bedding – I know I won't sleep tonight. Not like how I'd done when Darius was with me in that hut.

Memories of the Ardenti from Emberwell still plague my mind, and though I should tell Darius about it, I just can't bring myself to. I don't know how to say it.

The shame and guilt eat me alive.

Golrai enters, her white hair spun in a bun and an apron over her moss-plain servant dress. 'The King requests your presence for supper,' she says, walking over to the foot of the bed and neatly placing a gown on the bedspread. 'Would you like me to save a seat for you?'

'Yes,' I answer, jumping off the ledge not so gracefully. 'I will be there soon, thank you.'

She bows her head and departs, leaving me to stare at what she has laid out. I tread over to it, touching the emerald chiffon dress.

Scrunching it between my hands, I glance at the door leading to the bathroom chambers and sigh, feeling overwhelmed at the thought of changing into the dress. Surprisingly, it fits me just right with a lace bodice that cuts into a square around my neck and dramatic flaring sleeves. I was surprised by my appearance in Elven attire.

I leave my chambers, turning to each of the echoing halls with leaf-painted walls, searching for something familiar, equally confused and lost in this grand castle. A bright light flickers when I wander into another section, and I'm welcomed by laughter as I finally enter the dining room. A long table fills the entire room. Maids and guards stand at each corner as Dusan sits by the chair at the head of the table. Darius is smiling at the other end and now wearing a fine dark green jacket. He dangles a glass of wine between his fingers as Tibith sits on the marble floor, eating his bread. Aias laughs at something the King says while a woman in a white gown sits beside Dusan and Arlayna to her right.

'Nara,' Dusan greets me as he spots me loitering by the entrance. Darius's head whirls to me, and his eyes trace the finery of my dress. I inhale the air around me. 'Would you prefer it if I call you Nara or Naralía? Darius says you are quite . . . *opinionated* over names.'

I cast Darius a glare, and he chuckles, sipping from his glass. I don't think he will ever forget the Misty incident. 'Nara is just fine,' I say and sit beside Darius. The table hosts heaps of meats, cheeseboards, fruits and desserts that make me lick my lips, and my stomach growls in hunger.

I have not had a proper meal in so long that I have forgotten how much I adore it.

Serving myself an abundance of it all, my gaze connects with Arlayna's. She stares straight-faced as I plop a piece of bread onto my plate. Her turquoise silk gown differs from mine. It's beautiful with a halter neckline and off-shoulder sleeves. A sapphire circlet adorns her head, and I can truly see an air of royalty to her, differing from the hunting attire she'd worn earlier.

'So, this is the mortal you have been so fondly speaking of,' the woman in white beside Dusan says, and I almost drop my plate with all the food I have loaded on. I look at her, and a sense of enjoyment pierces her expression as she sets her grey eyes on Darius.

I bite my cheek with silly amusement. I almost feel superior for a moment, like I have the upper hand on him. I lean in, whispering to Darius, 'Fondly?'

He rests a fist under his chin, smirking in response. 'Don't get too ahead of yourself, Goldie.'

'Oh, I could never reach your standards of arrogance.'

We look at each other with conspiratorial smiles before my eyes are on the woman again.

She tips her head to the side. 'I am Meriel, Arlayna's mother.'

My eyes go wide, and I'm instantly embarrassed by my reaction. Well, I certainly see the resemblance. They have bronzed skin, and are wearing their dark hair up with tight curls framing their sharp faces.

'Apologies for my tardiness,' someone else announces, barging past a few maids. A slim girl, wearing a gown decorated in colourful flowers, grinning, with her raven hair wildly unkempt. 'I would have been here sooner, but Thallan opposed my greeting the guests naked.'

I almost let loose a laugh as Aias starts choking on some of his food, and a man with long brown hair tied in a low ponytail comes through the doors. Judging pale green eyes wander around the table before he walks over to Dusan and plants himself by his side.

Dusan coughs away the sudden awkward atmosphere as he looks at me with a strained smile. 'Nara, Darius, this is my emissary, Thallan.' He gestures to the man beside him, and Thallan sends us a curt nod, though his expression tells me he might never be pleased by anything. 'You have already met one of my nieces,' Dusan adds, 'so let me introduce you to Faye.' His gaze cuts to the girl that had just entered as her grin grows. 'They are daughters of my late brother.'

The Fallcrown Princesses. 'You're sisters,' I say.

'Unfortunately.' Faye sighs dramatically.

'Faye,' Meriel scolds her, raising a brow.

Faye lifts a shoulder and pouts mockingly at her mother. 'What? She is the favoured one, is she not?' She reaches across the table, grabs a strawberry, and turns to me.

I stiffen as she picks up a strand of my hair like I am a toy she can fiddle with and bites into her fruit.

'Humans are so remarkable,' she murmurs. 'They are just like us, yet without any power—'

'Faye, will you just sit down already,' Arlayna hisses, her knuckles turning white on the table.

Faye groans. 'Oh, you are such a bore, Arlayna.' She draws out the seat on my left and plops herself down on it. 'I am only messing around. I am glad we finally have visitors that aren't our cousins or –' She shivers '– Edwyrd.'

'Faye,' the King warns, and the table goes quiet save for the sound of Tibith continuing to munch on his bread. I turn to Faye as she slouches in her chair.

'Well, I am sure your cousins feel the same way about visiting you,' I say casually, grabbing an apple as Faye's head turns to me.

She starts smiling and straightens her back as she glances at everyone else. 'I like her.'

I crack a smile as she says that before Dusan changes the subject, swirling the mead inside his chalice. His ashen hair, like pure silk, flows down his shoulders, accentuating the sharp contours of his cheeks. 'Have your powers come through yet?' He directs the question at Darius, and my eyes flick towards him.

He nods once. 'I felt them when I passed the threshold from the forest into Olcar.'

I let a frown slip.

He didn't tell me.

'Hm, your dragon markings,' Dusan says. 'You do not have them.'

I chew my lower lip, realising that's also something I'd wondered back in Emberwell. He'd never given me a direct answer at the Noctura ball, and considering he was not wearing gloves like the first few times we'd seen each other, I was glad to have someone else confirm it too.

Lounging in his seat, Darius taps his fingers along the oak table. His gaze stays on his hand as he says, 'I had them removed.'

'By twin witches, I am assuming.' Arlayna includes herself in the conversation.

Darius nods again, but he looks uncomfortable. His jaw is set like that part of his life isn't something he wants to discuss. 'So.' He clears his throat, looking at Dusan. 'Is there anything we need to know for the tasks you've set us?'

'Well, each stone is stored in a way that makes it hard for one to just –' he makes a fist with his hand, '– take it. And even though Renward was stupid enough to keep one at hand, I am certain that won't be the case for the rest.'

Perhaps Renward had become comfortable with the idea that nobody would take them, yet I couldn't help but think about how he'd gifted one to me, perhaps thinking I'd be dead sooner or later.

'The first stone is in the mountain caves of Melwraith.' Dusan finely cuts his meat. 'As you have a dragon shifter that can fly you there, I'm sure—'

'I can't fly,' Darius says immediately, shifting his eyes to mine with a look I believe is disappointment.

He shouldn't have to be.

It was never his fault, the blame lies solely with the Venators.

'A flightless dragon?' Faye croons from her seat. 'How scandalous.'

'We can heal you,' Arlayna says in almost a whisper, her eyes staring down at her gold plate. 'Right, uncle?'

Dusan's running a hand across his chin, thinking, wondering. He's likely thinking the same thing that I thought the first time Lorcan mentioned Darius couldn't fly. 'High Elves in Olcar are healers, yes,' he considers. 'We were lucky enough to be gifted with such power alongside a few others.'

A drop of hope blossoms inside of me. 'What else can you heal?'

'We can heal even the deepest wounds, all but bring those back from death,' he says, glancing at Darius. 'Of course, that is only if you want your wing to be healed.'

Another moment of silence lingers in the dining room. Everyone's heads are turned to Darius, anticipating his answer. He's still lounging in his chair, contemplating the idea of it, when at last he sighs, looks at me, and says, 'I do.'

'Excellent—' Dusan starts, but I drown the rest of his conversation out, my eyes fixed on Darius and his on mine before he turns his head away without a word.

CHAPTER EIGHTEEN

I finish my letter before tying it around the foot of a pigeon and watching it flap its wings as it flies away. Leaning against the window, I smile, softly sighing, hoping it reaches my brothers and alerts them that we've made it safely through the forest.

My eyes catch Darius and Tibith out in the castle garden playfighting each other by a maple tree. It makes my smile grow as the sun hides behind clouds in Terranos and forget-me-nots sway to the gentle breeze.

'What are you staring at?'

I swing around as if someone's caught me stealing and huff a laugh when I see Aias standing at the threshold of the white-marbled hall. 'Have you been here the whole time?' I ask, and he walks in with a new cedar-coloured tunic.

He shakes his head. 'I was with the King.'

That perks me up a little. I haven't spoken to the King since dinner last night. 'All good things, I hope?'

'He does not plan to banish me this time if that is what you are wondering.'

'I wouldn't let him.'

He smiles and looks ahead. A pensive thought enters his mind. 'He said he knew my mother.'

Oh.

'It was before the woodland Elves were banished,' he says, a sad note in his voice. 'He knew her longer than I did.'

A chord of empathy lingers between us. I also know what it is like to no longer have your parents with you.

I stare at him, his eyes deep with pain. 'Have you ever seen a shooting star?' I ask. He shakes his head. 'Well . . . you only ever get to see a shooting star for a few seconds. But every time someone has witnessed it, they say it's beautiful, magical even.'

He looks at me, and it's almost like a star itself sparks in his obsidian eyes.

I lower my chin and say softly and reassuringly, 'Think of your mother as a shooting star because even though your time with her was brief, at least you still have wonderful memories of her. And that never goes away.'

He doesn't say it, but I can see the gratitude in his eyes and how he smiles.

I turn to the window and think of my family, knowing I'd spent such little time with my mother and father before they perished.

My gaze settles on Darius again, and I wonder if he is the same regarding his mother.

'Do you like him?' Aias snaps me from the turmoil of my thoughts, and I blink, turning to him. He clarifies, gesturing his head out the window. 'Darius.'

My whole face heats up, and I chuckle. 'Why would you think that?'

He shrugs, repressing a grin. 'No reason.'

I press a hand to my cheek to cool down and clear my throat. 'I'm going to get some fresh air,' I say, waltzing to the double glass doors of the hall and stepping out onto the patio.

'Try not to kiss him,' he shouts.

I freeze and look over my shoulder in panic. 'What?'

He shoots me a devious smile. 'I said try not to trip on the small steps.'

The cheek of him, honestly. I scowl and start walking fast along the gravel ground until Faye approaches me with a gleaming smile and a colourful gown.

'Enjoying your stay so far?' she asks, her hands behind her back.

My eyes flicker to Darius unwillingly as I mumble, 'It is definitely different from the forest.' And Emberwell.

Faye must gather where I'm staring as she looks behind her and sighs in exaggeration. 'He is ever so handsome, isn't he?'

My gaze jumps to her as she turns to me with a pout of her lips and a scrunch of her nose as if she's pitying me.

'Though it must be awful for you knowing that mortals and shifters can't have children together,' she continues, and my bones tremble. She thinks we're together, yet her comments make me stiff and feel like I'm about to suffocate from the millions of thoughts knotting into a rope inside my head.

'He is not—' I try to correct, but it's useless; I'm just flustering myself more. 'We are just working together on these tasks.'

Her brows rise with shock as she pushes a strand of hair behind her arched Elven ear. 'Well, you certainly had me fooled—'

'Faye,' Arlayna's voice interrupts from behind, and I'm incredibly thankful for it as she walks up to us. 'Must you always bother everyone?'

Faye rolls her eyes. They're emerald compared to Arlayna's grey ones. 'And you just like to ruin everything, don't you?' She walks around Arlayna, placing an unwanted kiss on her, and grins. 'Farewell, big sister.'

Arlayna wipes her cheek and glares as her sister walks off. Her waves droop to her thin waist, and I notice she still has the circlet on her head – a tiara. 'You shouldn't listen to anything she tells you.' She looks bored as she says it, like she tires of Faye's antics. 'She loves to stir things around, mostly for attention.'

'So, what she said, about mortals, is it true they cannot bear children with a shifter?' I detest the curiosity that makes me ask this. It shouldn't matter to me. I should be celebrating at the knowledge.

Solaris knows what a menace a child of Darius's would be like.

Arlayna's brows pucker, she's suspicious of my question, but she does not egg me on. 'A mortal's body is not compatible with that of a shifter,' she says, 'if a human is to conceive from them, they will perish before the child is even born.'

'Is that because, as humans, we are perceived as weak?' I chuckle scornfully. It is why Aurum once saw us as people who needed to be enslaved.

'I've never thought a mortal to be weak,' she says, no joke or mockery. She is dead serious. 'Sometimes having powers instead is a weakness. We can be too trusting of it at times.'

Silence falls on us as I repeat her words inside my head. She is not wrong. People in power can also be the ones that end up powerless. Sarilyn lost hers, but she succeeded in ending Aurum's life. He underestimated what a woman would go through to get what she wanted.

'Will you be attending the feast tomorrow evening?' Arlayna's voice cuts through my reverie.

I shoot her a surprised look. 'Feast?'

She nods ever so eloquently. 'It is something my uncle's courtier always organises. It might serve you well to forget the tasks you are set to do for a little while if you're introduced to some of our people.'

People . . . Elves, immortals that will likely be stunned by a human in their lands.

'I suppose so,' I say, not as excited as she had hoped at the idea of a feast. Luckily, Arlayna cannot question much about my lack of enthusiasm as a servant suddenly calls for her from behind me.

'I must go,' she says. 'I have other appointments I must keep.' The fake cheerfulness in her voice mixes with the bleak look in her eyes. I smile at her as she walks past me, but I'm quick to frown as I ponder whether being a dutiful princess of Olcar is what she wishes to be.

Regardless, I close my eyes, drawing in a breath before going to the tree where Darius is animatedly talking to Tibith. I stop at a safe distance where Darius won't notice me, but I can still hear him. He's telling a story, dramatically pretending to impale himself as Tibith giggles and tilts his head to the side.

I cross my arms over my chest, biting my lower lip as I stop myself from smiling, but it's hopeless.

'Magic then sprung to life –' Darius's palm creates a flame '– as the handsome thief grabbed the enchanted crown.' The fire creates a wreath-like crown, and Tibith's eyes brighten with awe. 'The curse was lifted; each person that was no longer stone was free from the evil warlock—'

'And the maiden?' Tibith blinks up at him, his voice not missing that child-like wonder.

'She stole the crown from the thief.' I decide to speak up, and Darius looks over his shoulder as I approach them. His eyes brighten as I stand beside him and say to Tibith, 'It was the ultimate betrayal, but he couldn't help but admit how he didn't hate being bested by the most brilliant maiden in all the lands—'

'For he knew he would see her again,' Darius says, our eyes meeting as we face each other. 'Because their story never ends.'

'They always find each other,' I say gently, thoughtfully. 'Like Solaris and Crello.'

'What about the warlock?' Tibith asks, and it takes a moment for Darius to break his stare from mine. 'What happened to him, Darry!'

Darius bends down as he says to Tibith in a dramatic whisper, 'He turned to stone.'

Tibith gasps, and my cheeks hurt from smiling. 'Like the curse he placed?'

Darius nods, and Tibith squeals with delight before forming into a cocoon ball and rolling towards the other side of the vast garden. From here, you can see how far up the castle is on the hill compared to the land of Terranos before us.

Darius rises and turns to face me as I tip my head to the side and lift a brow.

'Do all your stories end with a thief saving the world?' Sarcasm weaves through my voice as he saunters past me, and I follow his movement, turning to look at him.

'You would know that I don't always end them that way.' He grabs his gold coin from his pocket and flips it between his fingers. 'If you hadn't fallen asleep before I finished that story back at the hut.' He takes a step forward, grinning down at me. 'Which reminds me how much you snore during your sleep.'

I throw him a wry look. 'Well, then you should have left. What are you, a creep?'

He flips the coin again. 'I seem to remember you wanting me to lie beside you.'

Solaris, he loves to test me. 'I'd eaten something that made me act irrational.'

I'm on my toes, attempting to snag the coin from him before he can catch it. I fail as he grabs it and laughs as he reaches out and grazes my left ear. He then moves his fingers in front of me, indicating that the coin is not in that hand, while touching my right ear with the other. I watch him with bated breath as he retracts the coin like a magician.

If he thought I would be impressed by that, then—

My breath shudders out of me when he hooks his finger between the white ribbon tied at the top of my dress, almost undoing it. His smile fades, and his gaze focuses on my chest, rising slowly and heavily.

'Favourite childhood memory?'

It takes me a second to realise he's asking a question from when we'd made a new deal.

I step back in an attempt to breathe. 'I—' My head shakes, trying to get a grip of myself. 'It was when I would dance with my brothers on Noctura night, and the magic would erupt from the Isle of Elements.' Before he can answer, I ask, 'Why did you have your tattoos removed?' My eyes catch sight of his hand now at his side. 'Was it because of the Venators?'

He looks away, tense all of a sudden. 'My mother didn't want anyone figuring out I was a shifter.'

I narrow my eyes. There is clearly more to it that he won't say. 'Is that all?'

He slowly lets out a breath before facing me. 'No,' he says, which surprises me, but he does not add to that answer. 'Now, if you'll excuse me, Goldie, I'll be heading for a bath. Feel free to join me, though.'

I glower at him. 'Only in your dreams.'

He chuckles musically, penetrating my ears. 'My dreams include more than just you joining me.'

My eyes widen at the boldness of his words, and I'm sure my pulse is about to burst from how fast it's beating.

He leans forward. 'Only messing with you, Goldie. Always fun to see you blush,' he says and winks, sauntering back to the castle.

He is an absolute nuisance of a man.

'Dragon pig,' I mutter with a frown.

'Foul mortal,' he calls out as if he'd heard me.

CHAPTER NINETEEN

The feast indeed came, and though I wish I'd stayed in the guest chambers I'd been assigned to, I'm now leaning against an ornate sage wall in the vast throne hall instead. A great table of sizzling dishes is set out in front of me, and a group of female Elves plays harps and violins. I've only been staring at every Elf who enters the palace for a few hours. All crowded together in their gorgeous jewelled green tunics or jackets. At least focusing on them is better than attempting not to look in Darius's direction the entire night.

I lightly groan, shaking my head as I stare at my crystal glass of red wine. Even when I try to actively avoid him, mentally and physically, he still manages to interfere since . . . since he is the only person in the room wearing the colour of night. A dark, lustful look that has all the Elves looking his way.

Glancing up as I hear a group of girls admiring how Tibith can talk in one corner, I chuckle, watching him flap his ears. I then spot Aias by the feast, munching away at different platters while Darius speaks with Faye.

My look turns sullen, and I absently pout. He grins as Faye laughs at something he says before his gaze catches mine, and his smile dims when he sees I'm alone. I feel myself blush, so I force myself to look away, and quickly, my eyes settle on a painting at the right side of the hall, catching the light as people breeze past the crystal candlesticks on the walls.

A tree with marigold leaves at the centre of the City of Flames.

I frown, moving away from the wall, and walk over to it. Light brushstrokes of gold adorn the leaves, and I'm more than perplexed as to why this is here, in Terranos of all places.

'The Neoma tree.' Dusan's pleasant voice comes from beside me, and I look to my right. 'Beautiful, isn't it?' His gaze focuses on the painting as he drinks from his golden goblet decorated with glowing leaves.

My hand is stretched out towards the painting, barely touching the surface of the tree. I look back at it and lower my hand to the side. As I turn to face the King, I cock my head. 'Forgive me for asking, but why do you have it?'

His chuckle is short, amused by my question. 'Well,' he says, pointing his index finger at the painting. 'There was once a time when I could visit Emberwell, and the Neoma Tree so mesmerized me straight away that I had to get it painted.'

Yes, much like how I was when I arrived in the city. Even now, I often think of the tree and the harm it caused Darius.

'You mentioned you couldn't leave Olcar,' I say. 'Why is that?'

His pale lips curl into a grim smile. 'Your Queen.' He takes another sip, his woven crown shimmering as I stare at it. 'She cursed me to never be able to leave this place.'

My eyes jerk wide.

Cursed.

Sarilyn has shown her enemies no mercy. Why she cursed the King of Terranos is something I don't think I will get an answer to just yet, not with the look of absolute hatred within Dusan's jade eyes.

'Is there no way to break it?'

His chuckle leaves a bitter trail behind. 'She did it so that it's almost impossible to break.'

A breeze of silence passes us. I think about Sarilyn, how she must have also taken up the task of fetching the Elemental Stones when she came here. Or . . . she didn't. Someone cunning like her might have had another way, something that ended up having her trigger this curse on the King.

'You've heard of the myth behind the Neoma tree, haven't you?' Dusan says, and I lift my head up, not realising how hard I was biting my bottom lip. 'Solaris's and Crello's blood,' he prompts.

I nod. I've never forgotten the tale of it that night in the woods, the night—

'That one day, a reincarnation can make it sacred, heal it as some might say.'

Upon hearing that word, my body locks up like chains wrapping around me, weighing me down. 'I'm sorry.' I shake my head, huffing out a skeptical laugh. 'Heal it?'

Dusan nods, telling me something, but it buzzes in my ears. When Darius had Neoma blood on him from all the Venator's torturing, I'd healed him. Yet I haven't been able to since.

I drag my gaze back to the painting, a frown settling upon my features, even more confused. It's just a coincidence. How would that work? How is it I healed Darius? How is it—

'The Isle of Elements isn't the only place that is linked to Solaris and Crello, though.' Dusan's voice is still a distant echo. 'It's a power source for our continent, but what will happen once that power runs out?'

Panic coils in my stomach. I look at Dusan with sheer worry. 'It shouldn't run out. It's—'

'Everlasting?' he suggests, his eyebrows going up. 'Even the stars run out at some point, Nara.'

But that is not possible—

'Ah, Edwyrd,' Dusan says over my shoulder as if he hasn't noticed the impact his words have had on me. 'Have you met the lovely Nara yet?'

I turn to meet a tall Elf with light blue eyes, enough to make one believe they are glass. His long straight hair shines in a silvery light as he smiles.

'Nara . . . such a beautiful name,' he says, deep and curious, as he grabs my hand, gently pressing a kiss on it. The lace sleeve of my pale green dress narrows to a point by my middle finger, making me hardly feel the touch of his lips.

My smile is reluctant. My lips fail to curl upwards as they usually would as I remain lost in deep thought about the Neoma Tree and the possibility that the Isle of Element's powers could one day cease to exist.

'She is a mortal.' Dusan waves his goblet in my direction. 'Here to take part in collecting the Elemental Stones.'

Edwyrd's lips tip down at each corner as he nods. 'Impressively brave of you, Nara.'

I don't answer. Instead, I give him a meek smile before Dusan mentions how Edwyrd comes from the Valdern territory. A port city close to Melwraith and just a ship away from the land of Undarion. He shares the same traits as a mountain Elf, greyish skin and silver and white hair. A crystallised beauty.

'Are you a ruler of Valdern?' I ask, glancing at his cream and gold-threaded doublet.

'An Elven lord of Valdern,' he answers, then glances towards the King. 'The only *true* king in all of Terranos is Dusan himself.'

My cheeks flush with slight embarrassment, feeling as if everything I had previously learned from my brothers was not enough to inform me of the political history of these far lands.

When Dusan chuckles at Edwyrd, a familiarity of heat and rosewood shifts past me like a current. I look to my left as Darius stops just beside Dusan. He's looking at me as if I am the only one here.

I lift my head, staring at him with a delighted gleam in my eyes. My heart is thundering and clashing as Dusan introduces Edwyrd to Darius, informing him of what he told me. But Darius does not even look in Edwyrd's direction.

'Nara,' Edwyrd says in a cheery tone. I find it difficult to pry my gaze away from Darius's, but I manage. 'Would you care to accompany me to fill up your glass?'

I frown, glancing down at the wine, stuttering not to laugh as I'm to answer him, but Darius beats me to it.

'It's barely empty,' he deadpans, and I look at him in annoyance as he extends his glass out, blocking Edwyrd from my sight. 'However, mine is. You are more than welcome to fill it up for me since you are offering.'

By the sudden rise of Dusan's brows and Edwyrd clearing his throat, I want nothing more than to scold Darius for his childish behaviour.

Edwyrd chooses to ignore him, and finally, Darius lowers his glass. 'How about some food? They are serving a delicious lamb pie.'

I attempt to hide my grimace at lamb pie and smile. 'I would love—'

Darius's disdainful chuckle cuts me off, and Edwyrd and I look at him as he shakes his head, fitting a hand into his pockets.

'Is something amusing?' There's a strain in Edwyrd's words and a swirl of aggravation.

'Not at all,' Darius says, lifting a finger, pressing his lips together in thought. 'It's just from experience I know she has a preference for sweeter pies than savoury ones.'

I glare at him to stop. My irritation is reaching its peak.

'Strawberry pie, to be specific,' he continues, his eyes locking with mine. 'But with no other added fruit. She tends to pick others off if they're included. I learned that the hard way.'

My expression immediately softens, remembering how on one of the days after the trials, I'd gotten a slice of pie with strawberries, blueberries, blackberries and all sorts inside. I picked the other berries apart, still thankful and not wanting to be wasteful as I wasn't quite ready to leave my room. The next day, I opened my door to receive a whole strawberry pie at my feet.

'You seem to know her well,' Edwyrd says, annoyed, and Darius's gaze shifts to him.

An icy smirk sweeps across his lips, chilling the hall and Edwyrd. 'Better than you ever will.'

Oh, for Solaris— 'Darius.' I look at him with a tight grin, forcing his name between my teeth. 'May I speak with you privately?'

'Certainly, Goldie.'

I excuse myself from the King and Edwyrd, grabbing Darius by the arm as we drop our glasses onto a nearby table and walk into the castle's hallways. A few people stand conversing, so I look to my right, push through a door, and enter an empty servants, headquarter.

'What is wrong with you?' I hiss, smacking Darius's chest as soon as I release his arm.

His face is the picture of feigned innocence. 'I was just having a delightful conversation with Edwin.'

'Edwyrd.'

He glances around the small space of the room in disinterest. 'Quite similar if you ask me.'

'Solaris, how badly I want to slap you around the face.'

'Now, now, at least save those slaps for some more exciting body part.'

I shake my head. 'I am not up for your little games tonight, so why don't you go back in there and flirt with the entire Elf community instead?'

'Well, now look who is jealous,' he croons, leaning towards me. Thin slivers of moonlight from the windows line across his face, illuminating his tanned skin.

I focus on glaring at him. 'Oh please, I'm not the one telling Edwyrd to go and fill up your glass instead of mine.'

'He didn't seem offended.'

He likely was. I just . . . couldn't see. 'That is probably because he does not have the time to care about what a random dragon shifter has to say.'

'True.' His smirk widens into a grin. 'But it seems like you care, considering we are alone in a room.'

I become silent, too annoyed to speak because he is partially correct.

A half groan, half scoff escapes me as I turn to pry the door open, but his fingers curl underneath my upper arm and turn me to him. He's no longer smiling as his eyes search my face.

'Why are you at this feast if you're not enjoying yourself?' he asks, his eyes hooded.

He *did* notice.

Pulling my arm from his grip, I sigh. 'I am enjoying—' I stop my potential lies when his eyes trail down to my heart.

'It's interesting,' he murmurs, still staring at my chest, 'because the only time I have seen you enjoy yourself was when I took you to the den.' His voice is strangely husky, making my heart throb faster. 'Funny how things work out.' He looks up at my eyes. 'An ex-Venator trainee, a dragon shifter . . .' His words drift off, and he takes another step where the end of his boots touches the hem of my silk dress. As his hand slides down my waist, my breath staggers in my throat, light yet incinerating me whole.

The base of my throat pulses as I swallow. 'What about it?'

'Well, once you wished the worst upon me, and now, we are here in Terranos, working together.' His finger runs along my collarbone. 'I wonder what will happen once this is all over.'

I find myself wanting to melt into him as I breathe out softly, 'What would you want to happen?'

Our bodies now press together in a way that fits perfectly. The heat of him is all-consuming. His stare on my lips as I glance up at him is lustful, and his eyes . . . his treasure-coloured eyes enthrall me.

'Guess,' he says.

'Your own private lair of gold jewels.'

He chuckles, rich and sensual. 'Yes, what else?'

I roll my eyes. 'All the men and women to satisfy your needs.'

He lifts a brow. 'Nowhere near right, Goldie.'

My hands glide up his chest, feeling the tension of his muscles harden beneath his shirt. 'A new mask then.'

He clicks his tongue, sliding his fingers up my bare back. 'Getting colder now.'

The air between us is palpable with something so fierce and profound that it's almost magic.

'Then—' I screw my lips together, breathing far too heavily. 'Then—' I scrunch the material of his shirt into my fist. Frustration, burning, and the desire I had always tried to subdue yearning to break out of me.

'Then what, Goldie?' he whispers, and my lips part slightly, but the only sound I can make is a breathless whimper.

I rise on my toes, our lips almost meeting when the door swings open, and I jump, shoving myself off Darius as I turn to find Arlayna's gaze shifting between us.

'Sorry,' she says, cocking an eyebrow. 'I thought I'd heard something.'

Was it the sound of my thrashing heart? The strange tension between Darius and me? If Arlayna had come just one second later, she would have seen us kissing.

'No.' I swallow, looking up at Darius defensively. 'It's fine, he—'

'I was just telling her about the plans for the upcoming tasks,' Darius concludes hoarsely and walks past Arlayna before whirling on his feet to us. 'I will see you both in there.' He inclines his head, his eyes catching mine from behind Arlayna like he is just as shocked as I am.

He looks off to the side, his jaw working back and forth, and I wonder what he is thinking as he turns and leaves to go back into the throne hall.

When Arlayna's gaze returns to mine, she studies me. I feel like I've been caught doing something that did not happen, yet almost did. 'You're sweating.'

I rub the back of my neck. 'It's quite warm in here.'

She nods with a low hum, obviously not believing it. It's cool here at best. 'You know . . . High Elves are known for practising the magic of Elvarune. We draw it from the earth, and from a young age, we're taught to heal and manipulate energies and objects—'

'And I assume knowing if someone is lying is also one of them,' I say, tired of yet another use of power that can catch me out.

'Not at all,' she says, 'I merely wanted to tell you about the history of Olcar's magic.' Her brow quirks as she gives me a secretive look. 'I assumed you'd be interested.'

My lips form into a smile because that is not what she truly meant, and we both know it. Her grey eyes twinkle with enigmatic amusement, a monochrome hue that you'd think is painted on.

'Is everything okay here?' Aeron appears to the side of Arlayna, clad in armour, and even with Arlayna's tall height, her head barely lines with his chest.

Arlayna stiffens at the sound of his voice, and I notice her breathing go slower as her gaze shifts to the floor. She closes her eyes, licking her lips like she's built enough courage, and then turns around. 'Why wouldn't it be?' she says before pushing past him.

There is a moment – a snippet gone in the blink of an eye – where the corners of Aeron's lips lift into an affectionate smile as if he remembers something.

I narrow my eyes at him, but he straightens, bids me goodnight, and returns to his post of guarding the castle.

CHAPTER TWENTY

There's a serenity to the lands of Olcar. Perhaps it is the fresh mountainous air or the views from the library's balcony that have me resting the heels of my palms against my cheek. Tendrils of hair spill over my shoulder as I look to my left, where a book I'd grabbed lies on the ledge.

I wanted to learn everything ever since the King spoke of the Isle of Elements potentially losing its power. The first thing I asked this morning when Golrai fluffed my bedsheets was whether the castle had a library.

Indeed, there was not just one but two libraries. The grand library was located on the upper floor of the castle, and the other, near the throne room.

And, while I haven't discovered anything on the Isle of Elements, I have learnt a lot about Terranos's history and inhabitants. Something worth researching for when Darius and I go to recover the stones.

Yet the second Darius starts to infiltrate my mind, a flare of green light bursts from the side of my peripheral vision. I turn my head, to see the gorgeous silver scales of Darius's dragon form. Elves surround him, and his left wing is outstretched, casting a shadow over them. Veins course through it as it slowly heals, and that same green light disperses along it.

'It's remarkable how something can be healed with magic.'

I bolt upright. A soothing woman's voice has me wrenching away from the window and my awe over Darius being healed as I look over my shoulder.

It's Meriel. Faye and Arlayna's mother.

I've not spoken to her as much as the rest, but now looking at her properly, she exudes beauty. Her deep bronze skin shimmers with a glow much like gold dust, and her halter-necked gown is a beautiful shade of emerald.

'Yes,' I finally reply, twisting towards her. 'I suppose it is useful in life. I am just thankful he finally has a chance to be what he is without being affected by his severed wing.'

Her grey eyes study me as she saunters over. Tall and elegant, she dips her head to the side, dark curls swaying. 'You care deeply for him.'

My heart pinches at her conclusion, and I disguise it with a slight shrug. 'We have gone through a lot together.'

She lifts a brow. 'But?'

I shake my head humourously. 'He is a pain.'

She laughs, bright and dulcet. 'Ailwin was the same.'

King Dusan's brother.

All I know is that he'd perished. How and why is something I've not been informed of yet.

'We met when I was just a seamstress in the city,' she continues, darting her gaze into the gardens. 'I'd never known what the two princes of Terranos looked like, never seen their faces until Ailwin tumbled into my shop one day. He was hiding from people. At the time, I thought he had robbed someplace nearby and decided to take shelter at mine, considering he was only clothed in dirty rags.' The sun captures a glow in her eyes, reminiscent and melancholic. 'His arrogant charm made me dislike him from the start, but that eventually grew into something more, and later on, I came to find out he was just simply trying to escape from his duty as a prince.'

Listening to her, I begin to think of love. You could tell she loved him. Deeply. You could hear it in her voice, even after all this time.

She tells me that he gave up his right to be King so he could be with her. Elven views in the Terranos hierarchy are a tricky thing. It's forbidden to court someone that isn't of high power. But Ailwin fought hard, and it worked despite the judgment and pain it caused the Fallcrowns.

'If you don't mind me asking,' I say slowly, tentative about whether I should ask at all. 'What . . . happened to him?'

Her eyes find mine, and the glow vanishes. 'When Sarilyn cursed Dusan, many, including Dusan's family, ventured out to find her. Only when they did . . . she created the Screaming Forests, as a way to trap them.' She looks down. 'They never came back.'

My heart aches for her, for everyone. 'I'm so sorry.' The three dreaded words. I almost cringe at the hate I have for them.

She gives me a watery smile. 'It's better not to dwell. Heartbreak can be a tricky thing.'

And so it is, with many.

Silence collects like water droplets between us. Her eyes are pensive when I hear shouting and thuds from the grounds where Darius is. I whirl to see him slam against a few pillars; they quiver from the impact but do not collapse, luckily. He shakes his head, his wings out and sliding across the ground as he tries to take off again.

'I thought flying came naturally to dragons,' Meriel wonders, and

I sigh sadly, watching Darius barely get above a few feet into the air.

'It should do.'

Days rush by so rapidly that it's hard to keep up with what is happening or where my thoughts lie.

Each night, I read more about Terranos, fascinated by the Dark Elves. I familiarised myself with their belief that Solaris and Crello are our punishers, dark and powerful deities to scorn our world. Or how Elves' views on our world go beyond the sun and the moon, involving legends of the Elven star that can open up realms.

It was all fascinating, and every day from mid-morning, I'd watch from my window as Elves helped Darius with his flying. But truth be told, I was starting to believe he was faking his inability to fly.

Call it an instinct or not, I felt it, in the way he looked at me and the pain in his expression before he shifted. Another two weeks passed, and I finally got a response from my brothers. They're well, which relieved me though the letter was short, telling me how the Queen had ceased her search after reports of us entering the Screaming Forests.

I'd suspected as much.

Now, sparing a glance out the front bow window, I sigh and become slightly disappointed I can't see Darius outside. Usually, I'm here sitting in the library, reading and watching him. Some days I'd be out on the balcony, but today the warmth and comfort of vibrantly painted ceilings with Elven history, tall shelves of endless books, and a winding staircase leading to the patio made me feel more at ease.

I sigh, look out into the gardens, waiting to see him. When I don't, my mind returns to last night before supper.

I close the door to my room behind me as Darius emerges from his. Our eyes connect and we stop. Neither of us moves. Neither of us say a word for a minute as his gaze slowly scans my entire figure.

His brows meet, and then he smiles. 'You're not wearing a dress.'

I glance down at my hooded tunic and pants. Wiggling my toes inside my boots, I say, 'I missed the feeling of being able to move more freely.'

'And more freedom to fight your enemies, I suppose.' His chuckle is low and troubled as I look at him. There's a hidden ache in his eyes. I can feel it resonating behind the walls of my chest, urging me to step forward and comfort him with whatever might be running through his head.

'Well,' I say, leaning my back against the door. 'I haven't felt the need to kick you yet.'

He hums as if contemplating whether to say something irritating to me. 'That's because I'm no longer your enemy, Goldie.'

I'm quiet, resisting the bouts of emotions hanging off me. I want to say that he never once was my enemy, even when I tried to believe that he was, and still stubbornly do sometimes. But I don't because Faye's boots thud against the floors as she appears beside Darius and grins, hooking an arm around his.

The memory fades, and I recall how she dragged him away for dinner. Even so, our eyes had remained on one another from across the dining table.

'Nara?' It's Aias's loud but muffled voice as if he's been saying my name multiple times.

I blink twice and peer up from the table at him standing at the edge.

'Where did you go?'

'Nowhere,' I mutter, too out of it to say anything else.

Aias stays quiet. The only sound is the chair scraping and echoing around the library walls as he sits opposite me and reaches across the table to grab the book from my hands. 'Thalorians? Are you trying to prepare yourself to recover the final stone in the supposed shadowlands of the Dark Elves?'

'I'm just fascinated by their views, that's all,' I say, perching my elbows up on the table and resting my cheeks between the palms of my hands. 'Did you know their history dates back centuries, to a woman named Kilya? Supposedly she already had dark magic within her and a black heart that made her turn others just like her.'

Aias doesn't answer, seeming enthralled by each page, hand-painted and full of wondrous detail.

'I read that if you are not careful, an Elf's heart can turn dark through heartbreak, betrayal . . . all sorts.' An aspect even Meriel had mentioned.

'Yes, well, not only are Thalorians mighty powerful in dark magic, but they also seem to be plaguing the lands of Terranos with shadow creatures they created themselves.'

'Where did you hear that?'

He's too captivated by each page he turns to notice I'm staring at him. 'The King mentioned it earlier today. Apparently, it's been happening for decades now.'

'Is the King not doing anything about it?'

'He can't while he is stuck here, though I do know his Emissary Thallan takes care of it all, such as sending spies to Thalore in case of a war between High Elves and Thalorians.' He gasps lightly despite the impending worries this poses to the kingdom. A kingdom that is not even mine or my home. 'This book must be centuries old; it dates back to the battles between the Elves and trolls eons ago.' He shakes his head, awestruck. 'Quite fascinating, I must say.'

I muster a smile, endeared by his reaction as he flips over the page. However, it ceases when my eyes focus on the large sketch front and centre.

'Wait,' I say, my brows scrunching as I slide the book over to my side of the table. It's of the deity Solaris, the sun and its rays beaming behind a delicate figure. Animals, plants and creatures surround the deity as it bares its hands out to the world.

'What is it?' Aias tries to pry, but my frown intensifies as I stare at the sketch. When I go to flip the page, I'm startled by the patter of feet and accompanying squeals.

I look up as Tibith climbs the table legs and says to me with fright, 'Miss Nara! Miss Nara! I cannot find Darry anywhere!'

My eyes go wide. I don't wait for Tibith to finish because, in seconds, I'm up on my feet, leaving the book behind as I rush out of the library. Aias and Tibith are on foot behind me while I hurry along marbled hallways.

'He might have gone into the city—' Aias tries to reason, but my mind is too hasty to think the worst—

A melody coming from one of the rooms stops me. A slow yet mesmerising sound that grows louder the closer I get to the doorway at the end of the hall.

I reach for the handle and silence Aias and Tibith with a wave of my hand. 'Stay here,' I whisper and enter, closing the door behind me. Standing ahead of me, facing the large stained-glass window, sits Darius playing the piano. A tone that weaves through my heart in the most heavenly way. As I look around, the whole room is reflected with the different coloured lights from the window, an art piece detailing the coronation of an Elf, with white lilies and vines decorating the borders.

'Are you just going to stand there and watch, Goldie?' Darius says, and the music stops. My eyes narrow, and I wonder how he knows I have entered. 'I saw your reflection on the piano.'

Ah.

I walk towards him, passing a harp and a few other instruments in what seems to be a music chamber. Darius doesn't turn to face me, so I slip beside him and sit on the piano stool. 'I didn't know you could play,' I say.

'I can't.' He is so focused on the keys in front of him. 'That was all I knew.'

'Whose music was it?'

'My father's.'

The answer surprises me.

'It's the only other time I can remember when my mother mentioned him.'

'Have you . . .' I halt my words, trying to think carefully about what to say. 'Ever tried to search to see if he is alive?'

He shakes his head. 'After Rayth and Lorcan, I spent most of my time learning to survive. Searching for my father wasn't something I had on my mind.' When he finally decides to look at me, too much is happening in his eyes. It's devastating, even as he fakes a smile. 'Why waste my time trying to find someone who left me?'

'And flying again? Is that something else that wasn't on your mind either?'

His smile slips. 'It's been too long, Nara.'

That is why he has held off from flying since he was healed. Flying is no longer so simple for him, especially when all it does is bring back dreaded thoughts.

'And it reminds you of that day.' I lean into him, my tone soft and understanding. 'Doesn't it?'

He stares at me and doesn't utter a word, but I know he agrees.

I hold my wrist, looking down at it. 'Do you want to know why I always covered this scar?' I don't wait for his answer. 'Because I thought it made me weak, like a constant reminder of what happened to my father. But now . . . now I realise it never did. It made me more determined.' My eyes flash up at Darius. The colour of his usual tanned skin is now mixed with the pale blue bouncing off the window art. 'It made me a fighter.'

My heartbeat quickens from how his features soften as he looks at me like he is not used to this but can't run away from it, not how he would after a theft. This wasn't what he was used to either.

Rarely have we had moments like this, and even then, something always interrupted us.

He exhales a short huff of air through his nose and shakes his head, his voice a low mumble. 'You are starting to sound like Gus there, Goldie.'

I give him a half smile. 'Well, I am certain he would say the same if he was here. Now.' I stand, clearing my throat as he watches me with peculiar amusement. 'Get up and be the shifter that everyone was so afraid to even speak of in Emberwell.'

He laughs, slowly rising to his feet. There is not much space between the piano and the stool, and the intensity in his gaze as he looks down at me sends a wave of electric nerves up my back. 'They were never afraid, Goldie,' he says, 'most wanted me. Well, most except you.'

Yes, most such as that Lillian I had eavesdropped on back in Emberwell. 'That is because I wanted to kill you – still do at times.'

Humour burns bright in his eyes as if he has caught me in something dire. I shake it off, getting up from the stool and heading for the door.

'Nara,' he says as my palm touches the handle. I half turn to find him in thought. 'If you had the choice to stay on land or travel the seas, which would you do?'

My eyebrows draw together; still, I smile at the question. 'Travel the seas. And you?'

'Land,' he answers. 'There is something about the warmth of the earth I enjoy.'

A smile lingers on my face. 'I suppose that is how Crello felt with Solaris.'

He laughs, agreeing with me, as we leave the room together.

CHAPTER TWENTY-ONE

I stand at a safe distance from where Darius lands on the green fields and assumes his human form. Faye claps and cheers loudly as Arlayna tries to tame her from the side.

When Darius sees me approaching him, our eyes meet, and I see that familiar glint of gold amber shimmers that catch my breath. He's matching me stride for stride, and we close in on each other with every step.

'How did that feel?' I ask, smiling after witnessing his ability to fly again. He deserves this after suffering for years with the memory of the General killing his mother and the Venators tearing his wing.

His grin is effortless, a spark of life reignited in his eyes as he looks up at the sky, contrasting with the saddened expression I had witnessed in that music chamber. 'After your pep talk? Outstanding, I would say.' He expels a breath, relief and triumph in one. Glancing back down at me, his brow lifts. 'Would you like a ride?'

'Me? A ride?' I snort, crossing my arms over my chest and slipping him a teasing smile. 'So you can drop me? I'd rather not.'

'I'd love to be dropped,' Faye says wistfully. 'Imagine the thrill of falling through the air right before you're caught again.'

'That is *if* you're caught,' Arlayna retorts, and I don't have to look their way to know Faye is rolling her eyes at her sister.

Darius chuckles, shaking his head, and I watch as his inky hair sweeps across his forehead with the motion. 'I wouldn't let you just fall to your death, Goldie.' His stare is unshakeable, dripping with mirth. 'I promised your brother I'd keep you safe, remember?'

Vividly.

He takes another step towards me; the corner of his mouth turns up. 'So, what do you say? Care to let me take you on an adventure?'

Giddiness has my lips part into a smile. He had me at the word 'adventure'. I lean into him, pressing my palms to his chest. 'We already are on one.'

A wave of his scent, so familiar, has me closing my eyes before I retreat and I wet my lips, gesturing my hand out. 'What are you waiting for?'

He tips his head back, chuckling when Tibith whines, waddling towards us as he looks up at Darius with large solemn eyes. 'Don't worry, Tibith,' he says, lowering himself to stroke the back of Tibith's head. 'I'll come to get you after. You know how it is. Ladies first.'

'We will let you both be,' Arlayna says as my gaze shifts to her and Faye. Darius and I had been in our own little world for a minute; we'd not realised they were still there.

Arlayna grabs Faye by the arm, then looks over at Aias, whose timid eyes are on us all. 'Aias? Care to accompany me inside? I heard my uncle was hoping to converse with you.'

Aias's head shoots up hesitantly before he nods, and they all start retreating. I watch them for a few seconds, a silent charge passing through Darius and me, and then I turn to him.

The silence grows stronger, more fervent.

He takes a deep breath, rolling his shoulders, and soon disappears between shadows and silver flecks. Wind sweeps my hair back as he reveals himself as the powerful dragon he is.

I inhale, staring at his large stature – a beautiful creature. He turns his head to me, lowering it as the sun catches sight of his horns. Gold eyes are on me. Even in his dragon form, his softening expression travels to my core, strengthening a trust . . . a bond deeper than any other.

He lowers himself onto his hind legs, allowing me to climb up his side.

Nervous, I reach out to hold on to his leathery skin. A small sound climbs up my throat as I breathe. It's almost a whimper as I remember the Ardenti fledgling.

I close my eyes, chest heavy and my heart swelling before I jump, swinging one leg around him. Placing my palms on either side of his neck, his body rumbles to the vibrations emitting from within him. He rises, looking over at me once more. I nod, eyes locking, and then I squeal as he leaps forward, gaining momentum before we're up in the air.

I'm squeezing my eyes shut, my stomach dipping the higher Darius flies upward. I clutch on to him harder, the heel of my boots tensing against his body as I do everything to hold on, breathe and focus. The errant breeze pulls and threads through the strands of my hair. And slowly, loosening my grip, I count to three and blink.

A flash of white and then crystal-clear skies appear in my line of sight. I turn to look at Darius's wings, his healed one so full and shimmering in the rays of sunlight.

A half chuckle escapes me. I'm shocked, in awe, too stunned by the views.

I'm flying.

I throw my arms up in the air, wide and free, as I tip my head back. The sensation is like nothing I've felt before. It's as if I am the wind that carries birds. I'm freedom incarnate, a rush of life I never want to let go of.

We go through clouds, and I look below me at the city, rivers, hills and mountains. It's surreal, beautiful, like a painting of earthly colours: greens, blues, mahogany and greys. And when Darius skims past clouds, I stick my hand out again as if I'll be able to feel them through my fingertips.

A surge of happiness forms in my chest, slowly growing and growing. Here, I realise that above the trees and the land itself, something that seems so grand to us can also look vulnerable up in the air.

A world that is also so easily destructible.

Darius suddenly descends, and the jolt in my stomach makes me laugh, earning myself a rumble of approval from him as we near the woods and he dodges between trees.

As he rises once more, he starts going faster. I grab on to him again, shouting, 'Slow down!' But he doesn't, and I lose my footing on him. There's a moment of panic before I realise what he's doing when he swivels his head at me, showing part of his fangs as if he's smiling.

I raise my brow, giving him a look that says, 'Don't you dare,' before he stretches himself into a straight angle and I fall backwards, screaming. My breathing quickens, my arms flail to the sides, and I can't see Darius because my hair is flying all over my face. Raging, I shout his name, and as I lock my eyes shut, hurtling into the trees and the earth below, something grabs my arm and pulls me into a secure position.

Prying one eye open, I look to my right, where talons are curled around my waist. As I glance up, I see Darius tip his head to the side before diving into the woods and releasing me onto the ground. I'm coated in sweat, adrenaline charging through my veins. I press a shaking hand to my chest when I hear the sound of Darius shifting behind me.

I turn and hardly give him a second before I shove him. 'You said you wouldn't drop me!'

'I said I wouldn't let you *fall* to your death. There's a difference,' he rephrases it with a grin. It makes me want to punch him – no, it makes me want to rub dirt all over his clothes and watch him whine like a child about it.

'I knew I should have said no—' I start muttering, moving past him, but he clutches my arm and swings me around to him.

'And then what?' His eyes narrow as pine trees block the sun from his face. 'I heard you up there. You were happy for once.'

His words strike me for a moment because he sounds so genuine.

My expression falls before I build it back up again with armour at the ready. 'I don't need you to fly me around so that I can feel happy.' *Yes, I do. Fly me everywhere. Fly me to the stars, the moon, and the world beyond us. Please don't stop even when I'm too stubborn to say otherwise.* I shudder those thoughts away and lift my chin at him. 'I'm content as it is.'

He doesn't listen to the beat of my heart this time, despite me attempting to hide how fast it is currently beating.

Instead, he shakes his head, and a forced chuckle escapes him. 'If you think I can't tell when you're lying without me listening to your heart, then –' He closes in, and my mouth dries at how he lowers himself to whisper close to my ear, '– you underestimate how much I know you by now, Nara.'

My eyes betray me as I stare at the curve of his mouth, its closeness, and how if I were to just jolt forward, our lips will touch. 'Then—' I swallow, 'Then you tell me what makes me happy if you know me so well by now.' I step back, flustered and heated, but Darius's heavy gaze flickers past me.

'Nara—' he starts to say, but I shake my head.

'No, don't. You know what? I don't want to know; in fact, I will tell you right now—'

'Nara—' His tone is more of a warning now, and I scowl at him as he tries to reach for my hand.

I slap it away. 'Will you stop—'

A twig snaps behind us. Darius's arm wraps around my middle, spinning me around as he places his palm over my mouth and drags me behind a tree.

What in Solaris?

I attempt muffled words into his hand, dropping my head against his chest as I glare up at him, but his eyes are alert, peeking past his shoulder. His grip on my mouth loosens as I follow the direction in which he's looking. At first, all I notice are huge crusty feet with long mouldy toenails attached to moss-toned flesh. Then I see the two massive trolls those toes belong to, walking through where we were just moments ago.

I scrunch my brows, staring at their bulbous noses and wart-filled faces. Flies swarm them as they scratch and pick at their noses.

'Wait until Yago sees the animal I've got,' one of them, built and hairless, says. His voice is nasal and old as he lifts a branch in mid-air.

'That's no animal, you idiot.' The other smacks his head, grunting before pausing and sniffing the air. 'Oi, you smell that?'

Panic threads through me as they both start looking around.

'Human,' the troll says, a sinister excitement blending in with his voice.

Darius's grip around me tightens. I look up at him, eyes wide as I try to reach for my blade.

'Impossible.' The first troll hacks up phlegm. 'A human can't be here.'

'Believe it, Fleet. Looks like we've got ourselves a treat tonight if a human is about.'

Their grating laughs have me wincing. I begin thrashing in Darius's arms, knowing the trolls will find us if we do nothing, but when I look over my shoulder at him, his eyes are closed – concentrating.

A sound like a tree tumbling in the opposite side of the woods crashes, causing a distraction. I tilt my head enough to see the trolls look at each other and mumble about checking it out.

They turn away from us, and I exhale with relief.

'Illusion?' I whisper.

'Illusion,' Darius breathes as we're left panting the second their voices are nonexistent, a blur the further they disappear into the woods.

We don't make any movement, and there is no sound, except our harsh breathing and the birds chirping from within high branches.

Minutes pass, and whatever words I had on my lips vanish as Darius's palm trails down my chest, curving to the dip of my belly button. I hold back a gasp as his fingers hesitate before reaching up and underneath my tunic. We don't need to say anything. We let our bodies entwine with need, his hand radiating a warmth that sets me ablaze. I close my eyes and exhale slowly as my head naturally falls back. His finger teases circles around my abdomen, sinking lower and lower but never more than that.

Whatever is in the air, the crash of lightning along my skin . . . it has me wanting to reach for his hand so that he doesn't stop. I'm desperate to feel, and I'm aching for more.

A shameful whimper tears from my throat and his unrestrained breaths meet my neck as I press my body further up against him, making him still.

His hand clenches into a fist and then withdraws, leaving a mark behind on my skin.

Frowning and coming to a vulnerable reality, I step forward before turning to him. He's averting his gaze from me as he says, 'I think we're safe now.'

It's unbelievable how little I care about that right now.

I look at him with chagrin, my eyes narrowing. We were getting into dangerous territory back there, something I cannot believe I wanted.

A side of me thinks he stopped himself because of what happened last time, or maybe he doesn't want to feel what he once felt for the woman who hurt him.

'We should go then and prepare ourselves for tomorrow,' I say so quietly that I feel the need to repeat myself, but Darius's head shoots up at that, and his brows furrow, so I add, 'Over two weeks have passed . . . I think it's time we got on with collecting those stones, don't you?'

It's a dismissal. I'm forcing my defences up, and he notices as he jabs his tongue to the side of his cheek and falters on a nod. 'Naralía,' he whispers, looking down at the ground, not 'Goldie', not the warning he gave me before when he'd realised trolls were nearby. Just my full name. Plain, yet an indescribable pain soars through my chest at him saying it.

I blink the gloss away from my eyes and shake my head before I lose my little resolve. 'Let's go.'

I awaken from a gentle nap as the fabric of my clothes sticks to my back, and my hair is in a plaited mess. My room is already dark, and as I glance outside my window, I can see it is night.

Arriving back at the castle, Aias had attempted to talk to me about how flying went with Darius, but I'd said I was too tired to explain while Tibith got to ride. At least it seemed like they had fun, even though I couldn't stop thinking about Darius. My confusion over him makes me so irritated that I escape to the only place where I feel I can let go by trying to sleep.

But even that is always a struggle. The Ardenti nightmares won't stop, Lorcan telling me he loved me won't stop, and my father's death is always there whenever I drift off.

Settling myself into a seated position, I stretch out my arms, unsure of where to go as I walk out of my chambers and stare at Darius's door. For five contemplative minutes, I try to reason with myself about whether I should knock, but truthfully, after thinking it through, I just want to ask him what the hell this is between us.

Finally deciding to knock, I rap my knuckles against the door and wait for him to answer.

No response.

I try again.

Nothing.

With a huff, I decide to enter anyway. His room is similar to mine in that it has silk sheets, hand-painted walls with floral sketches, gorgeous goldwork, and a platform leading to a tub. His bed appears to be untouched, and he is nowhere to be found within. I know I missed dinner, so perhaps he's still there. I start along the halls after closing the door.

'Golrai!' I smile as she walks towards me, 'do you know where Darius might be?'

She ponders over my question, her honey-brown eyes narrowing. 'Last I saw him, he was heading into the city with Aias and that adorable little Tibithian. Why do you ask? Do you need anything, dear?'

'No, I—' A pause. 'I think I will go and fetch them. It is getting late.'

If Golrai had anything further to say, I don't let her get a word in as I turn on my feet and untangle the strands from my plait. Perhaps something *was* about to happen between Darius and I earlier, but as I stomp along the marbled floors my lips are pursed with aggravation. Not even Aias or Tibith had mentioned they left.

Darius and I must leave for Melwraith in the morning for Solaris's sake.

Blowing an exasperated breath, I step out into nightfall and the heavier breeze of the approaching autumn. I inform the sentry of my departure, and as the gates roll down, I make my way through the curving pathway leading towards the city's central areas. When I'm at the bottom, I take in the busy streets at night. They're full of joyful laughter while Elves sit outside taverns. Lanterns shake above closed shops while some others are still open, letting customers inside.

It always baffles me to notice the difference between Emberwell and Terranos. The difference in clothing, how flamboyant women's dresses are back in the City of Flames compared to the toned earthen colours here, the leaf-like patterns on some of them, and then . . . the atmosphere. It's far tenser in Emberwell. City people always judge you there. But after being here for a while, Elves glance my way and never give me a rude gesture. They smile instead, genuine and welcoming.

I stroll past a few shops, fascinated by their gowns as a few bless me in the name of Solaris, and I smile back until a tavern at the end of one of the streets catches my eye.

The door is wide open, with cheers and music filtering out of it. Then I hear a voice – a cocky, insufferable, and all-enticing voice.

Darius.

I hurriedly make my way up there, and once I enter, I squeeze past a few men to see him standing on one of the tables, swinging his brew around. Half of the ale spills and seeps into the cracks of the wooden floorboards as Tibith joins him, tapping his feet to the music, and Aias claps along by the bar.

They're all drinking, and Darius, well, he is genuinely, unapologetically drunk out of his mind.

Chapter Twenty-Two

I make my way through the crowd, excusing myself, in order to approach Darius. I grimace at the possibility of him toppling and falling off the table as he stumbles on his feet. Not that he would care.

When I reach the edge of the table, he turns, his face brightening the minute he sees me. Spreading his arms out, he shouts, 'Goldie!'

'Are you out of your mind?' I shout over the raucous noises of the tavern as I watch him hop onto a stool and smoothly land on the ground. 'We have to travel to Melwraith before sunrise, and you're out here drinking?'

He runs a hand through his hair, his face glossed with a faint sheen of sweat as he smiles. 'Dance with me.'

What in Solaris's world— 'Did you listen to a word I said?'

'I'm always listening, Goldie. I just love to see those damned freckled cheeks redden whenever you're annoyed with me.'

My eyes widen, and his grin doubles in size.

'Now.' He makes a mocking bow, extending his hand out. 'Will you dance with me?'

I am standing still with my arms crossed over my torso. He taps one foot against the floorboard before sighing and lifting me by the waist and whirling me around. I squeal and hiss his name as I pound my fists on his chest to stop, but he takes hold of my wrists and lowers me back to the ground.

'You took too long to decide.' His lips tease a smile as he twirls me away from his arms and then spins me back to him.

My chest collides with his as I roll my eyes. 'You're truly inebriated.'

'And you are too sober.'

'Last I recall, when I was far from sober, you picked me up against my will and dragged me back to my hut in the Screaming Forests.'

His laugh is a dangerously low quake, and I feel it reverberate against my chest as we move slower than the speed of the fiddle. 'It was either that or harming those Elves staring at you.' He darts his eyes around for half a second. 'Kind of how most are staring right now.'

I give the tavern a quick look. The whole crowd seems to be looking our way. Glancing back at Darius, I cock a brow and whisper, 'I think they're staring at you.'

He gives me a pleased smile. 'Well, I am the looker.'

I roll my eyes, huffing a chuckle, when I feel a tug on my boot. Glancing down, I see Tibith rocking on his feet.

Darius and I stop dancing, but he never lets go or loosens his grip on my hand.

'Miss Nara!' Tibith exclaims, 'I saw another me!'

Darius chuckles, saying, 'Yes, a Terranos Tibithian.'

'But— but he didn't speak.' Tibith pouts, only causing my heart to grow ten times more before his expression changes, and he beams at us. 'Perhaps he can be my new friend!'

My smile softens as I release my hand from Darius's and bend down, ruffling Tibith's head. 'Perhaps.'

When I look up, Darius's drunken smile has me glowering. 'We should go,' I say as I rise on my toes and point my index finger at his chest. 'Or you won't be able to wake up tomorrow.'

'Might I stay?' Aias walks over to us, swirling the contents of his drink around in his tankard. 'The drinks here are delicious.'

I pull a face as he takes a sip and grab it off him before I have to deal with another drunkard. The night already has me flashing back to the moments Iker would come home intoxicated, and Illias and I would get him to bed.

'No.' I yank the drink from his spindly fingers and smack it down on one of the barmaid's trays as she walks past. 'Now, let's go.'

I stumble into Darius's chambers with one of his arms slung around my shoulder as he holds on to a leather flask he'd stolen off an Elf in plain sight. I had attempted to pry it from his hand, but the number of times he'd swung it around made it far too difficult to grab it, and if I had managed, he'd likely take it from me within seconds again.

'I can't believe you left the castle grounds to intoxicate yourself,' I mutter as I drop him onto his bed, and he sits up. 'And Aias, really? He shouldn't be dragged into your childish outings!' I had tried not to chastise Aias, considering he and Tibith had fled to their chamber as soon as the castle gates rolled up.

'He is not a child, Goldie,' he says, rolling his shoulders as he massages the back of his neck. The motion of it, for some reason, has me staring at the cut of his tunic, showing his chest more than anything.

'Even so, it wasn't a good time for you to start drinking tonight.'

'When is it not a good time to drink?'

'When we have to be somewhere in the morning!' I quell the temper in my voice as he slowly rises from the bed. 'Are you forgetting we aren't here because we want to be?' Through the dark, the lack of sconces, and the pervading scent of sweet honey ale, I can still see him clearly as I carry on, 'If our only hope of protecting Zerathion is the Isle of Elements, then we can't just keep wasting time, Darius.' I draw back a breath knowing his eyes are still on me. Folding my arms over my chest, I shake my head and stare at him. 'Why were you drinking?'

He escapes my gaze and shrugs. 'Must there be a reason?'

Considering he'd acted off today and how Gus had mentioned that at times when he'd not been himself, he would drink until he could hardly say his name . . . 'Not at all, but why now? Why today?'

His eyes pin me right here on the spot as he draws the flask up to his lips. 'I thought it would make me forget.'

I huff out a breath, slapping my hands against my thighs. 'Forget what?'

He takes a long sip. 'Forget how badly I want to kiss you.'

My heart jumps.

I can't voice what I want to say. Every ounce of my flesh melts at what he's just said and how his eyes don't leave anything to the imagination. He's looking at me like he's one step closer to dropping everything and doing exactly what he's been wanting to forget.

Kiss me.

He is drunk, that is all.

Drunk and—

He tosses the now-empty flask onto his bed. 'I'll be honest with you, Goldie, because I'd be lying to myself if I didn't tell you how I've considered taking you up against every inch of this castle.' His words strike a shockwave through my system, and I find myself stumbling backwards as he walks over, so leisurely and smooth you'd think he hadn't been drinking. And as he approaches me, he leans over the wall to rest his palms on either side of my head. 'Every single night, knowing you're just across the room from me . . . it's torture.'

I swallow slowly. 'Darius—'

He groans, low and frustrated, as he drops his forehead against mine. 'Don't say my name like that.'

'You're not thinking straight,' I murmur, half closing my eyes. Drunk, he's foolishly drunk.

'I've never thought more perfectly in my life, Goldie.'

'Get some sleep.'

He smirks. 'With you, I hope.'

I shoot him an unforgettable glare. 'Do you want me to dunk your head in a water barrel?'

He chuckles, our noses touching. 'Make it a barrel of wine.'

My legs quiver, my heartbeat too loud for me to hear myself as I press my palm against his chest and gently push him back. 'Sleep,' I repeat, walking past him as I try to regain my breath despite the lack of exertion. As I look back at him, he's leaning against the wall, his eyes on me with a mesmerizing smile. 'I'll come back to check on you.'

He stiffens, cocking his head to the side. 'Why would you do that?' he asks with a deep frown, but beyond that, there's a glimmer of sadness in his gaze, like drops of amber turning dark and cold in winter.

'To make sure you've not gone and caused any havoc.' I raise a brow, humoured by the thought, yet Darius does not tease back or smile as he lowers his gaze.

My stare reflects his, but when I try to ask, he stalks over to his bed and sits down without a word. Even though he's not looking at me, I nod and rush out of his chambers, heading straight into mine. Closing the door behind me, I place a hand on my chest, searching for a beat, a thump, *anything*. My feet are heavy on the floor as I pace towards the dresser by my bed and fumble to light a wooden wick. With trembling hands, the candle ignites, and I draw back sharp breaths.

Forget how badly I want to kiss you.

I close my eyes and shake my head.

I'll be honest with you, Goldie, because I'd be lying to myself if I didn't tell you how I've considered taking you up against every inch of this castle.

I scrunch up my hair by digging my fingers into the sides of my skull. 'Even in my mind, you annoy me, for Solaris's—' A gasp hurtles past my lips as I turn at the sound of the door opening and closing.

Darius's gaze collides with mine, and my heart soars.

The candle flickers behind me, casting different shadows on the walls of the room.

'I said I was going to check on you later,' I say, but it might just as well be no less than a whisper.

'Did you want me to go further?' He ignores me as his hooded gaze takes me in. When I frown, he clarifies, 'Today in the woods, did you want . . . more?'

He'd been thinking about it earlier, just as much as I had. 'I told you to get some rest.'

He clicks his tongue, advancing towards me. 'Not an answer, Goldie, unless you're too stubborn to say yes or no?'

I scoff. 'If anyone should be asking a question, it's me. Why did *you* stop?'

That stumps him, and for a second, I don't expect an answer. It's hard to deny I'm not disappointed, because I am, and usually, where I am good at hiding my emotions, I can never do so with him. 'Seems like I'm not the only stubborn one,' I say and start towards my door in an attempt to make him leave.

'When we first met—' His voice is like an echo that makes me freeze. My heart stops as I breathe and spin to look at him. He slowly turns, his eyes brimming with an agonizing hold '—I wanted to hate who you were. A Venator bold enough to go up against me alone. And even so, I could never shake you off . . . I *wanted* to hate your smile.' He takes another step. 'The way it would sometimes slip out, whether it was with a lilt in your voice or a twitch in your body. I wanted to so easily find a way to despise it all because I knew I didn't even deserve to be near you, but then your laugh,' he breathes like the thought aches every inch of his mind and soul. 'The day you laughed inside the den, then the forest . . . it took every ounce of me not to kiss you, feel you, laugh with you, and damn anyone who dared to try come between us.'

I can't blame this on him drinking. I can't even breathe over him saying this to me with such determination and need because I'm not used to it.

'So, when you ask me why I stopped?' He forces out a husky chuckle, running a hand over his jaw. 'It's because I do not think I will ever be worthy of you. I don't think anyone is. I feel selfish even looking at you . . . always have, Goldie.'

My heart drums to a fast beat. I'm staring at him as if I'll be able to find a flaw in his words. Something that in the next few seconds, will say how he's lying, and he'll insult me, tell me how my hair is a mess today, mock my attire, and laugh at my anger over him.

But no, he does none of that.

He's drinking me in whole, waiting, pleading to hear my response.

'Kiss me,' I finally say, my words taking him back.

'What?'

My chest rises with each second. I can't think of anything other than the fact that he is over there, and I am here, and that I want him to do the very thing I have craved since that night in Emberwell. 'Kiss me,' I repeat. 'And don't stop.'

His jaw locks as his eyes travel to my lips. It's the confirmation he needs before he whispers, 'Fuck.' And takes two steps, cupping my cheeks as my back slams against a desk with the force of his mouth claiming mine.

The first few seconds do not register in my mind. It's a haze of ecstasy, wants, and a pit of dangerous desires.

Our tongues meld into one. It's not soft. It's an unending passion where we're gasping for air with each contact of our lips joining. His hand lowers from my face to my thigh as he hoists me onto the desk. My hands rake through his hair, vicious and wild, like I'm in need of more. As he jerks me up against him, my middle meets his as he situates himself between my legs. Our foreheads rest on each other's as a sound escapes from my throat, and I think I must have said his name because he practically devours me with another kiss, swallowing up any other noises I make.

Unable to resist, I arch my back and pull away as his lips graze my jaw down to my neck. The contact of his teeth nipping and kissing me leaves a trail of fire behind, igniting it, even more, when his hands grab me under my tunic, and that possessive instinct takes over as he grips my waist and tugs me closer to him.

'This still doesn't mean I find you less annoying,' I breathe, tipping my head back as I fist his hair between one hand while the other rests against the flat surface of the desk.

The heat of his breath on my neck has me almost curling in pleasure as he chuckles hoarsely. 'Like I've said before, Goldie, annoying you is something I love to do.'

I grin, feeling like I've drunk a whole bottle of wine, intoxicated by his hold on me. Lifting his head, our lips find a way back to each other—

'Nara? I know it is late, but—'

The desk vibrates beneath me as the door hits its side, and I jump off, gripping Darius's shoulders as my gaze widens to find Aias.

His obsidian eyes are blinking at the sight in front of him. His hand is still gripping the doorknob as he looks between us and clears his throat. 'Darius, I didn't know you were in here.'

I'm breathless as I touch my swollen lips and glance up at Darius. A lazy smile is plastered on his features as he hums, content and not at all embarrassed.

'Goodnight, Aias,' he says, stepping back from me and slapping a hand on Aias's shoulder. The action makes Aias jolt while Darius turns his head to look at me one last time, his eyes lingering on my lips before leaving.

Oh, I am in trouble.

Aias's forehead scrunches, expecting an answer from me, but my mind is unable to come up with one. 'It's—'

'It's exactly what it looks like,' he says, shutting the door.

I groan in defeat, slouching my shoulders as I trudge over to my bed and plop down. 'What is wrong with me?' I run my hands over my face, squishing my cheeks together as I turn to look at Aias sitting beside me. 'First, it was his brother, now him. I—' I stop to breathe. It's impossible to think straight. 'I said to myself that if I ever fell in love, it would only be if it was Crello himself.'

'So, you love him?' Aias concludes.

'What? No,' I rush out, scowling at him as I shake my head.

'He— he angers me, he's the worst person to talk to, he's pretentious, has an ego the size of Zerathion, and—'

'And yet you would do anything for him.'

I frown at him as he looks at me like I'm supposed to agree with him after the absurdity that has just happened.

'Nonetheless . . . he is a dragon shifter, and you are a human,' he adds slowly. 'So, despite it all, you are both from different worlds. If you were a shifter like him, maybe things would be easier.'

I let his words settle in, and my shoulders sag the more I think it through. 'I don't want to be a shifter,' I whisper. 'I can't be one.'

A mortal can't be bitten unless they want to bet on their life.

'Then the answer is right in front of you,' Aias says, standing up from the bed, his hands reaching out to my shoulder. 'You can't be with him.'

Something feels like it's gutting me from the inside out as I hear this. Freya would know what to say right now. She'd always have a positive mindset, so I find myself searching for comfort in Aias. 'What would you do if you were me?' I ask, and he lets out a long sigh.

'I'd risk it all and become what he is.' He shrugs. 'A dragon shifter with powers sounds better than having none at all.'

I half chuckle, half snort, and shake my head. 'Remind me not to ask for your advice next time.'

'Take it as you will, but I haven't seen a connection such as yours in a long time.'

'He has a connection with everything he comes into contact with,' I say, and he screws up his face with amusement.

'Well, anyway, my original intention had been to bid you good luck before you set off for your task in the morning, but considering everything, perhaps I should have waited.' He chuckles. 'I think I'll head back. Tibith is likely snoring away by now.'

I smile at him, but my energy seems to drain as I think about what he said.

'Nara?' Aias draws me out of my endless worry loop, and I spot him by the door. 'I know you will do brilliantly at each task; I don't doubt you once.' He closes the door behind him, and I'm left in the silence of my room.

How will I do brilliantly when I doubt myself about every little thing nowadays?

Chapter Twenty-Three

As Golrai fits me into a fur-lined sleeveless coat with a hood over my tunic, I stare far ahead at the painted walls of my chambers. She describes how much colder it is in Melwraith, a city of snow mountains and ice caves. I already know Darius will not wear such attire. He's explained how his body generates heat, and he even proved it to me that night in the forest.

Golrai wraps my sheath around my waist, her gaze widening with each dagger she examines. I almost smile at her, but my mind isn't entirely with it this morning, not since last night.

I'd pestered Darius about needing to sleep so much that I'd gotten *no* sleep. Instead, I stayed awake, carving jasmine blossoms into the wood of my bedposts as my mind replayed our kiss, his words . . . his confession.

I bite my lower lip absentmindedly, replaying it all over again. That possessive hold on me, a war with our lips and heart. Aias had been right, whatever it is between Darius and me, lust, a bond after what we've gone through, or burning curiosity, he's a shifter at the end of the day. And I am a human. We're don't work together.

'I can take it from here, Golrai.' Arlayna's calm and melodious voice has me looking over my shoulder as she enters the room. Her dark hair plunges down the right side of her neck as the left is braided back, and her halter satin dress shimmers in blue and green once the slit of sunlight catches hold of it.

Golrai stops fastening the laces of my fingerless gloves and bows to Arlayna before leaving us. Arlayna walks with precision and grace towards me and doesn't say a word as she laces up my right glove.

'Are you prepared?' she asks, focusing on her task.

'What should I be prepared for?' Death? Deadly creatures? Seeing Darius?

Somehow that third one is the most daunting.

Arlayna looks up at me once she's finished, her grey eyes like prowling clouds in a storm. 'Nothing at all, I suppose.' She twirls her finger, gesturing for me to turn around and head to the long mirror decorated with gold roses at the sides.

A shiver runs along my skin as her feather-light fingers sink into my hair. 'From what I know,' she says, 'Melwraith is the easiest task. Each place is a puzzle to solve in order to get the stone, but they are not the ordinary kind. Any magic you may have is useless for these tasks. It will not work and many who seek the Isle of Elements give up before they make it to Thalore.' She pauses as she looks past my shoulder into the mirror, her brows rising ever so slightly. 'Although you don't seem the type to give up.'

I trust her words. She's not saying it to boost my confidence or to have my belief in obtaining it flood me with doubt. She's saying it meaningfully.

'That is because I'm not,' I say, betrayed by the pensive sadness in my voice. Sometimes giving up is the better solution.

Arlayna doesn't notice, luckily. She pulls my hair from the sides, tugging it into a plait and leaving the rest of my locks down. 'Might I ask, once you have access to the Isle of Elements, what will you ask of it or wish for if you believe Zerathion is in danger?'

I mull that question over a few times. I do not have a set plan for what I'd wish for. Neither Darius nor I had previously spoken enough about it. Maybe we assumed we wouldn't be where we are now. 'I guess something worth uniting our kingdoms without facing wars,' I say with hope. 'Even if that requires something beyond creating the Northern Blade. What would you ask for?'

She stiffens. Her hands stop their actions, and a stretched silence fills the room. I turn to face her as she finally says, 'A High Elf cannot use the Isle of Elements for their desires.' That baffles me, causing her to add, 'The elders from when our world was first created made it that way. That is why we are the only ones who possess the stones. It would be far too easy for us to take advantage otherwise.'

I frown at the reveal of it all. 'That is unfair, though.'

She chuckles, but there is little humour in it. 'A lot is unfair in our world, don't you think?'

'Yes.' I nod solemnly. 'I realised that a while ago.'

There's a sudden knock stopping us from furthering this conversation. I go to open the door and I'm greeted by glinting emerald armour and a stoic Aeron.

'The King is ready for you outside,' he says, arms behind his back as the smallest trickle of light from my room caresses his skin.

I nod, unsure if I am ready, but Arlayna interjects to say, 'She was already on her way. You didn't need to come to fetch her.'

I'm startled by the blatant irritation in her tone as I glance between the two.

'I did it because of the King's orders, not yours, Princess.' Aeron's punishing smirk seems to rattle Arlayna. Her chest heaves as she lifts her chin and tries to remain composed.

I don't attempt to intervene between them. Whatever it is, it looks like they have some history together. From the moment I first saw them interact, I realised it. They don't look at each other how a sentry and a superior would look at one another. No, there's a hint of childish play, pent-up anger, and longing from both sides.

Arlayna's brows narrow, her delicate features tensing the more she stares at Aeron before she storms past us and out of the room.

I cast a glance from the hallway to Aeron's soft smile, but he straightens his face as soon as he sees me watching, and he clears his throat, guiding me with his arm.

The minute I walk out into the gardens, my eyes snap to Darius, his lack of winter attire and his dark leather jerkin fitting snug against his muscles. It almost reminds me of the first time we met.

He turns to look at me, and my heart flutters. It worsens as he smiles because I know it's not just a normal smile. It's one where he's staring at my lips, remembering last night despite his drunken state. It's one that tells me he doesn't regret it and one where he wants to do it again.

Finding the strength I need in my trembling body, I march and stand beside him. I don't greet him or flash him a smile as I hold my gaze straight in front of me, where Dusan is holding a rolled-up piece of vellum.

Darius's gaze on me is unforgiving. I can feel it penetrate through me. I try to focus on the King instead, the extravagant jewels upon his fingers, his forest green attire made of fine silk and thread, and his crown of thorns. I wonder whether if anyone tried to steal it from him, would it prick them? Or perhaps it's laced with magic that only the King of Terranos can possess.

'Nara.' His voice cuts through my thoughts as he smiles, and the open air filters through the long ashy strands of his hair, making him look ethereal. 'How are you feeling this morning?'

A multitude of things. 'Dreadfully fatigued.'

Dusan chuckles. 'You can have a celebratory nap once you have retrieved the stone.'

So, he also believes we can do this. 'I certainly will,' I say, mustering up some confidence as I see Tibith sleeping in the arms of Faye from the corner of my eye.

The view makes me feel better before Dusan says, 'There is something you should know for when you arrive at the glacial mountains of Melwraith.'

A chord plucks at my already anxious mind as he points a finger in the air and slowly begins pacing. 'You will see that it is guarded by an order of seven priestesses. They will not speak to you, and they will not look you in the eye, but you must tell them your name and your purpose as to what brings you there. You do that, and they will show you the path which will lead you to the stone.'

It seems easy enough, but it surely wouldn't be as simple as them leading us to the stone.

Dusan stops in front of Darius, handing him the piece of vellum. 'I wish you both good luck,' he says with a bow of the head and retreats to where Faye is.

I turn to Darius as he unfolds a map of Terranos. Melwraith lies towards the south, and Valdern's port city Edwyrd had spoken of.

Watching Darius roll the map back up and pass it over to me, I'm completely captivated by his eyes as his thumb caresses mine. It's just one second of us touching, but I know it was intentional.

His lip curls up at the side as he whispers teasingly, 'I promise not to drop you this time.'

My laugh is short and breathless. As I clear my throat and hold back a smile, I try to act normal, like last night was just a dream. 'Well, I'd like to think you wouldn't. Once can be a mistake, but twice—' I tut in mockery, shaking my head '—I'll begin to wonder whether you want me dead.'

His smile doesn't quite stay; it's as if my words took a severe turn for him. 'I wouldn't be able to live with myself if that happened to you, Goldie.'

My mockery fades. I'm in a state of shock. Suddenly, the winter clothing is too much for me; I want it off, I want . . . I want—

'Shall we?' he says, stepping aside like what he'd just said hadn't made me speechless.

I find it difficult to answer, so I hesitate with a nod, and he rolls his shoulders back, taking a deep breath as silver mist and darkness encase him.

Like yesterday, I mount him and press my hands against his scales. He takes off without a second thought, and our journey to find the second stone begins.

Chapter Twenty-Four

My boots barely thud against the snowy ground as I leap off Darius, and the cold wind comes down the mountaintop with enough force to push me back. It is definitely not something I'm used to, as my teeth chatter, breathing becomes difficult. Studying my surroundings while Darius shifts, I glance at the sloped pathway uphill. When Darius was flying over Melwraith, I could see the faint outlines of houses, huts, and lights within dips of mountainous areas. But where we are now is near the peak with no soul in sight unless I look down to my left, where I could easily fall to my death. Honestly, you can hardly see the ground from up here; an outer layer of fog covers most of it.

'I'm assuming we must make our way up there.' My breath creates a cloud of smoke from the cold as I jerk my chin towards the fang-white mountain soaring further into the sky.

Darius comes up beside me, and immediately a surge of heat from him has me warming up as I relax my shoulders in satisfaction. I turn my head to look at him and realise he's not doing anything except just standing there, analyzing the trek ahead.

I huff a breath, annoyed at myself, and before he can say a word, I start up the steep path.

'You know, Goldie,' he says, already having made his way next to me. 'If you plan to avoid me during this task after last night, you're going about it the wrong way.'

I stop and send his arrogant smirk a glare. 'I'm not avoiding you,' I say, even if that is precisely what I'm trying to do. 'In case you haven't noticed, I have much bigger concerns than talking about your drunken mistake last night.'

I urge myself to turn back around, but he grabs my hand, making me snap my head to him. My body tenses with the need to have him hold on to me elsewhere.

'You mean the one where you specifically asked me to kiss you?' His words have my heart trying to jump out of my chest.

I snatch my hand away and try walking away again. 'I was clearly delusional.'

'Then what was I?' he asks in a laughter-tinged voice. When I roll my eyes and don't answer, his hand snakes around my waist, whirling me to his chest. His voice is much lower than before as he says honestly, 'Because there's no mistaking how I'd like to do it again, Goldie.'

My feet feel light. There's that same lustful look in his eyes, and I know I'm staring at him the same.

'Every day,' he whispers, inching closer to my lips. 'Every hour.' On impulse, my eyes start to flutter closed. 'And every second.'

I gulp. 'We would surely pass out after a while.' My voice seems to be lost. 'Besides, you would go insane. I can be quite a handful.'

Yet, in reality, he's the only one who *can* handle me.

His vibrating laugh makes me want to ignore all the signs as to why last night shouldn't have happened. The truth is, that kiss left me needing more. It created a hunger worse than the first time. One that should be impossible between him and me.

'As can I,' he replies, and my eyes open.

I scoff. A handful is an understatement when it comes to him. 'I think you enjoy being a handful.'

He nods. 'True.' Then grins. 'Though I tend to enjoy a lot of things.'

'I know. Annoying me is one of them.'

'Now kissing you has been added to that list.'

It's like he's trying to say all of this on purpose for a reaction. And he is getting the right one. My throat knots, and I close my eyes, chuckling as I shake away the flutters in my stomach. When I open my eyes to look at him, his smile pulls me close with his warmth and forms a bond I cannot fathom.

But the moment withers like autumn leaves falling off branches as something skitters across my calf, sending me jumping back from Darius.

My hand flies to the blades along my sheath as I stare at the snow-coated ground. 'What was that?'

'What was what?' Darius asks, but whatever happened doesn't occur again, making it feel like I'd made it up in my head.

'I thought—' I pause, looking up at Darius, his brows drawing together before I shake my head. 'Nothing, let's just go.'

He's still by my side as we reach the top, and a group of seven priestesses, as Dusan had mentioned, appear from behind two boulders.

The mist makes it hard to see them, even more so as a white lace covering obscures the top part of their faces. Each has a silver staff with an opalescent gem affixed at the top, and as I step towards them, Darius presses a hand against my arm. Our eyes meet, and he sends me a look that tells me he'll take it from here. He then starts telling the Elven priestesses our names, why we are here, and what we've come for.

They're silent, not even moving an inch or giving us a sign before they part to each side, now standing in a row and giving us space to see inside the pitch-black cave. The two closest to the entrance tap their staffs against the ground, causing the gemstones to light up.

I watch with grave fascination as they extend their staffs and hold the gems to the floor of the entrance to the cave, sending beams of phosphorescent blue light inside.

We thank them despite their silence and enter, moving carefully, echoes of the crunching of broken ice following behind us. My eyes roam the cave with slight wonder, its reflective colours making Darius's hair look navy, and I notice that the ceiling is aglow with dots of emerald, almost resembling a night sky.

'After how easy it was to enter this cave . . . what do you suppose we'll encounter?' Darius offers his hand as we come across a dip, and for once, without argument, I accept it, skipping across. We're further away from the entrance, and I imagine we have a long way until we see at least some sign of the stone.

'Arlayna mentioned there are likely to be puzzles ahead, almost like tasks to solve.'

'Are you any good at puzzles?'

I turn to him and cross my arms. 'I'm excellent, of course.'

He half smirks, half laughs until his eyes catch something behind me.

'What?' I ask warily.

'There's something inside your hood.' He draws a step nearer to me, reaching his hand out. 'Stay still—'

Swatting his hand away, I huff, not up for his usual trickery when inside a cave that could potentially be filled with traps. 'If this is some plot just to get close to me—'

'Goldie, for the love of—' He stops himself, pressing his lips tight together before he exhales and says, 'Just let me—'

I go to raise my finger to stop him, but something tugs at my hair, and I look to my left, only catching a glimpse of fur before it slides down my leg, and I gasp, jerking backward with Darius catching me in his arms. He wraps a strong arm across my middle, and we pant, wondering what on earth just happened.

A little squeak comes from the ground, and as we glance down, we stare at what had been hiding in my hood.

A Tibithian.

One exactly like Tibith but with fluorescent green fur – likely from the phosphorous – and slightly smaller in size.

It blinks, tilting its head from side to side.

A chuckling breath escapes me. It must have followed us in here, I think it's the tiny thing I'd felt crawling around my leg before.

As Darius lets go of me, I kneel, stroking the Tibithian's silky fur. He purrs against my hand and closes his eyes in comfort, which is the most endearing sight.

'He's a male,' Darius says.

I glance up at him, frowning in question as he points back at the Tibithian.

'See the feathers at the top of his head?'

When I look, the Tibithian has the same feathers that Tibith has whenever he gets excited or frightened spreading across his head.

'Only the male species have those.'

My nose scrunches with a smile, and I whisper, 'Tibith would love you.'

'Almost as much as he loves bread,' Darius says, chuckling as he crouches beside me and runs his knuckles along the Tibithian's neck.

We glance at each other as he holds my gaze for seconds, perhaps minutes.

For a fleeting moment, I'm filled with something that brings back that homely feeling, but a rumble disturbs us, reminding me what we should be doing. We both stand up, looking further down the cave. The Tibithian squeaks, waddling before us and growling at the never-ending tunnel.

Darius and I glance at one another before we go on. The Tibithian stays beside me, cooing and clinging on to my leg at points. Darius mentions how fond he seems of me, to which I laugh at. I'd heard that phrase a lot throughout my upbringing with regard to various creatures. It is funny how it hasn't changed.

Opting for luck, we turn a corner straight into another, stopping short as we spot another much larger, almost square-shaped opening.

My eyes drag up to a symbol of a weighing scale carved into the ice above the entrance.

Weighing scales could mean many things. Good and bad, truth and lie, life and death.

Perhaps this is part of the puzzle.

A heavy drop in my stomach has me hoping we come out of this with the stone in our hands. Another has me wondering if my reading of Terranos history at the castle library was enough.

I press my hand against the side wall and lean in to look. I see stalactites hanging from the ceilings, dreadfully dangerous and obstructing most of my view.

'Ladies first,' Darius says when I turn to him.

My brow quirks. 'Ever the gentleman.'

He chuckles, and I hate that I've come to adore that sound so much. 'You know I always am,' he says, dramatically stretching his hand out for me to proceed.

I roll my eyes and with the Tibithian still clinging to my side, I walk inside. I'm immediately struck by the grand view. A long bridge on my left extends to a circular platform of pure ice. The surrounding area is a pitch-black void that, if I am to drop a coin, I doubt I'll ever hear it land on the ground.

The hairs on my skin rise at the thought, and as I take another step, a sudden sharp sound like swords being drawn slices through the air. I whirl, and it's too late as a wall of ice separates me from Darius.

CHAPTER TWENTY-FIVE

P anic seeps into my bones as I bang my hands on the wall.
'Darius!'

He responds with my name, and I run my palms along
the ice, searching for a way out or an alternative that will perhaps
break the wall.

'Use your strength!' I yell, noticing two carvings of a crescent and
sun entwined above.

'It won't work. This wall seems to be protected by magic,' Darius
says in frustration from the opposite side, then sighs, collecting his
thoughts. 'Goldie, I need you to listen to what I ask you, alright?'

The Tibithian, having managed to squeeze in with me, peers up
as I nod, even if Darius can't see my face.

'What do you see right now?' he asks, and I scan what's around me.

'A bridge of ice leading to another platform,' I answer, as my eyes
focus on something gleaming atop the platform. 'I think the stone is
there.'

'Go there—'

'But what about you—'

'Never mind me. Just focus on the stone and get out of here.'

I sigh, dropping my forehead against the wall. There's no point in fighting this when we need that stone. 'I will,' I promise him. Glancing down at the Tibithian, I order him to stay here and I start towards the bridge, but two steps in, I find him following me. My shoulders drop in resignation, and I wave a hand over at him to join me. His ears flap, rushing to my side as I reach the narrow bridge. There's nothing to hold on to, and I can only rely on pacing myself carefully.

I put one foot out onto the bridge, cautious to see if it can bear my weight, and take a trembling breath, leveling my eyes with the platform ahead rather than the dark nothingness below. The Tibithian whizzes by without a second thought and I hold my breath, hoping the bridge doesn't collapse. When he comes to a halt, he blinks and uncurls himself, emitting animalistic garbles as he waits for me.

I chuckle as I step onto the bridge. 'Just so you know, I'm not usually one to be afraid,' I tease as I waltz towards the Tibithian, and he looks up at me with a twitch of his ears.

We spend the next few minutes walking across. The cave is so vast in size, and after a minute or two, I look back to where Darius is. He seems so far out of reach, even with a wall blocking us. I sigh, trying not to get myself so worked up. *This isn't like the trials, Nara.*

A glimmer of light from the sky above the mountain peak shines upon the platform. A staircase made of ice greets us at the end of the bridge, and we take the few steps we need to reach the top, coming face to face with a lustrous pedestal in the middle of it all. The Tibithian's gasps echo inside the cave as I walk around, gazing at a weighing scale carefully placed on top of the plinth.

What on earth am I supposed to make of this?

My attention quickly catches an inscription of cursive writing on its side, and I tilt my head to get a better view. '*A prize awaits for those who confess what their lips have dared not say,*' I read out, over and over, slowly and carefully.

I draw back from the pedestal and quickly analyze my thoughts.

It is asking for a confession.

My eyes jump back and forth from the left scale to the right.

'I do not have a—' The scale on the right tips and part of the platform starts to rumble beneath us.

Right, it did not like that.

I blow out a tense breath and brace my arms against the pillar as my nerves start to get the best of me. I wipe my forearm across my forehead while the Tibithian's soft murmurs reach my ears like a bird's melodious coo.

Worry bubbles over me as I repeat the phrase out loud.

'*A confession I have dared not say . . .*'

But I have too many, some I don't even know myself. I assume most of us do, but which one will get me that stone? If the scale on the right side tipped when I spoke, that could only mean it's equivalent to a lie and the left . . . the truth.

Glancing over my shoulder, I wish to have Darius here beside me. He would have an answer. Likely a terrible one that would annoyingly somehow do the trick—

My body tenses, and a memory so fierce and vivid plays inside my head.

So, this . . . must belong to you then.

My carving, my sun.

You – you were the one to drop it. And you kept it all these years.

'Lorcan . . .' I whisper as the echo of his words inside my head disappears, and I look towards the scales, repeating, '*A prize awaits for those who confess what their lips have dared not say.'*

The Tibithian tilts his head to the side, possibly wondering what is the matter with me. But realising my answer, I shut my eyes, count to ten in my head, and release a slow, steady breath. 'When I found out who the crescent carving belonged to,' I start, 'part of me was disappointed.' Once I open my eyes, the revelation makes it all that more real. 'I—I didn't know *why* at that moment, but now I think it is because I'd wished it to be someone else deep down, and I hate myself for that. I hate that I believed so much in a little carving, thinking it was tied to my luck, and I hate that while I knew who the crescent belonged to, I would think of someone else.' I lower my head. 'Maybe that is why I tried so hard to despise— why I still try to . . .'

A charged silence descends on the cave. I lift my eyes to the scales, silently hoping, and then – the left scale drops, and a beacon of silver light bursts free.

Grimacing, I raise my forearm to cover my eyes until the light dims, and I blink through the blinding flash. A sense of wonder clouds over me when I realise it is the stone – an iridescent opal floating in midair.

It worked.

A confession I wouldn't dare to admit, even to myself.

I reach for the stone, examining it closely in my hands. It bears the same sign of a crescent and sun interwoven, Solaris and Crello. I half grin, half chuckle in relief, glancing down at the Tibithian. He squeaks in approval though it is not long before the ground beneath me vibrates, and the Tibithian wobbles on his feet.

The walls roar, and within moments large chunks of ice crack off and fall.

My gaze darts towards the entrance. Even with the success of getting the stone, I should have realised there is always a catch. If I stay here one more second, the entire cave will collapse, burying me within it.

More chunks of the wall break off as I spring into action, sprinting across the bridge.

'Come on!' I yell to the Tibithian as a rumble splits the air, and my head shoots up. Shards of ice begin to smash onto our pathway, and I cross my arms over my head, dodging the sharp fragments that are flying in the air as each piece of ice crashes around us.

I'm not so lucky when another comes crashing down, shattering straight into the bridge. I stumble to a stop and as I slip, the stone falls from my grip. I gasp, trying to grab it, just as the Tibithian jumps into the air, capturing it between his paws. He throws it at me, and as I catch it, I call out to him, sprinting towards the bridge's edge.

A feeling of dread begins to spread across my chest, but then I see him clinging to an icicle. He looks up at me, fangs peeking through his tiny smile. 'Grab my hand,' I shout, straining my arm to reach him. His paw waves through the air. 'Almost got it, that's it—' The bridge trembles, making him slip further down the stalactite.

This bridge won't hold us for much longer. My mind races to find a solution as the ice fissures under my legs. I yank a blade from my belt, flipping it so the handle faces the Tibithian. I don't care if it cuts me. I just need him to grab on to it.

He shakes his head as the blade cuts through my glove, and blood begins to drip from my palm. He whimpers, but I smile at him as I say, 'It's fine. I'm okay. I will heal.'

His small paw reaches out for the handle hesitantly. He's almost there, but the shafts of ice approaching the platform we were standing on begins to break apart individually. The ice splits as I turn my head back to the Tibithian. He retracts his paw as he looks at me, his eyes wide with affection instead of fear.

No.

Not again. Not again. Not again.

I no longer feel any pain in my hand as I urge him to grab it.

He doesn't. He hugs the icicle instead.

I squeeze the blade, letting out a whimper. 'Please,' I whisper.

He smiles and squeaks obligingly, almost as though he's thanking me, but I'm shaking my head, half my body already over the ledge.

It is too late. The crack in the ice ruptures, and my heart plummets, watching the Tibithian fall with it.

Agony floods my chest, a deep burning sensation, and time slips, slowing down as I stare at the dark pit. And as another patch of icicles break loose, I know I can't stay here. I retreat, dropping the knife, smudging blood all over the ice, and an ache burrows itself deep in my chest as I rise, and with the stone in my other hand, I begin to run.

I don't look back; I don't want to.

Still shielding myself when more ice tumbles down, I hear Darius calling out my name from the other side, giving me enough determination to keep going.

My heart drums and thuds, almost as fast as my legs clamber across the floor. I finally reach the bridge when part of it breaks off. I start to sprint faster, and just as the rest of the path caves in, I leap across, my legs swinging in the air helplessly for what I count as an eternity before I land on the ground. Scrambling to my feet, I race to the entrance, my distress heightening as blood from my hand smears all over the symbol as I place it against the wall.

Seconds pass, and the sheet of ice separating us slides upwards. I immediately push myself forward and collapse into Darius's arms, and he holds me in a tight embrace.

He smooths down my hair, his soothing voice a whisper against my ear. 'You're okay, you're okay.'

I must be shivering because he pulls back, his gaze landing on my hand drenched in blood and the other clenching the stone between my fingers.

He ignores the stone as he focuses on my bleeding hand and swears, and I notice the strain in his jaw as he swallows. Pulling back his sleeve, he goes to bite down on his wrist, but I stop him, not wanting to heal right now as I stand and walk past, staring at the ice walls around me. Everything feels too small, too tight, *too* much.

'Where is he?' I hear Darius ask, and from his low tone, I can tell he has realised. 'Nara,' he whispers, the ache reaching my ears. 'Tell me.'

My eyes screw shut, and the moment the Tibithian fell replays in my mind like a torturous nightmare.

When Darius repeats my name, I whirl to look at him. 'You really want to know?' My voice raises, my body fires up, and I'm suddenly untethered.

His eyes are serious as he attempts to walk over, to console me, but before he can, I whisper, 'I couldn't save him.'

And then I can't hold it in any longer.

The wave of sadness finally takes over me and I burst into tears.

Darius's expression crumbles. Pain, sadness, worry, and so much more comes over him as I weep profusely.

'To think, all my life, I knew what I wanted, and I had it just for a brief moment,' I say through gasps. 'I thought I could find some sort of justice for my father. I thought I could hate dragons the way I wanted to for so long. But no.' I shake my head, and the lump in my throat makes it hard to swallow. 'Instead, I met Lorcan. I met you, the General, the Queen.'

Darius shakes his head, walking towards me like nothing else matters. I look at him and wipe each tear as I continue, 'I believed she was protecting our land. I thought what she was doing was good, but she made me weak. She used me and then made me do things I wish

I never had.'

My lips quiver as I fight so hard to gain control.

I can't. I'm spiralling.

'I thought for once I belonged somewhere, but I never did.' I'm trembling. I'm hurting. 'I never have.'

'Nara, please—'

'And then she wanted me to prove my loyalty!' I release an abrupt laugh full of hysteria, and then slowly hunch over, clutching my chest as I break out into a wet sob. 'And then she made me kill a dragon.'

Darius's hands come towards me, but I shake them away as I wipe my cheeks. He still yanks me into his arms as I thrash and cry out, 'No— no, I killed her, I stabbed her in the heart, I— I—' My sobs become muffled as he holds me against his chest, whispering comforting words. I'm letting every part of me out, every single emotion I've kept to myself from what happened in Emberwell up until now.

His hand brushes my back as I clench my fist around the fabric of his clothes. My shoulders shake, and I sob silently. I can't feel my legs, and if Darius's arms weren't around me, I know I would fall. I would collapse here and want to stay until everything else disappears.

He draws back for a moment, clutching my face in his hands. His thumbs brush my damp cheeks, and he looks at me like I'm his entire world. 'She did not make you weak; do you hear me?'

I'm trying to blink past my tears, but they fall. Fall. Fall.

'You never gave up.' His voice has such conviction that every thread of determination forces its way through me. 'You did everything to protect your brothers, save me. Hell, you're here now doing everything in your power to save Zerathion.'

'But I couldn't save the Tibithian back there,' I gasp through tears. 'I couldn't save the dragon . . . I couldn't save Lorcan.' My voice breaks at his name, my tears cascading with the heavy ache of my chest as I blink enough to see the torment in Darius's eyes – torment and heartbreak, shrouded in worry.

'There are times when you have no choice other than to watch life slip away, but I'll be damned if you believe even for a second that it could be your fault. I'm with you, Goldie, through the good and the bad. You can hate me, push me away, but I will always do anything in my power to take any bit of pain you feel away from you.'

I'm nodding, trying to purge this agony out of me.

'See this?' He grabs my right hand, pushing down my thumb and pinky so the rest stays up. 'Place them on your heart.'

Not wanting to ask questions, I place the three fingers against my heart and feel the fast rhythmic drumming.

'Remind yourself of these three things—' Darius holds his gaze with mine '—that you're here, you have a purpose, and you cannot and *never* will be daunted.'

The burning pain in my chest subsides as I repeat in my head that I am here.

I have a purpose.

I cannot and never will be daunted.

Darius pulls me towards him and I lay my head on his chest as we stay in this embrace for a while. I listen to his heartbeat as if I'm in a trance. The rhythm of his life force, my salvation.

I am here.

I have a purpose.

I cannot and never will be daunted.

CHAPTER TWENTY-SIX

D ropping my blade on top of my bedside table, I marvel at the Tibithian I've carved out of a small piece of oak wood that I'd asked Golrai to fetch me.

The soft light beaming in from the moon caresses the carving, and I smile. It's been hours since we came back from Melwraith. Darius took his time to heal my hand, and the stone went straight to the King like the other I'd gotten from Renward.

I didn't go down for supper; I did not feel like it. Even the pie Darius had sent to my door was left untouched.

Bringing my legs to my chest, I rest my cheek on my knee. From this angle, I watch as Tibith lies on my pillow in a foetal position. His snores melt my heart, and the little twitch in his ears has me feel at peace. When we arrived, I rushed to him and did not leave his side. He'd giggled and that innocent warmth radiating off him constantly made me tear up.

I slide off the bed and walk towards my window, taking in tonight's subtle stars. My eyes trail from the sky down to the gardens where before, I'd go in search of something to trap.

I no longer feel like doing that.

Glancing at Tibith over my shoulder, I watch as he carries on sleeping, and then I head out of my chambers in search of a place to go. I pass the library and various rooms I've never been inside and then find myself by the kitchen entrance. It's dark, and no servant is in sight, so I creep forward, admiring the polished wooden counters full of fruits, a pitcher of milk, and a panelled window to my right.

'Come to complain about the pie?'

I jerk back on the spot, turning to the other side, where Darius sits atop a counter. He's shirtless, as he leans back I can see specks of flour dusting his cheek and his chest, and annoyingly he still looks handsome as always.

'What are you doing here?'

He shrugs. 'Thinking.'

My eyes cut to the counter in the middle. A golden pie crust pastry rests on top with various strawberries scattered around and flour scattered everywhere. 'You baked the pie yourself?'

'I always do, Goldie.'

The answer goes straight to my heart.

I always knew that he was aware I loved pies, but hearing he has been baking them himself feels wonderful.

I nod slowly as if processing his response. 'Why?'

He tilts his head, admiring me from the opposite side. 'You said it was your favourite.'

A soft chuckle flickers from my lips, and after a minute or so, a wave of emotions comes flooding through. I bite down on my lower lip, and tightness engulfs me whole.

'How are you feeling?'

I shrug, folding my arms over my chest to keep the sudden draught of air filtering through my thin nightgown. 'I think you already know the answer to that.'

He hums without saying a word as he flips the coin he was holding and fits it into his pocket.

Even after we left Melwraith, he never asked me what I had to do inside the cave or what the puzzle was. He'd stayed by my side, and once we were in the air, his soft murmurs were the only thing to console me. Yet . . . he doesn't know a thing about my confession, the very confession involving him.

'There was a scale,' I say, hoarse and quiet, as Darius's gaze lifts to me. *A prize awaits for those who confess what their lips have dared not say.*'

He studies me through the dark haze of the kitchen, and not a word falls from his lips.

An unbearable second passes. There is all the time in the world, but why does it feel like there truly is none for us.

I suck in air. 'My confession involved Lorcan . . . and you.'

He tenses. I don't think he realises I noticed.

It takes me a great deal of courage to say the following words, but I must, for my sake, for Lorcan's, and for Darius's. 'I said how part of me didn't want that carving to belong to Lorcan. That I felt guilty even in his death because it was supposed to be our moment, yet I'd hoped it to be someone else.'

A long shallow breath releases from his lips, and a cord of tension, unknown and almost grief-filled, extends between us. I know he has so much to say, but for whatever reason, I don't think I will get that response today. I didn't intend on getting one. I just wanted him to know.

'Why the three fingers to the heart?' I whisper, the moonlight casting shadows upon his hair.

He stares at me for a long time. The revelation from before clearly still lingers inside his mind. And as he looks away, he says, 'It is something my mother and I used to do.'

My heart thrums against my bones. I am hit with an intense feeling. I couldn't believe he had shared something so private that he would do with his mother, and he did it without any hesitation.

I link my hands in front of me and glance down at them. 'You must miss her deeply.'

He breathes a joyless chuckle. 'As much as you do yours.'

'What did she look like?'

He tips his head against the wall, and a wistful smile spreads across his face. 'Beautiful . . . green kind eyes, forgiving – too forgiving.'

'You must have gotten your eyes from your father then.'

'No, not at all. My eye colour is the one thing my mother said was unique, much like my powers. For whatever reason Solaris and Crello had, I was blessed with all three.'

I walk towards him, and a smile pulls at my lips. 'I'm assuming that's where all your arrogance stemmed from.'

His chuckle is such a rich, seductive sound that it reaches me in my core. 'That, and also, I'm pleasing to the eye.'

We both laugh, letting it subside into a comfortable silence.

'Goldie?' he says as soon as I stand before him. Even from this position, he's far taller than me. 'Why did you never tell me what the Queen had you do?'

I meet his eyes, and I can see how badly that has affected him. Looking away, I sigh. 'I did not want to burden you with it.'

A stiffening silence. 'That's not why.'

No . . . it is not.

He doesn't need to listen to my heart to know it's a lie. He doesn't need to do anything. He just knows me more than I've allowed anyone else to before.

Defeated, I look up at him; my breath stutters at his intense gaze. 'I've always kept a lot to myself . . . my emotions and worries, just like Idris. Telling you meant I was opening up.'

'You were afraid,' he confirms the thoughts I'd tried to bury. When I don't answer, he adds in a soft consolation, 'It's okay to be afraid, Goldie. It doesn't make you any less vulnerable.'

A sharp breath leaves my lips. How is it that all I ever feel is vulnerability? How is it that I can't think straight when I'm around him?

'After my father died,' I say. 'I promised myself I wouldn't be afraid again or at least show it openly, against any creature.' I shake my head as I reflect on a time of great grief. 'Because standing there when—'

'When Lorcan killed him,' Darius answers for me, his words leaving me frozen in shock.

'You . . . knew?'

He nods, coming down from the counter as he rubs a hand over the scruff of his jaw, and a bitter smirk tilts at the corner of his lip. 'The General made sure to tell me down in the dungeons.'

My hand curls in anger, remembering how much the General and the Queen had done in torturing Darius. I can't help but have those memories cloud my mind. The whipping marks along Darius's back, the arena fight . . .

Suddenly, it's so quiet, but none of us make a move. We look at each other, and that's enough. I do not think he will say whether it hurts him knowing what Lorcan became or how he died, his eyes tell me it does either way.

'You should know that I didn't mean to kill him,' he says softly, and my brows come together before he clarifies, 'Lorcan's father, Rayth. I didn't want to.'

I didn't expect him to say this. 'So why did you?'

'Because he asked me to bite him. He wanted to bet on his life, knowing he would likely die, and when I refused, he forced me to do it.'

If I wasn't mad before about how Rayth treated Darius, I am now.

Darius closes in on me. My eyes fly up to his as he stares at me and says, low, powerful . . . 'You asked me once why it is I so badly want to be hated by many.' He pauses, and a worrying frown pulls at my forehead. 'When Rayth was dying, he told me no one would love me, that I deserve to be hated, that I'm a murderer, a disgusting dragon with no family. So, when I saw the look in Lorcan's eyes that day Rayth died, it stayed with me. I believed in those words, and I've never thought differently.'

Because he thought he deserved it.

I'm locked into silence at the thought of all the pain hidden beneath those layers of gold in his eyes.

All this time, I'd searched for an answer as to why he wanted to be hated so badly. And it is all because of tainted words from a horrid man.

'You were only a child,' I whisper.

He scoffs, clearly thinking otherwise. 'A foolish child.'

I place my palm against his cheek, turning him to look at me. 'A child no less. Rayth's death is not your burden to carry.'

He stares into my eyes, dark and raw with emotion.

'Tell me,' I say. 'If I asked you right here, right now, that I wanted the bite, would you do it?'

He sighs. 'Nara—'

'When he asked you, you were too young to know right from wrong. As you said, he forced you to do it, there was no choice, but now you wouldn't do that to someone else.'

He shakes his head, and a muscle in his jaw ticks as he looks off to the side like he is reliving all of it. I've come to find out that as much as I kept things hidden and locked away from everyone, Darius, too, had done that with his own emotions.

'I could never give anyone a shifter's bite,' his whisper is full of anguish; it cuts a gash deep in my heart. 'Not again.'

I don't hesitate as I clutch his face and say quietly, 'And you will never have to. I promise you.' I stare at him, ensuring he understands how much I mean it.

His hand travels up my arm, the backs of his fingers brushing against my skin. The air grows heady with anticipation and need. We can't help but hold each other's gaze. It's eternal . . . *beautiful*, and then he wraps that hand around my neck, pulling me towards him as he claims my lips like the dawn does twilight.

While our kiss is intense and wild, his touch is tender and gentle, tracing his fingertips down my spine. We can't and won't stop, not even for a breath of air. Our kiss deepens as he hoists me up against him and pushes us ahead until he's lying me against the flour-covered wooden countertop.

'You're maddening,' he whispers against my lips, heavy and lustful.

I smile. 'And you are infuriating.'

His chuckle vibrates to my core, and my hands run along his chest. I can feel his taught muscles tense and harden upon my touch before he says, 'I doubt you'll think that about me for much longer.'

Despite the solid desirable affirmation in my chest, I hum contentedly. 'I will always choose to believe you are infuriating.'

If he has a reply to that, I cut him off as I bring his face down and kiss him with as much intensity as I can give.

We part for a moment. He's looking at me with a heavy-lidded gaze, our lips touching, our breaths mingling as he undoes each lace strap of my nightgown and exposes the lightest parts of my round breasts.

My legs clench around his waist as he takes a second to admire my figure.

Paranoia skitters across my back, wondering how many he's been with before. Men, women, whoever he desired, yet I am so inexperienced and new. Not even my times with Lorcan could come close to the panic I feel right now, and it is something I have never had to deal with before.

He shakes his head, awe filling his eyes as he breathes, 'You sure know how to ruin a man.' And leaves me breathless as he kisses his way down my neck. I can't contain the thrill from those words, grinning as I rake my hands through his hair, craning my neck to give him more access. He grips my hands, and I release a whimper as he pins them to each side of my head. He doesn't stop there as his lips continue tracing down my chest.

His hold is so tight on my hands I can barely move them. My chest heaves. Heat slowly builds up and begins to spread everywhere on my body, firing me up with every soft touch of his lips. I almost plead for him to keep going when he lets go of my right hand and reaches across the counter, grabbing a few strawberries. He crushes them, the sweet scent wafting in the kitchen as he smears it over my breasts. I suck in a breath before he takes my nipple into his mouth.

My body jerks at the warm strokes of his tongue, circling, *tasting*. I try to hold back a moan, but it's pointless the more he teases me. My back arches, my hands clench, and my entire body tingles with each swirl of his tongue.

Pleasure unfurls inside my stomach as I glance at him, and he comes up to kiss me.

A strawberry has never tasted any better.

'Darius,' I gasp his name in between, looking at him as I stroke my hand along his jaw. His gaze almost undoes me, and causes me to blurt out in a moment of panic. 'I— I have never done it.'

Darius releases a relieved smile, his forehead dropping onto mine. 'Touched or untouched, I'd have you either way. And only when you desire it, Goldie.'

My heart swells, not knowing what to say to that except grin. 'Well, if we continue here, we might get caught.'

'So be it.'

'Miss Nara?'

My eyes widen as Tibith rubs his tired eyes from the doorway, and both our heads immediately turn to him.

Mortified, I sit up as Darius calmly straightens himself, and Tibith beams at us. 'Hello, Darry!'

I don't have time to do up the laces of my nightgown, so I cover myself with my arms as I jump down from the counter. 'Tibith! Why—' A surprised glance his way. 'Why are you up?'

'You weren't on the bed, Miss Nara. I thought you might have gotten lost!'

I plaster on a tight smile, my heart racing with exhilaration from minutes ago. 'Wait for me there. I will be with you in a moment.' As Tibith nods, I glance at Darius firmly, throwing a mocking curtsey his way. 'Goodnight, Darius.'

He runs the pad of his thumb along his lips as if the imprint of our kiss still lingers there. 'Goodnight, Goldie.' He bows, then slides his gaze past me. 'Tibith,' he says. 'Take good care of her.'

'Of course, Darry, I am her second protector!'

Darius chuckles.

If Tibith's excitement wasn't obvious before, it is now as his ears flap, and he jumps in the air and pads his way out of the kitchen quarters.

Warmth blooms in my chest as I smile, starting to head after him when Darius tugs at my hand, and I turn to look at him. His gaze dips to my lips, my half-exposed breasts, and then he's whirling me towards him. I almost trip, pressing my hands to his chest and gasping as he swallows in one final kiss.

He lets me go, and I walk backward, my fingers skimming my bottom lip as our eyes stay on each other, and I smile grandly.

Perhaps, avoiding him was always going to result in failure.

Chapter Twenty-Seven

I'm flipping through books when Aias barges into my chambers without a knock or even a hello and he drops onto the bed.

I look at him.

He looks back at me.

I flip a page and sigh in resignation when he says nothing. 'What is it?'

'Do you realise the significance of what is going to happen in two days?'

My body locks up. 'I—'

He doesn't let me finish. 'It will be the first of September, when the Elves celebrate and worship the moon and the hope that there will be a ruler of the stars one day. They call it Llerune. It is one of many celebrations that Terranos holds yearly.'

Curious amusement has me scrunch my brows at hearing about the Elves' different beliefs compared to mortals. 'Did you not also call it that, then?' I ask Aias. 'You are an Elf even if you've lived in the Screaming Forests most of your life.'

His smile strains. 'Renward was never one to celebrate it.'

I nod slowly, regretting having brought that up.

Desperately trying to change subjects, I glance at his spindly fingers. He twirls a ruby crystal ring, and I point to it. 'Where did you get that ring from?'

He looks at it and tilts his head. 'The King gifted it to me.'

My eyes widen at such a beautiful gift, although I'm confused about his generosity. Ever since Sarilyn, I consider all royalty to have dubious morals.

I rise off the bed, waltzing over to my window. Resting against the ledge, I say, 'Has the King said anything odd whenever he has spoken to you in the comforts of his study?'

'He's been kind . . . telling me he understands my past and—' He stands beside me, glancing out into the gardens. 'If I want to, I don't ever have to go back to the Screaming Forests.'

Oh.

I turn my head to him. 'That's really nice of him, considering he banished your kind.'

Aias nods, his gaze flitting to the gardens again before he goes, 'What's Darius doing out this early—'

My ears stop working when I hear him say the name Darius. I whip my head to the window, spotting Darius out front, flipping a coin as he looks around and leans against a tree.

I smile like a complete fool as I stare at him. Aias continues speaking, and I will never know what he was saying because it's simply muffled noises in the background.

Clouds part, making way for a ray of the sun to burst through and shine against his raven strands. My heart jolts the more I look, remembering our heated kisses from last night.

I see Faye join him from behind, and my face immediately

becomes clouded with envy. I almost want to roll my eyes at how Darius would love the fact that I am looking at him. He'd likely make fun of me, and being the vain man that he is, no doubt his head would grow bigger—

My smile fades, and I blink.

Darius's hand is reaching out to touch Faye's cheek.

Delicate . . . soft like a lover's touch.

He leans in, and a sharp pain shoots up my chest.

I suddenly feel sick.

He's kissing her.

They're kissing.

In plain sight.

'I hadn't realised he was interested in an Elf, much less a princess,' Aias comments beside me.

'Neither had I,' I say, my heart splitting. I want to look away, but it's hard to do so.

They stop.

She smiles, flirtatious and bright.

And then they start to walk away together.

Rage conquers my despair, and I stand up, my fingers curling into my palms as I storm out of the chambers.

'Where are you going?' Aias calls out, his feet pattering behind me as he tries to catch up. Determination sets in between each of my strides. To think he likely believes he can do as he pleases without consequences—' 'To speak with him.'

'Nara, shouldn't you—'

'Seducing, dragon pig,' I mutter, scowling as I stride down the hallway. 'You know, I should warn Faye of him.'

'I thought you did not want to fall in love?'

The heels of my feet draw to a stop before I twist to face Aias, horrified. 'I am not in love.'

He blinks those glossy eyes at me with disbelief.

'I am far from that,' I say. 'In fact, I feel . . . *disgust* and anger over that insolent—'

'Nara,' I hear the King's voice from behind us. 'So glad to see you out of your chambers.'

This is not what I need right now.

I slowly turn to face him.

He's not wearing his crown, but his fine jewelry and his luscious emerald clothes make him look supremely royal. 'I was preparing to have Thallan fetch you,' he says.

Burying Darius's and Faye's kiss, kindness has me plastering on a broad smile at Dusan instead. 'Is there anything you need?'

He inclines his head, glancing towards the entrance of his study. 'A chat, if that is alright?'

It takes me five seconds to let that sink in, and then stupidly, I'm nodding. 'Yes— yes, of course.'

I wave Aias a small goodbye, then enter after Dusan into his study as he makes his way towards his desk and sits.

Standing idly before him, I fidget with the laces of my corset.

'I wanted to discuss the plans you have for gathering the next two stones,' he begins, not looking up at me as he takes a feather ink pen and writes on a piece of parchment. 'As you know, you'll possibly encounter trolls for the third stone.'

'Nothing we can't handle.'

'Well, trolls might be ruthless creatures, but they are also daft. Galgrs are the ones to watch out for.'

'Galgrs?'

'They're ancient creatures from Terranos that live to torment,' he says mockingly, rolling his eyes as he dips the pen in ink. 'They mainly reside in lakes, but if captured, they can be used to enchant others, carve out their deepest forgotten memories.'

My body turns to ice.

Forgotten memories.

Back in the forests . . . that lake.

I glance to my left, trying to picture that memory I saw, wondering if I will face another Galgr during my time here.

'Nara?' Dusan says, and my head turns to his furrowed gaze.

I clear my throat, casting those worries aside. 'I see you have gifted Aias a ring,' I say. 'That was very kind of you.'

His shoulders straighten out, the long locks of his blonde hair spilling over them. 'I thought it would suit him.'

'Trying to win him over?'

He lifts an eyebrow at my brusque comment.

It goes deathly silent and an awkward sensation rolls over me.

'I'm sorry,' I say. 'I didn't mean to be rude.'

But I did.

I really did mean to do so and he can see that.

His smile is tight, a string pulling at either end. 'You don't need to apologize.'

'Your expression would suggest otherwise.'

He chuckles, but it's too bitter between us. 'Your honesty is charming.'

I smack my lips together, my hands clasped behind me as I take in his sage-touched study.

'You can ask the question you are dying to ask, Nara,' he says. 'I'm not afraid to answer.'

My eyes shoot back to meet his. Truthfully, I have a lot on my mind, and I'm still not so sure of trusting him, regardless of his nobility. However, I take a risk with my next words. 'When you mentioned how you would do anything for Sarilyn, did that mean you were in love with her?'

He stares at me blankly like the question means nothing, but the grip on his hand against the pen tells me otherwise. He looks down. 'Once I was. Sarilyn was beautiful, ethereal, strong-willed, and for that, I wanted to do anything for her.'

'Then what happened? What went so wrong?'

'She had already been hurt by Aurum, so she no longer craved another half. I already knew that Aurum thrived on the idea of suffering love, and because she was so driven with rage because of him, I tried to make her see things could be different. That we could put this feud between kingdoms behind us, that *love* could be different.'

But it was not.

Not for Sarilyn.

'I tried to destroy the Northern Blade.' His eyes are back on me, his expression the same. 'But she saw that as me betraying her; hence, why I cannot leave my land. I would perish if I did.'

My brows scrunch together, my mind eager to devise a solution. 'Are you certain there is no way to break your curse?'

He gets up, striding towards me, smiles, and rests his hands on my shoulders. 'You are doing enough, Nara.'

But what if it is not enough.

What if everything I am doing is going to be in vain.

'I hope you manage to free yourself one day,' I say, my smile striving to forge the trust I so fear.

'I can only hope.' He returns to his desk, my eyes grazing his movements before they land on the sun sketch atop his parchment.

'Might I ask you something else?' I say as he takes a seat and looks up at me. I gesture to the parchment. 'I saw in one of the books I'd taken out at the library an illustration of the deity Solaris.'

Dusan frowns, curiosity filtering through him at what I am about to say.

'It looked like she was summoning animals.' My head tips to the side. I haven't been able to find that book ever since that day. 'What does that mean?'

'It is an old tale of how Solaris is supposed to be the bearer of all animals and nature . . .' He waves a nonchalant hand. 'A connection to them, if you will, just how Crello is depicted as the ruler of the tides.'

I have more questions than answers; all that has done is leave me wondering what it means. And even if I want to ask more, Dusan seems to end that topic as he returns to his pen and parchment.

I step back, nodding as unease creeps its way up my spine. When I turn to the door, Dusan says, 'Oh, Nara.'

My back is still turned to him as I look over my shoulder to see him writing.

'I'm not sure if you have heard, but an important event is coming up for us Elves this week.'

I nod, my face a little sad as I recall something *else* that is coming up. 'Yes, the celebration of Llerune.'

He smiles at my knowledge and glances up. 'I will be hosting a masquerade here in celebration that evening.' His eyes narrow to focus on me. 'I do hope you will attend.'

His hope sounds a lot like I have no choice. I'd rather be holed up in my chambers.

'I will be there,' I say, walking out into the hallway.

I'm resting my head against the door when Darius appears at the other end, making his way over to me. My blood pumps through my veins, my heart racing at an intense speed that has me momentarily forget I wanted to confront him as I start heading in the opposite direction.

I feel his grip around my upper arm as he turns me towards him. A smile blooms on his lips, and I hate how my stomach flips over.

'Where are you heading to that you're so eager to get there?'

'Somewhere far away from you,' I mumble, agitated.

His low and penetrating chuckle soothes the slightest bit of anger in me. 'You always know how to enamor me with your words, Goldie.'

I glare at him without saying anything and yank my arm free.

His smile disappears, and any trace of flirtatious amusement is gone. 'What's wrong?'

I shake my head, a light scoff emitting from my lips. 'Do not worry about me, Darius. You finally got me at your mercy last night, and now you can have anyone you desire. Congratulations.' I spin around, but he grabs my hand this time. My scowl meets his confused gaze.

'What are you—'

'Faye is a perfect match,' I say calmly, disguising the hurt beneath my words. 'Beautiful, a princess, immortal. She is better suited to you.'

'Where is this coming from?'

From seeing you kiss her.

'Do you think I care about whether she is a princess or not?'

I drag in a slow breath. 'I just think that you and I are a mistake.'

That hits him like a punch to the stomach.

'Seriously?' he says, a frown stiffening his anger. 'After everything that happened last night?'

I stay deadly silent.

He shakes his head, letting go of my hand. 'You know what you are doing right now, Nara? It's not stubbornness. It's not you wanting to have pride in yourself; it's you fearing.'

Irritation crackles within me and fires up the cruel mockery in my words. 'You couldn't possibly be more wrong.'

He huffs a laugh, his tongue darting to his cheek. 'Really?'

I nod vehemently.

He takes one step towards me, my eyes in line with his chest, before I drag them to his face. 'I think you're afraid of anything going beyond what happened last night.'

A rush of annoyance coursing through my veins, hot and painful. 'I felt *nothing*. I never have.'

He lets out an incredulous chuckle, shaking his head. 'Have to stop lying to me, Goldie.'

I lift my head in defiance even when I feel otherwise. 'Then *stop* listening to my heartbeat.'

'Solaris, look at yourself, Nara. You're still so quick to put up your defenses when any inconvenience comes your way that—'

'That what?' I stare at him right in the eye, my fists clenched at my sides.

Our gaze holds for one, two, a thousand seconds, and then I watch as his jaw tightens, his darkened eyes turning a deep colour of gold, and the frustration billowing out of him.

I'm the first to break our stare. 'If anyone is lying here,' I say quietly. 'It is you after kissing Faye—'

'What?' He looks baffled. His head rears back as he frowns like I have told him the cruellest joke there is. 'I never kissed Faye!'

I huff out a loud laugh, full of disbelief that he could even say that. 'Would you look at that, lying again? I saw you two with my own eyes!'

His jaw clenches. 'If you believe I kissed her, fine, go ahead, but it never happened. You want to know why?' He moves even closer to the point where I have my back against the wall. He looks so determined, so . . . hurt. 'Because I have not been able to kiss someone that hasn't been you ever since we met. You're a pain, Nara, in all the best ways. You get on my nerves. You have me breaking when you're down, and even now, with all your guards up, I want to kiss you.' Our brows touch. 'I want to *worship* you.'

His words power something so profound inside me, I don't understand why I can't despise him. Why am I closing my eyes and letting him in like a fool?

My palm flies out to his chest as if I'll have the power to push him away, but I have none, not even a glint of strength. 'Darius—'

'Oh.' A voice interrupts us, and Darius pushes himself off me. When my eyes blink open, I look to my left, where Arlayna is staring at us. 'Pardon, I didn't mean to intrude—'

'No need to apologize,' Darius says, his voice low and hoarse. 'I was on my way to find Tibith anyway.' He inclines his head at Arlayna in a farewell bid. 'Your Highness.' He then turns to me; our eyes lock, and I'm paralyzed. 'Goldie.'

I watch him walk away and place my hand on my chest as if I can feel it squeezing the air out of me.

'Twice,' Arlayna says. 'That's twice now that I have walked in on you both.'

I barely have the energy to say anything.

'I think it's becoming a rather annoying habit from my end, don't you?'

'Actually . . .' I trail off and look at her standing outside one of the doors. 'It was perfect timing.'

She makes a thoughtful sound, unsure about my answer.

I turn to leave, not knowing what to do with myself, when she calls my name.

'Nara.' Her voice echoes around the empty hallway. I look over my shoulder as her palm hovers over a doorknob. 'I think you two would make a wonderful pair. Human or not, I have not seen people care like that for one another in a long time.'

A smile colours my lips, which truly masks the ache within me and how that confession makes me feel . . . alive.

I watch as she steps inside another room, and I'm left to wonder what on earth it is I am supposed to do with myself.

CHAPTER TWENTY-EIGHT

'Lady Nara, are you in need of anything?' Golrai places a bucket on the hay-strewn ground as I pass by her on her way into the stables.

I shake my head, stopping at a distance to look at the horses. 'I just felt like wandering the castle grounds.'

I also felt like I couldn't stand being near Darius right now.

'Ah.' Golrai smiles. 'If you would like, I can fetch one of our servants to show you around?'

'That won't be necessary.' I glance at the bucket beside her. 'May I?'

She looks momentarily confused before she nods for me to take it. It's filled up to the brim with carrots. A horse's favourite treat.

'I'll take it from here, Golrai.'

Golrai titters, amused to find me wanting to feed the animals. She doesn't know it is the most likely thing to calm me down since seeing Darius and Faye yesterday. 'Well, I can't deny you. Although, it is the stables boy's job to do that for us.' She looks around, huffing. 'If only Aeron hadn't decided to leave that position.'

The mention of Aeron nudges my brows together, but there isn't enough time for me to question Golrai more as she gives my shoulder a gentle squeeze and leaves.

I look down at the bucket and the few horses inside here. A beautiful mare with a white and brown coat catches my eye, and I walk over to her, smiling. 'Well, aren't you gorgeous?'

The mare snorts, her nostrils blowing air my way as I laugh, caressing her snout. I feed her a carrot and watch her munch on it before I move on to the other horses.

'Charming the horses?'

I turn to find Arlayna fitting some white riding gloves on. Her dark hair is in a braid, swinging across her back as I bring my gaze towards the horse in front of me. 'Rather, they charm me.' I exhale, looking at Arlayna. 'Where are you off to?'

'Somewhere . . . anywhere where I can escape my mother's gruelling activities to find a husband.'

A grimace pulls at my features. I may not have lived a royal life, but the thought of having to find a husband makes me glad I never grew up that way.

She gestures a thumb over her shoulder. 'Would you like to come?'

I blink, not necessarily expecting her to invite me, but it is an opportunity to escape that I don't want to turn down, not when I long to get out for a bit.

Lowering the bucket of carrots to the ground, I place my hands on my hips and nod, already knowing which horse I will pick for our outing.

For half of the evening, Arlayna takes me through the outskirts of

Olcar, showing me the beautiful landmarks and nature of Terranos. We have a handful of sentries travelling metres behind us, I don't mind it as much as Arlayna, but this is a common occurrence every time she goes out.

I watch as she points with her gloved finger to the left of us, where the sunset cloaks over hills and valleys. Smoke clouds the skies through chimneys far ahead within villages, and I tilt my head to smile at the lingering scent of damp leaves from the rain this morning.

'Across those rivers right there.' She points ahead. 'You will see the remains of ancient ruins from when our elders fought epic battles beyond the historical timeline.'

I nod mindlessly.

'You seem pensive,' Arlayna says, noticing I haven't paid attention to her stories about Olcar. 'Have I bored you?'

I shake my head. 'Not at all. Though I can see the need for guards chaperoning us annoys you.'

Something slips in her regal expression for a moment, and she sighs, looking away. 'It always annoys me. But when you are royalty, you learn to appreciate the little freedom you do have.'

I hum, staring back at the guards. I'm frowning deep in thought when my gaze cuts to Arlayna. 'Have you ever thought about sneaking away from them?'

Shock flares across her face before it falls into an amused smile. 'You're trouble, aren't you?'

'Me? Trouble? Never.' If Idris were here, he would crack a smile on that grumpy face of his.

Arlayna laughs, shaking her head at me. But then she looks towards the people who are always there to watch her every movement, protect her from any danger, and keep her freedom away from her. She nudges the horse with her heel and cries out for it to gain speed.

The guards behind all look our way as I follow after Arlayna. I can hear them shouting for us to slow down, but I know Arlayna won't.

The wind streams past us as I grin, jumping over puddles. My mare gains speed to match Arlayna's horse, and we break out into laughter, clutching our stomachs as we stop by a hill overlooking the Elven lands on the east.

'Usually, this would be Faye's idea,' Arlayna says as soon as we have calmed down. 'She has snuck out of the castle too many times.'

I can imagine. 'Are you two . . . close?'

Trees shield us from the sunset blooming across fields. A bold blaze of Solaris's farewell.

'Not like we once used to be,' Arlayna says, looking at her lap, and my gaze falls along with hers.

I had wanted to speak to Faye since I saw her and Darius, but her mother soon sent her off to visit family members in Valdern along with Aeron as her guard. It is as if fate had done it on purpose or it was Solaris and Crello's way of messing with me.

I ask Arlayna, 'Is it because of your duties as a princess?'

She shakes her head slowly and thoughtfully. 'Faye never wanted to be part of anything royal from a young age. She would hide, spend time in the town with seamstresses or drag me out into the forests to dance with butterflies.' She fights off a smile, attempting to hide it by clearing her throat. 'But since I was the eldest, I had to obey, and then we simply drifted apart one day. I cannot recall the true reason.'

'Why don't you try to fix it?'

She chuckles as if I don't understand. Perhaps I truly don't know their relationship, but I thought about my own brothers. 'You sound exactly like Aeron,' she says, looking at me, and the emerald gem of her diadem glistens, shining against her riding attire.

I wonder about something. 'Why didn't you go with them to

Valdern?'

Arlayna looks startled for a split second before facing the fields. 'I only ever go there if I am needed.' A sigh escapes from her lips. 'Whereas Mother sends Faye to learn how to be a royal.'

Unable to contain it, my eyes widen, and I let out a small chuckle.

She frowns, confusion taking over her grey eyes as she looks me up and down. 'Why do you laugh?'

I shake my head, laughter still present on my lips. 'When I was young, I always imagined royalty meant you could do whatever you wanted. I guess I was wrong.'

'Royalty in Terranos hold different responsibilities to the other kingdoms of Zerathion.'

I don't miss the disappointment in her voice as she looks off towards the fields. We are so different in our upbringings, yet we crave the same thing.

Freedom.

She huffs a big breath, turning to me. 'We should go. This area is too dangerous at night.'

I frown. 'What is it?'

'Shadow Calps,' she says. 'Creatures that belong to Thalore. Ever since my father's death, they seem to be lurking everywhere.'

The name alone makes my stomach twist. Not even the thought of capturing one sounds the least bit exciting as I follow behind Arlayna.

CHAPTER TWENTY-NINE

Star-shaped lanterns decorate the palace gardens ready for the Llerune festivities.

Arlayna and I come out of the stables laughing, having annoyed the palace guards in charge of ensuring Arlayna's safety.

One of them chases after us. A new guard who had recently been sworn in. The layers of his metal armour clash against each other as he catches up. 'Your Highness, you must know—'

'Relax, Ruvyn,' Arlayna says, peeling off her riding gloves. 'I won't tell my uncle you lost sight of me on our outing.'

I chuckle, and she nudges me with an amused look before my smile dies as soon as I spot Darius coming towards us. Immediately, I excuse myself, turning the other way and quickening my steps to escape him. He calls after me, but I ignore him as I enter the maze, thinking I will lose him here if I walk fast enough.

My plan fails when his hand grips my elbow, and he whirls me around to face him.

Great, just great.

His hair is damp, and water droplets fall on his shirt. He must have bathed not so long ago, and I hate that he has to look this perfect when I am supposed to be angry at him.

'What do you want?' I snap, trying to free my arm from his grip.

He relents. 'To talk.'

I roll my eyes, finding a chance to turn my back on him and head deeper into the maze. 'We already are.'

'I wouldn't consider you walking away from me talking.'

I spin, almost bumping my head against his firm body. 'Fine, what is it you want to talk about? Is it to do with what I supposedly did not see happening?'

He quietly laughs in disbelief, shaking his head as he rubs the pad of his thumb along his jaw. 'How many times do I have to say I did not kiss Faye.'

'I saw it happen right in front of me, Darius!'

'And have you wondered if maybe it was someone else, or that maybe somebody was playing tricks on you?'

My mouth snaps shut. Maybe he is right. Maybe he is *absolutely* right, and I should trust him.

Yet I can't seem to do so as I walk away from him again.

'You need to stop running away from me at every opportunity, Goldie,' he yells after me, hot on my trail. 'Are you that afraid of me?'

I halt, clenching my eyes shut. I take a deep breath, looking up at the starry sky before I face him. 'I do not want to be another one of your conquests.'

He looks genuinely hurt as his jaw tenses. 'Not once have I ever thought of you that way.'

'Then what have I been to you?' I begin breathing harshly through my nose.

His silence enrages me.

'Someone to pass the time with?'

Our eyes lock, and anger darkens his face like an overcast sky.

'What is it you really want, Darius?' I ask, feeling ready to explode. 'To have fun?' I push him slightly. 'I mean, that is all you ever cared about before, so is that it?' Another push that does nothing to move his tall frame. 'Tell me!'

'I want you!' The words stun me as he closes in, seizing both my wrists. 'In every lifetime and in any universe, if the sun and moon will allow it. And if that means I have to sacrifice something in order to get it, so be it. Because it is you, Nara. You are all I want in my life.'

I can feel my lower lip tremble and my temper immediately dissipate in defeat. 'Don't do that,' I whisper. 'Don't tell me these things if you don't mean it.'

'Do you think I'm lying?' He is not asking but challenging me because he knows it's a weak argument.

Everything within me is aflame as I stare back at him, and instead of responding, I rise to my toes, giving in to my desire and landing an urgent kiss on his lips. He seizes control instantly, releasing my wrists and diving his hands into my hair as we stumble back against the hedges.

The moan I let out against his mouth pushes him over the edge. We're both frantically devouring each other, allowing our primal instincts to get the best of us. As his kiss intensifies, he threads his fingers through my hair and pulls it back.

I want him to ruin me, in all the best ways, through the good and bad.

'Do you have any idea what it is like having you near me all the time?' Desire coats his voice. 'What it does to me?' He grabs my waist and softly kisses down the side of my neck. As I grind my hips over him, I'm lost in a fog of want and hunger. All I can think about is running my fingers through his hair and messing it up.

'You say one thing, but then your body tells me something else.' When his hand reaches my inner thigh, my whole body feels like it's on fire. I don't care if he notices it. I am past that, too aroused to say otherwise, as my lips part, releasing a moan and I tip my head back.

I try not to squeak or make a sound as his fingers grab my thighs, adding to my arousal until—

He stops, and his hands leave my body altogether.

Why is he stopping?

My head lolls forward as I look at him, panting. 'What are you doing?'

Taunting delight flares across his face, and he whispers, 'Punishing you.'

Punishing you.

Scorching anger rumbles throughout my body.

I let out a dry laugh, and I am about to push him off me when he beats me to it and takes a step back. 'You are such an ass.'

'But you enjoy it.'

I do.

And I hate that I do.

'You're the most annoying person, Darius Halen,' I hiss, crossing my arms over my chest as I drag myself forward.

His laugh is deep and tinged with sarcasm. 'Is this the first time you have said my full name? It sounds exotic coming from your lips.'

I glare. 'You know, this is as much punishment for you as it is for me.' My eyes dip to the tightening of his pants, and I raise a brow, doing my best to rein in how my body naturally reacts to him. 'Don't act like you weren't having as much fun as I was.'

All the amusement on his face vanishes.

I smirk, and begin to step past him when he grabs my arm and spins me around. Our gazes meet for one split moment before his lips are against mine, and I feel his tongue trying to overpower mine. I shove him, and he stumbles back. We both breathe heavily as we hold each other's stare, we are so close to bringing each other to our knees.

No longer able to hold back, I grab him, pulling at the collar of his shirt and bringing his mouth to mine like two comets colliding. I don't know how we land on the ground, but I am suddenly beneath him, grabbing at every inch of his body. Our moans ring through the air in the maze as his grip on my thighs becomes tighter. Passion explodes between us as we kiss and grab each other harder.

'I thought you wanted to punish me.' I smile against his lips, trying to untuck his shirt.

A funny noise rumbles in his throat making me vibrate to my core. 'I changed my mind.' I gasp as he rips my pants – my clothes are just a barrier for him to break through. Caressing my breast in his right hand, he leaves open-mouthed kisses along my collarbone, shattering my sanity.

He lifts my legs and slides his hands between my thighs. I can no longer breathe; I can no longer focus. His gaze as he looks up at me from between my legs has my heart going out of control. His fingers squeeze my hip bone, and a moan climbs up my throat as his mouth moves to my centre, drenched in arousal.

As his tongue begins to stroke me, my hands grab fistfuls of the surrounding grass as I arch my back, uttering sounds I have never before. His tongue continues to ravish me without giving me a chance to talk or rage at him. *He knows exactly what to do.* I am breaking in the best possible ways where only he can put me back together.

My moans grow louder and more desperate as he works his finger into the mix, and I know I am ready to shatter.

I push against him, and the sound of pleasure he releases lights the flame of my incoming orgasm.

'Come on, Goldie. Show me how much you despise me,' he whispers in my ear.

I'm gasping as he uses his finger to speed up inside me and he lands one final kiss on my lips. A warm sensation explodes throughout me, and my walls clench around Darius's fingers. He groans into my mouth as I breathe into his. My body quakes, and I can barely contain myself as he kisses me softly, savouring every moment.

CHAPTER THIRTY

'Miss Nara, do you like bread?'

I smile, sitting by the vanity inside my chambers as I brush my damp hair. Looking at Tibith through the mirror, I reply, 'Of course I do. Why wouldn't I?'

As he thumps his bottom and sits on the floor, he crosses his arms and pouts. 'Aias has said he does not.'

'Well, then Aias is missing out.'

He nods so quickly and heavily that he loses his equilibrium when sitting. I chuckle as I watch him fondly. Just the idea of knowing he is here and alive sends a jolt of happiness to my heart.

'Tibith?' I say, thinking of my words carefully as I turn to face him. He nods. 'Can I tell you a secret? But you mustn't tell anyone, especially Darius.' I'm drawn back to when I woke up in Darius's cottage, and Tibith told me *his* secret.

I don't think you're a creature murderer any more.

Tibith angles his head, waiting for me to tell him. I lean forward, smiling as I whisper it into his ear. I hear him gasp before there's a knock at the door, and Arlayna peeks her head through.

'I thought you might not be ready yet,' she says, entering wearing an off-shoulder emerald gown. It has sleeves made of hand-woven lace, intricately designed to look like flowers, and the silk train of her dress spills across the floor behind her. In one hand she's holding a crescent-shaped mask – one that flares at the edges like the sun – and a silver gown in the other.

I gaze at it with one brow raised in alarm. 'Is that—'

'Your gown for tonight?' She lifts it up with a smile. 'Yes, I got it from my mother. Now what are we going to do about that hair?'

I blink. I wasn't aware this masquerade required a princess to help me get ready. 'I already have something to wear.'

She looks behind at the washed-out blue kirtle and scoffs. 'That's not fit for a celebration, it's an unfortunate garment.'

Excuse me?

My mouth half opens in protest, but she quickly sets everything over the chair and looks at my robe before ushering me to try the dress on. Tibith blinks at the both of us and finds comfort in climbing up the bedpost to rest on the so-called 'unfortunate garment'. Once I return from the bathing chambers wearing the silver dress, I pause by the threshold, gazing at the shimmering heart-cut bodice. It pushes my breasts up and cinches at my waist flatteringly, layers of gossamer spreading outward to create a wide skirt. I place my arms out in front, looking at the sheer batwing sleeves and how, in essence, this whole gown is just perfection. And if I look close enough at my bodice, it's decorated with sequins that remind me of stars in the night sky. They catch the light when I move, darkening and then glowing with the sconces of my room.

I glance over at Tibith, now curled up and snoozing on my old dress, and then at Arlayna's pursed lips as she studies me.

Her sapphire circlet sits across her forehead, and her obsidian curls are in the most gorgeous half-updo – braids, pearls and gold shimmer. 'Acceptable,' she affirms, and I chuckle, ambling towards the vanity chair and sitting down as she rakes her hands through my long tresses. 'Your little Tibithian loves to sleep, doesn't he?'

I glance in the mirror at him again as he makes slight cooing noises. 'He also loves to steal and eat bread.'

She nods, gathering my hair up. 'And Darius?'

My eyes cut to hers.

She mentioned him on purpose.

I look at my hands, my nails clipped short. 'What about him?'

I haven't seen him since last night in the maze, not even during supper.

'I imagined you would have made up by now.'

'Why do you say that?'

She arches a brow, leaving some of my waves to frame my face. 'It is pretty obvious something has happened between the two of you since the other day.'

Well, there is that. I snort out a chuckle, shaking my head. 'He and I are always on bad terms. He angers me, I annoy him, he is just—'

'Someone you've come to care for deeply.'

My chest compresses against the tight bodice. I meet her stare. Yes, I have, and regardless of how I feel, him kissing Faye has not changed that. 'Don't ever tell him I said that, he would rub it in my face,' I joke with a smile.

It almost makes her smile too, but she still seems so distant, like smiling would costs her dearly.

'And Aeron?' I ask, and she pauses, placing a crescent hair brooch in my updo. 'What is he to you, other than part of the sentinel?'

She's silent, staring at the brooch in an effort to avoid answering.

I twist around and rest my chin on my knuckles like a child peering up in thought as I say, 'You're not the only one who notices things.'

'It doesn't matter what he is to me,' she whispers. 'Everything changed when he became part of the Terranos army.'

'Why?'

'A royal like me cannot marry someone like him.'

I bite my lower lip, pensive and curious. 'Your father did it with your mother.'

She lets out a humourless laugh. 'That was under different circumstances. She was a commoner, yes, but Aeron . . .' I watch her suck in a breath and turn away from me as she walks around my room. 'When you swear into the Terranos army and become a soldier for the King, you are also making an oath where you must give all your life to it. You may never marry, you must serve and protect the royals until your last breath.'

My shoulders sag at that thought. Even a princess suffers.

She leans against the wall. 'I knew him from a young age.' Her gaze is elsewhere, lost in nostalgia. 'He was a stable boy, and I a quiet girl – a stuck-up princess, he used to call me. We grew up despising each other, so I'm not sure what changed, but it just did. And from then on, we made plans. We even wanted to run away together until he decided to serve my uncle instead.'

Arlayna seems to have been transported back to that time, she's still not focusing on me, and I imagine she likely thinks of this a lot. I know I would.

'I don't think I've ever felt such pain as on the day of his ceremony.' She huffs out a laugh – a lonely, miserable laugh. 'It's the cruellest thing to have witnessed.'

I decide to ask her a question I already know the answer to. 'Were you in love?'

Her eyes, grey and almost like a strike of thunder, connect with mine. 'Everyone thinks they know the meaning of loving someone, but very few know how to love.' She takes a breath. 'So, yes, you could say I am one of those few.'

I believe her.

I believe she still loves him. She deserves to fulfill a love like that, to truly experience its joys.

She sucks in a breath, straightening and feigning a smile. 'Shall we head off? Tonight is a special evening, where we hope for the stars to shine brighter than most nights, and I'd hate to keep you in here too long.'

There isn't a chance for me to say otherwise. She's already marching towards the door, and I am heading over to Tibith to wake him up.

I've been idly standing against the outdoor pillars, watching Elves chatter and dance merrily along the garden path. Silhouettes of their dresses and masks bounce off the walls from the festival lights strung over our heads. I'd thought about walking through the maze. Getting lost sounded like a grand idea now, even if it means remembering what Darius and I had done.

I don't fit in with the Elves, same as how I didn't fit in with the Venators back in Emberwell

That only reminds me how I have not received a letter from my brothers after the last one they sent. The thought they could be in harm's way unsettles me.

Letting out a sigh, my eyes travel through the crowd, spotting Arlayna looking uninterested as she converses with a male Elf. To my left, beneath the castle archways, a few of the Terranos sentinel stand. Among them, I see Aeron. His eyes are glued to Arlayna, unbeknownst to her.

'Goldie.'

My heart jumps. Any higher, and it'll be out of my throat.

I turn, my eyes hook on Darius's boots, then they trail up to his black jacket threaded with intricate gold designs, framing his broad shoulders, and then a silver mask.

'Darius.' My voice comes out unusually breathless. 'Ready to insult me?' I tip my chin up at him, waiting for his usual perusal before the words 'hideous' or 'terrible' can leave his lips.

He doesn't say anything but the tense energy between us is too much, *too* thrilling.

'I always knew you would run out of insults for me,' I say.

He laughs, rubbing his thumb across his brow. 'Not quite, Goldie.'

'How so?'

'Well, you despise compliments,' he says, fitting one hand in his pocket. 'In essence, complimenting you is actually an insult in your eyes and—' He edges forward, his rosewood scent mixing with that familiar smell I cannot figure out hits my nose. 'Right now, I'm about to give you the biggest insult of your life.' His eyes hook on to how I lick my lips. He's well aware we are in public, and he is also *well aware* that I still haven't shaken off last night's conversation. 'You are devastatingly beautiful, Naralía.'

I swallow my nerves, hearing my full name roll off his tongue. 'Really?'

He nods, firm and resilient. 'But beautiful isn't enough,' he adds.

'I could list a million words to describe you, and they still wouldn't be enough. Remarkable, breathtaking, utterly enchanting? Those words don't do you justice.'

I can't hold it in; I break out into a sheepish grin, my cheeks heating up under his gaze.

'And anyone in this palace would be lucky to see that smile. Actually, the entire world would be.'

My grin widens until my cheeks hurt, and his statement loops around my heart in a tight hold.

'I don't think they realise how you practically shine.'

I look away, suppressing the little voice in my head. It tries to remind me that this is just his thing, what he usually would say to impress someone. I couldn't help but tease him. 'Is that what you also said to Faye?'

Unlike his baffled reaction when I first mentioned Faye to him, he now remains calm. 'Like I have said, Goldie, I never kissed her. Irritatingly enough, I've only had my eyes on a blonde with striking blue eyes and a bad temper for a while now. She likes to tease me.'

I bite my lower lip, shaking my head. He sure knows how to weaken someone with his words.

He takes a step to walk past me, smirks, and leans into me. 'By the way.' His lips brush the arch of my ear. It makes my chest tighten and my skin pebble with goosebumps. 'Happy birthday, Goldie.'

My eyes widen as he carries on walking. With lips parted and a hand to my chest, I watch him manouevre through the guests. When I try to go after him, a delicate grip on my elbow has me turning to face a smiling Edwyrd wearing a royal blue mask covering half his face.

'Nara,' he says, his silvery hair plaited on either side. 'You look absolutely divine. Care for a dance?'

Divine.

Dance.

Birthday.

Darius.

I snap my head in the direction Darius went, but he has disappeared.

'*Tibith? Can I tell you a secret? But you mustn't tell anyone, especially Darius,*' I'd said earlier before whispering, '*Today is my birthday.*'

'Nara?' Edwyrd repeats my name again, and I look at him, too dazed to think straight, as I smile and agree to dance.

Chapter Thirty-One

I t was the birthday following my mother's death that I had decided I no longer wanted to keep celebrating them. I'd started working for Ivarron, and my loathing for creatures grew stronger by the day. Not to mention that I'd had my fair share of run-ins with my fellow villagers. Idris was always explaining to families why his younger sister had smashed their son's nose, and even his apologies couldn't clear the Ambroses' name. And the more birthdays I had, the less I wanted to remember them. But Illias and Iker attempted to change that. They would buy gifts with the little money they had and organised parties that resulted in complete anarchy on numerous occasions.

I suppose I should have known that Tibith would still tell Darius even if I had bribed him with bread. I might be closer to Tibith now than when we first met, but Darius is his companion, friend and family.

'You seem quite distant tonight. Is everything alright, Nara?' Edwyrd has me blinking up at him, my expression likely doltish as he guides me through this dance.

I shake my head, clenching my eyes shut for a second. 'I— sorry, it has just been a tiring week. Tasks and whatnot.' And also, my night with Darius against the kitchen table, my breakdown, his kiss with Faye, the maze—

'I can imagine,' Edwyrd murmurs in agreement. 'I only wish I could help, considering the last task in Thalore won't be easy.'

I laugh to try and humour myself at the thought of my never-ending dangerous situations. 'Worse than encountering trolls?'

'Well, I hardly think trolls possess dark magic.'

A pensive frown forms between my brows. 'You say dark magic, but what does that really mean?'

He moves me around the floor with swift motions. The music is loud and the atmosphere feels sweet enough to taste. 'Not even we know the true extent of it. Thalorians have practised it for eons, far longer than their king has been alive. It's said even an ordinary Elf like me can quite easily become dark.'

I remember the book I had read in the library; I'd got as far as learning that dark Elves worship a side of Solaris and Crello far too dangerous for our world. 'How?' I Inquire, my nose tickling beneath my mask as I scrunch it up and Edwyrd inhales deeply.

'All Thalorians' hearts blacken the more they practise that magic – Kilya magic is what it is called. Named after the first ever Thalorian. It is said she became insane for reasons not many know. From then on, it was just a matter of corrupting other Elves.'

'Are you not afraid for your people?'

'There is too much to worry about, Nara. Our kingdom is already plagued by the shadows of Thalorians. They just happen to be a small part of all the dangers out there.'

Such as the Isle of Elements losing its power. Our world potentially suffering at the hands of more powerful beings – ones the General had mentioned.

Edwyrd becomes a blur as my eyes wander from his to the cheerful people surrounding us. An Elf beside us has her pointed ear decorated with a crescent dangling from it, and another who happens to be a child is dressed head to toe in a twilight gown with the sun and moon adorned on it. They do not even know the peril that is to come if the Isle of Elements is to fail us.

'May I?'

The sound of that voice takes my attention, dulling my worries as I cast a glance to the side, where Darius is waiting with a smirk on his lips.

Edwyrd releases my hand, looking at me for a response.

'I'd hate to be rejected twice for a dance, Goldie,' Darius says. 'The first time already bruised my ego.'

I try to hold it in, but it just happens. I burst out laughing.

'First time?' Edwyrd chuckles, confusion contorting his lips.

Darius waves a careless hand. 'Noctura night. Nara learned how much she loved to say no to me.'

Darius holds my stare.

'I—' Edwyrd tries to say, but neither Darius nor I budge. 'Well, I'll leave you both to it.'

'Thank you, Edgar,' Darius mocks, and I give him a look despite Edwyrd not even bothering to correct him. He knows Darius is trying to irritate him by saying his name wrong.

Once Edwyrd leaves, Darius practically dominates the small distance between us, raising his right palm and inviting me to grab it. As I take it, I roll my eyes, the sound of the violins carrying through the soft breeze. His other hand comes around my waist, and then he pulls me towards him.

Our eyes meet once again through the masks and he tilts his head as we move at a slower pace than the others. 'So, Goldie, did you ever plan on telling me today was your birthday?'

'Does it matter if I'd told you or not?'

'Yes, for starters, I would have made you a birthday pie.'

I snort. 'I'd have refused to eat it.'

'And wasted a delicious pie?' He tsks. 'That's terrible manners, Goldie, though that doesn't surprise me coming from you.'

I smack the side of his jacket, and he laughs. 'When is yours?' I ask and add, 'Your birthday. When is it?'

He doesn't answer straight away. Instead, he dips me and brings me back up again. 'The 21st of June.'

Shock climbs its way up my throat, the realisation spearing me like a sword.

Summer Solstice . . . Noctura. 'You—'

'Attended the Noctura ball on my birthday?' His lips stretch out into a grin. 'I quite like to think seeing your surprised face that night when I appeared was the best gift of all.'

All that time, it had been his birthday. A day he risked everything to see *me*. 'Was stealing the pendant part of your birthday gift too?'

He chuckles. 'Something like that.'

'I suppose we are even on not telling each other when our birthdays were.'

'Well, I had a reason, Goldie. You—' he lowers his head, our lips almost touching, 'You, on the other hand, I'm not sure what the reasoning was.'

My throat bobs. 'Are you hinting at a question?'

'I have infinite questions I can ask you, Goldie, and *that* I can promise you will never change.'

I look away in resignation and sigh. 'Birthdays no longer meant anything to me after my parents died.'

His silence is agonizingly painful.

I glance back at him. He's staring at me like the other day in the Melwraith mountains.

'Mine too,' he says with similar solemnity just as the music picks up and everyone begins to cheer and dance. Other Elves are chatting excitedly, staring up as the night sky is cloaked in the brightest stars, scattered evenly in shining clusters.

Darius draws back. The space where his hand was on my waist turns cold and empty as he lets go.

I don't want it to be over.

I want to be selfish.

'Wait,' I say, not daring to look at his eyes. 'I know I'm angry at you, for everything – for Faye, for kissing me . . . I just—' I exhale. 'I don't want to let go of this just yet.' Glancing up through my mask, I see how he's staring at me, like something is squeezing his heart just as it is squeezing mine. He nods without a word, and I don't have to say anything else for him to understand what I mean as he pulls me towards him in a soft embrace. His arms encase me with warmth, and my cheek rests against his chest as he lowers his chin on my head.

I nestle into him like I can't get enough, and all we do is sway slowly, even though it isn't to the tune of the upbeat music. Closing my eyes, I breathe him in. It makes me think of home. I can share my vulnerable side with him. I don't hate it. In fact, he puts me at ease, guides me, and, more so, it feels . . . just right.

An hour later, I am back to staring at the Elves celebrating. Except this time, I'm inside the grand hall. I would have been content to stay outdoors with Darius, but a male Elf had asked him to dance, and despite my selfishness, I recognised we couldn't stay that way forever.

Even if every part of me wished it to be so.

'You danced beautifully with Darius,' a sweet, wistful voice says from behind me. I turn from the pillar I'm resting on, and my stomach curls as I face Faye, who is clutching a glass of wine. She is stunning in a shimmering white halter-neck gown with a colourful cape draped from her shoulder, yet no mask shields her deep bronze skin. 'I think I even saw you glow,' she continues, her pouty lips tilting up at the sides.

'That was a one-time thing.' I fiddle with the side of my dress, suddenly uncomfortable in it. 'I don't want to come between you two. I think you both look wonderful together.'

She spills her wine as she jerks back. '*Between you two?*'

'Look, I was meaning to speak to you the other day, but I just assumed you're both courting each other—'

'Darius and I?' She makes a face and then bursts into laughter. 'Oh, I would never court him.'

'I'm sorry.' I shake my head, trying to grasp what is being said. 'Do you not—'

'He's infatuated with you!' She grins, gesturing her hand towards me. 'Don't get me wrong, he is a dream, but . . . he is not who I want.'

This brings me more questions than answers. Frowning, I ask, 'Where were you the morning before you left Olcar?'

'So inquisitive,' she says, her emerald eyes bright. 'But if you are so eager to know, I was having tea while my mother scolded me for—'

I silence her voice as I try to piece the puzzle. None of it makes sense. I'd seen them kiss right outside my window. Aias had witnessed it—

Aias.

Where did you get that ring from?
The King gifted it to me.

'Could you excuse me for a moment?' I say to Faye, barely hearing her response as I careen through the crowd, searching for Aias. I squeeze past a group of young Elves when I spot him talking to one. Reaching him, he smiles at me, but before he can even open his mouth, I demand, 'I need that ring.'

His forehead furrows as he stares at his finger, the ruby glinting off it. 'What, why?'

'I have something I want to test out.'

He chuckles. 'If you wanted it from the start, you could have—'

'Aias,' I say, my tone stern, and more like a warning.

His eyes widen, and he quickly removes the ring and places it in my palm. I don't respond when he asks why I need it again as I sprint the opposite way into the gardens. As I stalk up to the maze, I clasp the ring tightly in my fingers. My feet start to hurt, and I slide off my heels, kicking them to the side with a quiet grunt. The grass feels cool and damp under my bare feet. It's relaxing in comparison to my pounding heart.

Dipping into one of the maze sections, I lean against the hedge and lift the ring out before me. At a closer inspection, I can spot how the red gem has a glow to it, some form of magic seems to be swirling within it.

I tap it to see if it does anything.

Nothing.

I shake it.

Nothing.

'Great,' I mutter, tipping my head back and not caring about whatever leaves get tangled in my hair.

Maybe I am going out of my mind.

That would explain everything that is going on with Darius.

At least if Idris were here, he'd scold me for thinking it.

Illias, on the other hand, would be thrilled to just speak to me.

And Iker, he'd flirt and grab whatever animal he finds.

I chuckle, but it turns into a whimper until a burst of light and echoing voices travel from the corner of the hedge. Frowning, I push myself off the row of bushes, treading warily as I peer through the vines.

My pulse shoots into the air.

It's Darius and Faye again, just like that morning, with the same scene repeating before me.

Him kissing *her*.

I glance at the ring, then at what is unfolding before me, and as I stare at it, everything I've just seen disappears.

Darius and Faye are no longer there, and the ring's brightness dims.

I look back to where the festivities are – to where the king must be – and clench the ring tight in my palm as I think of what to do next.

CHAPTER THIRTY-TWO

I push through the King's study doors, interrupting him and his second-in-command, Thallan.

As I march up to the desk and place the ring in front of Dusan, Thallan's head turns towards me. Barefoot, my mask long forgotten and with leaves tangled in my hair, they must know I'm not here for a friendly discussion. 'Is this part of the tasks, or are you that bored staring at the castle walls each day that you feel the need to test me?'

Dusan studies the ring with a frown marring his forehead before he looks up.

Thallan's pale green eyes are on me, wondering why someone who doesn't belong here has just barged in to question the King.

'The ring you gave to Aias, whatever it can do, magic, illusions, tricks, it worked. You made me doubt myself.' My words taste bitter on my tongue. 'Congratulations, Your Majesty. You had me convinced you are on our side.'

He drops his head, heaving a sigh. 'Nara—'

'Were you ever in love with Sarilyn? Do you want us to fail? What is—'

'Nara, that ring belonged to Sarilyn.' That shuts me up. 'I gave it to Aias because it reminded him of someone. I didn't think it still worked, but when Sarilyn was last here—' He glances at Thallan '— She cast a magic spell over it to create hallucinations, to conjure up fears of others. She also used it to trick me, and it is the last thing she left behind.'

I open my mouth but immediately shut it at the humiliation settling in at the base of my stomach.

'I understand you are cautious, Nara, but you were not the target of some cruel trick. I should have never given this ring to Aias and I apologize for that.'

'Mortals,' Thallan's scoff sends a wave of anger through my veins as he shakes his head.

It's the first thing that has me reliving every moment the General taunted and belittled me. Rage roars in my ears, and I step towards Thallan with my hands balled up in fists. I'm acting on blind emotions when something hard blocks me. I look down at the firm hand splayed across my bodice and then to sharp golden eyes laced with wrath at my side.

'I hope that comment implies how important you think mortals are. Much like us.' Darius slowly looks Thallan's way. The fact that he is no longer wearing a mask lets me see the fury in his brows and the tension in how he stares at Thallan. 'Nara here managed to complete the first task in Melwraith without my help. Back in Emberwell, she subdued a herd of dangerous creatures. And if she wanted to right now, she wouldn't hesitate to hurt whoever gets in her way.'

Thallan's complacent stance towards me disappears as he stiffens.

I'd seen him a couple of times around the castle, heard him and Arlayna arguing about her duties, and from the looks of things, I'd figured he was a pompous lackey, looking to rise among the ranks.

From the corner of my eye, Dusan smirks, dropping back against his chair. Darius's hand slides from my bodice to my hand and grips it as he turns to Dusan and bows his head. 'Your Majesty.' He then gives Thallan one final glance. 'Happy celebrations.'

He drags me out of the study before I get the last word.

I squeeze his hand as he takes us through the castle, continuing until we reach his chambers. He lets go, his back turned to me as he strides to the end of the room and runs his hand along his jaw as if debating something.

The moon is brighter than ever tonight, bathing the room in an ethereal glow. In my mind I go over what the King just told me in his study.

She placed a magic spell over it to create hallucinations, and sometimes it could also conjure up fears of others.

Are Darius and Faye kissing one of my fears?

I place a hand over my heart, wondering if it is still beating, and clear my throat. 'I could have handled that on my own.'

Darius's chuckle is soft and husky. It reverberates through the room. 'I know you could have,' he says over his shoulder before turning to me. 'But I also know we can't risk getting into trouble. We are the King's guests. Now, if that *Thallan* had laid a hand on you, that would have been entirely different.'

I roll my eyes, a sarcastic comment brewing on my tongue. 'Would you have jumped to my aid and rescued me?'

He chuckles. 'It is our thing, isn't it, Goldie? You save me, I save you, the only difference is—' He starts unbuttoning the top part of his jacket, revealing his chest as he moves closer. '—If someone so much as touches a hair on your body, I'd leave them in a state beyond what anyone would consider worth saving.'

The sharp threat behind his words makes my pulse rise and my cheeks heat up. 'Well.' I swallow. 'I'd hate to inform you that a vicious hedge did harm me.'

He leans against the door, inclining his head so I can keep going.

'Scratched up my back, pulled my hair,' I list. 'It was really violent.'

His lips quirk up at the sides, and he picks out a leaf from my hair. 'I guess this hedge needs to be chopped down.'

My smile turns dreamlike.

'So,' he says, 'the ring. Is that what made you believe Faye and I had kissed?'

My smile fades, and I bow my head. 'You were listening.'

Of course he was. He came into the study at the opportune time.

'I saw you storm out of the hall,' he says. 'I thought you were hurt.'

I peer up at him and see the concern on his face. 'Well, I was not.'

'I can see that.' Humour creeps up on him again. 'Besides the hedge, of course.'

I don't have it in me to laugh. Reality seems to sink in too fast, causing me to look away as I confess pensively, 'I'm sorry.'

'What for?'

'The ring . . . me not wanting to believe you hadn't kissed Faye.' I sigh. 'Dusan told me not long ago how he had fallen in love with Sarilyn before she cursed him. And now that ring is all that's left of her.'

There's no response.

That unnerves me.

I release a breath, walking over to the edge of the bed. 'He also told me a few weeks ago that the Isle of Elements could eventually lose its powers.' The thought has me exasperated as I spin to face Darius.

'What if we don't have much time? What if everything we are doing is pointless? If the Isle loses its powers, then our world will lose all its magic. It could destroy so much.'

Darius just stares at me, his eyes narrowing like at any moment he's preparing to catch me, hold me, do something so I don't spiral out of control.

I can't stop shaking my head. 'You were right. I *am* afraid and— and I hate it because I'd always been so good at keeping it hidden. I'm afraid for my brothers, my friends, what could happen in the future, I'm afraid of failing, and most of all, I'm afraid I will lose you like I lost Lorcan.' The confession barrels out of me; I have no time to stop it. I bite my lower lip, staring at him as my chest feels ready to collapse from his analyzing gaze. 'Will you please say something?'

The air hums with a tense silence. It's hard to focus. His scent, mingling with my worries, is confusing enough.

I wonder if he will say anything at all. He takes a deep breath, and makes his way over to me.

His hands cup my cheeks, eyes locking with mine, making sure I can tell how serious he is as he runs his thumb along my skin. 'Look, I can't promise that what we are doing will work. I can't promise that the Isle won't lose its powers. We can try to stop it, but that still might not work; however, what I can promise you is that you will never lose me, Goldie. You're stuck with me whether you like it or not.'

'I don't want false hope, Darius.'

He takes one hand off my face and presses three fingers to his heart. It wrecks me deeply. 'You won't lose me.'

I close my eyes, nod, and place three fingers on my heart.

I tilt my head, nuzzling my cheek further into his hand as I grip his wrist and breathe. 'I suppose I did deserve that *punishment* for believing you and Faye had kissed.'

An amused smile darkens the corners of his lips. 'It was entertaining to see your jealous side.'

I glower, pushing his hand away. 'I don't get jealous.'

He cocks a brow in response to my defensiveness.

'I never have before, especially over someone like you who doesn't need their ego—' I don't get to finish the rest as his hand settles on the nape of my neck and pulls me into a searing kiss. My annoyance disappears in an instant as a moan travels up my throat. He devours, consumes and ravages me with each movement and each flick of his tongue against mine.

When he draws back, I'm left disappointed. His voice is rugged, like he's just woken up from the most splendid dream. 'I meant it when I said I have not been able to kiss anyone else that isn't you.'

I bite my lip as desire vibrates through my body. 'Then I should likely tell you that—' My eyes meet his as the moonlight shines on his face. 'There isn't anyone else I'd like to argue with unless it is you.'

A sly smile graces his lips. His hand still touches my neck as he lowers his voice into a teasing whisper, 'So, Goldie, what do you wish to do before your birthday ends?'

I pretend to mull it over. 'To trap a dragon shifter.'

'I think I spotted an extremely handsome one roaming around here.'

'Really? I didn't know Gus was here.'

He frowns, looking far from impressed at my joke. I laugh and swing my arms around his neck.

'Dragon pig,' I whisper, nudging his nose with mine.

His chuckle tickles my lips. 'Foul mortal.'

And then our mouths meet, our tongues entwine, and the whole world fades around me, there is nothing and nobody else but Darius.

As his fingertips stroke my back, slowly and torturously loosening each lace of my bodice, his touch is like velvet against my flesh. My fingers then undo each of his buttons before resting my palms on the warmth of his chest, probing each coiling muscle of his, feeling the cut and definition.

When my gown falls at my feet, goosebumps scatter along my skin as he pulls back. His eyes betray his lustful thoughts, and I almost cover myself as he stares at me. I'm not used to this side of myself, even if I've done certain *acts* with him.

I think he can see my sudden apprehension because he hooks his thumb under my chin and raises my head.

'You shouldn't have to cover yourself for me, Goldie. You're perfect.'

I exhale a sigh of relief as I lift my hand and trace a couple of fingers across his cheekbones, the sharpness of his jaw and the light beard beginning to coat it.

We don't say a word. We just look at each other, never losing eye contact as he lifts me up. My legs wrap around his waist with my breasts against his chest, causing an involuntary moan to loosen out of me.

He walks us forward and splays me on the silk bedsheets. The coolness calms my heated skin but doesn't tame my racing heart. His arms wrap around my body, and I watch him keep his eyes on me as he slowly lifts the palm with my scar to his lips.

'Darius,' I gasp as his bottom lip starts tracing from my palm up my arm, firing every nerve inside me and bringing me to the verge of tipping over the edge.

'When I met you,' he whispers, kissing along the scar. 'This was one of the first things I noticed.'

'Not my fighting skills?' I can barely tease him as he continues sweeping across the sensitive parts. Who knew someone kissing my scar would give me this amount of pleasure?

And who knew that someone would be the person I once thought I detested with my whole being?

'That too.' He laughs, his breath tickling my skin. 'But after that night, you plagued my thoughts, my dreams.' He lowers his head, and our lips touch as he whispers, 'My world.'

With that, he ruins me once more with his kiss. If I could bottle it up forever, I would. The way his sensuous lips part mine, how slow and passionate he can be.

Maybe once, I might have thought that kissing Lorcan made me feel this way. But I was so wrong. He was special in his own way because he was my first kiss, the first person to look at me, more than just a helpless girl wishing to avenge her father.

With Darius, however, it felt like an end and a beginning.

An obsession.

A craving that could last a lifetime.

Destruction.

'Darius,' I breathe, grasping the sides of his face so he looks at me. I realise how determined I am as the following words come out of my mouth, 'I know what I want for my birthday.'

CHAPTER THIRTY-THREE

I see a glimmer of shock and yearning in his eyes. I can just about
see my silhouette in them. He knows. He understands exactly what
I am implying.

'Are you sure?' His voice is rugged and dripping with desire.

I nod.

I've never been more certain in my life.

'It might hurt,' he says, his voice with a hint of concern.

'I don't care.'

'But you're not—'

'I will ask Golrai for some Rucca leaves in my tea tomorrow morning.
I should be fine,' I pant out, knowing what he meant to ask. Even if
mortals can't bear a shifter's child without perishing, I still want to be
protected from unwanted pregnancies. A brew made of Rucca leaves have
been used by creatures of all kinds for their contraceptive properties.

Darius looks torn for a minute. I'm concerned he will say no,
leaving me mortified.

Instead, he drops his head by my side and whispers, 'Thank you . . .

for letting me be your first.'

As he fondles one of my breasts and begins pinching, squeezing, and causing sparks of pleasure to shoot down my legs, it leaves me breathless, yearning and unable to respond. My hands scramble to grasp something, and I end up sinking my fingernails into his back. He grunts but doesn't let go of me as he starts kissing my neck. My spine arches and my eyes flutter as I gasp and bite my lower lip in response to the frenzied strokes on my breast.

More, more, more—

A yelp claws up my throat when his hand moves between my legs and presses his thumb against me, lighting up my whole body with the pleasing pressure he's inflicting.

I am already wet as he stares up at me with a seductive smile, reminding me of every time he's used his charms, trickery and attractiveness to entice me.

If I had it my way, I'd have made a comment, anything to keep my sanity in check, but he doesn't let me, he knows me too well by now. He slides two fingers inside me, and I cry out. I immediately cover my mouth, but he yanks my hand away, welcoming my moans, his gaze hardening at each sound.

Desire pulses through my body as I groan while he pumps in and out of me. Slow, teasing and tormenting.

I don't realise his lips are grazing my ear until he says, 'Hips up, Goldie.'

I do as he says and feel him move, taking his pants off.

Propping my elbows up on the mattress, I stare with half-closed eyes at the V-shaped carving on his lower torso and at the largeness of his frame.

Arousal pools between my legs and I can hardly swallow.

He climbs on top of me again and looks at me as if to make sure this is what I really want.

It is.

I'm full of anticipation, excitement and nerves as I nod.

I want him to be inside me. *I need him.*

Darius will be my first.

And I wouldn't want it any other way.

He positions himself, his arms on either side of me, and when I feel his tip inside me, I wince as he finally slides in.

A sting, a burn, an intense sensation that's so foreign fills me right at once. My hands dig into his shoulder blades, worried I will jerk back as he goes in further, but a low moan emits from him before his mouth finds mine.

As he pulls out and thrusts back into me, I tip my head back with both pain and pleasure. *I never thought this could feel so good.*

He moves slowly, sweat glistens on our bodies, as his hands grasp mine, sliding them up to the sides of my head.

My eyes water and my teeth clench, but I've never wanted this more.

'If it hurts too much, I'll stop,' he says, panting.

I shake my head. 'I'm not a quitter.'

He chuckles. It's hoarse as our hands sink into the mattress. 'A competitor even in bed. You're insatiable, Goldie.'

I only manage a sigh as he stretches inside me and moves.

It starts as a gentle rhythm, soft enough to lessen the pain.

We stare at each other, our mouths touching but never kissing. Thrust after thrust, we pant, I whimper, and he moans my name like a prayer.

Our foreheads touch, each movement becomes deeper, and heat crawls up my spine as pressure builds and builds.

This time we kiss, but it's raw, intense and blinding as we breathe into each other.

My legs clench tighter around his hips, begging for a release as he continues harder and faster this time. I moan against his mouth, and in one swift movement of his arm, he scoops me up so I'm on his lap.

I'm a mess, drenched in sweat. He's so full inside me as he smooths strands of my hair away from my face.

'Use your hips, not your legs,' he orders softly, resting his hands on my lower back.

My breath shudders, and I attempt a nod before tentatively lifting myself up and then sliding back down with a whimpering moan. I keep doing it, slower, then faster, as I rock my hips. It feels even more intense when I have all the control.

Lust coats the air, thick and heavy enough to turn us insane. My lips part with endless moans, our noses touching as he grinds against me.

'That's it.' His encouragement turns me on even more. 'Keep going.'

I apply more friction, and our movements become synchronized.

Again, and again.

Harder, slower, deeper.

Pricks of pain and sexual pressure make me whimper. It doesn't feel as if I'm here. I'm somewhere between desire and need, breaking me apart and putting me back together.

Heat coils beneath my skin, my muscles contracting against his length. I hold on to him tighter, my fingers burrow into his skin as he plunges into me with more force, and I cry out, riding through a wave of bliss. Trembles travel through my body as I feel him jerk and shudder.

I'm far from recovering. My legs go limp around him as I try to catch a break. He doesn't slide out of me, and I don't move to push myself off him.

I don't want to.

I don't ever want to.

I rest my cheek against him as he chuckles. It's breathless, mingling seductively in a way that makes me want to go again.

He tucks a strand of hair behind my ear and then kisses my temple before whispering, 'Happy birthday, Goldie.'

CHAPTER THIRTY-FOUR

I wake up to Darius tracing his fingers along my spine. Up then down. It's the best feeling in the world – after last night, of course. There'd been no regrets, no takebacks on what we'd done. It was indeed a birthday worth remembering because we didn't just do it once. We did it again, then again, and finally, a fourth time until pain meant nothing and pleasure meant all.

The bedsheets hardly cover me as I turn to face Darius. It's vexing how handsome he looks when he's just woken up. His raven hair is ruffled, golden eyes are fresh and alight from the morning sun. He has one arm propped up on the pillow, and a lazy smile on his face as he looks at my nude figure.

Thrill and dreamlike contentment tickle my skin.

'Glad to see you sleeping on an actual bed,' I comment, as his fingers lightly skim over my arm, eliciting goosebumps.

'Couldn't resist listening to your snoring.'

I roll my eyes. 'I don't snore.'

He raises a customary mocking brow.

I return one with a level of defiance. 'You hog the entire bed. You're a right nuisance, shifter.'

His chuckle is a seductive sound, making me want more. I want to bask in it all day. 'And a shifter—' Despite the humour lacing his tone, lust darkens the edges of his eyes '—You thoroughly enjoyed sleeping with last night.'

Heat spikes in my blood, my cheeks warming up at just the memory of him inside me. I send him a playful glare before attempting to slap his shoulder, but he snatches my wrist, causing me to squeal as he rolls me over and pins my hands above.

I laugh.

His eyes flare with admiration, our bodies heating up at the skin-to-skin contact.

'Are you hurting?' he asks, his voice soft, almost protective.

I shake my head.

'Good,' he murmurs, his gaze fixed on me as he drops his mouth by my ear. 'Because next time, I won't be so gentle.'

His words are playful as ever. Smooth, addictive, the perfect mix.

I don't want him to be gentle. I want him to unequivocally ruin me forever.

'Is that a promise?' I say with a slight moan as he kisses below my ear, trailing towards the base of my neck.

'A warning,' he whispers, and my back arches as his teeth graze my skin.

Before he goes any lower, he stops, lifts his head, and dangles an earring over my face.

My earring.

Sun-shaped golden ones I wore last night.

'Thief.' My voice holds a teasing tone.

He laughs as his mouth covers mine and gives me a lingering kiss.

My eyes stay closed for a few seconds longer as he gets up from the bed, leaving me with the disappointment of wishing he could have stayed longer. Though watching him waltz to his dresser is a view I do not mind. The ripples of muscle along his back, the firm tight—

'You're not very subtle when you stare, are you, Goldie?'

Ugh.

He still has his back turned as I roll my eyes and push myself off the bed. I saunter up to him, letting my fingers trace his arm before he turns with a piece of brown rope and the gold coin he always carries in his other hand.

'I hope you're not going to try and strangle me with that because then I would have to find a way to hurt you back.'

He chuckles softly when he sees the severity on my face. 'This—' he drawls as flames release from his index finger, aiming it towards the top part of the coin. It's not long before he's melted a hole through it and loops the coin through the string. 'Is for you.'

Confusion and hesitation wring a knot inside my stomach.

Is he giving me a gift?

His hand is stretched out to me with the newly made necklace in his palm. A smirk lifts the corner of his lips as he says, 'My hand won't bite, Goldie – well, not unless you provoke it, of course.'

My hesitation turns into something strange hearing those words.

I stare at the coin, then slowly gaze up at Darius. My heart thumps at the sight of the boyish smile on his face. I must be frozen still because he comes around and places the coin around my neck. Its coolness shoots shivers up my spine and takes me out of my hypnotic state as he ties a knot, letting his hand linger on my back, branding me with the heat of his palm.

Looking at the coin, I run my fingers over the dragon crest. 'Why are you giving this to me?' I ask, turning to face him.

Like the crescent I used to carry, Darius always has this coin in his hand.

This feels like I'm taking something precious that's his.

'It's your birthday gift.'

'And last night was not?'

He steps towards me, his gaze looking over my naked body and darkening to resemble an eternal night. My breath turns ragged, and I try not to look down at the arousal settling between his legs. 'You've lived on this earth twenty-two years, Goldie. Expect more gifts for all the birthdays I've missed.'

I barely manage to swallow. My hand grips the coin tighter, certain that if he's to come any closer than we already are, all my willpower will crumble.

'Hello, Miss Nara!'

My eyes widen.

Looking down to my left, Tibith waves at us. I scream and rush to the bed, yanking off the bedsheets to cover myself. I'm horrified, panting as Tibith beams as if seeing me naked is nothing. On the other hand, Darius looks too calm, baring his entirety to Tibith as he spreads his arms to the side and grins.

'Tibith!' He cheers. 'Enjoy the festivities last night?'

Really?

'I did, Darry!' Tibith lets out an excitable squeal as Darius pets him. 'Miss Faye danced with me before Miss Arlayna took me around the mazes and argued with a very tall man, then kissed and slapped him,' he describes animatedly. 'Like you and Miss Nara do!'

I can't hide my frown, I have my suspicions on who that could have been. 'Did that man happen to be wearing the Terranos armour?'

Tibith whirls to me and nods.

I conclude it is definitely Aeron.

'Should I be aware of something?' Darius questions, eyeing us both with furrowing brows.

I fire him a lopsided smirk. 'I believe it is none of our concerns.' I don't want to imagine the trouble Aeron could get into if anyone else found out.

'You're right.' Darius starts towards me. It's highly inappropriate for him to look this sensual with no clothing while Tibith is in the room. 'My concerns only lie with Tibith—' He points a finger at me. '—And you.'

Months ago, I'd not dared believe this would be the case.

His hand rests by my waist as I pinch the bedsheet behind me, and he hooks a finger through the necklace he made.

I draw an eyebrow up. 'And here I thought your first concern would be how you look in the morning.'

'Devilishly handsome?' His debonair smile works wonders to prove how right he is.

Giving in to that, though, is not on my list.

I tilt my head, and an amused sound rumbles from my chest as I smile. 'No, an absolute mess.'

His gold eyes light up in his usual mischievous way.

My response didn't offend him in the slightest.

As always, he already knows it's a lie.

Dragon pig.

'What do I look like in the morning?' Tibith asks innocently as he appears beside us.

I throw my head back and chuckle, lowering myself, so I can scratch his ear. 'Like a king,' I say, scrunching my nose with a smile. 'Now—' I stand and glance at them both, '—If you'll excuse me, I should head back to my room.'

They both look at me as I bunch up the bedsheets like a dress skirt and lift my head as I walk out of the chambers with deliberate confidence. I quickly cross the hall, enter my room and close the door as I press my forehead against the wooden frame, reeling from what happened with Darius last night. It still seems almost too surreal, yet the pleasurable pain throbbing between my legs tells me otherwise.

'You made love last night.'

Upon hearing Arlayna's voice, my body jerks as I spin around to see her sitting at the edge of my bed, poised and observant. Not at all someone who cares that they are intruding.

I arch a brow. 'You kissed Aeron.'

She stands, fluffing out her gown. Despite her outward composure, the tension in her shoulders tells me otherwise. 'He kissed me, and how did you know that?'

'Tibith.'

'Ah.'

Silence clings to the walls of the room. It's not ideal to be naked beneath bedsheets in front of royalty, yet here we are. 'Have you been in here for long?' I ask, striding across the room to find something to wear.

Arlayna follows my movements, swiping a finger along the wooden bedposts. 'Enough to know you are fascinated with carving most of our furniture.'

I bark out a dry laugh, sorting through the bedside drawers. A draught of air on my backside has me gasping, thinking I've exposed myself.

It's only my imagination.

'Here,' Arlayna says, and I turn as she throws clothing my way.

I catch it with one hand and glance down at the forest green shade of the tunic and pants. 'You will need it tonight – it's laced with fruit extracts to cover your human scent from trolls. They're known to detest all nice-smelling things,' she adds when I sniff it and cock a brow in surprise at the citrusy smell. 'The stone should be within a well which hides the entrance to an oubliette.'

It seems too simple.

And that can only mean it's not.

I put on a brave smile. 'Anything else?'

'Don't get eaten.'

An uneasy laugh scatters out of me at her stoical tone. 'I will try not to.'

She bows her head and moves to leave. I stop her just as her hand reaches the doorknob. 'Arlayna.'

She turns halfway.

'As to your thoughts the other day. You were right,' I confess as she cocks her head in mild curiosity. 'I do care deeply for him.' I always have, and perhaps that means more than something. Perhaps Darius's version of love is just a fraction of a much greater act.

I hate everything about you as a person and as a shifter.

The memory of my words back in Emberwell stings the back of my mind.

And I promise you, once I get the vial and you get your stupid little pendant, I will hope to Solaris I never see you again in my life.

What a terrible lie that wound up being.

'I thought so,' Arlayna muses. She turns again before stopping. Silence pierces the air before she says, 'I must say . . . through an Elf's eye, sometimes we can see beyond what any other being can. Yet last night was the first time I saw a glow surrounding you both as you danced.'

My stomach twists, and I'm paralyzed as she looks at me.

'It was blinding.' A twitch of a smile. 'Like the sun.'

CHAPTER THIRTY-FIVE

L ike the sun.
   Like the sun.
   Like the sun.

As I get ready, I can't stop repeating Arlayna's words inside my head. After she left this morning, I kept thinking about it. Faye had said the same last night.

That we practically glowed.

I did not think anything of it in the moment, yet now . . . something digs into the pit of my stomach.

'Solaris incarnate,' I whisper what I'd once heard in the Screaming Forests. 'Protector of land and life alike.' I stare at myself in the mirror. My hair cascades over my tunic, and dazed, I brush my fingers through it.

Until the door to my room slams shut, and Aias strolls inside, tapping his foot against the floor. 'What was that last night with the ring?'

I should have gone to Aias and explained the ring situation right after. 'Nothing,' I say, fixing the leather braces on my arms. 'It's just—' There's a pause when I focus on him. Aias telling me how he'd also seen Darius outside flashes in my mind. 'You saw Darius kiss Faye, too, didn't you?'

'Yes?' he says slowly, confused. 'What does that have to do with the ring?'

That nothing ever makes sense any more. 'If I'm honest, I'm not entirely sure.' I sigh. 'Look, I do not trust the King, despite what he might say or how he acts.' Given my past with royalty, I would say I'm not overreacting. Paranoid, perhaps, but I just have this foreboding sense that something will go wrong sooner or later.

Like the scales in Melwraith.

A balance.

At one point, that scale has to tip one way or the other.

'Do you think he could betray you if you let yourself trust him?'

I glance down at my hands. 'Most have before,' I admit quietly. 'That has always been my downfall.'

Ivarron.

The Queen.

Lorcan.

I sigh, not meaning to put Aias in a bad mood when I soon have a task to do. 'Listen, I need you to keep an eye on him,' I say. 'He seems fond of you. Perhaps you can try and get information out of him.'

Aias doesn't look convinced. 'That sounds like an impossible task – *but* since you helped me,' he continues as he watches my expression go from disappointment to hope, 'I want to do the same for you.'

I say thank you, breathing out in relief as I walk over and squeeze him into a hug. His arms are stuck at each side, and I chuckle, wondering if this is too much for him. It likely is. Then again, everyone always mentioned my hugs were too tight.

'You should probably get going,' he says, his voice high and strained. 'You won't want to keep Darius waiting.'

A laugh draws out of my lips as I release him. 'I'm sure he will manage just fine. I can imagine him staring at himself in the mirror now and saying how handsome he is.'

Aias nods, shying away. It makes my smile fall.

'What is it?' I ask.

'Nothing, it's just you remind me so much of—' he stops and shakes his head. Something I can't quite decipher washes over his eyes. 'You know what? It doesn't matter. Shall we?' He offers his arm, and I take it, deciding not to press him on what he had wanted to say.

After Darius had taken me into the skies and landed in the woods outside of Olcar, I'd thought that they reminded me of ones near Emberwell, except now, with the change of climate and green foliage to browns and oranges, I see how different that is. Emberwell's nature never changed. Only the people around us did.

As I watch Darius take deliberate steps in front of me in the night, leaves crunch beneath my feet. We want to be as quiet as possible. I peel the hood of my tunic down to see better and steady my grip on my double-ended blade.

Darius soon stops, looks down at the ground, and kneels. He traces a finger over the set of footprints. Large . . . fresh.

'How many trolls do you think might be guarding the well?' I ask.

'A few, maybe less. We shouldn't worry, though. Trolls are daft creatures.' He rubs dry mud between his thumb and forefinger before rising to his feet. He turns to me. 'They'll be easy to fool.'

And easy to catch.

'Then we will build a trap,' I say, heading past him. Vines drape off one of the trees, long enough to tie branches together. I rise on my toes to grab one before I notice from the corner of my eye that Darius is watching me. I huff at him. 'What?'

'Has anyone ever told you how desirable you look in trapper mode?'

I glower. 'Concentrate.'

His eyes languidly travel all over me. 'I am.'

Flutters go off in my stomach. I'd smack him if it wasn't for the daring smile on his face, itching to get beneath my skin.

I go back to pulling the vine. 'You may think those compliments are working on me –' *They are.* '– But I know you've likely told hundreds of people how desirable they look.'

His hand rests over mine, making me stop what I am doing. We look at each other, and I part my lips to say something when he speaks before me, 'Are you always going to assume I used to be this philanderer?'

'I don't need to assume,' I tease. 'You've mentioned it many times before.'

'I had my desires,' he says, eyes staring straight into mine as if hoping I understand. 'But there was no one that could quite quench them before.'

I frown despite the heavy thump of my heart. 'Not even the person you fell in love with?'

He takes his hand off mine, glancing to the side. His brows furrow as what I'd just said sank in.

I might have overstepped with that remark.

'I didn't mean to—' My voice fades, knowing an apology won't do much, and instead get back to building a trap.

I'm halfway through tying a few branches together when he says, 'It wasn't someone else in my past that hurt me, Goldie.'

I pause, my eyes fly up at him, and a look of tortured sadness sweeps across his features.

'When you asked if I'd ever fallen in love, I had. What I failed to explain is that I still am.'

Words bubble up my throat, yet nothing spills out. I'm too startled to speak.

'See, there's this girl.' He chuckles to himself. 'A human girl. Who can be quite persistent with what she wants in life. She also hates it when you try to beat her at something and makes sure to insult you, such as calling you something silly, like a dragon pig. But you should see how her face lights up whenever she finds a slice of her favourite pie by her door . . . when she mentions her brothers or when she leaves bread for Tibith to snack on and sings him lullabies despite how awful she sounds.'

I can only stare, baffled, as his eyes radiate such affection.

'She doesn't know it yet,' he says, leaning forward and whispering covertly to me, 'but one day, when this is all over, I hope for her to be my wife, even if that might only be possible in my dreams.'

The cool air does nothing to help the heat spreading like wildfire through me.

He takes another step. 'I could have all the riches in the world, rule all of Zerathion, and it still would not be enough if I didn't have that person by my side.'

My eyes are wide, my lips parted without a word in sight.

Me.

He is in love with *me.*

It has never been someone else.

'It *hurt* seeing the way you looked at him,' he reveals, looking down at the ground, and my ribcage shrinks, realising whom he means. 'It *hurt* seeing you injured, on the verge of death that day in the woods.' His eyes, agonizing and beautiful, meet mine. 'And it *killed* me, knowing you'd never want anything to do with me. But I accepted that because you hated me, and I wished to have hated you in return.' He steps back, and it is here I understand the gravity of every word he is saying, how it still hurts him now. 'I realised too soon that I could not.'

I can hardly breathe.

When Lorcan had told me he loved me, he'd said it in a moment of fear. I don't think he meant it; I don't think he truly loved me. But as I look at Darius, I feel it. I feel it in his voice and how his gaze reaches my core.

I release the vines, branches – everything within my grip. 'Darius,' the name hardly reaches him. I try to move closer, but a clash further into the woods interrupts us.

Our heads swivel towards the noise.

Bickering voices, rough and nasally.

Trolls.

There's not enough time to finish the traps. Darius turns to me and grabs my hand as we sprint through the trees. He makes us duck behind a bush after skidding to a halt. Looking up, I observe a glade surrounded by trees with a brick well covered with moss in the centre.

My gaze flickers to the two trolls standing guard dressed in animal skin. Flies buzz around them as one scratches their behind, grabs the fly in midair, devouring it.

The meal Golrai had left in my room swirls inside my stomach, and bile rises to my throat.

Trying to shake that image out of my head, I lift my blade, but Darius's hand covers my fist and lowers it. I frown at him, perplexed, and then watch him tilt his head as he stares at the trolls with an intense flare in his eyes.

'Did you see that?' one of the trolls says, glancing in the opposite direction of the woods. The other raises his chin, his nostrils flaring.

'I don't smell—' They freeze, then start chuckling. 'Looks like we got an intruder, Slig.'

Slig shoots him a rotten, crooked grin before they creep towards the trees, away from us and away from the well.

When I glance at Darius, a self-satisfied smirk appears as he watches them fall under the ruse of whatever Merati powers he must have used.

'Come on,' he says, but I grab his arm before he can charge towards the well.

His head turns, and my eyes linger on every part of his face. I still cannot forget his confession.

'Darius—'

'Later,' is the word he whispers as he pulls out of my hold and walks into the clearing.

I close my eyes with a sigh and clutch the gold coin around my neck as I follow him, unable to think of the task because of what he had said.

CHAPTER THIRTY-SIX

I have never been afraid of wells before. I was once forced to climb down one by bullies in our village, but now, from a certain angle, it appears as if I am staring into the pit of a monster's mouth.

I look across the well towards the lake, dark and uninviting. 'I'll go down while you look out.'

Darius's incredulous chuckle has me whip my head around to face him. He shakes his head, grabbing hold of the rope. The screech and hiss of metal sting my ears as he pulls out an almost disintegrated bucket and looks at it as if it is useless. He throws it on the ground and begins fastening the rope around him.

'I'll go down first,' he says, tugging on the cord so it is secure. 'Make sure no trolls are lurking there, or you know –' He eyes me humourously '– creatures with an insatiable hunger for blondes.'

'Such as yourself?'

He clicks his tongue, effortlessly standing atop the ledge of the well. Turning to me, he says, 'I can't deny that you do taste sweet, Goldie.' My cheeks flame. 'I'll whistle to let you know I've landed.'

One second, he is there in front of me. The next, he's going down the well. I rest my hands against the stone masonry, watching as he disappears. I'm on the verge of shouting his name when seconds pass, and there is no response. I grip the ledge harder, sharp edges indenting my palms.

He finally whistles.

It echoes on and I release a breath.

I pull the rope back and mimic Darius by wrapping it around my waist. As I raise myself on my feet and turn away from the lake, my chest feels like it's twisted around a tight coil. And as I lower myself, I look up at the sky, a ring of stars and green hues whirling in the darkness. It shrinks and shrinks until I feel hands touch my back and I leap into Darius's embrace. An odd stale scent hangs in the air – a smell that brings me back to my childhood.

Darius twists me around, and I can't help the overwhelming joy of seeing his face. It is maddening, yet it makes me smile.

'No creature to slay?' I say, bracing my hands against his chest.

His laugh warms up my palms. 'The night is young.'

And clearly, he is hoping for a lot more later.

If we succeed.

I move to his side, staring at the damp walls surrounding us. The moonlight lands on a cluster of jagged rocks on the wall, almost indicating a path. I trace my fingertips along the wall's curves and land on one block protruding outward.

My eyes find Darius, not for reassurance but for the confidence that glows within his eyes. He encourages me as he tips his chin, so I nod, pushing down on the block.

A groan splinters the well, and then I let out a startled cry as I fall through an opening in the ground, rolling and tumbling onto hard concrete flooring.

A cough splinters through my throat before Darius lands beside me.

'Fuck, Goldie,' he says, immediately coming towards me. 'Is anything hurting?' He curls an arm around my waist, lifting me up, and I shake my head, thankful that nothing feels broken except for my sanity. After the last time at Melwraith, I was determined to keep it together this time.

And yet here we are.

I'm on the verge of replying when I catch sight of the right side of the oubliette. I turn, widening my eyes at the hundreds upon hundreds of brass keys – all identical – hanging off hooks.

'Well, the good news is that I know where the stone is,' I hear Darius say behind me, and I look over my shoulder, seeing him standing by a vault carved into the wall – a safe. 'Bad news is that I assume we have to search through all those keys.'

I shut my eyes, exasperated, as I rush over and glance at the cracks in the wall, the keyhole, the sun and the crescent carvings . . .

Certain areas of the oubliette are too dark to see despite the gold light bursting through the keyhole of the safe. I can see there is an etched inscription beneath it.

'To survive,' I read out. 'Here is a test. *There are those who cannot see me but know I am there. When you lose me, you live life in despair. Everyone knows the world isn't fair. But I am what keeps you pushing through when life seems hard to bear.*'

A riddle.

I open my mouth to ask Darius what he thinks when a rumble shakes the oubliette, and water starts gushing out from the cracks of the walls.

Panic registers within seconds. I spin to where Darius is as he mutters a curse word and starts grabbing keys from the wall, lobbing them at me.

I fumble for the lock as freezing water begins to fill up the passage, but nothing works.

Every key he throws, I realise, is the same. None have a distinct pattern. It really could be any of them.

Frustration churns my stomach, making me grit my teeth. 'It's not working!' I say, tossing the worthless key.

Water covers the entire floor, and I take a sharp breath as I go under. I'm desperate for a way inside. By the time we try every key, we'll be drowning at the bottom of the oubliette.

I study the gap of light through the hole, illuminating the riddle.

There are those who cannot see me but know I am there.

All I can hear is the beating of my heart in my chest.

I reread the next part, intent on figuring out the riddle, but Darius pulls me up, and I gasp at the contact of air. He presses a hand to my cheek, looking at me with concern, but all I can think about is the riddle.

When you lose me, you live life in despair. Everyone knows the world isn't fair. But I am what keeps you pushing through when life seems hard to bear.

The world isn't fair.

No, it is not.

It never is.

But I am what keeps you pushing through when life seems hard to bear.

Hard to bear.

I glance to my left as if I can still see the safe despite it now being underwater. I think of the crescent . . . the sun. Solaris and Crello. Something snaps inside my head. My gaze settles on Darius. 'We have to let the water rise all the way.'

He looks at me as if the low oxygen level has gotten to me.

'The keys are there to trick us,' I add, breathing heavily as my chest compresses. 'Just trust me.'

Beads of water drip from his dark hair. 'You should know by now that I do.'

And that is all I needed.

My teeth chatter. I slide my hand behind the nape of his neck, and he brings me closer to him as the water batters against our chests. I lean in, pressing my lips softly to his for warmth. My tongue glides along his bottom lip before he gives me access, consuming me with his taste and his . . . *love.*

She doesn't know it yet, but one day, when this is all over, I hope for her to be my wife, even if that might only be possible in my dreams.

Wife.

I kiss him harder, not for fear that this won't work, but for actual fear that I will lose him, which I now know I could never deal with.

'It won't be a dream,' I whisper, pulling back slightly, the water now at our necks. 'Me becoming your wife. I will make it a reality.'

He stills. It's as if he is not breathing.

For too long, he has believed he only deserved hatred.

And whatever lies ahead, I know he deserves a chance at a better life.

We have floated to reach the ceiling, taking in our last breaths, and then there's nothing to do except wait.

I cling to Darius, our lips connect, exchanging air. I pray to be right about the riddle, and that the vault opens, I pray that Darius's trust in me is not in vain.

But seconds tick by, and the safe doesn't open.

Come on, come on, come on—

Like someone cranking a lever, a sound emits through the water, and the safe pops open. A golden stone, similar in shape to the ones we retrieved from Melwraith and the Screaming Forests, hovers inside the vault. I kick my legs, the weight of the water heavy as I swim towards the stone and pry it from the safe. I'm smiling as I admire it in my hand before glancing up at Darius.

He's staring at me as if wanting to ask how I knew.

Faith.

That is what I want to tell him.

It is what kept me from deteriorating for so long. Faith in Solaris and Crello, faith in my brothers, faith in my friends, faith in Darius.

I can't see or feel it, but I know it is there, and Darius put his trust and faith in *me*. That is what the test wanted.

My hands curl around Darius's in lieu of an answer, and over his shoulder, part of the wall opens. I point to it and motion to Darius for us to swim towards it. We exit the cave and swim into the lake. It's darker than inside the oubliette. Nonetheless, we continue swimming upward.

To freedom.

To air.

'*Solaris,*' something hisses in my ear.

I stop, my head whipping in the direction of the sound.

'*Stay with us,*' it says, and I turn again.

Darius is up ahead, unaware of this. I shake my head, eager to get out as I move my arms. I hardly make it halfway when I hear the voice once more. It's so feminine, so sweet yet cold at the same time . . . like a siren, tempting me.

Galgrs.

'*Crello is in danger.*'

I shut my eyes and cover my ears while holding on to the stone as if that is the only way to stop the Galgr.

'*Death, reign, resurrection.*'

Stop, stop, stop.

'The phoenix is—'

Stop!

My eyes pop wide open, and the first thing I see is a dull, grey, deathly face with hollow eye sockets and gills on its cheeks, centimetres away from me. Long hair flows across its gangly naked body before its mouth opens, and rows of sharp teeth greet me as it releases an ear-splitting cry. My screams come out gurgled, bubbling in the lake. I jerk back, but skeletal fingers grab my ankle, and another Galgr appears from the right.

Even as memories begin to flood my head, I strive to envision reaching the surface.

Then a specific moment cuts through my field of vision.

Me smiling at a boy.

Marbles of Solaris and Crello . . .

'Do you believe in them?'

'I believe that—' the boy pauses, staring at the marble. 'I believe that they once existed, yes.'

I beam up at him, squinting past the rays of the sun. 'Well, would you like to play a game with my marbles?'

He grins and nods as I take his hand and run with him along the street. Laughter echoes from our lips as sellers yell at us to stop playing around. We ignore them by stealing a few apples and a rose which he then gives to me. I tell the boy that I have three brothers whom I adore with all my heart. He mentions he has one and that his brother is always furious at him for the stupidest of reasons.

I'm laughing, throwing the marble and knocking it on the ground.

I have a friend.

A boy my brother Idris wouldn't like me being with, but a friend nonetheless.

'I'm sorry, I didn't mean to lose it,' the boy says, grimacing apologetically as the marble disappears into a crowd of people.

I don't want to tell him how upset I am that the marble is lost. I fear I'll lose him as a friend if I get mad. It wasn't his fault. 'Don't be sorry.' I reach into the pocket of my pinafore and take out a golden coin I'd grabbed from my father's pouch. 'You can have this instead.'

He frowns. 'A coin?'

'Not just any coin.' I wiggle my brows. 'A gold coin. You could get yourself anything you like with that, maybe a jewel or strawberry pie!'

He narrows his eyes, pocketing the coin and smiling as he brushes dark strands out of his face. 'You're strange.'

I wave the rose he gave me around. 'I get that a lot.'

'It's a good thing.' He smiles, dimples appear, and a cool confidence radiates from him. 'I like strange.'

I smile in return, content at the idea of having a new friend liking me for me, even though I still don't know his name.

Tilting my head, I try to ask him what it is, but something unexpected happens. His eyes . . . turn gold. 'Your eyes, they are no longer brown?' I stretch out my hand to his alarmed face. 'And you – you look different—'

'Darius!'

I coil backward at the furious cry of a man who looks like he could be my father's age save for his copper hair cut above his shoulders. He storms towards us from one of the stalls and grabs the boy – Darius – by the arm. It's rough and clearly hurts Darius as he winces from the touch.

'What did I tell you about leaving the cottage?' the man says, his tired features hardening as he shakes Darius.

'Stop, you're hurting him!'

The man's head slowly tilts my way as if he hadn't registered me before. He eyes me up and down then scoffs. 'Get out of here, girl. This doesn't concern you.'

'Actually, it does.' I step forward, my chin raised high, as Darius looks at me with fearful eyes and shakes his head, telling me not to say anything else. 'I am his friend, and friends protect each other.'

The man stares, stupefied. And then, he laughs so loud it hurts my eardrums.

'Friend?' He glances down at Darius for seconds, minutes. His grin is not at all comforting. 'Why don't you bid your friend a farewell, then, Darius?'

Darius looks up at the man, the confidence from before now completely gone as he ducks his head. The man shoves Darius towards me. I give him an angry look, wondering if he is Darius's father. If so, they look nothing alike.

'I'm sorry,' Darius mumbles, looking lost and distraught.

I'm not sure why he is sorry. He shouldn't be, not for that man.

He huffs out a breath. Golden eyes interlock with mine. 'Close your eyes,' he whispers, and a heavy weight pulls them shut as if I cannot help it, no matter how much I fight to keep my eyes open. 'If this works, then you are not to remember who I am, this moment, or my name. You were playing with your marbles alone. You lost one and will now go look for your mother.' Silence. 'Goodbye . . . Goldie.'

A wave of air tickles my skin, and an arcane wildness blooms. I'm staring at a street full of merchants and shoppers as I blink back to reality.

I spin on my feet, slowly and confused, as I look down at the rose in my hand.

How did I end up here?

CHAPTER THIRTY-SEVEN

As the Galgr wails, I'm drawn away from that recollection, and I open my eyes to see the creatures scatter. Next, my arm is grabbed by Darius as he hauls me out of the lake. I gasp, feeling the cool air hit my face as we swim to the bank, and rest our forearms against the grass.

Our measured breathing is all you can hear, and my heartbeat is the loudest it's ever been.

Darius's laughter-tinged voice breaks through my daze. 'We should really have a point system for how many times I save you.'

You are not to remember who I am, this moment, or my name. You were playing with your marbles alone. You lost one and will now go look for your mother. Goodbye . . . Goldie.

Goldie . . .

'I remember.' My voice cracks as I speak quickly. I look towards Darius; he turns his face as I try to stabilize my breathing. 'It was you all those years ago. You made me forget who you were.'

It takes him a moment to understand what I am saying. Water droplets slide down his face as he parts his lips in shock, and I push myself onto the grass, storing the stone away in my pocket.

He knew me. All this time.

He made me *forget* him.

And it took a Galgr to bring that memory back.

'Nara,' Darius says, his tone pleading as I start walking off.

Hurt sinks into my skin like the talons of a creature – a dragon. *His claws.*

And his scent . . . it'd always been so familiar.

He catches up to me just before we enter the woods and spins me to face him.

'Have you always known it was me?' I ask because I'm hoping he didn't. I'm hoping there is some reason why he *didn't* tell me.

His heavy sigh as he runs a hand through his hair tells me everything I need to know, and his words are equal parts pain and regret. 'It was the night I asked you to steal the pendant. You mentioned your brothers.'

Goldie. I think you look like a Goldie. Wouldn't you agree, Tibith?

'When we met, you reminded me of her – of the girl I'd seen all those years ago, and when I saw your carving, I knew for sure it was you. You always carried it with you every time you visited the town with your mother. I'd see you from afar—'

I shake my head, the revelation knocking me back. 'Lorcan's carving.'

He doesn't meet my gaze as he whispers, 'It was never his.'

For a moment, I don't consider what he means by this. Then I remember.

On one of the days of the trials, when Lorcan was in my arms, he kept repeating how he'd lied while handing me my carving. He

274

did not mean that he'd lied about what he was or that he'd tricked me. He meant that the carving never belonged to him in the first place.

As soon as I realise, I turn back around and begin storming away as I furiously wipe the damp water from the lake off my cheeks.

He knew, he knew, he knew.

'Nara, wait, just let me explain—'

I turn to him, my eyes burning with tears. 'Why didn't you tell me?' I press my hands against his chest and shove him before he can answer. 'Why did you keep it hidden from me?' Another push, and he takes it. 'Why did you make me forget you?'

Because he thought he didn't deserve you, my mind whispers.

I stare at him, the troubled tension in his eyes, he still looked so beautiful and vulnerable under the moonlight. The boy who I'd befriended. The boy who'd turned out to be Darius.

My voice breaks as I point to myself. 'Where was my choice?'

'If I hadn't,' he says quietly, so painfully it hurts me more than a blade ever could. 'Rayth could have gone as far as to harm you.'

I shake my head. 'There were people around, he wouldn't—'

'He never cared,' Darius says. 'He was cruel, Nara, and if anything had happened to you—' he winces, his jaw clenching as he looks down at the ground without finishing his sentence.

My lips tremble, not even from the cold any more, and I edge forward. I tilt my head, a tear slides down my cheek, and tentatively, I reach for his face as if feeling him here with me would fix everything.

He watches me, paying attention to my movements. He looks torn and ashamed, yet stops me before I can touch him by grabbing my wrist. His eyes look away from mine and scan the forest. 'Nara,' he whispers. 'We're not alone—'

From the trees, trolls make their way towards us. One, two, three . . . maybe ten or more of them.

Darius pulls me behind him as the same two trolls that were guarding the well lunge towards me, green tongues slithering out to lick their lips.

Disgust fills me.

'Told you there'd be dinner for us tonight,' the troll says.

A few chuckle, low and repulsive, like they have something permanently lodged in their throats. They advance forward, stopping short when Darius begins to shift.

I step back as Darius transforms into his dragon form. Leathery wings and silver scales gleam in the night as his rumbling growl shocks the trolls.

Yells come from every direction as Darius charges at them. I swivel around just in time as one troll tries to grab me. I duck, unsheathing my blade and ramming it into the back of his thick-skinned neck.

It does nothing. He doesn't even notice I've just stabbed him.

The troll barks out a horrifying laugh. Up close, I can see warts and rotting flesh on his face. Over his shoulder, Darius slams his claws into one of the troll's backs.

'You don't look like an Elf,' says the one before me. He takes one long sniff and grins. 'Human.'

The disguising scent Arlayna laced my clothes with must have washed off in the lake.

I take a few steps back, and more trolls approach me, attempting to block me. I don't second guess it. I turn and run further into the forest.

I'm jumping over tree trunks, as the sound of feet shuffling through the leaves grows closer. I start looking for berries, beehives, anything to cover my scent, when something whacks the air, and I tumble onto the ground as rope tangles around my ankles. I roll onto my back, glancing down at the bolas and then towards the trolls coming closer. I can see their vile grins and waste no time trying to free myself. I'm up soon enough, but it's almost too late as the trolls are metres away from me. I turn to flee in the other direction, but I smack into something large.

I land on my backside, staring up at the grinning troll.

Shit. I'm surrounded.

'You're a feisty little human,' he says.

I kick him in the groin.

He howls, and I sprint, spotting a gap between two trolls. I slip by them as they bump heads, and I start making my way back to Darius, panting as I try to get my legs working. The trolls are in pursuit again, and I'm unsure what prompts me to stop, but I do.

As I glance up at the trees, I notice bats among the branches, their beady eyes staring at me.

Peaceful and nocturnal, yet vicious creatures when provoked.

Slowly, I twist on my feet. I can hear my fast-paced breathing. *Inhale, exhale.*

Grotesque green shapes swarm my vision, closing in before my eyes flutter, and I bring my palms out to the sides, focusing on my senses.

The smell of dew and pinecones.

I'm sorry.

Fresh swaying grass underneath me.

Close your eyes.

Gusts of late autumn wind brushing my skin and hair.

If this works, then you are not to remember who I am, this moment, or my name. You were playing with your marbles alone. You lost one and will now go look for your mother.

Sounds of the forest coming alive at my fingertips.

Goodbye . . . Goldie.

There's so much hurt, so much anger and energy in me. I need to release it. My eyes fly open, and the trolls chuckle as they spot me. I glare at them, and soon their faces fall, no longer staring at me, but at something else.

A swarm of bats flies past me, screeching as they latch on to the skin of the trolls, who shout and wave their arms, but it's pointless. The world buzzes around me. My chest is like steel, expanding from the heat within my body and shrinking at the cool air. I glance at my palms, squeeze them shut, then look up at the retreating trolls, the bats clawing away at their faces.

I—

'Nara.'

I gasp, my body weakening as I turn.

Darius is covered in blood.

Worry takes over me until I realise it's not *his* blood.

He looks shocked. He witnessed everything.

Before he can speak, I'm already saying, 'I want you to shift again.'

He looks at me for a few seconds before he nods, conceding my wish. He doesn't question why I want him to transform. He does it without hesitation, changing once more into his dragon form.

I walk over to him, extending my palm to his neck as his golden reptilian eyes tear through me. He looks so dangerous, so powerful. Others would see him as someone capable of slaughtering them in half, burning them until they are soot, unrecognisable, ruined. I see him as that boy sixteen years ago who was afraid to even look me in the eye.

His heart beats slowly beneath my hand. Mine speeds up.

My hand now traces each outline along his scales. He quivers, a rumbling murmur emerges from him, and like moments ago, a buzzing energy courses through me – through *us*.

I absorb every detail of him and start to think of Emberwell.

How he helped me pay my debt with Ivarron. How he didn't hesitate to save me from Lorcan in the forests. How he came back for me when the trials commenced.

I'd hated him, I'd gotten him captured because of my foolishness, and he'd risked so much just for me because he knew who I was all this time.

I jerk my hand away, swallowing the tears flooding down my face.

'Take me back,' I whisper, looking away.

Though I wanted to say 'home'.

But home is not Dusan's palace.

Home is where my brothers are.

Except part of me now feels Darius is my home too.

I hear the sound of his hind legs thumping onto the ground for me to get on, and I climb up onto his back.

My hands rest on his skin, and I let him take me higher and higher into the clouds.

CHAPTER THIRTY-EIGHT

The King's voice is distorted within the walls of the throne room. Arlayna, Faye and Meriel are standing by Dusan's side, and I notice his lips moving and his smile deepening as he glances at Darius and I.

I don't care for his praises, and I don't care that all eyes are on me.

I'd kept my briefing simple: we'd retrieved the stone successfully but then we ran into some trolls. I didn't mention what happened with the bats, nor did Darius, though he did not stop looking at me.

'I should mention it is best you do not fly into Thalore for your last task.'

That snaps me out of my stupor.

Dusan sees the confusion written on my face and waves his bejewelled hand. 'Thallan suggested you travel there discreetly and gather information along with the stone.'

'So, you want us to be your spies?' Darius speaks up, and Dusan presses his index finger to his lips.

'Spy or not, I will go with them.' Arlayna steps forward, and from the corner of my eye, I notice Aeron shift from his stiff posture. 'I'm familiar with our lands. I can be of service.'

Thallan, who is to Dusan's right, laughs and runs a hand through his long dark hair. 'Don't be absurd, Your Highness. It is not your duty to protect outsiders.'

'As a royal, shouldn't she be allowed to decide whether she wishes to protect us or not?' The words fly out of my mouth, and I huff when his eyes widen at my audacity. 'Apologies, I just think it should be her choice. We –' I don't look at Darius as I gesture between us '– Are used to working independently.'

The King is thinking, his fingers toying with a jade ring. 'Arlayna,' he says, looking at me with a scrutinizing gaze. 'You may take your bow and arrow.'

I think Arlayna is just as shocked as Thallan.

'If Arlayna is going, I might as well too, right, uncle?' Faye asks. 'I know the woods inside and out—'

Meriel is shaking her head when she cuts in, 'You will not go. Arlayna is more equipped to handle herself in dangerous situations than you. However—' She turns to the King. 'Dusan, I do request some of your men travel with them for extra security—'

'Mother—' Arlayna tries to protest, but Meriel silences her with a hand.

I realise Arlayna not only wants to join us to help, but she also wants an escape. Her life as royalty keeps her trapped. I can see when there's a drop in her expression, a crease in her brow at the mention of meetings, or travelling into the city with guards at her side all the time.

'Very well.' The King claps his hands, rising from the throne. 'It is settled. You will ready yourselves to retrieve the last stone in a few days.'

I do not know what time it is. I imagine it is far too late for me to be awake. But here I am, sitting on the edge of my bed, dressed and ready for the task. On my dresser, I'm watching a candle burn and waver, the wax melting away.

I feel as if I am the wax right now. I feel like someone has lit a match, and I'm drifting . . . disappearing beneath its heat.

'Miss Nara?' Tibith's groggy voice comes from behind me. I turn to see him crawl over to me. He rubs his eyes and stares up at my face. 'Why do you look so sad?'

I smile, look away, then glance at the coin Darius gifted me. 'I'm not sad.' I'm torn. I'm torn because I no longer know myself, I'm torn because I miss my brothers and my friends, and I'm torn because Darius kept something from me.

But . . . What hurts me more is knowing so many things in my life have been kept a secret from me. That I am so easy to trick.

It happened with Ivarron.

It happened with Lorcan.

It happened with Sarilyn.

It happened with . . . Darius.

Who next?

'Did you argue with Darry again?' Tibith asks, and I chuckle quietly.

'No,' I say, still laughing. 'We just—'

A knock.

It comes from the door, and I rise so fast, hearing Darius say my name.

The door is locked. He could use any of his powers to get in, his strength even, but he chooses not to. He just calls my name and waits patiently.

I stare at the doorknob, frozen in place.

'Don't shut me out.' His voice is rugged and desperate. 'Don't push me away. Just please, listen to me. I know you're awake. I know you can't sleep. And I know that because you told me you only ever sleep well with me by your side.'

I'm so silent, trying to channel my heart into beating slowly.

'I think you should answer the door, Miss Nara,' Tibith whispers, now by my side, looking despondent for the both of us.

I wonder if he knows everything.

'You're all I've ever thought about since I met you in that old town.' Darius's words wreak havoc in my chest. 'I was never allowed out. Rayth made sure I wouldn't step foot anywhere unless it was to wash myself outside in the rain. But that day, I'd rebelled. I did it occasionally as a way to practise my magic, except that day was different. I don't know why or how, but I felt like I needed to find something – *someone*.'

It's hard to swallow.

'I was losing myself, Nara. And then you appeared.' He laughs a little, and I can picture him shaking his head at himself. 'A dream in a waking nightmare. You didn't know what I was. How frightened I would feel if you found out I was a dragon shifter. But then you smiled, and for the first time, I knew what it was that I needed to find. It was you.'

I cover my mouth with my palm and blink, the tears trickling down my cheeks.

'You want to know what I said to Lorcan later that day?' He sounds so breathless, and I nod. I nod desperately as if he can see me. 'I told him how I'd met the prettiest girl to ever exist, that you gave me that coin you have around your neck right now, and that . . . Even if I had to wish for it, I'd see you again.'

I'm sobbing now, my shoulders shaking as Tibith climbs my leg and rests his head on my shoulder.

'You're all I've ever wished for.'

Hearing him say that felt like a stab to my chest. I can't find any word, idiom, or phrase to express myself.

'That night,' Darius whispers through the silence. 'That night in the hut, you asked me why I always left gold coins after every theft in the city.'

That's something I can't tell you right now, Goldie, he had said.

Many say he does it to irk sellers so that they can use that gold coin to replenish stock and then for him to just steal it all again, Freya had told me back in Emberwell – back when I'd first arrived at the city.

'I didn't tell you then because the answer always led back to you. My regret has always been how I made you forget me. I'd always hoped to see you again, to find you. Leaving those coins behind was my way of searching, and then one day, you walked into a store I happened to be robbing.'

That night, that fateful night, is when everything changed.

'A girl with the same golden hair, same blue eyes. I thought it had to be you, but there you were, dressed as a Venator, intent on capturing me.'

Shame reddens my cheeks. I'd harboured such hatred towards dragons and shifters, I regret it all.

'I went home after that, thinking about you, wondering if it was just a cruel joke. That my mind was messing with me. The girl I'd met all those years ago couldn't be a Venator. But when I realised it was truly you the night after the attack . . . I broke.'

I glance at Tibith, and he nods to confirm that it's true.

He *did* know.

'And even when you hated me, I did everything to keep seeing you. That's why I decided to attend the ball despite the risks, because all I knew was that—' A pause followed by a deep exhale. 'I was irreversibly in love with you. I *am* irreversibly in love with you, Nara.'

More tears spill.

My heart squeezes against my ribcage, and my hands are suddenly on the keylock. I'm ready to open the door, jump in his arms, and tell him I'm afraid. I'm afraid of so much. Too much.

Tibith slides off my shoulder, beaming as I twist the key.

Except . . . a chilling scream coming from outside stops me.

CHAPTER THIRTY-NINE

My body locks up, and I turn to Tibith, who is whimpering. I tell him to wait here and I open the door to find Darius's panicked expression reflecting mine. We look at each other for a few more seconds, we're both hesitant to let go of the moment he'd confessed his secrets to me, his profession of love, and bolt down the castle's corridors. We rush outside, where guards and servants are heading towards the maze. When we arrive at the main hall, and I peer over one of the sentry's heads, my stomach constricts, bile travels to my throat, and I stumble backward into Darius's arms.

Golrai's lifeless body lies on the ground in a foetal position. A tray is scattered to one side, and half of a broken teacup is covered in blood. From the jagged line along her neck, I assume someone had slit her throat, and half her head is caved in, making her look almost unrecognisable.

How . . . ? Who could have—

'Out of the way!' Meriel shoves gasping servants aside, her curls falling out of her plait as she steps forward to the view of what is in front of us. She presses a hand to her chest and turns to Aeron. 'Who was patrolling the gardens when this happened?'

'Alwin and his men, Your Highness.'

Meriel is about to ask more when Aeron clears his throat and answers before her. 'I already had them questioned. They did not see any suspicious sightings of Shadow Calps nor any other break-ins.'

Meriel shakes her head with an exasperated breath and mutters, 'Incompetent—'

I disregard Meriel's complaints, focusing on Golrai's dead body. Not long before Darius came to my door, I'd requested Golrai bring me herbal tea. She was taking longer than expected, but I did not care by then. I'd been too focused on Darius's words.

Blowing a breath, I count to three, then slowly pull myself away from Darius towards the other shard of the teacup.

I kneel, pick it up, and stare at it.

If this wasn't a break-in and there wasn't any attempt from the outside, then someone from the castle must have done it for whatever unknown reason. I glance at everyone around me as Aeron orders people to head inside. I rise and meet Darius's gaze. We both step towards each other – to comfort, know that the other is safe. But Meriel grabs his arm and causes us both to halt.

'We may need you,' she says, raising her brows to imply they needed him in his dragon form, his . . . powers.

His eyes shift back to mine, and I can't help it. His stare, the intensity of his words from the other side of the door; it is soul-aching that I must look away.

I hear the hesitancy in his voice as he says to Meriel, 'Lead the way.'

More orders are shouted out. Some to stay vigilant, others to protect the princesses and King from any possibility they could be next. When I finally find the courage to look in Darius's direction, he already has his back turned, a small figure in the distance. I fiddle with the coin around my neck and press it against my heart. I'm still standing there as others try to tell me I must leave, go back to my chambers, and lock the door.

Instead, I breathe heavily, frustrated and furious as I think of the King. Be it my distrust or because an innocent Elf such as Golrai was violently killed, but I march back inside the castle, intent on finding the King.

The sage walls look dark and terrifying in the dimness as I pass the many empty halls and rooms. I'm nearing the King's study, unsure if he is in there—

'Nara!' Aias's voice stops me from behind. I turn to find him coming out of his room, confused and worried. 'What is all the commotion? I heard screams—'

'Golrai,' I say, unable to hide my distress. 'The maid. She was found dead.'

His mouth drops. 'What—' He looks around as if we shouldn't gossip. He lowers his voice. 'Murder?'

I nod, and he blinks, placing a hand against the wall to steady himself. 'Is the killer still out there? Was it a troll's doing? Did they breach the walls?'

'There was no break-in attempt,' I sigh, darting my gaze elsewhere. I'm unsure whether I should tell him I believe it was the King's doing. Saying it out loud might sound stupid. And even if Aias confides in me the most, I don't want to bother him with my theories. 'I think you should—' I pause as I see Thallan walking out from one of the rooms and heading straight to the King's study.

What does he think he's doing?

'Look, Aias,' I say in a hurry. 'I need to speak with someone before I return to my room. Please, could you go there and make sure Tibith is okay?'

He nods a few times. 'Sure, of course, I'll go there now!'

I thank him, and as he leaves, I stalk towards the study, entering without even a knock. I'm pressing the door closed behind me as I look straight at Thallan shuffling through some paperwork. The King is not here, no sconces are lit, and Thallan's attire is only a white shirt, breeches and a green tie holding his hair back.

Far from his usual forest-green garments.

'Does the King know you are looking through his stuff?'

Thallan's head lifts, and he looks at me, his hand still holding a parchment. 'The King asked me to fetch something that deals with his niece.'

My brow goes up. 'At this hour?'

'Should I not ask you the same, considering you are here too?' He's approaching me now. All I see is the frightening glow of his green eyes through the dark until some light from the glass panel windows forms a halo from behind him. He raises the parchment in his hand, and I make out the name Arlayna Fallcrown, then the words *successor* and *queen*, before he lowers it and looks at me as if waiting for the answer.

'Someone was killed,' I say, crossing my arms over my chest. 'I assume you must know that by now.'

'Ah, yes, the maid.'

'Yes, Golrai. Her head was caved in, her throat slit, and it appears the one who did it wasn't an outsider.'

He laughs unkindly. 'And you suppose I am a suspect?'

Actually, it is the King I first suspected, but I would not rule out his emissary.

'I did not kill the maid.' He turns away from me, strolling around as he drops the parchment back onto the desk. 'What use would I have for killing someone so worthless?'

I swallow hard, despising his use of that word.

'Have you thought –' He pivots in one mocking movement '–perhaps it was one of our own guards?'

I don't have a response.

He sighs and shakes his head. 'Why must you be so quick to judge?'

'I've mistakenly believed something before only to be wrong.'

'Then perhaps you're wrong again,' he snaps, staring at me like I am foolish. Like I am just as worthless to him as Golrai apparently was. Ever since I got here, he's looked at me like I am a disturbance, a useless mortal wanting to collect the Elemental Stones.

I narrow my eyes. 'You dislike me, don't you?'

He laughs once. 'I dislike a lot of things. The King's choices are only some of them.'

I tilt my head, seeing this gets to him. Too much has changed for his comfort. 'And you hate that he let us into his castle, accepted us despite the treaty, even if I am a human, and Darius a shifter.'

His jaw twitches. 'Ever since your arrival, my opinions on this kingdom no longer matter. Dusan focuses more on you than his duties to Terranos. And that . . . dragon shifter . . .' He shakes his head, sucking in air through his teeth. Glancing at me, he spits out a hateful chuckle. 'You want to know what he did after the meeting in the throne room? He choked me because I'd mentioned how he should keep you in line.'

My arms drop to my sides. Darius . . . defending me like always, through the good and the bad. I grasp the coin again, running my thumb along it, and almost smile when Thallan scoffs.

'Dragons—'

'His name is Darius,' I seethe, interrupting him before he can think about an insult. 'Darius Halen, a shifter far more powerful than you could ever be.'

Thallan's eyes widen with interest. He stares at me for a few uncomfortable seconds and then bursts into laughter. 'Of course,' he says. 'You're in love with him.'

I'm quiet, so very quiet.

Hearing someone say that. Even if it's Thallan, it . . . it sounds real.

My heart is in my throat, I'm trying to stay calm, but that word has thrown me off balance.

Thallan laughs once more and claps his hands. 'I already knew *he* was; he's made it far too obvious on many occasions, but you, *you* were hard to decipher.'

I lower my eyes, and I can feel my cheeks heat up.

'I must say I thought you were of no interest the moment I met you, but now—' he pauses, his footsteps sounding closer and closer until I glance up and see he is standing before me. 'I think you might be on a par with the beautiful princesses.'

My thoughts land on Faye, Arlayna and Meriel, but he closes the gap between us, pressing his face against my hair and inhaling.

'What are you doing?' My voice is firm, though I flinch at the touch of his filthy fingers stroking the side of my neck.

His arms have me caged in as he ignores me. 'You smell like her too.'

I'm pushing at his chest. 'Get away from me.'

I can feel his grin on my face, and I swallow my nausea. 'Why should I? That dragon of yours is nowhere near here to save you.'

'I don't need him to save me.'

'What can a measly mortal like you do?'

He's pushing up against me. I'm trying to shove him and squirm away. A shiver of revulsion goes down my spine as he kisses my neck. I close my eyes and breathe, then his body jerks, and a grunt slips from his lips as the bones in his finger crunch beneath my hands.

What can a measly mortal like you do?

Much more than you can imagine.

I lean forward and say into his ear, 'Your fingers are not the only thing I can break if you don't get away from me right now.' His pained groan grows louder when I let go of his broken hand. He stumbles back, his features hardening into a glare as he stares at his fingers.

I raise my chin. 'I wonder if the princesses will be thrilled to hear the King's trusted emissary tried to hurt and molest their guest.'

He laughs but stops to wince. 'You won't tell them.'

'Why won't I?'

'Because.' He's finding it hard to breathe. 'Then I will tell Dusan that his darling niece and one of the guards were kissing the other night.'

My defiant demeanour crumbles.

His eyes are wild flames of green as he smiles. 'Would be a pity if Aeron Hawthorne had to be executed for breaking his oath to the King.'

Sick, sick bastard.

'Sooner or later, the princesses will be set to marry someone worthy of Terranos. And a romance between a guard and Princess Arlayna would spark too much uproar. Think about it . . . mortal.'

I grind my teeth, anger creating a vortex in my chest. If I say anything, he will just turn it against me. I might have injured him, but I will not jeopardise Aeron. Arlayna would never forgive me.

Thallan's staring at me as I open the door. I level him one harsh look and walk out, eager to forget the horrid feel of his hands on me.

CHAPTER FORTY

Under a dove-grey sky, I watch how guards patrol the fields from the garden terrace. Since Golrai's death the other week, the King requested us to wait longer before completing the last task in Thalore. The princesses' safety is his priority, and if Arlayna had not fought to still accompany us, she would not be coming.

Things have been quite strange lately. With Darius busy helping the King's warriors and Thallan's threat to expose Arlayna and Aeron hanging over me, I've lost all sparks of life in me.

It's as if no matter everything Darius and I have gone through, the universe does not want us to be together.

We had no time to discuss the night he'd come to my door. And when things finally calmed down, he told me he would come by my chambers and that I should wait for him.

I did. I waited for hours, but then fell asleep after an eventful day where Meriel and Faye took me horseback riding through their lands. For once, I fell asleep, and I wish I hadn't.

I woke up that morning to blankets covering me and a strawberry pie beside my bed. When I had asked where Darius was, Tibith told me the King needed him.

For his powers.

Always his powers.

Merati magic to seek out a perpetrator.

'Nara, dear, you've not touched your tea.'

I blink, darting my head to Meriel seated in front of me. She'd invited me for breakfast on the terrace this morning alongside Faye and Arlayna. Tibith had joined us, sitting beside me with cushions beneath him so that he reached the table's height.

Shaking my head, I take a long sip. It's cold, long forgotten, but I smile anyway. 'Apologies, I find my mind seems to wander off lately.'

She laughs in delight. 'Don't we all?' Her expression seems to change to sympathy as she sighs. 'With a maid's death and your final task to come, you must be feeling anxious.'

You have no idea.

'Not as stressful as Arlayna's duties to the kingdom,' Faye remarks, spinning a jade circlet around her wrist as she looks at Arlayna. 'I heard Uncle is making you visit the Mordinthrens.'

The name probes my curiosity. 'Mordinthrens?'

Arlayna nods. 'Edwyrd's family from Valdern. They are quite close to our cousins who also reside there. It's why our uncle is so fond of Edwyrd, and since the Mordinthrens are High Elves of great social standing—'

'Yes, I hear Tanyll Mordinthren plans to marry and is looking for a suitable wife.' Meriel's smile could not be more ecstatic. 'Did I ever tell you how he survived against a Rippling while travelling through the Ocean of Storms?'

I frown at the possibility of someone surviving against a savage whirlpool known as the Rippling. Iker had always tried to scare me by saying he would take me all the way to the Ocean of Storms and wait until a Rippling appeared so he could push me into it. I had always replied that I would take him down with me.

'Several times, Mother,' Arlayna says grimly, downing the last bit of her tea in a very unroyal manner.

I'd grimace at the awkwardness between us if Tibith wasn't stuffing his face with bread and jam.

Faye straightens from her chair and clears her throat, turning to me. 'I heard you encountered a Galgr while completing your previous task.'

I cast a sideward glance at Arlayna, and her shoulders seem to relax after the quick conversation shift. 'I did,' I say, doing terribly at hiding the change in my body as I think about what I learned about Darius.

That we'd met before.

That he'd loved me since we were children.

And that the coin I carry around my neck is the same one I gave him all those years ago.

'We thought with Golrai's death, there might have been something odd involving them.' Meriel keeps her eyes trained on me as she motions for one of the servants to take away Arlayna's cup. 'Though Darius feels that might not be the case, considering Galgrs tend to hunt their prey from lakes and stepping on land would come at a great cost for them, especially when we are far from their watery homes. They perish from being exposed to sunlight.'

'What about a Shadow Calp, Mother?' Faye asks.

'Golrai dying from an attack of a Shadow Calp would seem highly unlikely given that they feed off your soul, not your blood. Golrai's wounds suggest she was murdered by some other creature, maybe even an Elf.' Meriel looks at me, her lip curling at the side. 'I must say, though, that Darius does not seem to trust easily. I mean, he certainly never follows the advice from the sentinel. Instead, he does whatever he wants.'

She's amused and curious, but I can no longer hide certain feelings. Hence, I look away, staring at the entrance's glass doors, and say, 'He is accustomed to doing his own thing.'

Meriel doesn't seem to accept this, she narrows her eyes and hums. 'Except he loves to work with you.'

'That is because Darry and Miss Nara also like to sleep naked together, Miss Meriel!' Tibith says through a mouthful of bread, and I go bright red.

Faye is laughing, looking my way as Tibith cocks his head to the side. An expression of pure innocence.

'Could you tell me more about the Galgrs?' I ask, not glancing at any of the four in particular, wanting to change subjects. 'What happens if they are on land during the daytime?'

Meriel laughs at my obvious embarrassment. 'Certainly,' she says. 'Galgrs are creatures that thrive in deep waters and disintegrate if the slightest ray of the sun catches them due to their skin sensitivity.' She stirs her tea, deep in thought. 'They've resided in Terranos for centuries, ever since our Elf ancestors existed. Still, as you already know, they're dangerous beings since they tend to draw in victims using core memories or their deepest secrets before devouring them. A terrible way to go, if you ask me.'

Yes, I'd gathered that after they lured me the first time during our journey through the Screaming Forests.

'Although some know more than just secrets,' Arlayna adds. 'They are similar to Seers, if you can put it that way. They have excellent knowledge of life, drawing their powers from the moon's reflection upon the water.'

'Can you get answers from them?' I ask.

'Of course you can.' Faye chuckles. 'If you can trap one without perishing.' She smirks, throwing a blueberry in the air before catching it in her mouth. 'I'd advise visiting a clairvoyant if you want answers, though they are hard to find nowadays in Terranos.'

'Or a witch.'

I glance at Arlayna, whose face is blank.

She continues, 'I was told that some are known to have visions.'

Faye scoffs. 'Those are just superstitions, Arlayna.'

Arlayna glares in her direction, but I'm instantly wondering about Freya and if she is okay.

Faye and Meriel carry on speaking while I take no notice of them.

Is Freya finding it easy tackling her new life as a witch? Is Leira teaching her? I know so little. The letters I'd received from my brothers weeks ago only mentioned certain things about them. I know my brothers, and I wouldn't be surprised if they left things out because they didn't want to worry me.

I blow out a breath, pressing a hand to my chest as I look towards the garden, the maze, the fields. I know Arlayna is staring at me, her grey eyes studying me as I remain lost in my own thoughts.

Glancing down at my palm, I remind myself how I'd controlled the bats. Tamed even the rümens during the trial with the other Venators and conjured hundreds of frogs when Adriel and Oran attacked me.

I have no explanation for how these things have happened.

But I deserve answers, and I deserve to no longer be in the dark about my own self.

I'm opening the door and sheathing my blade as Arlayna walks past me into the room.

She faces the bed; her dress shows off her bare back before she huffs and spins around. 'You're terrible at hiding your emotions.'

'What?' I say, even though I know exactly what she is talking about.

Funny, months ago, one would have said I was impeccable at hiding emotions. Lorcan used to think it, as did my brothers.

'You thought I wouldn't catch on to your sudden interest in Galgrs, didn't you?'

No, I knew she would. Her eyes gave that away.

I gaze at my boots, clicking the heels together.

Arlayna sighs, her voice softening the minute she walks over to me. 'So, what is your plan? Search through every lake or pond, risk your life to relive distant memories, or receive answers?'

My head snaps up. I already know what lake. I just . . . 'I have questions.' I draw my bottom lip between my teeth. 'Theories that, yes, may sound stupid initially, but—'

'When do you plan to leave?'

I blink back at her, startled by her nonchalance. 'Tonight.'

'Then I will meet you here and bring some equipment to help you trap one.' She strolls to the door. I think I'm still blinking in surprise.

I'm turning on my feet, my mouth half open, when the other door to my bathing chamber creaks open, and Faye casually emerges.

'You may count me in, too,' she says, and Arlayna and I glance at one another with a frown.

I point towards the bathroom, looking at a smiling Faye. 'How long have you been in there?'

'A while. I was hiding from my darling mother. She's intent on giving me a headache with piano lessons.' She waves a mocking hand around. 'I thought this room would be the perfect hiding spot.'

That does not make the situation any better.

'You're not coming.' Arlayna sounds determined.

Faye makes a face, slapping a hand to her chest in offence. 'Excuse me, but I'm not allowed to travel with you to Thalore. At least let me enjoy the possibility of trapping a Galgr or encountering a Shadow Calp. Uncle says they seem to be getting restless, casting shadows along the mainland.'

'You do realise how dangerous they both are if—'

I wave my arms in the air to catch their attention. 'I would prefer it if neither of you came, considering there was a death not long ago within the castle walls.'

Faye chokes out a laugh. 'Last Yulemas, trolls tried attacking the guards to enter the castle. We aren't new to threats. Besides, out of all of us, Arlayna is the one in danger, and if anything happens to our uncle, she is the next in line to be queen—'

'Faye,' Arlayna scolds her though it comes out in a half whisper like she's suddenly so exposed, scared, miserable.

I feel terrible, which is the worst feeling because no one ever wants to be pitied.

She turns her head my way. 'Tonight,' she reinforces before grabbing Faye's wrist and yanking her out of my chambers, leaving me no choice but to accept it – they are coming with me.

The night arrives fast. Arlayna and Faye meet me by my door, both clad in pine-coloured fighting attire. Arlayna holds up some nets and rope before swinging them over her shoulder. Faye takes us along the castle corridors, careful to avoid any guards. It seems as if she knows when and where they will be. Once outside, she leads me past an archway covered with ivy leaves. It takes minutes for us to walk under bridges and through different sectors of the castle until we reach the borders.

A stone wall greets us as we stop metres away from it. I glance at Arlayna and then watch her pull a thick looping vine that's hanging above us.

'Princess.'

The three of us freeze.

'Shit,' Arlayna mutters under her breath.

There is something particularly shocking about witnessing a princess as she swears.

She turns slowly, followed by us, as we see Aeron standing there, eyebrows raised, hazel eyes focused on Arlayna and Arlayna only.

'Aeron,' she says indifferently, as if we weren't just attempting to escape the castle walls. 'Shouldn't you be focusing on the safety of the castle?'

'That was before I found two princesses and the King's guest trying to sneak out.' A curt glance my way, and then his eyes are back on Arlayna. 'Interesting weapons, princess. Trying to track Shadow Calps again?'

Arlayna forces out a single laugh, shoves the nets towards Faye without looking at her, and storms up to Aeron. 'I don't need to track Calps any more, when I have other more interesting matters to deal with.'

I hold back from smiling as the corner of Aeron's eyes crinkle in amusement. 'Get back inside, Your Highness. Both of you,' he adds, not looking Faye's way.

Faye groans. 'Hawthorne, you are ruining our fun.'

'Believe me, I am trying to save your lives. Do you realise the dangers you are putting them in?' he's addressing the last part to me, his jaw suddenly set.

'It's as dangerous here as it is out there,' I say, unwilling to take the blame for something I'd refused in the first place. 'There's already been a murder. Chances are they will be safer—'

'From those who want to use the princesses to get to the King?' He cuts me off. 'Or how about trolls who would love to wear them around their necks like trophies?'

I'm silent immediately.

I am putting them at risk for my own stupid adventurous desires and curiosity. I can see Aeron would do anything to ensure not only Faye's safety but also Arlayna's above all.

He crosses his arms over his broad, armoured chest, those golden strands of his blonde hair shining brighter under the stars.

'You, out of everyone, should know that I can take care of myself,' Arlayna steps up, and Aeron's frustrated gaze cuts to her. 'Or have you forgotten every sparring session we had as children?' His eyes soften at that, like the memory remains with him to this day. 'If you want to keep us safe, you will do as your princess says.'

Tension cuts through the cold air. Arlayna and Aeron stare at each other as if unaware that the rest of us are still standing here.

After a moment, he shakes his head and almost looks like he already regrets what he's about to say next. 'Fine, then I will come along.'

What?

'What—' Arlayna voices my thoughts out loud as Aeron sidesteps her to take a look at the wall.

He tugs on the vine and glances over his shoulder, mumbling, 'The back walls, really? At least be clever.'

Arlayna's mouth drops open before Aeron motions for us to accompany him to the stables.

CHAPTER FORTY-ONE

'No sign of trolls,' Faye says as we dismount our horses.

I rub my knuckles soothingly under my mare's snout. We are scouting for signs of life around the clearing. My eyes catch the well at the centre, and something flickers inside my chest. It makes my legs unstable.

'We didn't have time to cover our scent.' Aeron draws out his sword and tips his chin in my direction. 'Or hers, which is more likely to catch their attention.'

'Then I suggest we capture one straight away.' I head straight to the lake, knowing three pairs of eyes are on me. It's colder than the other night, a temperature switch signalling winter is coming.

I can never get used to it. Sometimes I used to wonder what snow looked like. Now I have a feeling that the longer I am away from Emberwell, the more likely I am to witness it.

Crouching, I wave my hand over the grass and exhale sharply as it tickles my palms. 'This shouldn't take very long.'

'Nara,' Arlayna says softly over my shoulder. 'These creatures are not easy. They get inside your head and might twist whatever you say.'

I stare at my distorted reflection in the ripples of the lake. What more can they do other than show me a memory I had long forgotten? 'I'll manage.'

Arlayna heaves a sigh, placing a hand on my shoulder. 'Nara—'

'Looks like the four of you could use some help.'

My head snaps, my heart stuttering at the teasing tone of the voice. I stand and turn. 'Darius.' My voice comes out startled, seeing him leaning against a tree. 'How—'

'You're not the only one who found out that Galgrs hold valuable information,' he says as he walks towards us. 'When I heard noises, I thought it might have been some trolls, but instead, I find you four.' He gives Aeron a nod. 'Aeron.'

Aeron nods in recognition.

I huff. 'What information do you possibly need?'

He stares at me for too long. I feel faint under his golden gaze. 'The same as you.'

I take a breath. All I can do is stare back at him, my eyes softening.

'Well!' Faye claps her hands, snapping our attention away from each other. 'This cryptic conversation definitely interests me, but how about we get on with trapping one?'

Right, yes, the Galgr. 'Are you sure you can help?' I ask Darius.

He rubs the pad of his thumb across his brow and chuckles. 'It's insulting that you think I won't, Goldie, after all this time.'

I'm about to roll my eyes at the smirk on his lips when he turns to everyone else and continues, 'Illusions don't work on them, I tried that before, but shadows do, and their own strength also seems to be their biggest weakness.'

'So, will Nara be the bait in this case?' asks Faye slowly, pointing towards me.

All heads turn to her.

'What? No offence, but I don't feel like getting soaked or eaten.'

'Then why did you come?' Arlayna hisses.

'Because this is better than sitting inside my chambers doing nothing.'

Arlayna rolls her eyes at her sister and glances my way. 'Nara, you do not have to—'

'I want to.' My decision sounds final. I already knew I would be the one going in there. 'Aeron, if you could be on the lookout.'

He nods even if he seems skeptical of everything. On our way here, he seemed anxious and I can imagine why.

I tell Faye the same, and like a young child, she pouts, trying to catch up with Aeron.

Arlayna gives me a pensive look, and drops the net in front of us and says, 'I will give you two a moment.'

How ironic that this is the only time Darius and I are finally alone.

Once Arlayna joins Aeron and Faye, I turn my focus to Darius, fiddling with the material of my tunic. 'Did you come to get answers about me?'

He nods, and I find myself wondering.

'Would you have told me?' I ask quietly after a moment.

He exhales in resignation, fitting his hands into his breeches pocket. He looks at the ground, then up at me again. 'There are certain things I still have yet to say to you, Goldie. For years I've kept so much to myself. I don't want to do that any more.' He looks at me so deeply. 'Especially to you.'

I'm overwhelmed.

I hadn't told him how I felt when he appeared at my door. That he'd made me cry. Not from hatred or anger but because of how wanted I felt. I had blamed him when I found out he'd taken that memory away from me, yet I might have done the same in his position.

He was so young and scared of Rayth, and now he is here, wanting to help me figure out what is happening to me. No matter the hardships, he has never left my side.

I glance down, tucking my bottom lip between my teeth to stop it from quivering. 'Do you think there is something wrong with me?'

I sense him.

I'm afraid to look.

'Nothing could ever be wrong with you,' he whispers, and my eyes shoot up to him. 'You're indescribable, ethereal, and morally perfect in every way. Whatever it may be, you should not feel that it is a bad thing. You're too strong to think so little of yourself.'

I shake my head regardless of my racing heart. 'I'm not the same as I used to be, before joining the Venators.'

He nods slowly, digesting my words. 'You're right,' he says. 'You're not.'

Everything goes quiet, yet I'm not sure what is beating the loudest, my heart or his.

'You're better.' He takes another step, his hands cupping the sides of my face. 'You're finally you, which makes you strong.'

My stomach stirs with emotions I never thought I would have. I want to say so many things, but I don't know where to start because none have ever made much sense.

Now they make all the sense in the world.

'Darius . . .' I've lost my voice. 'I—'

Someone clears their throat.

We both turn our heads to the left, where Faye has her hands on her hips and is tapping her foot impatiently.

She arches a brow. 'As romantic as this is . . .' A pointed stare between us. 'We don't have all night.'

Darius laughs, but I still don't have the strength.

She is right. We do not have all night.

Although I wish we did.

I pull Darius's hands away from my face and look up through my lashes.

'You will go in first,' he says. 'It shouldn't take long for them to attack. I will go in not long after, alright?'

I'm nodding, checking my blade is still inside its sheath. He looks hesitant to let me go, but I don't give in to his worries and amble to the edge of the lake.

I clench my fists in and out. I look once over my shoulder. Darius's eyes are fixed on me as Arlayna moves towards us, and then I'm diving into the waters.

Cool, wet pressure batters against my skin as I sink further. My eyes are closed, my pulse steady as I let the weight of the water lift my arms. One minute passes, and I can feel my chest tightening at the lack of air until I hear that same name whispered.

'*Solaris.*'

I keep my focus on the mission.

'*Solaris.*'

I can tell the Galgrs are getting closer, trying to entice me to open my mind to them.

'Join us,' one whispers; it feels as if they have caught up to me.

I'm reaching for my blade, my closed eyes tightening as I try not to let past memories flash inside my head.

A skeletal finger caresses my shoulder, and I work up the strength – the strength Darius knows that I have – and unsheathe the dagger, jamming it into the side of the Galgr's arm as I open my eyes.

I'm staring directly at the Galgr's hollow sockets as the creature screeches in pain. Others surrounding me dart away, swimming to whatever depths of the lake they came from. I swing my arms back and forth, trying to maintain distance.

Black blood tints the water as it leeches out from the Galgr's arm. She clutches on to it, and then a net comes over her. She's hissing, her inky hair flowing around her before I notice Darius holding the net and swimming upwards. I come up after him, gasping as I swim to the edge. Arlayna grabs my hand, pulling me onto the grass. I'm still trying to regain my breath when I realise Darius is dragging a thrashing Galgr away from the lake. He deposits her somewhere close to the well and ties the bit of rope onto the wooden rod holding the well's roof.

He pants, running his hand through his hair, and looks at me. His eyes practically ask me if I'm okay, and I nod.

The Galgr is still flailing around in the net, snarling at us like a wild animal. She bares her teeth and looks like she is about to chew through the rope when Darius casts a shadow flame from his palm.

'I wouldn't do that if I was you,' he says, and the Galgr stops, raising her head to sniff us out.

I take a step forward when Arlayna clutches my arm. 'Careful. They can still manipulate your mind even on land.'

'Why think so lowly of me, Your Highness?' The voice comes from the Galgr. It sounds old and echoing, almost like many are speaking at once.

Our heads slowly turn to her. Between the net slits, I can see her sharp-toothed grin.

'Are you so afraid that I will see your thoughts?'

Arlayna tenses, not having let go of my arm. 'No.'

The Galgr looks in Aeron and Faye's direction as if she can see them – as if she is not eyeless. 'What about your love?'

Arlayna's grip on my arm tightens. She's breathing too fast, too hard now. 'He is not my—'

'No, he is not . . . and he won't be your last.'

'What are you talking about?'

The Galgr clicks her tongue, shaking her head. 'Such heartbreak, such betrayal set to come for you, Princess Arlayna. Your journey will not be easy; neither will it be for your sister.'

I lower my voice as Arlayna stares at her as if she's torn between asking more or doing something drastic. 'She is just trying to get to you, you know that.'

She finally looks at me, her eyes glossy and her lips tight with struggle.

'Go with Aeron and Faye,' I say. 'We will let you know once we're finished.'

She doesn't give me a response as she numbly lets go and walks away.

'Naralía Brielle Ambrose.' My name coming out of the Galgr's mouth sounds as if it's vibrating throughout the entire clearing. She inhales, and her smile almost looks pleasurable. 'I can sense your power from deep within you wanting to break out.'

As if I am back in the lake, my oxygen is cut. 'What –' An exhale. '– Power?'

She pays me no heed. 'Darius.' She grins, lifting her head. Her body jerks for seconds as if she is receiving every little bit of knowledge though she is far away from him. When she stops, she cocks her head to the side. 'You gave the Rivernorth pendant to a previous trapper. Why?'

I glance at Darius, confused. Why is the Galgr deliberately asking that when she can find it out herself?

He's not looking at me; his jaw is tight as if his patience is slowly slipping away. 'You know why.'

'Yes,' she says, hollow eyes slicing across to me. 'But *she* does not.'

She is getting in our heads; she is getting in our— 'What is she talking about?' I'm looking back and forth between them, my head spinning profusely.

'His biggest secret,' the Galgr whispers in a taunt. 'Isn't that right, Darius?'

He laughs once. It sounds cold, almost tortured. 'You're a deadly thing.'

The Galgr flashes her sharp teeth and bows her head. 'As are you, Your Majesty.'

Your Majesty?

I shake my head one too many times.

'What . . . ?' My heart is pounding. I can barely finish what I want to ask him.

He takes my hand, seeing the distress on my features. He looks nervous. I've not seen that look on him the whole time I've known him. It's new, it's . . . worrying. 'Nara, I wanted—'

'He is more than just royalty, though,' the Galgr interrupts him, her voice taking on a disdainful edge as I turn my head to look at her.

'He is a Rivernorth.'

The world spins.

Trees, stars and the land blend into one.

I hear the Galgr laugh. 'Darius Rivernorth, you are nephew to Aurum Rivernorth, and the rightful king of Emberwell.'

CHAPTER FORTY-TWO

'You're a Rivernorth,' I repeat in complete disbelief, turning to face Darius.

Aurum Rivernorth's nephew.

He has the Rivernorth bloodline in him.

He is the rightful heir to Emberwell.

'No one knows,' Darius says quietly. 'No one *can* know.'

I'm in complete shock, holding his hand – a Rivernorth's hand. And the pendant, it belonged to him. He wasn't trying to steal it because he was a thief. He was retrieving what was rightfully his.

'You're a king,' I whisper as if saying it out loud to him will trigger me out of this perplexing state.

'Though Sarilyn Orcharian, sorceress and tormentor of dragons, rules your kingdom,' the Galgr adds further to the building fire. 'You do not believe you deserve the title of a king. Am I right to think that?'

Hurt cracks through my chest as Darius's gaze cuts to her. His jaw works back and forth, trying to contain his anger.

The Galgr's grin widens until I can see the backs of her fanged teeth. 'However, you do believe she is your queen.' Her head travels my way. 'Our Solaris.'

Solaris.

I yank my hand away from Darius's, stepping far too close to the Galgr. Darius pulls me back by my waist, but I still have to ask. I still have questions I need to be answered. 'You said you could feel my powers from within. What did you mean by that? What do you mean by *our* Solaris.'

An eerie glow shines upon her greyish skin. It's as if her hollowed eyes are staring straight through me. 'Millennia ago,' she says. 'When the deities of Solaris and Crello created this world, they couldn't stay in it forever. The skies needed them for the world to survive and knew they had to eventually sacrifice something.'

'What did they sacrifice?' Darius asks, not even attempting to soften the harshness in his voice.

The Galgr looks up. Silk hair caresses the ground as she tilts her head and whispers, 'Their lives.'

Her answer sends a chill up my spine.

'They promised each other the skies, but not without promising that their love would one day be reincarnated,' she says. 'Eventually, the Isle of Elements will cease to exist. Its power is slowly fading unless two people, chosen by the deities, can help restore it.' My whole body tenses, knowing what will be said as she looks my way. 'Solaris. Ruler of life and land alike.' Her eyes then flicker to Darius. 'And Crello, ruler of the tides and night.'

It's as if someone has dumped a bucket of freezing water over my head. The Galgr has now revealed something I could have never expected. Was this the answer I was searching for?

I press my full weight against Darius and am thankful he is here to support me. I turn my head and look up at his eyes.

Reincarnates.

Solaris and Crello.

'Why?' My throat feels like I'm swallowing a thousand thorns. 'Why us, why—'

'Two souls that are night and day, different yet the same.' The Galgr hums as my gaze darts to her. 'A shifter that holds all three powers of a dragon, and a mortal who grew to hate his kind.'

I shake my head, confident that I'm still at my cottage, having the craziest dream from which I'll awaken and tell Illias. 'But how are we— how am I supposed to restore the Isle of Element's powers when I hardly know anything about who I am? All I can do is connect with creatures I—'

'Your connection to Solaris was dormant until it all aligned when that marble led you to your Crello.'

'What?' There is frustration in my voice when I pause and remember Leira's vision in the backroom of that tavern.

The sun blooms again, for she has found her moon . . .

That day I met Darius, my marble landed by him. It was not a matter of coincidence, but fate. That is all it has ever been. When we bumped into each other and dropped our carvings, then when we saw one another years later in that jeweller's shop.

Every grand moment of ours flashes in and out of my mind.

One of their greatest wishes was to unite and dance among the stars, he said to me the same night he was captured.

For no love greater shared than the moon and the sun, I'd replied, realising now deep down that in that moment something had changed.

'Now,' the Galgr's voice doesn't quite reach my ears. 'You must awaken the rest of the powers you have deep within you.'

My head snaps up.

I have so much more to ask her, but I'm quickly interrupted by Arlayna, Aeron and Faye dashing over to us.

'We need to go,' Arlayna says, her eyes scanning the rustling trees, and I hear the distant grumbling sounds of trolls.

'Seems like we are out of time.' The Galgr grins, humoured by the distress lingering in the air.

I step out of Darius's grip. 'How do I awaken the rest of my powers?'

She says nothing.

'Tell me!'

'Nara,' Arlayna urges, but I need to know.

My eyes are focused on the Galgr. Faye has already mounted her horse, with Aeron grabbing Arlayna by the elbows and dragging her away.

'Soon,' the Galgr finally says. 'When certain choices are made.'

The cryptic words do nothing to help my manic mind.

'Go,' she says. 'I know how to free myself.'

I shake my head. We're not done. *I'm* not done.

'Goldie,' Darius whispers and I take my eyes off the creature to look at him. He's holding out his hand, the grunting coughs of trolls drawing closer.

He knows we can't stay.

I place my hand in his and nod, rushing to where my mare is stationed. She's braying, spooked, as she rises on her hind legs.

I'm lifting my palms in the air, trying to hush her. I touch her neck, and immediately she calms down. Darius mounts her and pulls me up with him. He could as well shift and flee the scene, he could have asked me to go with him, but he knows I would never leave the horse here. He knows I'd rather stay and fight the trolls off if it meant protecting an animal.

The Galgr is staring in our direction, still not having freed herself. I look at her soulless face as I wrap my arms around Darius's abdomen, and he gets us out of there.

Chapter Forty-Three

I'm looking down at the ground as Darius and I pad back to our chambers. We've not uttered a word since leaving the Galgr. Numbness has taken over, and neither of us knows what to say or how to start.

I stare at my palms.

Solaris, ruler of life and land alike.

I look up at Darius.

And Crello, ruler of the tides and night.

So much of it is indescribable.

We reach my door, and I glance at its wood-panelled rose decorations. I can't decide if I should say goodnight or if I should think everything through first. It all still feels like a dream.

'The carving.' Darius's voice seeps into my skin, soft like silk.

I suck in a sharp breath; I'd thought he was in no mood to speak with me. He must have a million thoughts racing through his mind too.

'It was my mother's,' he says. 'The initial stood for Rivernorth.'

I'm stone, standing still without facing him.

The letter R that was engraved into that carving. Lorcan had told me it stood for Rayth, yet it had been a lie. So much of what he said had been lies. My eyes drift to the floor before turning to Darius. Slowly, I look up at him, and my heart doubles in size. 'Did she . . . carve it?'

'Yes.' He smiles wistfully. 'She loved carving, anything from toys to simple things such as a spoon out of wood.'

A small, sad laugh releases from my throat. I shake my head, biting my bottom lip. I want to cry out of frustration for not ever seeing this, for not thinking even after Lorcan had lied to me so much that perhaps there was more he hadn't told me.

'The crescent, though.' Darius's smile falls. 'She carved it for me because I reminded her of the night sky, and it is the last thing she gave me before her death. Then . . . when you and I had bumped into each other that day, I had been running from nearby Venators. I didn't have time to check what I was doing, and when I realised I had the sun – *your* sun – it was too late to go back.'

'How did it come to be in Lorcan's possession?'

He pauses, looks aside, and then runs his hand along his jaw. 'The day of the Emberwell attack. He must have grabbed it as he wrestled with me on the ground. I realised it wasn't there when I got back home and felt in my pocket.'

I take a step closer. I don't know how to comfort Darius. I feel that this is something one cannot do without breaking him further. Once, I'd believed Darius was the one to attack Lorcan, but the General, the Queen and Lorcan himself spun different lies and fed them to me.

My gaze drops to Darius's arm as I place my hand over it, allowing him to be at ease with my touch. My other hand falters as I reach his chest and press my palm against it. Upon contact, a memory of the night at the Noctura ball resurfaces. 'Your tattoo markings,' I whisper, staring at his hands. 'They were the Rivernorth's symbol, weren't they?'

Three rivers within a compass pointing north.

That is what the shifter drew on the ground down at the dungeons.

Darius is quiet. He nods, fixing his gaze on the floor.

I tilt my head to try and catch his eye. 'Why did you give the pendant to Ivarron when you'd risked so much just to get it back the first time?'

'Because I knew how much getting here meant to you.'

My heart cracks. 'But it was your mother's.'

He looks away. 'It'd already been tainted by Sarilyn.'

I'm struck with silence. I have to force myself to breathe. He is being too harsh with himself, reminding me so much of myself.

'I saw her that day,' he says, detached. 'When Erion killed my mother, Sarilyn was there. I watched from the place my mother had hidden me. Sarilyn had told her that she'd always favoured her compared to the rest of my mother's siblings, but it was such a pity she had to end her life just so there was no trace of the Rivernorth bloodline . . . Aurum, Aurelia, Eleodora, Auryn, Cressida and Idalia. The six golden children.'

His family . . . all gone.

'After my grandparents passed the crown down to my uncle, my mother did not agree with everything he did for the kingdom. She told me what I could understand at the time, but it was never enough. I spent five years with her, hiding from our enemies, unable to see what the sun even looked like, and then—' He finally looks at me, eyes glossed over in the moonlight shining in through the windows along the corridor. 'I had to stay silent as I watched my mother die right before my eyes.'

It's as if someone is splitting my heart into pieces. I can hear the fragments of them break just as Darius's voice does.

'Darius—'

'I don't want pity, Nara; I've survived all these years without it.'

I back away from him and frown. 'I don't pity you. In fact, I wish to shout at you.'

He lifts a brow, and a glimmer of humour returns to his face.

I'm huffing, shaking my head at him as I cross my arms over my chest. 'And if anything, I want to be mad at you,' I whisper, vulnerability in my voice. 'But I can't be. I understand why you did the things you did, but still, I cannot deny that it didn't hurt, Darius . . . you've made it known that you are here for me through my weaknesses, my moments of bliss or anger. You know parts of me that no one else has ever witnessed. Not even my brothers.'

He stares at me, and a thousand emotions flicker through his eyes. Sadness, relief, maybe hope.

I move towards him again and reach out for his hand. His eyes are trained on every movement as I pluck three of his fingers up and rest them against his heart. 'You have a purpose, Darius.' I stare into his eyes. 'You are the ruler of tides, the ruler of the night.'

And I am the ruler of land and life . . .

He's not saying anything despite my beseeching eyes wanting him to.

'You can still be king,' I say.

He shakes his head. 'It's a risk against Sarilyn—'

'And a risk for those who believe Aurum can be brought back, I know.' I sigh, pressing myself even closer to him. 'But you are the rightful heir.'

He scoffs, a self-mocking smirk etching his lips. 'I am a wanted criminal in Emberwell, Goldie.'

'I thought you loved being wanted?'

That gets a chuckle out of him, and I smile because I'd never realised how Darius smiling or laughing could be my favourite thing to witness. I'd taken it for granted before.

He lowers his hand, clutching mine in his. He rubs my knuckles with the pad of his thumb, and a pensive murmur hits my ears. 'She was right, you know.'

I tilt my head as his gaze shoots up.

'The Galgr. When she said I believe you to be my queen.'

My breath catches.

'I always have since the moment we met again.' He closes the distance between us. His gaze is heavy as he looks down at me. It's so deep, so meaningful. 'You have always been my queen . . . my Goldie.'

A surge of painful desire thrums between us as he whispers those words.

My Goldie.

I make a noise deep in my throat. It comes out as a helpless whimper, and then with one look, his hands are on my face, his lips on mine, and he's pushing me against the door with enough force to break a dam. I'm fiddling with the doorknob, prying my door open. He kicks the door shut, and my hands travel everywhere, on his neck, chest and abdomen. I can feel the fine lines of muscle tensing at the run of my fingers as I try to yank his shirt off.

Our lips press together with a sensual urge that cracks against my back like a whip. He's not as tender as at other times. This feels primal. This feels like we've gone so long without breathing that we are each other's oxygen.

We're fumbling to get our clothes off, and once my tunic is on the floor, our lips meet fervently. He twists us around, backing me up against the wall, careful not to knock over any candles. My breasts are flush against his chest. It's chaotic, just as we have always been with one another.

'I have to ask you something,' I gasp, pulling back. My eyes are closed, and my lips long to be on his again.

He chuckles. 'Really, Goldie? Now?'

'Yes.' I open my eyes, breathing raggedly. It's hard to even form the following few words. 'I know what would have been my fifth question,' I say, and he cocks his head to the side at this thought. 'I would have asked if you truly do love me.'

He looks at me as if he cannot believe I'd think otherwise.

A sensual grin carves his lips. He lifts my legs up and wraps them around his waist, making me gasp before he says, 'With a passion.' And kisses me.

My lips smile against his.

That's right, because you hate me, don't you?

With a passion.

Months later, those words we'd exchanged on the night of the Noctura ball mean nothing to what we feel now.

Darius takes me from the wall onto my bed. He lays me down, and my hips lift as his fingers dig into the waistline of my leggings. Carefully, he draws them towards my ankles. Our eyes meet while he does this, and my whole body goes up in flames.

He presses soft kisses against my inner leg, trailing them up my thigh. I drop my head back, sighing with pleasure at the contact.

I want to tease him back, but it's hard enough as each of his kisses reaches my core, and I bite my lip to stop a moan. He stops above me and kisses the column of my throat. I grip his hair and breathe, 'I want you to take me from behind.'

Darius stills. 'Nara—'

'You said next time you would not be so gentle.' My words come out in a sensuous breath. 'So don't be.'

A tortured groan eases out of his lips as he drops his head beside mine. His arms bracket me, and the rhythm of our hearts beat together on cue.

Skin to skin.

Sweat and arousal.

'I'll need you on your knees then, Goldie,' he murmurs provocatively into my ear, and I make a startling noise as he flips me around.

The anticipation hangs over the air as I heave out long breaths. His hands curl around my hips, and my veins pulse with excitement and longing.

He leans over me. I can feel his thickness behind me and warmth pools between my legs. 'Hands against the headboard.'

I do as he commands. He takes his time tracing his fingers up my thigh, and my head hangs between my shoulders.

'Darius,' I plead, my legs trembling.

'Darius, what?'

I can picture the teasing smile on his lips. He thrusts me further up against him, and I gasp, bordering on a moan.

'Inside,' I manage to blurt out. 'I want you inside of me.' I don't care about the desperation. I know he wants the same thing. I can feel it in the tenseness of his hands, his arousal hardening against me. It doesn't take a second before he slams into me, and I cry out in pleasure. One hand tangles in my hair, pulling my head back, and the other rests on my hip, guiding me with each thrust.

Fast, wild and rough.

He doesn't hold back.

He is not gentle, and I never thought how much I would love it.

I moan. He moans.

He grunts. I cry out in pleasure.

The sounds linger through the room for minutes as my walls clench around him. I'm whimpering, teetering on the edge of release. He pulls me upward so my back is against his front. I tip my head up, closing my eyes as his hand splays across my neck. My hair is sticking to my skin, sweat drips around me, and I feel like I am crashing.

His breaths are jagged on my skin; he's groaning, saying my name.

And when he whispers, 'Come for me, Goldie,' I become undone. I'm consumed whole by him, quivering as his body smashes into me. I'm bursting with euphoria, never wanting to come down from this.

He is still inside me; his thrusts slow into a steady rhythm, and I grind against him as I turn my head to my left and look at him. Dark inky hair sticks to his forehead as I wrap an arm around his neck.

We kiss, panting with each second, just as his muscles go taut. He jerks harder, and we ride out his orgasm together.

When he smiles at me, I realise right here, right now, that I am just as in love with Darius as he is with me.

CHAPTER FORTY-FOUR

S team billows out from the vast golden tub in my bath chamber. I watch Darius swirl his finger along the water, the tip of it igniting in bright light as he keeps the bath warm.

I roll my eyes and grin as I tip my head against his chest and look up at him. Sunlight spills from the obscured windows to his left, shining on the right side of his face. 'Must you always show off?'

His hand is draped across my middle. Humour laces his voice. 'Does it impress you?'

I shoot him a superior smile. 'Nothing does.'

'You've come to be quite the liar.'

'And you just won't ever keep your mouth shut.'

He hums sensually, smiling with contentment as I sit up and turn. 'If you like, I will keep my mouth shut and open it only when you find your designated seat, Goldie.'

'How tempting.' I grin, throwing my arms around his neck. I am so small compared to his muscular physique in this bathtub. As I position myself atop him, he releases a pleasured groan. His hands brace upon my waist, he has a perfect view of my breasts. 'Although I think I'm lost, care to help me find my seat?'

He laughs, and our noses touch. 'I would say you are quite close to finding it.' His lips skim mine as he whispers, 'But I can always guide you, of course.' He gives me a kiss, another on the corner of my lips and one on the side of my neck. I close my eyes, murmuring softly as I revel in every moment with him. His bottom lip skims along my skin, near my ear, then to my collarbone. Soft, wet and satisfying.

Knock.

We freeze.

'Miss Nara!' *Knock, knock, knock.* 'Darry is not in his room! Do you think he was taken!'

I lean back, forcing down the laughter bubbling in my throat. Darius grins as I shout, 'Don't worry, Tibith, he is here with me.'

Tibith's gasp makes me chuckle. 'What are you doing there, Darry? Is your bath chamber too small?'

'Of course not, Tibith.' Darius's gaze holds mine, shameless and full of playful mischief. 'You know what Goldie is like. She just needs assistance with everything.'

I'm gaping, smacking his chest.

'Wait for me in the King's dining hall,' he says, half laughing. 'I'll be there shortly.'

Tibith squeaks excitable words we can hardly understand before hearing his footsteps pad away.

I snort a laugh. It makes Darius smile so wide, and my pulse flutters. I can feel it all the way in my stomach.

His hand emerges from the water as he pushes back a strand of damp hair behind my ear. I catch sight of his bare skin without a trace of his shifter's tattoo. My gaze lingers on that hand as he withdraws it and submerges beneath the water.

'Is there a way to get your markings back?' I ask, meeting his eyes.

Does he want his markings back? I wonder, or would it remind him too much of his mother and true heritage?

He looks towards the window, leans back, and rests an arm against the side. 'If I ever encounter twin witches, they could return them.'

I nod silently, making sense of it. 'Do you want them back?'

He takes a moment to think about it. 'No,' he says, and when I cock my head, imploring him for more, he adds, 'I am a Rivernorth, but I am also a Halen. I do not want something that tells me I am one thing when I would like to believe I am both.'

His answer feels refreshing to hear, despite the yank in my heart.

He will always see himself as Lorcan's brother.

I question whether they would find a way to make peace again if Lorcan were still alive. After Lorcan killed Erion, I want to imagine so. 'If Lorcan was too blinded by Erion's words, why did you not try to change that? Why not use your Merati powers to make him see?'

'It's not so simple, Goldie. Merati powers only work to a certain extent. Illusions, glamour . . . changing one's thoughts can truly destroy someone's mind in the long run.'

'Erion did it without any power.'

He gives me a pointed look. 'He was also a master manipulator. Besides, Lorcan was always easily misguided even when we lived together.'

I glance down and let the thoughtful silence ripple throughout the bath chamber. It's true. When Lorcan had his mind set on anything, it was hard to change. He chose to believe Rayth before Darius because Rayth was his father. Then he'd thought of Erion as another father figure he did not want to let go of no matter the price he had to pay, even if it meant being half rümen.

Darius is silent, likely thinking the topic has ended, as his hand slides around my waist and pulls me towards him.

My hands reach out to his chest, and I straddle him once again. Sighing, I say, 'When you said no one knows, does that include Gus?'

He nods, his brows furrowing as he looks off to the side of the tub like he is in some sort of whirlpool of thoughts. 'Although I think he has an inkling.'

'Why do you think that?'

'It's the way he would look at me. He knew I was powerful when I joined him, but he never treated me differently. There were times when I'd nearly revealed all, either on a drunken night or because he was the first person in a while that I could confide in.'

A smile of admiration plays on my face remembering the first time Darius had taken me to the shifter's den and I'd met Gus.

'Look, Goldie, the Rivernorth bloodline is a strange phenomenon.' Darius's voice holds a sense of exhausted frustration to it. 'And despite how I am perceived in Emberwell, if anyone found out I was related to Aurum Rivernorth, it could cause so many problems.' His eyes flicker to meet mine, and a sudden look of mischief shadows his face as if trying to hide other emotions that will bring him down. 'And it would simply do terrible things for my gallant reputation.'

I raise an eyebrow and push myself off him. 'You can be so terribly annoying.'

His deep chuckle resonates within the bathroom walls. 'And you can be terribly stubborn.'

I shake my head. 'You always tell me to say what is on my mind and not hide what I feel or am afraid of, yet you do the same. Why?'

Amusement flickers away from him like a dying candle flame, and he sighs. 'You have bottled everything up for years. You became desensitized to so many things. Why must I bring you down with me after everything you have already gone through?'

'That is my cross to bear, do you not think?'

He stares at me.

'Would you not do the same?'

'In a heartbeat,' he says softly.

I inhale a steady breath, my smile hardly there though my heart squeezes at how much love there is in his eyes. The same I feel for him.

Is this why we were chosen?

Did Solaris and Crello foresee this moment?

Now, most things make sense. The talk of reincarnation, the Neoma tree. My ability to heal only Darius when he had the Neoma blood in his system.

'What is it?' Darius asks, and I hadn't realised I'd been frowning.

'The Galgr,' I say. 'Everything she said . . . I can't shake it off.' Nor can I forget the idea that I have a bond with creatures and animals. *Intriguing.* That is what Lorcan thought of me . . . what the *beast* in him thought. 'Do you believe our purpose is to restore the powers keeping our world alive?'

Darius looks pensive. 'I'm not sure. But if we were chosen, that must count for a reason.'

'I am mortal, though, Darius.' I feel useless, and I wish I did not. I have the answers I sought, yet I do not know what to do with them. And the reality is Darius will live longer than I ever will.

I don't even notice he has moved closer to me until damp fingers lift my chin.

The way he looks at me is so soft and heart-wrenching. 'There will be another way.'

I stare at him, and pain cinches my heart. 'What if there isn't?' I whisper. He's looking at me like the idea of that is something he cannot bear. 'I am not a dragon, Darius. I am not a phoenix nor an Elf. I am a chosen mortal who does not know how to awaken the entirety of her powers.'

His jaw twitches. 'I refuse to watch you grow old, and I refuse to watch you die.'

'One day, I will have to.' I press a palm against the side of his face. 'And for the years I will live, I want to live them with you.'

He hates the idea, and he always will.

He's shaking his head.

I decide I can no longer bury the words I want to share with him. 'I love you.' I say what I have never uttered to any man. It is relief and anguish at once.

When it hurts.

It would only hurt if I no longer had him with me. It is a thought I cannot bear.

He closes his eyes; his forehead touches mine as he produces a heartbreaking sound from his lips. It's all he has ever wanted to hear from me. 'Say it again.'

'I love you, Darius Halen Rivernorth,' I whisper. 'Dragon shifter and all.'

His lips capture mine, and my beat pulses as his hands dive into my hair. Lust explodes between each movement of our lips and tongues gliding together.

It is a kiss that emphasises the truth behind my confession.

He is my first love, and he will be my last. And I make sure he knows that as I keep my eyes on him, lifting myself up slightly before slowly settling against his hard erection.

We then spend the next minutes making love inside the tub, safe from the storm brewing in the world outside.

CHAPTER FORTY-FIVE

I'm the last to arrive for breakfast. Everyone is already seated and eating away when I join them. As I settle on one of the cushioned chairs, Darius and I share a secret smile. Tibith is by his shoulder, snuggled close to him, while Darius tears off pieces of his bread and passes them to Tibith.

I don't think anyone suspects much about last night. Faye hums as one of the servants pours her tea, and Arlayna simply stares my way. Like always, she's more observant than others.

Aias then comes and sits beside me. He nudges my shoulder softly, and I smile up at him. He is the reason I'd stayed behind. After bathing with Darius and getting dressed, Aias stopped me along the corridors to inform me what he'd been doing with the King.

Disappointment had run through me when he'd said nothing out of the ordinary happened and that Dusan had only shown him the castle grounds.

I now watch as Dusan leans back against his chair, his emerald attire shimmering with silver dust as he stares at everyone along the table. I've begun to question whether my mistrust towards him stems from the trauma of Emberwell. I've always trusted too quickly. Maybe I am just more conscious of it now.

Coughing, I clear my throat and reach across the table to where the pastries are. 'Any news on the night of Golrai's death?' I ask. By now, Dusan knows I'm not convinced about certain things. I didn't know much about Golrai, but I do know that she had come here relatively young and served long before King Dusan and his brother were born.

Someone inside the castle had killed her, but I do not know or understand for what reason.

'I have my best soldier looking into it still,' Dusan says, sipping from his cup. 'Aeron Hawthorne, I believe you've seen him around. He is Faye's personal guard.'

At the mention of Aeron's name, Arlayna's fork seems to tumble out of her hands. Everyone turns to look at her. She seems lost in her own thoughts before she shakes her head and apologizes.

'Sadly,' Dusan is saying with a slight drawl as if the interruption had annoyed him. 'We know nothing so far. And though Darius has done his best to help us, winter is approaching, and we can no longer delay your task.'

'Dusan—' Meriel tries to intervene, but against Dusan, she has no luck.

'My niece will be in safe hands, Meriel. When encountering Thalorians or their leader, I'm sure she will show how truly ready she is to take on the crown.'

My head bows at the realisation that this is our last and final task. With Golrai's death, learning Darius is a Rivernorth, and that we are a reincarnation of the deities of our world, it had slipped my mind.

'Who is their leader?' asks Darius from his end of the table.

He's staring at Dusan calculatingly, he is just as suspicious of him as I am. Tibith rolls from his shoulder, unaware of the tension emanating through the air as he lands on Arlayna's plate with a splash.

Dusan clears his throat. 'Kirian Tryskalyn.'

The name causes unwanted goosebumps to appear along my skin. Despite it being inevitable, I hope I never have to meet this leader. Still, from what I have read inside the castle's library and knowing how Thalorians came to be, I ask the King, 'What happened to the previous leader?'

Dusan's brows rise as he releases a short chuckle. 'He killed her.'

The silence around the room lasts too long for my comfort.

'Well, one must assume he grew tired of serving her,' Aias says with a chuckle, and I glance at him, confused as to why he would say that. He's swirling a spoon in his tea when he looks up. 'Sorry.' He waves a hand. 'I just thought of Renward. I'm sure Kirian had his reasons, that is all.'

'Still,' Arlayna says, her lips thinning. 'Kirian Tryskalyn deems himself worthy of Terranos. Who knows what he will do next.' Her laugh comes out dry as she leans back and crosses one leg over the other. 'I wouldn't be surprised if he tried to make a deal with you, Uncle. I heard he loves political negotiations.'

Deals.

It is outright embarrassing, of all the bargains I've made to get to where I am now.

Dusan looks as if he is about to say something when one of the sentinels opens the doors for Thallan. I grow cold as his eyes swerve in my direction, and a grumble of dissatisfaction leaves his lips as he makes his way towards the King. He whispers something into Dusan's ear while Darius presses a hand to my knee under the table, relaxing me with a simple action.

Darius inclines his head at me, and I look at him from this angle. With how his short hair recklessly falls across his forehead and the unique nature of his beauty, I can genuinely imagine why he would be Crello.

The moon lights the magic of the night.

And he is exactly that. He always was.

'Nara?' Dusan's voice flickers across the table, and I blink, whirling my head towards him. His face is grave as Thallan stands back. 'May I speak with you?'

Something sharp twists inside my stomach over what it might be that he feels he needs to speak to me about. I look from Thallan to Dusan and find it hard to form the right words. So, I nod.

Dusan excuses himself from the table. Everyone's eyes are on me as I rise from my chair, and Darius doesn't waste any time doing precisely the same. We lock eyes, and I'm ready to tell him to stay here, but he shoots me a look that tells me that no matter what I say, he will accompany me whether I like it or not.

I exhale sharply, spinning on my heel as I follow the King and Thallan out of the dining hall and into Dusan's study. One of the guards closes the door behind us as Dusan makes his way around his desk. I'm standing by the threshold, my fingers digging into the side of my leg before Darius slides a hand across my back, bringing me to his side. I wish to close my eyes and live last night again with him instead of waiting here in this room, most likely for news I do not want.

My patience deteriorates once Dusan purses his thin lips and taps his fingers on the wooden desk. 'Is there something I should be concerned about?'

His head darts up, silvery blonde locks spilling over his shoulder. 'We've received word from Emberwell.'

Dread squeezes my throat.

Emberwell.

The Queen.

My brothers, Freya, Link, Rydan . . . the dragons— 'How . . . I— I thought you'd shied away from any news from Emberwell over the last three centuries—'

'Sometimes it is unavoidable, Nara.' His face is tight, his expression a fit of unidentifiable anger. 'Thallan,' he calls, and his trusted aid walks over, handing him a crumpled piece of paper. 'This came through today. It wasn't addressed to anyone so Thallan opened it and read what was inside.' He extends it out towards me.

I look at it as if it will come alive and bite me. Slowly walking up to him, I snatch it out of his grip, keeping my eyes on him as I unfold the stained parchment. When my gaze drops down, a thousand knives jab at my heart.

Nara,

As Iker writes this out for me, I want to tell you how much we miss you dearly. Idris, most of all. He is going insane in this den, and even Freya's rambling does not calm him as it did at the beginning. Food rations are getting smaller by the day here, shifters are weakening while the dragons have become restless. We know that you would not wish to hear this news, but it is best that you know from us that no human turned rümen survived after their release from the dungeons.

I grip the letter even harder.

This means that Adriel is no longer alive, that what I had hoped would give freedom to those turned by Lorcan and Erion failed.

We are not sure how long it will be until the Queen's Venators figure out where we are, and though we don't want to get our hopes up, Gus might have found a way for us to be safe and if all else is to fail

The words trail off as the black ink is smudged, and my chest seizes. I reread each sentence as if it would magically manifest the remaining parts of the letter.

'We believe Sarilyn's army must have attacked before your brother could finish,' Thallan says, but my eyes are stuck to the parchment, the curves of Iker's writing, and the ink sliding off the page.

I shake my head. 'They said they might have found a way to be safe—' *Breathe.* 'There must have been a mistake. I—'

'Nara, we beg of you to calm down—'

My gaze shoots up at Dusan. I'm panting and scrunching the parchment in my hands.

No.

'Sarilyn would not kill them when she can still use them to bait us. She knows what my brothers mean to me. She—' I press my lips together in frustration. Darius reaches out to me, but I take a step back with another shake of my head as his eyes are awash with concern. I glance at Thallan and the hidden smirk itching to reach his lips. 'What did you do?' I demand and raise the letter in my hand. 'For all I know, this letter is fake, conjured up by you!'

But I know it is not. No one else knew about the den, plus I would recognise Iker's hand writing anywhere.

'Thallan was just doing his duty, Nara,' Dusan says, his voice taking on an edge. 'I know you might be upset, but you do not need to take it up with my emissary.'

My gaze snaps to him, and I march to his desk, slamming my fists down. I grind my teeth, hating how he would defend a man like Thallan. 'Even if he was passing on news that made me euphoric, I would gouge his eyes out just for speaking to me.'

Dusan's stare grows wide at my fury. He might be King. He might have let us stay inside his home out of kindness, but my brothers come first.

Always.

Especially when it is over royalty.

'Leave her, Your Majesty.' Thallan's laugh breaks the putrid silence. 'She is clearly not in the right state of mind right now. Might I suggest locking her up until she calms down?'

Fire burns throughout me. I'm shaking with rage as I slowly turn my head towards Thallan.

He's grinning, amusing himself with his jokes.

My legs start moving, fists clenched and ready to wipe that smile off his lips when I'm stopped mid-step as he goes slamming against the walls. Garbled sounds come out of him as swirls of shadow magic wrap around his throat.

I look over my shoulder. Darius is there with his hand extended outward and a look of pure wrath flooding his eyes.

'You were saying?' He smirks, and Thallan's choking gasps become louder.

'Darius,' Dusan warns, but it's no use. Darius's shadows slither up Thallan's now blue face until they begin digging into his eyes.

Squelching blood slides down his face as he cries out in pain.

'Darius!' Dusan yells again, and his voices ushers other guards into the study room.

Swords are unsheathed, and Thallan's screams are still bouncing off the walls, but Darius doesn't care.

I walk up to him, circling a hand around his arm. 'Let him go,' I whisper, even though I want to smile at Thallan's misfortune. 'Darius.'

The tension in his shoulders lessens, and our eyes meet.

The warmth in his usual gold eyes returns, and he exhales a breath as if in relief. He drops his hand, and Thallan falls to the floor. His gasps and agonizing groans sound haunting. I don't look his way. I don't believe he deserves that much. Instead, I glance back at Dusan.

His expression is blank, eyes only on Darius and me.

My grip tightens around Darius's arm, fearing he will be taken, fearing I will relive the moment Sarilyn captured him once again.

Dusan's gaze slides to his guards. 'Stand down.'

'But, sire—'

'I said stand down.' Dusan turns to me. He doesn't say anything else, but the look he gives me is clear.

He is giving us one final chance.

And for what reason, I'm not sure, but I'm grateful enough to take it as I curl my fingers around Darius's hand and walk out of there alive.

Chapter Forty-Six

I'm storming through the maze as the fresh air beats my face, yet it does nothing to ease the frantic state I am in right now. I arrive at the centre with Darius behind me. I start pacing back and forth, running both hands through my hair. I'd expected Darius to be less than calm, seeing the way he used his powers on Thallan, but no, he's leaning against the hedge, watching how panicked I am.

Sarilyn.

My brothers.

The letter.

I pause, patting myself down, wondering if I'd dropped the letter through the chaos at Dusan's study.

My name comes out of Darius's mouth softly to soothe my nerves.

I look up at him.

Worry and anger swirl in his eyes.

I can't stop it; my legs collapse.

My hand reaches out behind me as I try to find something to steady myself on but fail, landing on the ground, depleted and lost.

Darius is straightening off the hedge, taking immediate steps towards me and not waiting another minute as he lowers to his knees and embraces me. My fingers curl around his shirt, and I close my eyes while he strokes my back, resting his hand on my head as he holds me in a protective cocoon.

'They have to be alive.' My voice disappears amongst the rustling sound of flowers and dried-out leaves inside the maze. I refuse to believe in rumors from the King, much less Thallan. And yes, I am certain that I wanted Darius to inflict even further pain on him. But I dare not think of the consequences that would fall on him.

On us.

On our future.

'They are,' Darius says with conviction, cupping my face and making me look at him. He traces the pad of his thumb along my cheeks as I stare into his amber-golden eyes. They're almost hues of brown now in the shadows of the maze. 'Dusan's heart. It was beating too fast while you read the letter.'

All tears cease from my eyes. He'd tried listening to Dusan's heartbeat. 'What—'

'I know you don't trust the King. Neither do I. In a world like this, not even trust can be earned, and if he had a history with Sarilyn, who is to say it is not finished?'

'Do you . . . do you think he's working with her?'

It wouldn't make sense; she cursed him, and the King has never affiliated himself with Emberwell since then.

Darius shakes his head. 'Someone else, perhaps.' He sighs. 'Listen, Goldie, when I was assisting him after Golrai's death, he didn't care who had killed her. He'd already assumed that whoever had murdered her was male before I could say anything.'

The first person that comes to mind is Thallan when I spoke to him that night. He denied all my allegations, threatened me with exposing Aeron and Arlayna, and my feelings towards Darius. It definitely could have been him, but it also seems too easy if it was.

'What if Golrai knew something grave?'

Darius thinks about it for one moment. 'She was killed inside this maze,' he says. 'It was clear she was trying to hide from someone.'

Too much around us is dangerous.

It's been months since I last saw my brothers and friends. They *have* to be safe, and right now, all I'm clinging on to is Darius's words that the King might have lied.

'We need the last stone.' I stare to the side where the statue of an Elven man riding a horse in armour stands. Looking back at Darius, I get up and mean each word I say next. 'And once we have it, we'll leave this land behind. We will get our friends and family and take back what is rightfully yours.'

He's kneeling before me, and a smirk I'd regard as full of pride fills his face. He gets up slowly. One leg then the other. His chest aligns with my forehead, and I have to lift my chin to face him.

My breathing stills as his fingers trace my collarbone. One, two, hardly a third second goes by as he lowers them and stops by the coin pendant around my neck.

He smiles and lifts it between his thumb and forefinger. 'You truly want me to be king?'

I rest both my hands over his. 'You are the last remaining Rivernorth,' I say. 'For Emberwell, you are already king, Darius.'

His gaze fixes on my eyes with raw and unfiltered intensity, and as we stand here in the stillness, he whispers to me, 'Goldie . . . marry me.'

My eyes widen and my heart thumps and ricochets inside my chest with absolute happiness. But I know the depths of everything we will face are much more dangerous.

I sigh, dropping my hands to the side, and say, 'Darius—'

'Don't.' He shakes his head. 'I already know you will say not now, that it isn't the right time, that I am stupid to even suggest such a thing, but I have never been clearer about anything in my life than I am right now.'

He is looking at me in such a way. How can I say no?

I release a sigh. 'There is too much in our lives that we must deal with first—'

'And what if we don't get a chance again?'

I stay quiet because that is a possibility I do not want to even think about.

He cups my face. 'Goldie, from that day I first met you playing with your marbles, I've known I wanted you to be my wife.'

I shoot him an amused look. 'You were a child.'

He smiles so wide that his dimples appear. 'A very intelligent and dashing child who'd met the most beautiful girl in existence.'

I roll my eyes and grin. Turning my head, I reach for his hand on my cheek and gently kiss his palm.

Before I add another reason, he says, 'Come on, Goldie.' He lets go and takes a few steps back. 'I'll marry you a thousand times!' He raises his arms to the side without caring if anyone outside the maze will hear him. He picks off a blue hydrangea from the hedge and walks up to me again, offering it in his hand. 'If you'll only let me.'

I laugh, shaking my head. I am a fool completely in love with a dragon shifter I once desperately wanted to hate.

Taking the hydrangea, I twirl it between my fingers, smiling as I stare at each cerulean petal. 'How about we make it a little game.' I glance up at him, my lips curling into a smile at the sudden frown on his face.

'Not the most ideal answer,' he drawls with a smirk. 'But I do always love winning against you.'

I shake my head, then raise my chin and wrap my arms around his neck as I hum in pensive mockery. 'Well, if you ask me three more times to marry you, then I might say yes, but remember, you mustn't ask one right after the other. That would be cheating.'

He cocks a brow, his hands curving at the small of my back. 'Why three?'

'It is my lucky number.'

'Not five?'

I drop my forehead onto his chest and chuckle before looking up. 'Back then, five questions to ask you was far more reasonable than three.'

His eyes are half closed as he smiles down at me.

My dragon shifter.

'Well,' he lilts and clears his throat. 'Naralía Brielle Ambrose, will you be my wife?'

If my heart could swoon, it would. I rise on the edges of my boots, my lips a breath away from his as I whisper, 'One down, two to go.' And kiss him with all the promises of eternity lingering in the air.

CHAPTER FORTY-SEVEN

Five of the King's warriors trot up ahead on their horses. Aeron and Darius are at the front, leading us all through the wooded lands of Terranos while Arlayna and I hang back. With the last task looming over us, everyone seemed to be tenser than before. Only yesterday, Darius had told me he wanted to marry me, to be his wife, to be a . . . Rivernorth.

It is hard to believe so much could happen in such a short time. And though Darius and I knew the worst was not over, we still spent the entire evening in his room, under his bedsheets, against the wall, with our bare bodies tangled up.

I've never felt such blissful serenity before, as when I am with him.

My lips twitch with a smile as I stare at the back of him, riding his stallion. If I admitted that to him, I'd never hear the end of it.

'You two have certainly made up, haven't you?' Arlayna asks with humour in her voice.

I glance at her, gripping the reins of my mare. 'Sadly,' I joke, and she chuckles lightly. I look back at Darius, now conversing with a few soldiers. I whisper, 'He asked me to marry him.'

'A dragon shifter asking a mortal to marry him? History is truly changing.'

That made me think of how we are supposed to be reincarnations of Solaris and Crello, which in itself is a historic change for Zerathion. But I turn my attention to her and say something else. 'What is it like here?' After hearing how Meriel wants to marry off Arlayna a few times, I imagine she's displeased by it.

A humourous chuckle slips from her. 'Marriage for Elves is very political. Not many marry for love as it's considered a weakness. If our hearts are to break, we risk becoming like these Thalorians.' She looks at me. 'Heartless.'

Such a tragedy for a kingdom that is so beautiful.

'What about your mother?'

'She is quite possibly the only one who married for love. Then there is my uncle, who'd found it with your queen, until she cursed him.'

I don't reply at the mention of Dusan, and though he is not a dark Elf, he might as well be one.

'You don't like my uncle much, do you?'

My shoulders stiffen, but I try and keep my expression impartial. 'Let's just say I do not have a great reputation amongst kings and queens. It's mostly Thallan whom I despise.'

She laughs. 'Yes, I heard about the incident between Darius and him yesterday. Our healers say he will regain his sight. Though I wonder what he'd said to get Darius so riled up.'

Thallan insulted me.

Darius gouged his eyes out as I'd said I would have done myself.

I don't know what I will tell Arlayna. I shouldn't tell her the truth, even if I consider her a friend.

When moments pass, and she sees I won't tell her, she asks, 'Are you . . . worried that perhaps someone might use what you and Darius have to their advantage?'

I frown at her, but a strange feeling sticks in my stomach. 'I haven't thought about it. Why do you ask?'

She shakes her head like she regrets asking me in the first place. Her eyes focus on Aeron, and she drags in a tense breath before my gaze catches on the satchel hanging off the saddle, shaking as if something is inside it.

'Arlayna.' I reach out and place my hand over hers. I jerk my chin towards the satchel, and she looks over her shoulder as I whisper, 'Animal?'

She narrows her eyes at it, and we halt our horses, causing everyone in front of us to notice. Darius is the first to dismount from his stallion, stalking straight to where we are.

'What is it?' he asks, with Aeron already at Arlayna's side.

I get off, brushing the side of my mare's mane. 'Nothing.' The rustling inside the satchel catches everyone's attention. 'A possible creature has infiltrated our trip.'

Darius cocks an eyebrow, moving past me. I turn as he approaches the satchel and flicks it open. Everyone is hushed. It's oddly dramatic for one simple creature. Until the rummaging inside stops, and an orange fur-coated head pops up.

'Hello, Darry!' Tibith says, grinning.

Darius stares at him, murmuring with amusement, 'You're not where I left you.'

'Tibith, what are you doing here?' I say, traumatized after my first task in the Melwraith mountains. 'Have you been inside there this whole time?'

'I did not want to stay with Aias, Miss Nara! He never tells me good stories!'

'It's too dangerous for you to come with us,' Darius says. 'You know that.'

Tibith whimpers, his eyes darting back and forth between us. 'But-but it never used to be before, Darry!'

Darius glances at me, and we share the same regretful look.

We have been so invested in these tasks that we haven't had the time to see how Tibith is doing. Before, it was just always him and Darius. I never thought to ask if he missed that.

'I can look after him.'

Our heads turn to Arlayna, still resting on her horse. Her lip twitches, staring down at Tibith. 'He's quite amusing.'

Tibith titters, climbing out of the satchel and onto Arlayna's lap. 'And I think you are very pretty, Miss Arlayna!'

I'm still reluctant to have him travel with us. I can sense Darius feels the same way. It's hard not to worry after what happened with that other Tibithian.

'We should make camp here,' Aeron says, staring skyward at the sunset casting red and gold hues through the trees. 'Any further, and we will be heading into darker territories.'

Another guard named Tregar agrees and begins to disperse. As Arlayna gets down, she and Aeron stare at each other for a few pensive seconds before she walks the other way, taking Tibith with her.

I'm sitting inside one of the tents whittling a knife out of wood I had found earlier. I would have shaped it into something else, but my creativity for carving has lost its spark, thinking of my brothers, the

King, and the last task.

I run my fingers through my hair, removing the tangled plait. It's become dark as a few guards patrol outside. A puffing breeze blows by. It chills my neck through the opening of my tent behind me, just as the sound of rain hitting the grass carries through to me.

A sound of crunching leaves begins to close in, and I freeze, turning with my knife. It's hard to see, but I can recognise the scent of rosewood anywhere.

'Even after everything we've been through, you will never stop pointing a dagger in my direction.'

I can envision the grin on Darius's face as he says that.

Dropping the knife, I hiss, 'What are you doing here? Shouldn't you be guarding the princess?'

His chuckle is dark and sensuous, not at all helpful. 'Last I recall, Goldie, I am not one of the King's guards. I should be guarding you.'

I roll my eyes, knowing he can't see me. 'No, you shouldn't.' I sigh, and for a minute, we are silent. 'Do you— do you think we should be more worried about Dusan?'

He doesn't answer, but I can only remind myself of what Arlayna had said earlier.

'Everyone knows there's something between us.' *We've not hidden it at all*, I want to add. 'What if Dusan uses that against us?'

'Are you saying that because of what happened in his study?'

'I am saying it because we've become too comfortable. Dusan already saw how you reacted when Thallan mentioned locking me up. What if he let us go unpunished because he guessed how vulnerable we are with each other?'

Like a match being lit, Darius's hand produces a flame, lighting up the tent, our faces aglow. He aims it towards the open hearth, kindling it so that we see better. He's kneeling before me, but his gaze is thoughtful, concerned, maybe unsettled by that anxious idea. 'Then we will act like we despise one another.' The look on my face must be expressive because the side of Darius's lip lifts as he takes it in. He says, 'We played the part quite well before, didn't we?'

I scoff. 'They would not believe us after—' I stop myself from revealing the moment Thallan told me I was in love with Darius and what everyone else has witnessed.

'They don't need to,' Darius says. 'But it would be fun to play around, wouldn't it?'

I make a frustrated sound and cover my eyes. 'Be serious, Darius, we cannot rely on the Isle of Elements to help us, and we can't trust anyone else but each other.'

'You trust Aias.'

'He has helped us every step of the way and he grew up without a family!'

'And is that all it takes for you to trust, Goldie?'

A groan rips from my throat, and I rise, turning away from him. A few seconds later, his hands come up to my shoulders, and I exhale, resting my back against him. He then slowly twists me around until we are face to face.

'Look, whatever you want to do, Nara, I'm with you,' he says in a soft gentle voice, like he finally understands how much this affects me. 'If you want me to back away from you, I will.'

I puff out an exhausted breath and shake my head. 'I don't want you to back away . . . I want you by my side.'

A speck of glimmering hope shines in his eyes.

'I told you that once this is over, we will leave. We will claim your throne and get my brothers,' I say. 'But that doesn't stop me from worrying something awful might happen.'

He nods. 'Then we will take each day as it comes. We will build our strength, and if anyone tries to stop us, we will defend ourselves, and I will help you win against those who dare wrong you.'

I stare at him, my gaze full of devotion. He has always thought of me as a fighter.

Wetting my lips, I breathe out a laugh. 'My biggest fan.'

He smiles. 'Always have been.'

One of the guards calls out Darius's name, likely wondering where he is as raindrops sliding down the tent's roof soften and then cease.

'You should go see what they want,' I whisper, and he sighs as neither of us wants to part.

'Or I could stay here.'

'Darius.'

He laughs, drops his forehead against mine, and runs his thumb across my chin. I savour his touch and closeness before it's gone as he starts to walk out of the tent.

I watch crestfallen, until he stops a few steps past the threshold. I don't have time to think or say anything as he turns and strides up to me, cupping my face in his hands and landing a kiss on my lips.

He hauls me up against him, lifting me from the ground as I swing my arms around his neck. His tongue is in my mouth, urgent and so profound I gasp between breaths.

It's a kiss where we are both afraid of losing each other.

I'm still trying to recover when he places me back down. My eyes are closed, my mouth half open, and once again, he lets go and leaves.

I press two fingers against my lips, already missing him, as my eyes flicker open and the fire goes out.

CHAPTER FORTY-EIGHT

A day and a half later, we had finally made progress.

Aeron mentioned we were close to the Thalorian border. And careful enough not to encounter trolls. I had wanted to believe we were entirely safe, but that is a foolish thought I'd brushed away. Nothing is ever safe, nor should I think too quickly before an outcome.

'Steady,' Aeron says, his palm raised before his boots slam onto the squelching mud. Branches and colossal trees with leaves of all sizes dominate the forest. It is nothing like the woodlands near Olcar. A foul smell hangs in the air and a certain darkness, the perfect hiding place for creatures that I do not want to tempt.

It is too much like the Screaming Forests.

I slide off my mare, walking towards Darius with cautious steps. There's a crack of a branch echoing in the air, and my heart jolts for a moment before seeing it was only a bird taking flight.

'We need to keep Arlayna safe.' I lean into Darius.

He looks at me, raises a brow, and crosses his arms over his chest as he glances past his shoulder. 'I doubt that she would like us taking extra care and being wary of her.'

I peer behind me, seeing how Arlayna is already off her horse.

Suppressing a smile, I turn my attention to Darius when a cold draught travels towards us. It lifts the leaves off the ground and blows my hair back. Everyone is unsheathing their weapons as Tibith waddles to my side and wraps his arms around my calf.

'What is it?' I whisper, even though Darius won't have the slightest clue either.

'Shadow Calps,' Aeron answers, looking at us.

I almost swear. 'What—'

'Your Highness, get down!' A guard yells, and I swivel just in time to see Arlayna tumble to the ground, and a dark humanoid creature with branches for limbs comes spiralling out of the dark. Tendrils of shadows surround it as it tries to lunge at Arlayna, but Aeron runs to her, slashing his sword across the Calp's body.

The forest turns into mayhem. Horses bray, scattering away as Shadow Calps come from every direction, creating a vortex of shadows to trap us.

'Monsters, monsters, monsters—' Tibith rolls into his cocoon, going in circles around my feet.

'Goldie, on your right!' Darius looks over my shoulder before he turns to ignite a flame and incinerates one of the Calps.

I twist as one tries to reach me, and I duck, falling into the mud. My double-ended blade clatters out of my hand, and I reach for Tibith, pulling him into my arms as a low growl comes from overhead. I look up as the Shadow Calp barrels towards the Elven guards, knocking one to the ground. The Elf cries out in agony before he is dragged out of the shadow barrier and deeper into the forest.

'Shit,' I mutter and look behind, but Darius is no longer there. I panic, looking everywhere as fear begins to pour out of me. All I hear are screams – guttural screams coming from different places. Amidst the shadows, I squint my eyes as it gets harder to see inside this whirling tornado. My blade isn't so far away. I can get to it. Glancing down at Tibith, hidden beneath my left arm, I say, 'I'm going to need you to listen to me, alright?'

He nods.

'When I tell you to run, you head straight to that tree trunk over there and hide, got it?'

He's blinking up at me, but he accepts as another Calp approaches, and I urge him to safety. He goes on all fours, rushing to the trunk as I stumble to get my blade. With the dagger in my hand, I turn and raise my forearms as the Calp attacks me. The branch-like fingers try to claw at me, and I find myself staring into a faceless creature. A memory infiltrates my mind. The time I'd faced rümen in my village. The first time I killed one before leaving for Emberwell. A spiral of shadow-like magic appears from the Calp's back, gathering into a point and aiming towards my face. I stop reacting in battle with the creature and tune into my surroundings, allowing myself to centre with the earth. Power cuts through my veins, and I can feel it. The energy I am always hiding.

It is so powerful, so strong, it longs to get out. But it can only go so far.

I lower my hands and arms to the side, giving the Calp access. The creature freezes. Growls lessen, and cries subside. I watch as the Calp backs away from me and retreats on four legs. It may not have a face, no emotion to show me, but somewhere through all that darkness, I feel it. And as all the Calps make a clicking sound, that's when I hear, 'Goldie.'

I slowly rise, looking across at where Darius is standing. Blood is smeared down his cheek, and he's panting, yet he manages to come over as the vortex of shadows stops. It's now much clearer to see who is safe and who is injured.

Ten guards came with us. There are only five left.

Arlayna is beside Aeron, her gaze as confused as everyone else's. When Darius comes to my side, we look at each other before glancing at the Calps. Counting how many there are is hard, but they all face Darius and me.

The sun blooms again, for she has found her moon.

Leira's words were always true. From the moment I found Darius again that night at the jeweller. The same Calp that had just tried to attack me floats towards us both; extending its hand out as if to touch me, it stops halfway, screeches, and vanishes away with the rest of the Calps.

'How did you get them to stop?' Aeron says between pants.

'I didn't.' I'm still not sure how I was able to connect with them.

'It does not matter how she did it.' Arlayna huffs, looking at me intensely as if she knows there is more to it. 'What matters is that we get out of here before they return.' She starts ahead despite the bodies of the deceased guards around us. I swallow as I glance down at one of the Elves. I struggle to move as I stare at the guard's hollow frame. What was once sun-kissed skin is now ashen. His eyes are vacant. You can see his cheeks and how caved in they are, just like the rest of his body.

Darius says my name gently, tugging at my arm to get my attention. As I raise my eyes at him, Tibith climbs onto his shoulder, and I nod, accepting his hand as set off on the remainder of our journey.

'This is as far as we go,' Aeron says as we near the townhouses on a sloping hill. A ghostly ambiance shifts through the houses and empty dry-mudded streets. Most homes are broken down and grey in colour, like no one seems to take care of where they live.

'Why can we not go with them?' Arlayna asks, and I whirl to face them, as the few remaining guards stare at the borders skeptically.

Aeron runs a hand through his light locks. This whole ordeal must be stressful for him after losing some of his comrades. 'You almost died at the hands of Calps; I'd rather not have Kirian Tryskalyn find out the Princess of Terranos is prancing through his lands.'

'I am more than capable of handling a dark Elf, especially one who hides within his own shadows—'

'Princess—'

'Don't "Princess" me, Aeron—'

Darius clears his throat, and it is almost comical how Arlayna and Aeron's heads swing our way. Darius can hardly contain the amusement on his face as he says, 'While this bickering truly brings me nostalgia . . .' He presses a palm to his chest and looks at me. I'm tempted to roll my eyes. 'I must say I agree with Aeron. We are grateful for your guidance, but this is a task that Nara and I must complete on our own. We can't risk any more casualties. If we find any valuable information, we will relay it back to the King.'

Arlayna goes quiet, looking off to the far left. Everyone is staring at her, waiting for an eventual protest, but seconds pass, and she sighs heavily in defeat. 'Then I suppose I should wish you both good luck,' she mumbles and darts a gaze towards Darius. 'And to not fall for whatever schemes Kirian might have. I hear he is cunning.'

'As is Darius.' I take a step forward and look over my shoulder, unable to conceal my teasing smile. 'We will be fine.'

Darius grins in return, and I walk up to him, looking at Tibith's curious wide eyes.

'I know you wish to join us,' I say, tilting my head as I run my fingers along his fur. 'But it is too dangerous.'

Tibith pouts and looks at Darius for a response, but he is met with an apologetic smile. 'Will I ever come on adventures again, Darry?'

'Of course you will. You're my partner through everything, remember?'

Tibith nods, his mood seeming to lift as he slides down from Darius's shoulder. He raises his head to look at me, blinks twice, then locks his arms around my calf. My heart compresses, thinking how much I have grown to love this little creature. This orange fluffball whom I'd first attempted to capture that night in the city.

I take a quick breath to compose myself as we part and he walks over to Arlayna. We bid our goodbyes, and Aeron tells us they will wait with weapons at the ready if anything is to go south. Darius and I set course onto the brittle pathway, noticing the streets are empty except for an Elven male sitting outside his house on a wooden stool. A few garments and cloaks are hanging on wooden poles to dry, and I deduce that they must belong to him as the wind picks up, causing the clothing to ripple and sway.

'Wait here,' Darius says, and I scowl at him, but he hides me behind a tree before I can object. He starts walking over to the posts, gazing around with a blasé look on his face. Stopping by one of them, he looks at the Elf on the stool, which is turned the other way. My face moulds into a grimace, wanting to tell Darius to stop taking his time, but the Elf's head drops as if he has fallen into a deep slumber, allowing Darius to slyly grab some cloaks.

Thief.

He's smiling as he makes his way back to me, and my arms are crossed over my chest as I shake my head at his cocky nature.

'May I ask how this is supposed to help us blend in?' I ask as I eye the raggedy pieces of clothing.

'Funny you should ask.' He raises a finger. 'When I grabbed the cloaks, there was a wanted poster on the wooden post for a female Elf who had stolen from Kirian Tryskalyn.'

'Sounds familiar.'

He chuckles and clicks his tongue. 'Regardless . . . it says to bring her to him in return for an immense reward.' He places the cloak around my shoulders, taking his time to tie it around my neck. 'I don't know about you, Goldie, but that screams opportunity.'

I hum, giving it some thought, and conclude that this is insane. 'Have you forgotten that I look nothing like an Elf?'

He snaps his fingers, and I feel the warm glow of magic covering me. 'Problem solved.'

The problem is not solved. 'Just because we can hide the fact that we do not have pointed ears with your powers for a little while does not mean this will work. I stick out, Darius. We both do.'

I'd read in books from Dusan's library what Thalorians looked like. Yes, they were Elves, but they lacked the grace that High Elves have. Their skin is a pale grey, borderline making them look unwell, and they are known for their blood eyes. And though I couldn't see the eyes of the Elven male Darius stole from, he still showed some of the features I'd read about in that book.

Darius sighs. He looks at me like he understands the consequences and says, 'We just need to get inside Kirian's castle, that's all. And if anyone notices something is off, then—'

'We break their hands.'

His laugh is melodic, but I am most definitely serious. 'Yes, we could break their hands, Goldie, although I would go for something more damaging.'

An amused smile dances on my lips. 'Yes,' I say and raise my chin. 'I imagine so.' I don't wait for his usual commentary because I strut past him and gaze at the road ahead as I prepare myself to travel towards the centre of Thalore.

CHAPTER FORTY-NINE

I pause by the busy crowds of Dark Elves strolling across the cobbled pavements and steep roads leading into different areas of Thalore. There are wooden shops and taverns in every direction I look, while up ahead, rocky paths and foggy roads trail towards the castle. It takes us a significant length of time to arrive at the central part of the city. And though I had expected worse, Thalore looks . . . normal.

As normal as a corrupted city could be.

My eyes drift to the female Elves walking around in obsidian gowns and frocks made of fine navy silk, their dark locks styled intricately into crown braids and jewelled headpieces. I realise I'm ogling each of them as some turn their heads. I duck my chin into my chest, and Darius grabs my upper arm, walking us forward.

We careen through the Elves as Darius keeps me by his side, and when I peer up to see where I am going, I spot the castle as we pass an archway.

Sable spires plunge into the sky, disappearing within grey clouds. Each side of me, townhouses with curved windows litter the narrow streets dominating the kind I'd seen in the City of Flames. Darius mumbles something, and before I can look at him, he's rushing me into a hidden corner. His arms rest on my shoulders as he presses me against a wall. He's looking the other way from me, and mild panic tightens inside my gut.

'What is it?' I whisper.

He lets go, jerking his chin for me to look. I twist and sneak a glance past the edge of the wall to where Elves dressed in black armour with two swords sheathed behind their backs patrol the entrance to the castle. One of them of muscular build walks up and down, his dark hair half shaved while the other half rests below his shoulder blade. I can't make out the symbol on his attire, but he soon stops as another Elf wearing tattered clothes limps towards him. The Elf in armour pushes him, drawing out his sword before the other Elf scampers away.

I grit my teeth, and since he knows my temper too well, Darius grips the sides of my arms, pulling me back against the wall.

'Easy, Goldie.' A humouring smile pulls at the corner of his lips. 'You'll ruin my plan.'

'What plan! We are already—'

He covers my mouth, silencing me as he presses his body against mine, and all my thoughts disappear at our proximity. My brows pinch together as I shoot him a glare, but he looks to his left, and the side of his lip curls into a smug smile.

'That plan.' I glance at a prisoner's carriage outside a noisy tavern when he takes his hand from my lips.

Why must he make my blood boil? 'Is this how you went about things back in Emberwell?'

He looks down at the ground, laughs, then glances up at me. 'You should know by now we've had many adventures together, all of which I've saved you from.' He winks, leaving me gaping at him as he walks towards the carriage.

I'm trying to catch up to his long strides. Even though we're on a mission, he possesses a regal posture. 'Are you forgetting when I broke you out of the dungeons?'

'You're right, but . . . who got you out of the trials again?'

'*Freya*. If she hadn't told you, I might have become one of Erion's rümen pets.'

He turns around on his boot, and I stumble backward before he catches my forearm. He's peering down at me, something odd twinkling in his eyes despite the curl of his lip. 'Yes, I recall the moment she told me what the Queen had done with you. It was enough for me to attack there and then, despite how weak I still was, yet I did not care because all I could think of was how you were suffering, thinking that your brothers weren't safe, and because of that, I wanted to destroy that castle, not caring if it rightfully belonged to me.'

Thank Solaris that he is still holding me because he has just made me completely breathless.

A wheeze comes from my throat as I look away and mutter, 'You win.'

His voice softens. 'I only win so long as I know you are safe.' He lifts my chin, and our eyes lock. An ocean meeting the heat of the sun. 'You find ways to save me every day, and I'll always find a way to save you too.'

I crack a smile, and he watches my lips, mesmerized. I don't think he will ever realise how much I truly care for him.

He steps back, opens the cart door, and gestures his hand outward. 'Your carriage awaits.'

I laugh, and before I turn to go inside, I glance at him with a sardonic smile. 'You're a fool, you know that?'

'You're the one stepping inside a prisoner's carriage.' He has that flirtatious look on his face. His chin is raised, and he's grinning wide. 'If I had it my way, this could be useful for other things.'

The last thing I see is the smirk on his face as he covers the cart with a threadbare blanket. It's not long before the cart jostles, and we start moving. I almost yelp as my body shifts to the right of the carriage, and hooves thump as we trot along the ground. I grab a hold of one of the bars and take two long breaths, hoping we get through. The cart jolts again, and I lose my patience. I'm prepared to argue, but the carriage slows to a stop, and I tense up. My hand is still clasped around one of the bars when I hear two men conversing.

Darius and a guard.

Possibly the one we had seen earlier.

'How'd you find her?' the guard asks in a grinding voice that matches the gruffness of a dark Elf likely serving Kirian.

'Outskirts,' Darius says. 'Think she was trying to run away.'

There's a pregnant pause. 'And you want a prize for this?'

'That's what it says on the poster.'

'Alright.' The guard sighs as if he has much better things to do than this. 'Let me see her.'

Gravel shuffles beneath footsteps nearing the side of the cart.

My eyes widen as I hear Darius say, 'Careful, I wouldn't look in there. Had trouble getting her to stay calm.'

The guard grunts a response, and I know he is about to lift the blanket. I shut my eyes with a wince, hoping he still falls for our glamoured exteriors. A snippet of light fills the cart before a clashing sound from outside makes me jump. The blanket covers the cell bars again, and the guard swears.

'Go on,' he grunts to Darius, and the carriage quickly begins moving again.

I sigh my relief and raise my knees to my chest.

'I told you it would work, Goldie.'

'Hardly,' I mutter and sit back, waiting until Darius draws the carriage to a halt.

He lifts the blanket, and I squint my eyes, raising a hand to shield the light from my face. I push the cell door open, and Darius helps me down onto the ground. As I am dusting the sides of my cloak, that is when I spot what is around me. Granite shards fill the cave entrance everywhere I look, and vines as dark as coal slink along the single pathway.

To each side of me, obsidian marble pillars shield us from falling into the sea's crashing waves. I sigh at the thought of having to go through it. 'Shall we?' I say, not looking forward to anything as Darius stays silent, taking me in with him.

My boots squelch against the ground, yet it's too dark to notice what I might be stepping on. I stay quiet in case another creature might be lurking. When I see an opening, I creep towards it and release a deep breath, bracing for whatever lies ahead.

We exit the cave into daylight, and surprised, I blink at what I see.

The castle is grand, a fortress much larger than Aurum's palace. Each tower and building are built of varying stones. They shimmer against certain lighting, and from here, sable mosaic rocks decorate the landscape. I glance at the bridge in the centre of the castle walls. Below there's a river too ethereal for this world. It glows the colour of midnight among stars, and I wonder if it's laced with dark magic and if it contains any Galgrs ready to feast on our memories.

I'm pulled along by Darius as the enormous stone doors of the castle begin opening. He dips behind the archway, and I follow him before any guard can spot us. We wait until they enter the cave and sneak past a group of who, I presume, are servants wearing black gowns buttoned up to their necks. Uncertainty bubbles in my stomach. It must be because we are so close to completing the tasks, and we must persevere to access the Isle of Elements.

When I slow down, Darius looks over his shoulder and stares gently into my eyes. He holds out his hand, and a weak smile flutters over my lips as his hand envelopes mine. After another arched hallway, we turn the corner into a torch-lit area. To my left sits the courtyard, and a female turned away from us laughs with another Elf.

'In here,' Darius says, guiding me through an opened doorway.

We stumble inside a dim chamber made of marble with ancient pillars supporting the carved ceiling. My eyes wander to the artwork depicting creatures, Elves, with more etchings spreading out onto the roof as if they are telling a story.

'Where do you think the stone is?' I ask, still staring at the artwork. Could it be a puzzle within this room? Must we solve what these carvings mean?

'Perhaps the stone isn't here,' Darius's words have my head drop to look at him. He's running his fingers along a pillar before glancing at me. 'I do not trust this place.'

My mouth opens to answer, but the voice that comes out is not mine.

'I'm not sure whether I should congratulate you on breaking into my palace or . . . discuss it with the guards who were so inept at their jobs that they failed to see two intruders.'

Solaris . . .

Kirian Tryskalyn.

CHAPTER FIFTY

I aim my dagger towards where I'd heard Kirian's voice come from, but the response I get is a rugged chuckle. It's hard to see where he is lurking.

'Please, there is no need to draw out weapons. I won't bite.' There's a sultry essence to the way he pronounces his words. 'Unless I'm asked to.'

Darius comes to my side and teases a smile onto my face in the darkness of the chambers. 'Say, why don't you show us your face? It's been a dreadfully long day, and I wouldn't mind a bite from an Elf, a dark one no less.'

'Darius,' I hiss. I'm too stressed to deal with his ability to flirt his way out of danger. He shoots me a sideward glance and smiles, but slow footsteps echo, and there, in front of us, walking out from the shadows, is Kirian.

I almost drop the blade.

He is far from what I had pictured and nothing like the Dark Elves. Though intimidating in how the side of his lip kicks up, as if he knows all my secrets, he is still as beautiful as any Elven being I have met in Olcar. His light brown eyes are the kind that can fascinate and bring chaos in their wake, and his ebony hair falls like untamed feathers across his ivory cheekbones and at the nape of his neck.

'I assume this is your first time here.' He gestures to his surroundings, sarcasm emanating from his voice. He is wearing a black and gold waistcoat over a brown shirt. His sleeves are rolled up, showing tattoos that look to be some kind of ancient inscription, the symbols wrapping around his muscular arms.

'We didn't come to stay,' I say.

'Obviously,' he drawls, and I wonder why – why does he lack the colour red in his eyes? 'You came for something.'

My back turns rigid.

'You are also no Elf of ours,' he surveys, pacing across the chamber. 'But you do wear the attire of someone from Olcar.' He stops and presses a finger to his lips before twisting on his heel. 'Clothing that belongs to royalty.'

'Your point?' Darius responds with a tight smile.

Kirian slowly grins, showing a flash of white perfectly straight teeth as he deduces, 'You're here for the last Elemental stone.'

Grinding my teeth, I step forward. Darius notices my impatience but lets me go on. 'We don't want to cause any trouble; we are here to solve whatever riddle, puzzle or fucked-up task we must do to get the last stone. So, if you could—'

'The stone is yours,' Kirian says, mildly bored, and I blink. 'So long as you understand the consequences of how this task will leave you if you were to fail.'

'What do we have to do?' My eyes remain on him as I lift my chin. 'Kirian Tryskalyn.'

His smile is a wicked sight. 'You've heard of me.' He fits his hands in his pockets. 'All good things, I hope.'

Darius chuckles beside me. 'You're wildly popular with the royals.'

Kirian hums. He doesn't seem amused any more. 'So I hear,' he says dryly, his features suddenly cold. 'You know, there's a saying that Thalorians use when it comes to High Elves.'

I think back to the books I'd read on Thalorians. Nothing comes to mind except what Dusan said and my curiosity about why Kirian killed the last Thalorian leader.

'What does it matter?' Darius asks, and it's a question I wonder myself.

Kirian simply smiles though it never reaches the polished amber of his eyes. 'Even the good can harbour a dark heart,' he says the phrase regardless, leaving a crack to fissure between us because he knows it is something so true to the world. He looks to his right and changes subjects. 'Those doors.' We glance in that direction, noticing two placed doors that were not there when we first entered. They aren't attached to a wall and have a marble-cut sphere handle on the left side. 'That is what you must go through to complete your task. You will each choose which door you want—'

'Why must we go separately?' My gaze goes to Kirian's. Weakness shows in the break of my voice as I say these words.

Kirian cocks his head to the side, noticing it himself as he looks from me to Darius, and his lip twitches. 'This is a task one must complete alone. However, if either of you is to fail, you must both submit to losing, and the stone stays here. It is all or nothing.'

That does anything but calm me.

Darius turns me to him, lowering his voice just for me. 'We'll get that last stone, Goldie, trust me.'

I nod. 'I know we will.'

His eyes pierce mine, and what I wish most right now is to be able to wrap myself up in his arms and for him to take me high into the skies.

I glance towards Kirian. He's staring at us like we are so extraordinary to him, so far out of what he must know in his world of blackened hearts and shadows.

As Darius and I make our way to the doors, we stand before them. Me to the right, Darius to the left. We look at each other, his fingertips hovering over the door handle like mine. A perfect mirror of each other.

'Good luck,' I say quietly, though I doubt he will need it.

His smile is small and full of worry. 'You too, Goldie.'

At the same time, we open the door and walk through.

I step into a place void of colour and just as empty. Everything around me, including the ground, is pitch black, and I look over my shoulder to see that the door I entered through is gone. Distressed, I rush to where it once was, searching with my hands for a way to find anything that could lead me back to Kirian's chambers.

'Giving up so soon?'

I go cold.

That voice, I recognise everything about it. I've had sweet nothings whispered into my ears with that voice.

'Out of the two of us, I thought I was the coward, not you.'

My pulse pounds, and I turn around so slowly, as if I'm too afraid to see the owner of that voice.

Copper hair, green eyes, and a smile that once trapped me in what I thought was love, stands before me. 'Hello, Miss Ambrose.'

I shake my head, and he starts moving. Each step pounding against the ground. I'm frozen. Everything in me wants to get out of here, but another part of me can't do that. He's inches away from me now, wearing his Venator armour. I glance at the dragon crest on his chest plate and then up at his eyes. It's him. How, how—

He grabs my coin necklace and eyes it with chilled amusement. 'I always knew it would be him.'

I don't know what to say. I don't know what to think.

'I saw it in the way you looked at him.'

'You're not real.'

His eyes fix on me. It sends a bolt of memories down my spine. 'But I am, Nara. I'm right here, can't you see?'

Behind him, flames spread like a bird's wings. Without a word of warning, I shove against his chest and bolt away from him, shaking my head frantically. I'm heading nowhere, only deeper into this black abyss that's never-ending. When I turn around to look for Lorcan, he's nowhere to be seen, and I suddenly find myself at a precipice. I shout as I stutter to a halt and take a step back, but the ground gives way and I fall. I try to twist myself into a position where I can reach for something, but I can't. My screaming reverberates as my body falls and falls into nothing but darkness. I yell Darius's name at the last second, closing my eyes and bracing myself to hit the floor when my body stops in midair. I'm suddenly afloat, my hair moving fluidly around me like it would underwater.

A source of light shifts above me, and I raise my hand to touch it. Specks of dust dance across my fingers, and in just one blink, I am no longer drifting in the air. I am no longer falling and my feet slowly touch the ground. Urging myself to take a moment and breathe, I inhale deeply through my nose and then exhale, inching one step forward and encountering a wall. My hands brace against solid, uniform bricks. Impenetrable and cold. The same barriers I'd been trapped behind in Emberwell.

The dungeons.

I take a step back and try to fight the panic. I'm shaking my head, scanning the chains along the ceiling when the same mould-infested scent clogs up my nose. A sturdy chain jangles beneath my boot, and I almost trip over it. I turn to follow where it leads. And at the end, the flare of a dull light in the cell shines on Idris, and to his side . . . Darius. The shackle is locked around his ankle as the other connects to my brother. They're silent, staring down at the ground.

They seem like they have been here for ages, my brother is almost unrecognisable with a beard covering his face. And yet he and Darius are still . . . so very still. I sprint towards them, tasting the potent fear on my tongue the more I run. No matter how long I keep running, I can never reach them. They seem so close but so far away. I'm shouting their names, waving my hands to get their attention, yet they don't hear me.

'You can keep calling to them,' a female voice says, 'but they will never hear you.'

Sarilyn.

Of course, she, of all people, would be the one to show up.

I can sense her behind me as she touches my shoulder and walks around me.

We soon are face to face. She, in all her golden glory and immoral grace. 'It is so good to see you, Naralía.' Her smile seems so serpentine.

This isn't real, this isn't real, this isn't—

'So brave.' She twirls a strand of my hair with her fingers before yanking on it hard. 'And so, so, so foolish.'

I cringe as rage festers inside me. It's so easy for anyone to be enthralled by Sarilyn. Even in my nightmares, I'd noticed this about her, but she is exactly like Aurum once was. The two, in theory, belonged together.

I grip her wrist and glare up at her. 'Let go.'

Her smile does not waver. 'What happened to you wanting to become a Venator, Naralía, or did you forget your one greatest wish?'

It was a wish I regretted the minute I entered Aurum Castle.

White-hot fury billows out my nose. I can practically see it between us as I breathe out harshly.

Sarilyn keeps her chin high. 'I see.' She loosens her grip on my hair and turns to Darius and Idris, still in this weird trance. 'Bite him.'

What—

I receive no other warning as Darius looks at my brother and grabs his arm, raising it to his lips.

'Stop!' Horror clutches my throat, and Sarilyn roars with laughter, lifting a palm in the air, which freezes Darius and Idris. I turn to her. 'Release them—'

Sarilyn clicks her tongue and shakes her head. 'Why would I do that when I'm having so much fun.' She places her hands on my shoulder, twisting me so I can look at them again. 'The eldest Ambrose, having to provide for his younger siblings since such a young age, and the Golden Thief, afraid to bite the ones he cares for, especially the woman he loves.' Her sigh is mocking. 'What a predicament.'

I stare at Darius, my heart waiting to burst from my chest as tears spring from my eyes.

Sarilyn turns me back around to face her, and she wipes my tears with her forefinger. 'But we can fix that,' she says. '*You* can fix that.'

I don't meet her gaze. I'm in a world of my own as she walks behind me. What can I fix? What can I do?

'You have a choice,' her whisper is a hiss, strangely making me glance at my hands where a blade now rests between my fingers. 'You can risk your brother dying from a shifter bite . . . . or kill the one you love.'

Kill.

I face her. 'I— I can't.'

'Make the choice, Naralía.'

I shake my head. 'No. I'm not going to kill any of them, not again, not under your control.'

'*Make* the choice.'

I won't. I won't, I won't.

'Make it!'

I can't seem to stop myself from shaking my head.

Her face contorts in anger. She keeps yelling, 'Make the choice!'

I need it to stop. I need everything to stop!

'Do you think you are better than me? Than Solaris!'

'Stop, please—'

'How can you be the reincarnation of Solaris when you are nothing but a weak human—'

My hands cup my ears, and the hilt of my dagger presses against my skin. I do not want to hear this. She's not here, she can't get to me, she—

She isn't real.

She isn't real . . .

I let my hands slip to my sides. Sarilyn is still hurling insults – insults that seem to be based on what I think of myself. As I look up at her, she stops and stares down at me with a wicked smile.

I whisper, 'You don't control me, Sarilyn. Not now, not ever.'

Her onyx eyes widen with surprise, and I conjure up every ounce of strength in my body to thrust the blade at my side into her abdomen.

I cut through flesh and muscle, listening to the hitch of her breath, and slowly, I raise my head high to see her mouth hanging open as she stares at me. I'm watching the life fade away from her eyes, and when I know for sure that she can still hear me, I lean into her ear and say, 'I may be human but I will make sure that nothing, not even *you*, stand in my way.' I yank the dagger out with enough power, letting her crumple, and as she hits the floor, she disappears like grains of sand in the wind.

Turning in a slow circle, I gaze around as everything else in my surroundings fades. Darius, my brother, the dungeons. And then there is nothing until a gasp ripples from my throat, and I fall onto my knees. My eyes crack open, and I'm back in the room with Kirian standing a few feet away. I look to the side as Darius pants on all fours, staring at me as if he'd also gone through hell.

'Congratulations,' Kirian announces. 'You both passed.'

I'm trying to gather what just happened. 'What did you do to us?'

'I tapped into your minds. I made you believe you were entering through a door and brought out your deepest fears in order for you to face them.'

'And if we hadn't passed?'

One side of his lip tilts up. 'You wouldn't be talking to me right now.'

Darius holds me up. I turn to him, scanning his face and holding back a sob thinking of what I'd seen while trapped in Kirian's mind test. My hands press flat against his chest, and I look at the wounded gaze he gives me.

What did he, too, have to go through?

'I believe this is now yours.'

We glance at Kirian as he opens a palm to reveal a stone resembling lapis lazuli. I'm dubious about taking it. Still, I pluck it from his hand and fit it into my pocket.

Kirian observes me with an unreadable expression that unnerves me more. 'You should know,' he says. 'Thalorians may be perceived as the most frightening Elves from Terranos, but two things we value most are valour and honour.' His eyes snap to where I'd placed the stone. He is genuinely not what Arlayna painted him to be.

He starts to walk away when I glance at Darius, and he nods to me to say what is on my mind.

'Kirian,' I call him, and he turns. 'Why are you being this kind? Why are you letting us go?'

His chuckle echoes within the chamber walls. 'Sweetheart, do not mistake this for kindness. I am anything but that. Consider this a one-off.'

CHAPTER FIFTY-ONE

I hang my tunic up to dry on a branch and sit on a log beside a stream. Huddling my legs up to my chest, I try to keep myself warm with my thin chemise. From someone else's perspective, I might seem callous to my emotions as I stare blankly at the pebbles beneath the water. In complete honesty, in the past year, I've shown more emotion than I ever have before. But every time I close my eyes, I see my brother and Darius, and Sarilyn telling me to choose.

Even if I passed the final test, the aftermath still awaits us.

I don't move from my position as someone sits beside me. I know it's Darius. I always do. Just breathing in his rosewood scent is enough for me to know.

He doesn't say anything as he rests his elbows on his knees, relaxing a breath, and for a minute or so, we stay like this, staring ahead. We are so far out that I can no longer hear Tibith's excitable voice or Arlayna and Aeron bickering. Instead, I hear the burbling sound of water tumbling over rocks and branches.

A deep breath escapes me. 'What did you see?' I'm the first to ask, the first to be curious. Did he go through the same as me? Did his fears involve him having to choose too?

He sighs, and I'm not sure what he wants to say.

I glance over at him. His hands are joined together, pressing against his forehead. He's as traumatized as I imagined he would be.

'You were in mine,' I say, trying to encourage him. As he turns to me with a silent look for me to go on, I do. 'I had to choose either to save my older brother or kill you.' A knot forms in my throat just remembering I couldn't even reach them.

Darius stares at me for some time, and I consider mentioning that I saw Lorcan too, but he gets there before me. 'Lorcan's father told me the only way out is if I were to give a dragon shifter bite to everyone I cared for.' He pauses, his eyes a fierce amber gold, making me understand that I was one of those people he had to bite. His worst nightmare. 'When I refused, he locked me in the cellar beneath our home. He always did that when I was young. Sometimes he kept me down there with no food or water for days. Once Lorcan tried to get me out, but he could never get the keys from Rayth.'

I shake my head just imagining it. 'What did you do? How did you pass Kirian's test?'

He plucks a piece of stray hair off my cheek and pushes it behind my ear. He seems fixated on it for a moment. 'Before . . . Rayth used to tell me I was a pathetic dragon, that I had the power, if I wanted to, to break out of that cellar, to do anything I wanted, yet I was too stupid to try because I knew if I did, I might not have been able to stop. And when Rayth was dying, he told me no one would love me, that I deserved to be hated, that I was a murderer, a disgusting dragon.'

I blink back the tears that are blurring my vision at the memory of Darius telling me all this that night in the castle's kitchen. My hand automatically flies out to rest on his arm, and I edge nearer to him. He hardly notices I'm touching him. It's like he's lost in his own thoughts.

'So, this time, I broke out,' he says, his voice stiff and tight with unclenched anger. 'I faced him again, and I won.'

A kernel of pride bursts within me, and I'm suddenly smiling at him.

He notices, his brows knitting as he asks, 'What is it?'

I shake my head. 'Nothing, it's just . . . you deserve so much more than what the world has given you.'

His gaze softens. It has a boyish charm as he rolls his eyes over my face and lips. 'The world gave me you.'

'Yet you thought you did not deserve me either.'

He lets out a quiet chuckle. 'I do not think anyone deserves you, Goldie. You're the reincarnation of Solaris. Not even the most powerful beings in Zerathion deserve you.'

'And you are the reincarnation of Crello,' I remind him, nuzzling my nose against his bare shoulder. Looking up at his face, my chest burns every second I stare at him. 'This world may be cruel to us,' I say, 'but we were always meant to find each other, Darius, regardless of who we are, and I would take fighting you for a million lifetimes in that jeweller's shop if it meant we got to be where we are now . . . together.'

We hold each other's gaze, and a silence full of charged energy buzzes between us. I have poured myself out to Darius in a way I have not with others. I have shown him parts of me that an outsider would consider weak, but it was strength to him. I love him with every part of my soul, and I am not afraid to acknowledge it, unlike before.

As my hand travels up his chest, resting on his heart, his breath slows, and I lift my eyes to his. All it takes is a hooded glance from me to get inside his head and for him to devour the tiniest space between us as he kisses me. His hand curves around my neck, pulling me towards him with such hunger that it makes me moan against his mouth.

A rush of power washes through me. It floods my veins, wanting – no, *needing* – to pour out of me. I mount Darius's lap, straddling him as I deepen our kiss, and heat gathers inside me. I rock against him, and his kisses become possessive as he hardens beneath me.

'Take me into the river.' My body is battling for air as I pant through the words. 'I need you to take me into the river.'

Whether it is a desire to quench this surge of fire doesn't matter, as Darius doesn't even question my odd request. He stands, lifting me up like I do not weigh anything. I slowly untangle my legs from his waist, my chemise riding up my thighs as we stay so close to each other, breathless. His hand never leaves my back as he leads me towards the stream. He gets in first, holding my hand before grabbing my hips and carefully guiding me into the water. My teeth chatter at the cold impact of the water hitting my waist the further I get in, though the fiery throb inside my chest does not yield. I wind my arms around Darius's neck, and he holds me, letting the warmth of his skin soothe each part of mine.

What is left of the sunlight dapples through the trees and onto the stream. Shadows carve parts of Darius's chest and face as he swims backward with me in his arms. He has always looked so handsome, but something about being in the water makes his skin glisten like he is aglow in the moonlight.

His hand strokes my back, and I tilt my head back as his fingers skim through the fabric of my chemise and then up my right thigh. He hitches my leg up, and I release a gasp, breathing out his name.

I look into his eyes, my nose against his. 'Someone might come looking for us.' Though I do not care. A Shadow Calp could appear, and I would still rather stay here with Darius.

His finger draws a circle along the crease of my hip, making me not want to get out at all. 'Let them,' he whispers with finality and leans in to kiss me deeply as two fingers slide inside me and find that I am ready for him.

My hips grind to the rhythm of his movements. In, out, circling over my sensitive parts, we kiss with such carnal lust. He keeps my thigh up, tightening his grip on it as I tremble from pleasure the quicker the pace goes. A desperate sound emerges from my throat, that overcharging energy inside me flowing again. I pull back, my mouth hanging open as the intensity of his fingers builds this pressure that I know will not last long. My eyes flutter open for a moment, enough to see a golden glow emitting from our skin like our powers have waited for a moment like this to meet.

I feel my energy source tumbling into his, joining and welcoming each other, but soon I moan with desperation at the deprivation of his fingers.

I'm pushing my body further up against him in protest when he drags his teeth across my jaw and whispers, 'You'll need to be quiet now, Goldie.'

I'm nodding feverishly, falling prey to the desire in his voice as he leaves sweltering kisses along my skin. I'm panting, grinding my hips against his. He cups my rear with one hand while with the other he positions himself by my entrance. I can feel the tip grazing over my sensitive spot, teasing me, and playing with me.

'Darius,' I beg, and he smiles as if he has all the time in the world to ruin me.

'What is it?' He mocks with a whisper against my ear.

A shriek rips from my throat, quickly swallowed by his devouring kiss as he slides into me inch by inch. My mind cannot think of words nor form sentences, for I had never been used to these sensations, not before meeting Darius, not before realising who it was I wanted.

It's as if the weight of the world has lifted away from us. Swirls of gold pour from our bodies as Darius picks up the pace, and a crescendo of ecstasy drifts over me as my body tightens around him. He pumps in and out of me, rough and wild, before he presses a thumb against a part of me that has me cry out his name, and I come apart as his hand covers my mouth.

My legs jerk, and I shudder out of pleasure. He slowly slides his hand away from my lips, and our breaths are ragged against each other's skin as he holds me against the river's rippling waters. He presses his forehead onto mine, it's a gesture I treasure.

'You've bewitched my heart, Goldie,' he says. 'Unconditionally in every way, I never want to be cured from it.'

A breath of laughter leaves my lips. 'I didn't know I could do such a thing.'

'Oh, you've been doing it for quite some time,' he says, capturing my lips as he smiles and lifts me up.

I laugh with delight, breaking away from the kiss as I smile down at him.

He stares at me, his eyes gleaming with affection. 'Nara?' His whisper ignites that magic again. 'Marry me.'

My heart thumps in absolute joy and it takes all my might not to eagerly nod.

I drop my lips to his and whisper, 'Only one more to go.'

L ike all dreams, eventually, you have to wake up. My moments of euphoria in Darius's arms yesterday are long gone, and now we are facing the King in his throne room with the last stone in my hand.

'Marvellous,' Dusan whispers in deep fascination, taking the stone from my grip and raising it to eye level. He glances at Aeron, standing beside what remains of the group we first left with, and Arlayna. 'I suppose I must thank you, Aeron, for caring for my niece. I hope she wasn't too difficult to work with.'

Meriel barks out a laugh from her seated position nearby. 'Oh, Dusan, Arlayna is a respectable woman. Faye, on the other hand, would have likely jeopardised all their lives.'

At that, Faye shifts uncomfortably beside her. She pouts her lips as she looks in Arlayna's direction, and I feel for both of them for a moment. Two sisters who are always compared to one another.

'I assume you both must want to rest after that long excursion?' Dusan says to us, and Tibith climbs onto my shoulder as I glance at Darius.

We both stare at each other, knowing the answer to that question. Resting means waiting longer, and we can't waste more time than we already have. I have to get back to my brothers. I need to make sure they are alright, or sooner or later, that letter I had received would consume me.

I shoot Darius a firm nod, and he turns to Dusan. 'We would rather journey to the Isle of Elements instead,' he says.

Surprise flickers across the King's jade eyes. 'Very well.' He raises his chin at us and clicks his fingers before Thallan comes forward. His eyes are healed, but the scars running along his skin show the damage Darius had caused. His gaze narrows in on us as he holds a polished oak box. He stands beside Dusan, who lifts the lid. Inside lay the three other stones we had collected on a velvet cushion.

My heart begins to thump too quickly with anticipation as Dusan plucks each stone from the box and—

'Wait!'

I wheel around as Aias comes rushing into the throne room. His dark eyes cut to mine, and I frown at him, not expecting to see him until after we had returned from the Isle of Elements.

'May I speak with Nara?' he says, and all heads turn towards me.

I clear my throat, nodding to say it is alright, and walk over to him, taking him to one side where no one else will listen to us. 'What is it?'

He takes a breath, and for some reason, I believe he is about to tell me the worst. 'I just wanted you to know that you should be proud of passing each task.'

Tension eases off of me in waves, a laugh almost escaping me for thinking something else.

'I know they are not simple, but I believed in you both.' He offers me a smile, and I return it, taking hold of his hands. 'I am glad we met, Nara.'

'Come back with us to Emberwell,' I say. 'You belong there, not here, not in the Screaming Forests.'

He laughs, rubbing a hand over mine in an affectionate way. 'Maybe you're right.' He nods. 'Emberwell does seem better suited to someone like me. I was never a nature person.'

My brows crinkle together as I stare at him in amusement. 'I thought your kind thrived in nature?'

Aias looks at me. An odd gleam shoots across his eyes before the King says, 'Shall we proceed, or do you need any more time?'

I step away from Aias, slightly on edge, as I go back to Dusan and glance over my shoulder. Aias gives me an encouraging nod, yet now the idea of venturing into the Isle of Elements seems more frightening than all the tasks I have previously done.

'What's wrong?' Darius whispers, and I glance at him. I am ready to say we need more time, but the truth is we don't have time, so I smile even when he can see right through me and turn my attention to Dusan.

'How will this work?' I know Darius's eyes are still on me as I lift my head, feigning confidence for the King.

Dusan nods once and steps back. 'Each stone once merged . . .' Vines slither along his arms as if he is summoning them as they wrap around every stone in his hands. 'Will open up a portal.' His eyes shift to Darius and me, casting us a steely look. The vines now seem alive, sprouting and lifting the stones into the air. Different colours from the stones start to glow as layers of that vine curve around them, tightening its grip while Tibith gasps with delight. 'But you must be careful.'

My awe at the view before me snaps away, and I narrow my eyes at Dusan.

'The Isle of Elements contains the most powerful magic in our world. You might betray even your deepest wishes if you let your emotions override you.'

I stare at him silently, and Darius's hand touches mine. 'I won't,' I promise, knowing the destruction Sarilyn's wishes to end the Rivernorths brought her.

A life surrounded by many yet always alone.

Dusan smiles, and as the stones form a circle within the vines, a spark of gold light flashes skyward. I shield my eyes with my forearm as the room around us plunges into darkness, contrasting with the luminescence of the stones. The sound of splitting rocks echoes through the castle walls, the floors awakening with life as they rattle beneath us, and then a rift cleaves it in two, opening a doorway in front of Darius, Tibith and me.

'It is so pretty, Miss Nara!' Tibith gasps, flapping his ears on my shoulder.

'And possibly deadly,' I whisper, staring at the swirls and ripples of rainbow colours within the rift.

Darius tugs at my hand. His jaw is clenched as he looks ahead at the oncoming possibilities. We don't glance at anyone else as we walk towards it together. My fingers reach out to the threshold, barely touching it, and with a deep breath, I glance at Darius once more before we both nod and step through.

Weight presses down on me, making my arms and legs heavy, but I never let go of Darius as we make it out onto the other side, hand in hand, standing on an island surrounded by the sea and nothing else. Thunder claps above us as grey clouds swirl almost cosmically. I drag my feet across the ground. When I look around, I notice the fields are dull in colour, and the river leading towards an uphill mountain cave is an inky shade.

It all seems as if it is slowly dying.

What will happen once that power runs out?

Dusan's question runs through my mind as Tibith gets off my shoulder and pads along to the decaying irises by the river. My gaze returns to that rugged mountain; the only thing that illuminates this island is the pouring of golden liquid from the sky into the centre of that cave.

The continent's power source.

I go to step forward when Darius stays put.

'Goldie,' he says, turning me to him. He looks at everything near us like he, too, knows this isn't how the Isle of Elements should look. 'If you think something is wrong, we don't need to do this. We can return, call it quits and leave Terranos behind us.'

I try to keep it together but sigh, edging closer to him. 'I don't know what I feel,' I confess quietly, glancing up through my lashes. 'I'm just afraid that if we don't try, we will endanger everyone else.'

The worried look he gives me makes me fall prey to my weaknesses when it comes to him. He brings me towards his chest, wrapping an arm around my neck as my cheek rests against his cotton shirt. I can feel him plant a soft kiss on my head before releasing a slow breath. I embrace him, not wanting to get away from this moment because I crave him, I want him, I love him.

'Whatever comes our way,' he says, 'I'll be with you even if the whole world goes against us . . . even if Solaris and Crello decide we are not worthy of being their reincarnations. You're stuck with me, Goldie, and I don't plan to ever let you go.'

Burning tears collect in my eyes as I hold him tighter and look up at him. 'My thief,' I whisper.

He chuckles, lowering his forehead so it touches mine. 'You and

I were meant for the skies, Nara.'

I smile, not wanting to let go of this embrace, when Tibith squeaks from the floor, 'Let's go save Emberwell, Darry!'

Darius and I ease away from each other as he grins at Tibith. 'Ready?' he asks, looking back at me.

I nod and bend down to grab Tibith as Darius steps back and shifts into his dragon form. I mount him, placing Tibith in front of me for safety, and I mentally prepare myself for our last hurdle in Terranos just as Darius takes off.

CHAPTER FIFTY-THREE

I hold on to Tibith as Darius lands outside the entrance to the cave. Sliding off his back, I step onto the dusty ground and glance towards the oncoming storm.

My lips pull into a frown. This isn't how I imagined the Isle of Elements. I know that for centuries the power has been dimming, but for someone who has watched from her window every Noctura night when the Isle would release its power . . . I thought the island would look like a haven.

'Is it going to rain, Miss Nara?' Tibith shifts in my arms as Darius turns back into his human form and comes up beside us.

'I thought you loved the rain, Tibith,' Darius teases him, and in return, Tibith purrs when Darius rubs his stomach.

I chuckle, and my gaze goes to Darius. He gives me a smile of his own that silences the thunder above.

'Shall we, Goldie?' he whispers, and I nod, entering the narrow threshold with an exhale.

Warm thick air greets me, tightening my chest as we take one step at a time to go down over the rocky ground. I watch as Darius leans forward and ducks to avoid the low ceiling. Still holding Tibith in my arms, I press my left palm against the humid wall as a luminous light reflects, casting a golden glow.

We near an opening where that light grows deeper. Darius moves aside, letting me enter first and then him.

My stomach drops as I witness the power source of our world for the first time.

Now this is a haven.

Fireflies buzz around us as a pit in the centre fills with the same sparkling golden magic of Solaris and Crello I see every year on Noctura night. A waterfall of that same dust pours from the sky as four crystal pillars surround it, each with its elemental power showing above. A flame for fire, a swirl of water on the other, a rush of wind, and finally floating rocks on the last.

I choke out a startled laugh as a firefly lands on my shoulder, and I settle Tibith on the ground remembering the moment I was with Darius in Emberwell. Back when I knew I belonged with him rather than the Venators.

We spend the next few minutes captivated by this place's magic and aura.

It's truly breathtaking.

'Goldie, look.' Darius's voice echoes around the cave, and I see him standing by one of the pillars. I reach him as he stares at the one with flames. 'It's burning out.'

I glance at it and notice he is right; the flame is beginning to die.

'We can restore it.' I look at Darius, the golden shimmer of power illuminating the side of his face perfectly. 'I am not sure how, but—' I take hold of his hand, a hypnotic daze taking over me. 'The Galgr, she mentioned I must awaken my powers. What if being here can do that?'

He sighs. 'Nara, we came here for answers, to protect Emberwell from Sarilyn—'

'Yes, but—'

He grabs my other hand and brings it to his lips as he kisses my knuckles. 'Let us fix one thing at a time. Remember what Dusan said, we can't let greed overtake us while we are here.'

There's promise in his eyes, and I bite my lower lip, realising he is again thinking more rationally than I am right now. I release myself from his clutch, resting a hand on his chest as I lean forward, pressing my lips against his. He cups my face, gliding his tongue between the seams of my lips, and I part them, letting him in with my thirst for him.

Darius's kissing intensifies, and I crave just as much. I bunch his shirt between my fists and sigh in pleasure until a pained grunt escapes his lips, and I pull back.

I frown, searching his face for what is wrong before he looks down at his chest.

My heart collapses.

Blood seeps through his shirt, and he grits his teeth, tipping his head back as I hear the slice of a sword retract from his body.

No.

I grab him as he almost tumbles forward and, from behind him, steps out— 'Aias?' I breathe in shock.

He wears a blank expression as he holds on to a blade dripping in Darius's blood.

'What—' Darius pants, holding his wound as it heals, but Aias cuts him off, rounding the pillars.

'Apologies for ruining such a tender moment.' His eyes flit past me, and I look over my shoulder at Tibith, unconscious on the floor.

'What did you do?' I shout, rushing over to scoop him into my arms.

'Don't worry,' Aias says. He does not look like the kind Elf I've come to know. 'He's alive . . . unfortunately. I had thought about getting rid of that incessantly talkative thing, but . . .' He shrugs. 'I felt generous today.'

Darius is confused, trying to gather his bearings, and a flame ignites in his palms, which he aims at Aias. 'Aias, if this is part of the King's plans—'

'Oh, Darius, for a Rivernorth, I truly expected more.'

Confusion and anger rattle my insides.

'Then again, I did have you both fooled.' He eyes the blade in his hand and hovers it over the pit. *Blood of a Rivernorth, release me from this body,*' he murmurs, and it only takes a second for me to realise what he plans to do.

'Aias, no.' I shake my head. 'Don't do this. You will only make things worse—'

'One thing you should know, Nara.' His voice is raised as coal eyes lock with mine, and a cruel smile takes over his lips. 'Is that I was never Aias.'

My heart hammers so fast, his words are slow to sink in as that smallest droplet of blood falls into the pit of golden power, and Darius has no time to use his magic as I watch Aias open his arms out wide and dive inside.

At the same time, Darius doubles over, crying out in pain. He shouts for me, and I feel helpless as I lay Tibith gently back down and run towards Darius. I press my hands to his face, needing to see what is wrong, but he crumples to the ground, clutching his chest.

'My powers,' he rasps, the golden tan of his skin now a pale shade as he tries to bring some of his power to life with his other hand, yet nothing comes.

This cannot be. No, no—

A bubbling noise emerges from the pit as liquid gold slides between the pillars. The cave trembles before us, and I quickly place Darius's arm over my shoulder, attempting to move us back. That liquid travels through the cracks of the ground as it begins moulding into a figure.

I freeze as that gold forms bones, skin, hands, feet . . . and a brown-haired man in black and white armour with the Rivernorth crest – three rivers pointing north – comes forth.

A handsome face carved with taut and chiselled features, but the man beneath that is far from beautiful. He is what one would see in dreams only to realise it had been a nightmare all along.

His emerald eyes cut towards me, a cold and twisted look swirling within them.

'Aurum,' I whisper, unable to hide my horror.

'*Aurum*,' he mocks in a high voice, fluttering his eyelashes at me before his expression fades to one of distaste. 'Oh, Nara, such a waste that the deities would choose you as the next Solaris.' He clicks his tongue and sighs as he takes in my seething stare. 'Don't give me that look. I thought you cared for me.'

Hatred shines in my eyes as Darius keeps his head hanging low beside me. 'That was when I thought you were someone else.'

Aurum laughs, glancing at his hand as if he is glad to be back in his body. 'Ah, well, true.'

I interrupt his self-admiration with a demand. 'What did you do to Darius?'

'Oh, that.' He looks over at us, swaggering his way to kneel in front of Darius. 'His powers belong to me.' He lifts his chin. 'In other words, I own every bit of him, and if he behaves well, I might share some of it with him since, after all, I am his uncle.'

Darius glares at Aurum, his jaw clenching as he builds enough strength to lunge at him. He swipes him across the middle, throwing him to the floor as Aurum's maniacal laugh vibrates through the Isle.

Darius wraps his hands around Aurum's throat, channelling all his rage when Aurum says, 'You will yield before me.'

I can see it; I can see how hesitation has Darius in a tight hold. His arms stop straining, and then he lets go of Aurum, collapsing onto his side with a wince.

None of it fazes Aurum as he rises, dusting himself off with a satisfied smile.

Rushing towards Darius, I kneel beside him. His pain-filled eyes meet mine, and I almost break.

'It is so great to be back in this body. I certainly do not miss being a powerless little Elf.' Aurum cracks his neck on each side.

'How?' I say. 'How can it be when Sarilyn—'

'Killed me? That is where Aias comes in.' Wild excitement flashes in his eyes before he places a hand on his heart and sighs. 'Poor Aias, an Elf who had wandered into our territories, looking for an escape after his mother's death, only to find the same destiny for himself.'

My teeth smash together. 'You killed an innocent boy.'

'See, but I didn't, Nara. That is the beauty of it.' He looks down at us with a grin as he starts to explain. 'I already knew I was losing against Sarilyn. Every Seer I requested to speak with would tell me the exact same thing as the rest. That I would die at her hands.' Lowering himself to the ground, his palm uncurls, and shadows dance between his fingers. His words form stories from his magic. A woman holding a newborn child in her arms then disappearing into a sun and crescent moon. 'But something else they mentioned was of a future Rivernorth to be born of my sister Aurelia and a reincarnation of Crello whose other half would happen to be a mortal.'

I stare as those shadows turn into different scenes. One of two children playing with a marble and growing into adults.

'This,' Aurum emphasises as another moment shows up of Darius and I entering the Screaming Forests. 'This is what they showed me. This is what they told me would happen if I played my cards right.' The times turn back, and a silhouette of a child with pointed ears walks through the threshold from Terranos into Emberwell. It switches to another man, showing him the way to Aurum Castle, and I wish to be there to warn Aias myself. 'Aias was my opportunity, so I took him in, a naïve child who adored me and saw me as their King. I told him he was safe, and when the time came, I made my trusted witch switch our bodies on the battlefield.'

The following images will haunt me forever as I watch it change to thousands of people fighting. Even the shadows cannot hide the chaos Sarilyn brought onto the Rivernorths. And Aias . . . I can see that he was confused by how he looked around, wondering what was happening. He had no time to speak, no time to plead that it was not him who was inside Aurum's body, because Sarilyn drove the Northern Blade through him, and the switch had already been made.

Aurum's shadows disappear from his hand, and I look at his face. Rage rolls through me, knowing I was trusting Aurum this whole time.

'Did you kill her?' I ask, and he knows who I mean.

Golrai.

His back straightens, not a shred of shame or regret in him. 'She overheard me sharing my plans with the King. I couldn't let her tell you, but it was entertaining to watch you blame it on Thallan.'

My body shudders. The look I give him is more than one of hatred.

It's repulsion. I raise my hand, prepared to hit him, but he catches it before I can so much as graze his cheek.

His grip is firm around my wrist as he pouts at me with disappointment. 'That wasn't very nice, Nara, or should I say Solaris?' He grins the vilest smile as he yanks me upwards, and Darius groans from the ground, trying to reach me.

Aurum traps me with his other arm around my waist, and I try to push him away with my free hand, but it's no use. He has me locked tight.

'Let go of her,' Darius breathes low and too painfully.

Aurum chuckles, a sadistic sound to match his rotten personality, as he tightens his grip, making me gasp, unable to breathe. He's crushing me. 'Oh, my nephew, ever the dashing rescuer.'

Darius is almost able to stand when Aurum kicks him down, and my anger bubbles through my veins.

'You are just like your mother, Darius. Loved too hard—' Aurum kicks him in the abdomen this time, and I shout out Darius's name in a plea. 'Cared too much.' He looks at me. 'Isn't that right, *Goldie*?'

I glare at him, and before I know it, I spit in his face, causing him to grunt with disgust as he releases me onto the ground. I gasp for air as I try to crawl towards Darius and turn him over, begging for him to be okay, but a bitter laugh leaves Aurum's lips as he glances at us.

I'm trying to lift Darius with me, but his weakened state drags me down. A blast of shadows then sends me back to the pit's edge. I grab on to one of the pillars to steady myself before patting the side of my leg in search of my dagger.

I do not care if it isn't the Northern Blade. I am going to kill him.

A guttural cry tears from my throat as I launch myself Aurum's way. He twists around as I raise my blade to his throat, and shadow tendrils wrap around my wrist, pulling me in Aurum's direction. The dagger is snatched from my hand while the other wrist is captured in another of Aurum's shadows. He pulls them forward, and I jerk with the motion until my chest is against his.

'Do you think you can kill me so easily?' he grits out, an unhinged look in his eyes. 'I was born from the Northern rivers of Emberwell. I *am* the true ruler of dragons. Nothing, and no one, can change that.'

Defiance sparks inside me as I struggle to break free from these shadow bonds. 'I can try.'

He laughs, shooting a flame at Darius's chest. I gasp with agony as he writhes in pain on the ground. 'And what will you gain from that?' Aurum asks. 'Plunging this dagger through my heart will only cause the death of the one you love.'

My eyes go round with fear as realisation dawns on me.

Aurum's slow smile feels like a knife twisting my insides as he says, 'His soul was tied to mine the moment I used his blood to bring me back. His power and his mind belong to *me*.'

Death, reign, and resurrection commence.

Leira's haunting lullaby.

Many believe there is a reason why she also slaughtered the rest of his bloodline, Renward had said.

She wanted to make sure there were never any remains that could possibly bring Aurum back.

'Don't look so saddened, Nara.' Aurum's scornful tone brings me back to the horrible truth I am facing. The shadows fade from my wrists, and he takes a step back. 'Falling in love with a Rivernorth was never going to be easy. Look at what Darius's father did. He ran away the first chance he had. Such a pity.'

My gaze is vacant as I look over at Darius. Even in this state, his eyes are filled with raw anger and hatred as he stares at the one family member he has left.

Aurum grips my chin between his fingers, forcing me to look at him. 'Now, here is what you are going to do. You will grab that annoying little animal of yours and take us back through the portal without so much as a fight, understand?'

No. 'Yes,' I grit out.

Aurum smiles, letting go of me forcefully. I glare at him, never taking my sight off that malevolent gaze as I pick Tibith up and walk towards Darius.

'Goldie,' he whispers, his eyes half closed as he tries to wrap his arms around me. Tears slide down my cheeks as I rest my arm around his waist and nod for him to stand up.

'It's okay,' I say, my voice trembling. 'We will figure something out.'

Darius nods, leaning against my side as Tibith lies in my left arm, sleeping with a small bump on his forehead, which fuels my anger even more.

'Perfect,' Aurum hisses, letting us lead the way out of the Isle of Elements.

CHAPTER FIFTY-FOUR

Darius and I sink to the floor once we push through the portal and into the throne room. Shocked murmurs circulate the chamber as I look up at Arlayna rushing down the dais steps.

'What is this?' she asks, kneeling beside me as she takes Tibith from me and assesses his injury before checking on Darius and me. 'Where is Aias? He was supposed to go in and fetch you both.'

Before I can answer and beg for her help, her eyes lift as a chuckle comes from where the portal is. 'How kind of you, princess, to worry for others.'

Arlayna looks from Aurum to me. Guards reach for their swords in case any action is needed, but they fall back when I spot the King lifting his hand as he rises from his throne.

'Who are you?' Arlayna asks, her gaze narrowing as she stands, clutching Tibith in her arms.

'Ah,' I hear Aurum say as he walks past us, the greaves of his boots clashing against each other. He stops in front of Arlayna, pries her right hand from Tibith's hold, and drops his lips to kiss it softly. 'Aurum Rivernorth *and* Darius's uncle.'

Meriel's mouth drops at the revelation, and Darius's grip around my waist tightens as he glares at Aurum.

'You're supposed to be dead.' Arlayna yanks her hand from his grip and backs away from him, but all Aurum does is laugh like he'd expected that from her, from everyone, in fact.

'Well, that is a rather long story I shouldn't get into right now. Perhaps your uncle might tell you more.'

Everyone looks towards Dusan as he makes his way over to Aurum. I try to keep my mouth shut as I already had a prior inkling that the King was up to something, but this . . . this is more than what I thought he would be capable of doing.

Once again, I had trusted, I had underestimated, and I had become too comfortable.

'You said you wouldn't harm them,' Dusan says harshly, grabbing Aurum's arm.

Aurum glances down at the hold on him and flicks him off like he is simply dust on his armour. 'That is rich coming from the person who covered my tracks with the servant and gave me that ring.' He turns to me just as Arlayna glances at her uncle with a horrified look. 'In all three hundred years of being stuck inside that frail Elf body, I must say I thrived watching you believe Darius had kissed one of the princesses. *Oh, Darius, I think you and I are a mistake. You have to stop lying to me, Goldie.*' He laughs at his own imitation of us before his eyes lock on to me, and his upper lip curls into something so vicious. He steps into my view, and every speck of hatred inside me grows, but not as much as Darius's anger. I watch his arms tense, and the veins on his neck protrude like the dragon in him is trying to get out. He lets go of me, managing to stand before Aurum.

They come head to head, both the same towering height, both kings in such different ways.

'You might have my powers within your grasp, my life at your hands, but if you so much as touch her or do anything to her, I will personally revel in severing your limbs until you are nothing.'

Aurum studies Darius, a shot of anger passing through his eyes before he puts on a tight smile. 'Beautifully said, Darius. Now.' He leans forward. 'Kneel.' A command, like Darius is a pet to him.

Darius tries to fight it, his muscles taut and fists clenched.

'Kneel!' Aurum bellows in his face before shadows form around Darius's wrists, pulling him to his knees and leashing him there.

'Stop!' I get up, my hands fisting as Aurum's eyes land on me. 'It is Sarilyn you want, not him.'

Aurum cocks his head to the side, deciding to make his way to me as Darius fights against his restraints. I don't back away as Aurum stares down at me like he owns and can control me too. 'I do not want Sarilyn,' he croons. 'I want something else.' His fingers caress my hair, and I turn my head in disgust as he adds, 'Something I figured I could have thanks to what the Seers showed me.'

'Uncle, this has gone too far,' Arlayna urges. 'We have already distanced ourselves from other kingdoms thanks to the treaty. Why would you help someone who only wishes chaos against our world?'

Aurum's hand stills on my locks, his eyes on me even as he says, 'Because your uncle figured out I could help him too.'

Dusan surges forward. 'I only wanted to bring you back to your original vessel so I could lift the curse, nothing more.'

The King's curse.

He had just doomed us all for the need to break free from what Sarilyn did to him.

Aurum rolls his eyes, twisting to face Dusan. 'You're right,

Dusan, but there is a reason I said lifting this curse might bring consequences.'

Dusan stares at him warily as Aurum brushes the lapels of the King's emerald coat.

'See, bringing me back may aid in lifting the curse, but I also made a deal with someone else. After all, I never much cared for you three centuries ago. Why should I now?'

Too much happens in a matter of seconds. None of us are fast enough to prevent it as Aurum's shadow magic materialises into two blades and impales Dusan's neck from each side. The guards draw their weapons out, but Aurum's power pushes them back with a shadow shield around us as Dusan's eyes bulge, and he clutches on to his neck with both hands. He looks straight at Aurum once more before he slumps forward onto the ground in a mess of his blood. Faye and Meriel come rushing towards him with horrified cries while Arlayna's chest heaves with fury as she looks at Aurum.

'You have no idea what you have just done,' Arlayna says in a deadly threat as she settles Tibith on the ground, and vines begin wrapping around her fingers as she raises her hands to each side.

Aurum chuckles. 'On the contrary, princess, I have fixed your little issue. You were the one who had shared her vulnerable feelings with Aias on how you did not want to be the next queen of Terranos.'

Arlayna's magic freezes, and her eyes momentarily meet mine in abrupt confusion.

But Aurum waves a hand to the guards, dropping the shield as he declares, 'There's a new King of Terranos!' He looks to his left, where Thallan walks through the sentries, grinning from ear to ear.

I shake my head, not wanting to process any of this.

'That is not possible.' Meriel jumps up from the floor alongside Faye, their gowns smeared in Dusan's blood. 'It is Arlayna who is next in line.'

Faye's eyes are on Aeron as tears stream down her face. Her uncle is dead. No Elven healer magic can bring him back.

Aeron goes to Arlayna's aid, but it is not her who needs him right now. It is Faye.

'That was before the King trusted me with all the paperwork,' Thallan answers, looking all smug. 'All he had to do was sign and put me forth as the next ruler.'

The paperwork.

That night I saw him snooping around Dusan's study. He was scheming, as was Aurum in Aias's body, and I had fallen for it all.

'Now.' Thallan claps his hands and looks over at Aeron with a shark-like grin. 'Everyone, *kneel* before your new King.'

Arlayna takes a protective stance before Aeron, making Thallan's brow rise in amusement. Other guards glance at each other, hesitant about what to do, but Thallan commands them to kneel once more, and they start to obey one by one.

Aeron does no such thing, neither do I, Faye, nor Arlayna; but Meriel, yes, with not a single fight. Thallan then waits for the rest of us, Aurum proudly by his side as if he tolerates him when he is likely using him like he does with everything else.

My eyes snag on one of Aeron's daggers sheathed across his armour, then I look to where Aurum stands. My anger spikes again, thinking about what he is doing to Darius and seeing him now on the ground, kneeling under Aurum's will and restrained. It unleashes something horrific in me.

I turn towards Aeron, yanking that blade off him before I lunge for Aurum and jab it straight through his eye. He cries out, stumbling backward as he reaches for the dagger lodged in the socket of his eye.

My triumph falls short as he backhands me so hard that I hit the ground. I brace my hands against the floor and bring my fingers to the side of my lip. As I draw my hand back, I glance at the blood staining them.

'You vile piece of human filth!' Aurum's hand fists the back of my hair and drags me towards the dais. I kick and buck in his grasp as I cry out my rage, hearing Darius bellow my name. Arlayna is trying to get to me, but Aurum's shield goes back up, blocking her, Faye and Aeron away from me. 'I always knew you would bring me problems,' Aurum says, ignoring Darius's insults and threats. 'But we can work that out, can't we?' I let go for a moment until he grabs me by the throat, and this time, I can see the ruins of his eye. The swelling, the blood, and the hope it is so far gone that it will never heal.

He lifts me to my feet, and I continue thrashing at him. 'Oh, Darius!' he sings. 'I hope you are prepared for the next part that is to come. I would hate for you to miss it.'

'Fuck you,' I hiss, but his hand tightens around my throat, crushing my windpipe as the word fizzles out on a choke.

He smiles at me before he takes the dagger I had used against him and plunges it into my abdomen, twisting and deepening it until all you can see is the hilt. My scream turns into an agonized gasp, knocking all the air out of me as Darius yells again. I can feel the broken panic in his voice just as searing hot pain travels through my core. My gaze latches on to Aurum's hateful face, and it's not shock that shines in my eyes. It's power, it's promise, it's confidence that I do not fear this moment. My adrenaline rides strong, and that smile of his loses its edge for a second as he takes in my countenance right before he withdraws the weapon.

I don't know what happens first.

The cold flame coursing through my wound or the impact as I hit the ground. I press a hand over my abdomen, blood spilling between my fingers as my head turns to the side, and I look at Darius. I stretch my other hand out towards him, and every bit of love I have for him floods me as he tries to free himself, fighting furiously to get to me.

Aurum steps over me and glances between us. His eye still bleeds, but that no longer fazes him as he admires our struggles. He turns to Darius, chuckles once, and breathes out in satisfaction. 'Bite her.'

Two words.

Two words that make my soul bleed.

Darius's arms slacken, his expression full of defeat and torture. I attempt to shake my head, but it only makes the room spin.

Aurum snaps his fingers, and Darius's shadow restraints disappear from his wrists. 'Go on,' he says. '*Bite her.*'

Unable to fight off that demand, Darius slowly rises, but I shout at him, 'Darius, no! Fight it!'

He looks at me in agony, and even in this state, I wish to kill Aurum. I wish he was not attached to Darius because I would do anything if it meant ending him.

'Darius,' I say, my voice brimming with despair.

He is now at my side, pulling me into his arms. His voice breaks as he whispers my name back and traces the side of my face with his fingers, wanting to feel and be with me.

'I am waiting,' Aurum taunts. 'And remember . . . you are not to heal her.'

Darius grabs my arm, and I am confident he is telling me to do anything to stop him, but I am too weak.

Please, is what I make out from the movement of his lips. He is begging.

'We are meant for the skies,' my whispered promise sounds gurgled from the copper taste of blood filling my mouth.

Darius squeezes his eyes shut, resisting the urge to concede to

Aurum's wishes, but the more he fights it, the weaker he seems to grow as he grits his teeth in pain.

'Bite her!' Aurum's echoing yell cracks the walls, and Darius can no longer fight it as his fangs lengthen, but the second they touch my skin, Darius is pulled away from me by Aurum and Thallan. I'm still holding his hand before the fiery flame of his golden eyes is the last thing I see as the tips of our fingers brush against each other, and I no longer feel him.

Elven guards are unsheathing their swords while swirls of fire start hurtling above me, followed by a large sound resembling a bird's caw. I drown it all out as I weep, thinking of everyone I love, knowing I have failed. And as the cries of an oncoming fight surround me, the world before me dies.

CHAPTER FIFTY-FIVE

I fight to open my eyes as my limbs feel weighed down by something soft and plush. It's difficult to figure out what when I can hardly see. I groan lightly, turning my throbbing head to my left, and I wince, looking at how everything is a blur as I try to adjust my vision.

With my sight returning, I blink at the person I am seeing right now and wonder if this is the afterlife I am in or if I am truly awake.

'Illias?' I croak, my throat parched, yet I'm full of hope at the sight of my brother.

He is seated beside me, with Iker standing behind, leaning against a cabinet. I attempt to sit up, but Illias presses his hand on my knee. My gaze goes to his two fingers and then to my abdomen. I'm wearing a soft white linen dress. Panic suddenly breaks through the barriers of my mind.

'Nara, stop,' Illias says as he watches me frantically run both my hands over my stomach, where I can feel bandages wrapped around—

'You're panicking.' Those words don't come from Illias. Idris says it as he stands at the edge of this single bed. His thick brows crease as he looks at me; the wave of concern washing his features bleeds into my heart, and I shake my head like a manic person.

My brothers, the three of them here before me.

I don't know what to say, I don't know what to do, I don't know how to calm myself, because my brothers are here. They are here and safe, and I am too afraid that this might be just a dream.

'You're alive,' I say when I find my voice, cracking a hopeful smile across my lips. 'You're okay.'

Illias's soft, reassuring squeeze on my leg has me wrap my hands around him as tears sting behind my eyelids. I pull back, pressing my palms against his face, hoping this is not a dream.

I turn to Iker and Idris, about to rush towards them for another embrace, when Illias stops me again. I'm suddenly frowning. 'Where are we?'

Idris looks away. The room is dark, and there are no windows, only sconces scattered along the walls. 'In Aeris.'

In Aeris.

The kingdom where phoenixes rule.

I feel the panic burrow into my veins now.

Illias says, 'We were hoping you would wake up sooner, but we weren't sure how you would react—'

'How long have I been asleep?' I ask, my head spinning; I'm suddenly breathing too harshly.

Illias doesn't answer.

'How long have I been asleep?' I ask again, my eyes flickering to all three of my brothers. They look the same as when I left them. Brown curls and Idris's long chestnut hair.

'Five days,' Iker answers and my eyes widen.

'What do you mean five days?' I rise from the bed, and they all come to my aid as if I might fall the second I stand.

'Nara, you are still weak from—'

'Where is Darius?' I cut Idris off as his arm stretches out to grab me, but I push past him, finding Iker blocking the doorway. I'm stumbling all over the place, and despite the need for answers, I only want to know where Darius is. 'Move out of the way.'

'I can't do that.'

'Iker!'

The door flies open, and the unmistakable colour of violet snatches my eyes from Iker.

'Oh, my Solaris— Nara,' Freya breathes as she barges past Iker, her arms wide open to embrace me. Lavender floats up my nostrils as she squeezes me, and her cries cut the tension in the room as she says, 'You're okay, oh, thank Crello, you're okay.'

The shock doesn't wear off me even as I slowly bring my arms up around her to reciprocate.

I don't feel okay.

I don't know what is going on.

As she breaks away from me, Rydan and Link come through the doorway. My eyes rest on Link holding Tibith in his arms, and a whimpering sob breaks free from my lips at the sight of him awake.

'Hello, Miss Nara,' he says, but there is no spark in his eye. No sign of the innocent joy that I am so used to seeing.

'It's good to see you, Ambrose.' Rydan nods at me, a soft smile cutting his usual mischievous features.

'How—' My throat burns with the desire to shed tears. 'How did you—'

'I felt it,' Freya says. She takes a breath. 'Actually, I felt a dragon's pain. Darius's.'

My heartbeat quickens.

Her hazel eyes shine as she wipes her tears with her hands. 'There is so much to say, Nara, that we—' She looks at everyone. 'Don't know where to start . . . I— I—'

'How are you all here?' I ask, trying to contain every ache inside me and every emotion begging to be free.

'Sarilyn,' Link speaks up. Soft blue eyes snap at me. 'She found our hideout, thanks to a shifter selling us out so that he could live freely.'

'We tried writing you a letter,' Illias adds, 'but it was too late, and they had begun attacking us, the dragons . . .'

The letter that Dusan had shown me.

'We knew we couldn't stay there for long, and we weren't sure how much longer you would be, but Gus – he sought out a way to help us, though he wasn't sure it would work. See, Leira's wife mentioned that the Aerians had always disapproved of the Queen's hatred for dragons, it was a long shot, but he thought if we sought out the Aerian leaders, perhaps they could help us.' Illias runs a hand through his curls and huffs a stressful sigh. 'We couldn't take everyone, but we managed to get enough shifters, dragons and children out to safety and made our way here—'

'The point is . . .' Idris walks over to Illias, his arms crossed over his chest. 'Is that the Aerians took us in and promised to help us.'

I feel like I have not taken a single breath yet. 'But . . .' I shake my head. 'The treaty—'

'Is broken,' Idris finishes. 'It's been broken for a while, Nara, but the moment the Aerians attacked Terranos to save you . . .' He winces, the words dying on his tongue.

Now we must prepare for everything.

For more attacks.

For a possible war.

For Aurum.

I glance at Freya. 'And this feeling . . .'

She looks at the ground. 'Do you remember when I felt a strange urge to help someone back in Emberwell?'

'I do.' In the Arena where Darius fought.

'While you were gone, Leira helped me find my strength and magic as a witch. That also led to these emotions and magic inside me that I couldn't pinpoint until Leira explained what it meant. When a witch is connected to a dragon, they are able to understand their emotions and even feel their pain.' Her eyes lift. 'I felt Darius's a few days ago. It was so intense, I thought I would die, Nara, and the only way to fix it was to find him, and since we knew you would likely still be in Terranos, we recruited the help of the phoenixes to get you out.' Remorse slices across her face, and I step back, not wanting her to look at me like that because I know what that usually means.

'And Darius?' The words quiver out of me.

Freya closes her eyes. 'Nara—'

'Where is he?' My voice cracks, nausea swirling inside me like a current.

'I think we need to get Hira here,' Rydan says to Link, and my gaze goes to Tibith's saddened eyes.

'Where is he?' I raise my voice this time, but I know where he is. I know the answer. I already knew the answer before everyone inside this room did.

I break, saying the word 'No' repeatedly and shaking my head. 'We have to get him, he— he—'

'We can't when he is bound to Aurum,' Freya whispers, but I can't stop the panic doubling inside my chest.

Idris tries to pull me towards him, but I push at his hands, saying that one word I can only repeat right now.

'*No, no, no, no.*'

But I am too weak right now, and I can't stop it as he succeeds in wrapping his arms around me and letting me finally cry into his chest. I had never done so in front of Idris. Even when tears slipped out in our cottage, I hid them. Now Darius had opened me to every emotion, made me feel like I was seen by him, by everyone, yet he is not here, he is with Aurum, he is a prisoner, he— he—

He almost bit me.

Aurum stabbed me.

And I am still here . . . alive.

My sobs turn into gasps as I try to stop. I push back from Idris so that I can breathe. The whole room is silent, watching me, listening to my sniffling.

I press my thumb over where Darius had almost bitten me that night. My mouth opens, and I stammer as I look at my brother. Regret traps his gaze as he looks off and runs a rough hand through his stubble.

'I thought I had died.'

He glances back at me, and I can swear there is a moment where he might cry. Cry for me.

'When we brought you back here,' he starts. 'We thought it was too late to save you. We waited for the worst and expected the worst. You lost a lot of blood, Nara. Not even Gus's blood was healing you.'

'But then, after days, you finally came to,' Rydan says, but I don't turn to him. I keep my eyes on my older brother.

'You're lucky to be alive,' Idris says, his voice hard, almost in disbelief, as he shakes his head.

My breaths heave in fast and sharp, I feel like I'm about to lose consciousness. I stumble backward, my body heating up with the idea I have survived. Everyone starts saying my name. At least, I think they are, because everything is fading away, and I'm nothing but air.

'Nara, wait—' someone says. I think it's Iker, but I'm pushing through them all, trying to get out of the room.

Nothing eases the burn travelling all over my skin, searing me alive. I step out into a hallway and take one look to my right, then my left, still struggling to determine what I see when everything becomes one mass of colour. I start to run, panting as I try to pick up my pace, yet I can't, and as I slow down, I clutch my wrist and stare at the untouched skin.

Aurum has Darius.

I am in Aeris, away from him.

I—

Something hard collides with me, but before I fall, hands come out to catch my forearms, straightening me. My breaths are sharp as I blink through the haze. I'm staring at a red gambeson coat and a white shirt peeking through the unclasped golden latches. I quickly tear my gaze free from the clothing and begin tracing my eyes over the person's fair skin before I pause on lips that I recognise and that fiery red hair curling at the neck.

Dread unravels from the knot inside my chest.

This isn't happening.

This *can't* be happening.

It takes every ounce of courage to look up, and when I do, my breath is ripped from my chest.

'Nara,' he says, his face pinched with apprehension.

'Lorcan.'

ACKNOWLEDGEMENTS

Mum – I want to thank you for being there for me when I would come to you emotional over my plot holes and thinking I could no longer write whenever I hit writer's block. Our late-night chats about what celebrities could play my characters will always stay in my mind as we laughed our heads off at the silliest of things. I love you and this book is for you and Yaya Mercedes.

Dad – What can I say? I am always wanting to make you proud and I hope I have with this as well as my first book. You're a tough cookie who I like to think of as a grumpy character to my mum's sunshine personality. I can't wait to have you embarrass me all over again as we go into bookshops and you ask the shopkeeper if they have a book by the author Rina Vasquez.

Angie – This book series would have never been made if not for you and your support through everything. We met just about four years ago through an online writing platform and quickly became close. From our chaotic chats to spoiler-sharing and headcanons, I could not have been luckier to have met you! We went through this writing journey together and now I consider you my wifey. So, please, please, *please!* Get yourself over here so that we can officiate our wedding!

My siblings – Although you both swear that you never read *anything*, I know you still love hearing about my book ideas. Eddy, you always tease me by saying 'You wrote a book?' and I laugh because you're the goofiest brother in the whole planet and because of that Rydan is written after you. Noelia, you're the craziest sister ever who loves to rile me up whenever I am writing. Yet you still hype me up for everything I write. For you, I wrote Faye.

George – Remember when I told you three years ago that I wanted to be an author? Well, here we are with book two and your support has been endless. You're always there for me, snapping me back into reality when I tell you I hate my writing or when I spend too much money on character art. You help me when I'm stuck and you're the first person to always read my book. The truth is, I have no words for how much I appreciate you because even then it wouldn't be enough. You are the Dean to my Cas. I love you.

Areen and the team at Wildfire – Areen, thank you so much for giving my book a chance and deciding to publish it. Without you and everyone at Wildfire, my book wouldn't be where it is now. I cannot wait to continue working with all of you and sharing my successes as a growing author. You're all absolutely brilliant (and thank you for putting up with having to read the rough, unedited versions!).

Para mi familia en españa – Los amo a todos con todo mi corazón. Ojalá pudiera estar allí ahora mismo y celebrar mi publicación. Sé que todos están orgullosos de mis logros pero yo estoy mas orgullosa de llamarlos mi familia.

Yaya – Aunque ya no estés, esta serie de libros siempre será para ti. Te extraño todos los días y sé que si estuvieras aquí serías la primera en pedirle a Yayo que compre el libro aunque no puedas entender lo que dice. Te quiero, Yaya, siempre estaras en mi corazón.

GET IN TOUCH

If you would like to find out more about the world of Zerathion and keep up to date with Rina's upcoming works, feel free to get in touch!

Instagram: @rina.vasq

Tiktok: @authorrina

Facebook: @RinaVasquez

https://www.rinavasquez.com/